NIGERIA JONES

IBI ZOBOI

BALZER + BRAY

An Imprint of HarperCollins*Publishers*

Balzer + Bray is an imprint of HarperCollins Publishers.

Nigeria Jones
Copyright © 2023 by Ibi Zoboi
"Revolutionary Dreams" from *The Women and the Men* by Nikki Giovanni.
Copyright © 1970, 1974, 1975 by Nikki Giovanni.
Used by permission of HarperCollins Publishers.
African wax print fabric illustration © 2023 by robin.ph / Shutterstock Images

Credit: Lucille Clifton, "i am accused of tending to the past" from
How to Carry Water: Selected Poems. Copyright © 1991 by Lucille Clifton.
Reprinted with the permission of The Permissions Company, LLC
on behalf of BOA Editions, Ltd., boaeditions.org.

ISBN 978-0-06-288884-6

Typography by Chris Kwon
23 24 25 26 27 LBC 5 4 3 2 1
First Edition

For my mother and her mothers before her.
For my daughters and their daughters after them.

CONTENTS

CONTENTS

I used to dream militant dreams
of taking over america to show
these white folks
how it should be done

I used to dream radical dreams
of blowing everyone away
with my perceptive powers
of correct analysis

I even used to think I'd be the one
to stop the riot and
negotiate the peace

then I awoke and dug
that if I dreamed natural
dreams of being a natural
woman doing what a woman
does when she's natural
I would have a revolution.

—*Nikki Giovanni, "Revolutionary Dreams"*

i am accused of tending to the past
as if i made it,
as if i sculpted it
with my own hands. i did not.
this past was waiting for me
when i came,
a monstrous unnamed baby,
and i with my mother's itch
took it to breast
and named it
History.
she is more human now,
learning languages everyday,
remembering faces, names and dates.
when she is strong enough to travel
on her own, beware, she will.

—Lucille Clifton, "i am accused of tending to the past"

PART ONE
FOUNDING FATHER

PREAMBLE

I, Nigeria Jones, in order to form a more perfect Black girl, establish justice, insure inner tranquility, provide for my defense, promote my general welfare, and secure the Blessings of Liberty to myself and my posterity, do ordain and establish this Constitution for the united, whole, and complete states of Nigeria Jones.

ARTICLE I
INDEPENDENCE DAY

"What to ~~the American slave~~ [this Black girl] is your Fourth of July? I answer: a day that reveals to [me], more than all other days in the year, the gross injustice and cruelty to which [I am not] the constant victim."

—A remixed quote from that OG Frederick Douglass,
July 1852

SECTION 1

My baby brother's name is Freedom, and today is his first birthday. I hold him in my arms real tight and sniff his little head. He smells like Mama—a mix of patchouli and lavender oils that cover up the scent of places I don't know, faces I can't name, and secrets I don't remember. We're fifteen years apart and he's not even walking yet, but it still feels like he could leave us, too.

We've rented out the community center over on Spruce Street for the birthday party, but it's not called a birthday party. In the Movement, nothing is ever that superficial. It's a gratitude celebration marking the one-year anniversary that Freedom Sankofa Jones chose us as his family. My father says that some African souls return over and over again to make things right, to heal generational wounds, and to fight for our liberation. We choose our parents, our families, and the lives we want to live before we are even born.

So I am a returning ancestor and I chose to be the daughter of Kofi Sankofa—the Black nationalist, revolutionary freedom fighter, and founder of the Movement, whose mission is to divest from oppressive systems and create an all-Black utopia. My baby brother did, too, and the members are coming together today to thank the baby king for choosing us.

The air in here is thick and warm even though the AC is on full blast. The aunties had smudged every corner with sage, and the scent lingers along with nag champa incense and all the different natural oils the members have on. Most of us are wearing colorful African print clothes and head wraps. When the members start coming in, a sea of braids, locs, afros, wooden beads, and cowrie shells will extend out to each wall of the community center. My father says that we're like a small African West Philly village in the big, white state of Pennsylvania. And it definitely feels that way, even though some people think we're a cult. Mama always says that the word "cult" comes from culture. We're just proudly celebrating our culture, that's all.

"Put that baby down!" my father calls out from across the room. "You're gonna spoil him." His deep voice is rolling thunder, his presence is parting clouds, and whatever words come out of his mouth today will be the sun shining on every member. He's moving about like a hurricane, putting the Youth Group to work, and I'm the only one who doesn't have to do anything because I'm holding my baby brother.

Freedom fidgets, babbles, and reaches for the floor, so I bounce him in my arms, shush him, and kiss him on the cheek, refusing to let him go. Even though this community center will be filled with people I love and who love me back, my eyes are glued to the front door, waiting for the person I want to see most in this world right now.

"Nigeria, come help us put up these posters," Jasmine says from the front of the room. She's rolling out the black-and-white photo of Malcolm X holding that rifle while looking out of a window. The words "By Any Means Necessary" are at the top, and that famous picture is my father's whole vibe—rifle and all.

"I'm busy with the baby," I tell her, even as Freedom cries for me to put him down. Besides, there are a bunch of other kids around to help her. She just doesn't like me giving orders.

About two dozen Youth Group members are setting up folding chairs and tables, throwing African print fabric over everything, and pinning posters of Black heroes over the old flyers on the bulletin boards. The baby king needs to know that by being born into the Movement, he'll be standing on tall and mighty revolutionary shoulders—Frederick Douglass, Toussaint Louverture, Harriet Tubman, and Marcus Garvey. On each side of a long table in the front of the room where the birthday cake and gifts will be are two wooden sculptures—one is in the shape of a bird with its head turned back reaching for its tail, and the other is in the shape of a heart where the curved lines curl in opposite directions into the center and twist out at the bottom like curlicues.

My parents told me since I was little that those shapes are what the Akan people of Ghana call Sankofa. It means to go back and fetch, or the way forward is to return to the past.

Sankofa is also the last name my father chose for our family because Jones is a slave master's name, he'd said. But Mama wasn't trying to hear that. She said she didn't want to erase the history that's in our blood, skin, and bones from our names. If my father's parents, grandparents, and great-grandparents had to carry the weight of all the Joneses that ever lived, including the slave masters, then I had to carry some of that load, too.

So that's why I'm Nigeria Jones on my birth certificate instead of Nigeria Sankofa. Or else it would've meant that I was trying to get back to Nigeria for some reason or other. We're not from Nigeria or Ghana. I've never been to any country in Africa. You'd think otherwise by the way my parents and the Movement talk about the motherland, though.

A huge banner with the words "We Are African Not Because We Are Born in Africa, but Because Africa Is Born in Us" hangs above the cake table. In just minutes, the community center looks like a throwback to the Black Panther Party headquarters. A few more tweaks would make it more like the Wakandan embassy; and I got Freedom a bunch of Marvel's Black Panther decorations, too.

"Let me hold him so you can put up the posters, since you know where they should go," Jasmine says, clearly trying to get out of doing her job.

I ignore her, hold my baby brother up, and say, "I bathed him and dressed him up real nice with his little shirt and matching pants. Don't he look cute?" I bring his face to mine and nibble on his little nose.

Jasmine shakes her head and rolls her eyes. I should tell her that doing this work is part of her community service for living rent free in the Village House, but right now, in this moment, I don't feel like being the president of the Youth Group. I just want to hold my baby brother and let him know that his mama—our mama—will be here for his first birthday.

I look around at the members, some I've known all my life. Most think that being here will change their lives and change the world. But some of them leave and never come back.

Makai comes in through the open double doors with a hand truck stacked with boxes. I quickly rush over to him and say, "Are those books? This is a celebration, not another seminar."

"We need to sell these jawns to get our own building," Makai says. I'm distracted by the ring of sweat around the neck of his T-shirt and his wire-framed glasses are slipping down his nose. "Capitalism don't sleep, Sister Nigeria. Especially when we're trying to dismantle it."

He starts to unpack my father's books to pile them on a table near the entrance. The newer ones—*Black Families Matter, Volume III* and *Flip the Table: The Global Majority's Guide to Dismantling Capitalism*—are front and center, and Makai stacks them into a pyramid. Postcards of the publishing date for his next book, *The Black Man's Constitution*, are spread out like playing cards. Another table holds brochures and flyers about the Movement's mission and its programs. One of the aunties puts out two giant glass jars for donations. A piece of paper with the words "Youth Group Trip to Ghana" is taped to one, and the other one reads: "Freedom School Building Fund." I was too busy worrying about Mama and Freedom that I didn't notice what my father had planned.

"Is he serious?" I say out loud, and catch myself. I can't let anybody hear me criticize my father. Not even Makai, who's been living with us for the past five years.

"Come on, Geri," Makai says all out of breath. "Help me set these up."

"I can't. I'm holding the baby," I say, turning my back to him. I'm keeping all my attention on Freedom just in case Mama shows up.

My father is in the front of the room and pulls aside some of the other boys and motions for them to set up the portable screen and podium. That's when I know for sure that this birthday party slash gratitude celebration will also be another one of his lectures.

Freedom must feel the heat rising from my body 'cause he starts to cry. More members are coming into the community center now, and they're not just members; they're like family. Every woman who walks in through those doors is an auntie, every man is an uncle, and every kid my age or younger is a brother or sister. The elders who are old enough to be grandparents are called Mama and Baba So-and-So, and they get the best seats in the room and are the first to get a plate of food. This is all to remind us that we are a family, that we may have been related way back in Africa, that we were separated during the Middle Passage, and that maybe, by joining the Movement, we are finding our way back to each other. A few of them rush over to hug and kiss me, ask me how I'm doing, ask to hold Freedom, and shower me with so much love that I can't breathe.

My father says that as long as there are women around, me and Freedom will never be without a mother. The thing is, I'm Freedom's only sister, and with our mother gone, maybe I'm like his mama, too. But I know she loves us way too much to just up and leave forever like that. She's coming back. She just needed a break, that's all.

I grab a seat in a nearby corner and put Freedom on my lap. He's tired from fighting to get to the floor, so he's a little drowsy, thank goodness. I pull my phone out of my back pocket to text my cousin, Kamau. He's not really a member anymore, but he's actually family, and he should be here. If not for me, then for Freedom. Are you coming? I type. I promise this is just a party, I lie.

Someone is suddenly hovering over us. A pair of beat-up Converses are in front of me, and I look up to see my cousin's halo of an afro that makes him look like a microphone, which is on-brand because he's always broadcasting his opinions out to the world (even though his name means "silent warrior"), just like we were raised to do. He's looking down at his phone and shaking his head. "Just a party, huh?" he says. "I swear the minute I hear one word from your father, I'm out."

"No, no, no," I say as Freedom reaches for his big cousin. "Please stay. I need you just in case something goes down."

He exhales deep, pretending to be annoyed with me, but I know how he is. He really wants to be here, but he'll try his best to avoid my father. "The way you holding that baby looks like you wanna carry him through life," Kamau says. "Isn't his name *Freedom*?"

"Be quiet and make yourself useful," I say, smiling wide because my cousin is like sunshine. He is my lifeboat and my lifeline. Kamau is the realest person I have in my life. We've gone through the same things, being children of the Movement and all: vegan our entire lives, homeschooled (until the eighth grade for him), and taught to see the world in black and white. Literally. We don't always agree, but he speaks his mind and keeps it one hundred. And sometimes that truth stings. He knows the sum total of me with all the pluses and minuses. And now that he goes to a real school, now that Mama left and we don't know when she's coming back, now that my baby brother is turning one and he'll be walking and talking and growing into his own, now that things are messy in the Movement and this is supposed to be what liberation is all about, I need someone who feels like sandy shores and trees and mountains and far-reaching land. Because here in my father's Movement, where I'm the daughter of his revolution, I'm drowning in an ocean of everything that I love and everything that loves me back, and none of it makes sense anymore.

SECTION 2

As the members pour in through the front doors, I don't need to keep watch to know when Mama has stepped into the space. She's a whole vibe. She'll shift the energy in the room as soon as she walks in wearing one of her tie-dye caftans and matching head wrap, her many beaded necklaces and silver bangles making music as she moves, and her waist-length locs swinging from side to side. And once she sees what's really going on, she'll definitely rearrange everything so that Freedom is the center of attention and not my father.

Kamau is biting his bottom lip and looking every which way, as if this whole thing is new for him. "Look at all these people. I told my mother I'd come because this was supposed to be just a family thing," he says.

"This *is* a family thing," I say as I get up from the chair with Freedom in my arms. I know what he means. Our celebrations used to only be with blood family. I want to distract him from the fact that my father will be lecturing, so I inhale and ask, almost whispering, "You think my mother will show up today?" It's a thought that isn't fully formed yet, like a hard, tiny seed that hasn't sprouted. I'd planted it there in my soul the moment Mama left us. *Is she coming*

13

back? I wasn't ready to speak those words, that feeling, that doubt into existence just yet.

Kamau looks at me as if I'm the saddest thing he's ever seen in his life. Then he takes Freedom from me and plants a kiss on his cheek while bouncing him in his arms. "I don't know, Gigi," he whispers. "But maybe she's always been here. You just don't see her yet."

"She's not here," I say as plain as day, smoothing out the wrinkles on my tie-dye sundress.

"Don't be pressed about it, though," he says, looking around as if he wants to change the subject. "And you knew damn well this wasn't going to be just a *celebration.*" With his free hand, he pulls out his phone and logs on to one of my father's pages where he posted about today's event.

"I don't be on social media like that, Kamau," I tell him.

"Yeah, you damn Luddite. If you would log on for, like, a minute, you'd see that he's arguing with half the country."

"I don't want to know," I say, taking the phone from him to get a closer look at my father's page. "And I'm not a Luddite. I just don't like seeing all the shit they say about us." My father being a radical activist and all means that if he's not out on these streets liberating our people, he's on the internet fighting for the cause. And by default, fighting everybody and their mama—Black or white. I try to avoid all of it.

But still, there's nothing on my father's post about his son's first birthday. The topic for his lecture: "What to ~~the American Slave~~ Black People Is Your Fourth of July?" It's a remixed Frederick Douglass speech from the mid-1800s that I was forced to memorize when I was twelve. I'd recited it on my father's podcast on Independence Day 'cause he was tired of seeing our people get all excited about fireworks when state-sanctioned murders, unemployment, crime and violence, and overall injustice were happening to us across the country. Since then, he's been talking about having a live lecture on this day. So, here we are. But the gag is, it's also his son's birthday. My father will be overshadowing my baby brother's big day with a speech about slavery and fireworks. When Mama comes back, she'll be pissed.

"You ready to get this *party* started?" Kamau asks with a smirk. Sarcasm is his second language.

"No, and this party is nothing like the one you went to last week," I say, bringing up the pictures he had texted me. "And you're part of Sage's little crew now? How come you don't take me with you?"

"'Cause you're still stuck here in Blacktopia," he says. "And I'm not part of Sage's nothing. I only let her sit with us 'cause she's *your* friend. Besides, you'll feel out of place hanging with the kids from my school. They live in the real world."

"Ouch. You outta pocket for that, Kamau." He stays, trying to make me feel bad for still being homeschooled. He doesn't have to try that hard. I live vicariously through my cousin as he navigates his fancy private school and goes to yacht parties on the Delaware River. "And Sage is not my friend anymore. You know that. That's why I need you here with us, cuz. You're family. You're still part of the Movement."

"No, I'm not. I only visit on holidays and weekends." Our eyes meet, and he sees that I'm hurt, like he always does. "Gigi, I'm sorry.

I don't know what to tell you, girl. 'Cause if I was your father's daughter, I'd be in the streets every day and night, just because. And it wouldn't be to recruit new members."

I laugh, and I hate how he can sting me one second and tickle me the next. "In the streets doing what?"

"Leading my own damn revolution! You can break free when you turn eighteen, Gigi. Or, I heard there's something called emancipation, when kids can divorce their parents. In this case, your father."

I squeeze Freedom a little tighter because even though Kamau knows what my life is like in the Movement, he makes it sound way worse than it really is. "I'm not trying to *divorce* my father, Kamau," I say as Freedom rubs his eyes. Still, I live for Kamau's stories about his school, all the drama, and all those different personalities. "I just want to know what it's like to be you. Especially now that you're out."

"You don't want to be me, Gigi. You just want to go to a regular school like everybody else." He gives me the side-eye, but he's smiling.

"I love you and I can't stand you," I say, laughing and nudging his shoulder. "And Philly Friends is far from a regular school—talking about socialism while partying on yachts and charging forty grand for tuition."

"I see somebody's been doing their research," he says.

And he read me like an open book, as usual. He knows that I wish I could trade places with him—to have one foot in the real world and one foot in this one.

My baby brother is almost asleep, so I take the fabric I'd tied around my waist, bring it up across my back, and have Kamau slide him behind me. I secure my baby brother to my back by tying the fabric across my chest and waist. I'm sure I look just like Mama when she used to carry me like this. Most of the aunties carry their babies like this because that's how they do it in the motherland.

"Are you ready?" I ask Kamau because he used to be my right-hand dude when it comes to organizing events for the Movement and keeping the Youth Group in check.

"Not really," he says, and I know what he means.

The community center is almost packed, and I'm glad that the members would rather be here than at some barbecue grilling meat or getting ready to see the fireworks at the Philadelphia Welcome America Festival over on Ben Franklin Parkway. I guess that's what makes them members. They refuse to celebrate independence in America while Black people are not free. They don't want to be part of this settler colonialist experiment called the United States, as my father says.

I take in deep, cleansing breaths, like Mama taught me. Freedom's breathing matches mine; his little belly expands and contracts against my back. I clear my throat, inhale, and start giving out the first set of orders to Kamau. "Make sure everyone walking in writes down their email address and phone number, even if they're already members. The presents for the baby can go underneath the table with the cake. Remember, no plastic toys, no electronics; only books and handmade gifts from Black-owned businesses. When the little kids come in, ask the girls from the Youth Group to take them down to the basement with some snacks. They can come up before we cut the cake. I'll be here if you need me," I say.

"Only 'cause I love you," Kamau mumbles. Then he leans in closer and whispers, "And if your father says one disrespectful word to me . . ."

"He won't," I tell him. "I promise." I want to add that my father didn't really mean all those things he said, but Kamau won't believe me. I'm not sure that I believe it myself.

Then he's off to delegate tasks to someone else. I miss having him around 'cause he used to love being a boss. He was good at being the Youth Group's president. But Kamau is still family, so other members will listen to him, even after my father stripped him of his leadership position when he started going to that school.

Some of the girls from the Youth Group are sitting on chairs, scrolling through their phones and being unproductive. They start making themselves look busy when they see me. With Freedom asleep on my back and a few minutes to go before everything starts, I call the Youth Group members to attention with one word: "Harambe!" I put my hand in the air and pull down with a closed fist. "Harambe!"

Most of them fall in line and repeat, "Harambe!" barely getting the "pull together" hand motion right.

"I thought this was a party," says Jasmine, the newly appointed Youth Group's secretary. "We have to organize on the baby's birthday, too?"

She's new and so are some of the other Youth Group members—Danika and Nailah in particular—who have confused and disappointed looks on their faces.

"Plus, it's Fourth of July!" Danika adds. She comes because her mother makes her. Otherwise, she looks out of place with her blond-ombre weave and lashes that almost touch her brows. "Can we get some grilled veggie burgers or something?"

"Y'all don't even have salmon burgers?" Nailah asks while

slipping her fingers beneath the front of her hijab to dab the sweat on her forehead. She's used to some of our rules, being part of the Nation of Islam and all. But she can't get with the plant-based lifestyle and the mandated monthly juice fasts.

My father is looking in our direction, and our eyes meet. *Please don't come over here.* So I get right in line, too. "All right, y'all," I say, motioning for the Youth Group members to form a small circle in the front of the community center. "As a reminder, 'Harambe' means 'pull together' in Swahili. 'Kombit' is the same thing in Haitian Creole. 'Mbongi' and 'Simba Simbi' in Kikongo." I start to say one of my favorite ones out loud in the Bantu language just to get them motivated. "Ubuntu ngu buntu . . ."

Then they all mumble, "Nga bantu!"

"That's right, brothers and sisters!" I say with as much enthusiasm as I can muster. "And what does that mean?"

"A person is a person . . ." Jasmine starts.

"Because we are people!" another girl adds.

"There's no 'i' in 'we'?" Danika asks.

They all give different answers, and I can't help but to laugh. "Y'all need to get it together. It's 'I am because we are,'" I correct them. I let it slide. It's early and it's hot and we're all hangry. But there's work to do because my father says leadership takes courage. "I need y'all to just greet the members as they come in. And I'm gonna need a couple of you to sing with me in the front."

"To sing 'Happy Birthday'? Why it gotta be a performance?" Danika asks, and she should've gotten a whole lesson on how we do things around here.

"No. To sing the Black national anthem," I say.

"'Lift Every Voice,'" Nailah whispers to her before she even asks what it is.

Danika quickly raises her hand, and so does Nailah. Jasmine shoots me a look as if to say, *Good luck with that*. Dani can't sing, and Nailah doesn't know all the verses to "Lift Every Voice and Sing," so one of the elders will be blaming me again.

Across the room, Makai starts to unfurl the huge Black Liberation flag to prop it up in the front near my father's podium—red for the blood of our people, black for the skin of our people, and green for the land of our people. It's to let everyone who walks in through those doors know what we're all about. No white people are allowed to any of the Movement's events. My father says that we need our own spaces without them poking their noses around and trying to figure us out.

In no time at all, seats are filled up, brochures are handed out, some of the uncles and boys have set up their djembe drums, and a line forms next to the food table where I am. This is Mama's spot. I'd made a couple of veggie platters with bowls of dipping sauce just the way she would. She believes she can have the most impact on the members by feeding them fresh fruits and veggies. Her voice echoes in my mind: "Eat to live, brothers and sisters! Eat to live!" I whisper those words to myself, as if she's speaking through me right in this moment.

Maybe she's already here, wanting to wake Freedom as he sleeps against my back. Maybe she'll show up right when we're ready to cut his cake. But even though the community center is buzzing with members, Mama's absence is a deep, hollow space in the middle of us.

One of the aunties is approaching me wearing a sky-blue caftan, and her colorfully beaded necklaces let us know that she's a priestess who serves the orishas. Her chunky arms are stretched wide enough to take in both me and Freedom. So I lean into her embrace, and everything about her reminds me of my childhood—tofu sandwiches and green smoothies for lunch, raw shea butter on our skin, and brown-paper-wrapped homemade gifts for Kwanzaa 'cause I've known her my entire life. "Peace, Auntie Fola," I say, and she squeezes tight.

"If he wasn't asleep, I'd take that sweet baby king from you," she says, and her voice is the ocean—wide and far-reaching and all-knowing. If the Movement has a village gossip, it's definitely her. And I know she's spreading all kinds of rumors about my mother leaving.

Auntie Gloria, Auntie Ama, Auntie Yvette all come over to kiss me on each side of my cheeks and tell me I'm spoiling my baby brother. These women are like Mama's real sisters. All of them are moving on with their lives and they walk along the edges of this hole my mother left. They know it's there, they see it and feel it, but none of them are reaching down to bring her back up to us. It's as if they like it this way; they like the emptiness because Mama used to take up so much space. She was larger than life, larger than the Movement. Both too much and not enough for this world. But even so, I'm leaving a little room for her to return to, because I don't want to ever take her place.

SECTION 3

I take my post behind the food table with the veggie platter, glass pitchers of water, biodegradable cups, and large wooden bowls filled with apples, oranges, organic chips, and gluten-free hemp-seed cookies that I had made from one of Mama's many recipes.

Some of the uncles and boys from the Youth Group take seats in the front of the room and set their djembe drums between their legs. The slap tone and the bass tone followed by a series of syncopated rhythms reach my bones and make the small hairs all over my body stand at attention. I've been hearing African drums since I was in Mama's belly. She always says that African drumbeat rhythms can awaken souls and dig up truths. That's why the drum was taken away from enslaved Africans. Here in the Movement, it's like a bullhorn letting everyone know that the event is about to begin.

Freedom wakes up. So I untie him from my back, take a seat, pull out one of his bottles from his baby bag, nestle him in my arms, and feed him.

But my father motions for me to join him in the front. Auntie Yvette, with her bright yellow African dress and salt-and-pepper locs, comes around the table and reaches for Freedom. I don't let her take him. "He's gonna start crying," I say.

"Then let him cry. Let me hold that little brown butterball," she says, making kissing sounds at Freedom.

I get up, hoist my baby brother onto my hip as he holds his own bottle, avoid eye contact with the other aunties so they don't ask to hold him, and make my way to the front of the room to stand next to my father. All eyes are on me now, and I bet they're wondering and whispering about my mama. The gossip and rumors swirling around the community center are like the little bit of cool air coming in through the vents.

It's only when my father reaches for my baby brother that I finally let him go, and it feels weird without him, as if someone has cut the strings that tied me to this world. Without Mama here, I need something real and alive to latch on to.

Freedom is out of my arms, and a microphone is in my hand. It's time to start today's event. The drumming has stopped to make room for my voice. I know exactly what to say. I've been reciting these words since I was six for my father's podcasts, his channel, his lectures, his recruitment sessions, and any- and everywhere he's given a microphone or a bullhorn to speak. His voice is like Shango wielding his giant hammer—commanding and thunderous. When he passes the mic to me, my voice is often like Oshun—smooth and undulating.

But now the words pour out of me like a raging waterfall.

"All power to the people!" I say with my right fist in the air. "In honor of the legendary Black Panther Party for Self-Defense, we invoke their vision of Black liberation in the twenty-first century.

Now repeat after me: 'All power to the people!'"

The collective voices become one.

"And we honor the great Marcus Garvey and the Garveyites," I continue, "and their vision for Black autonomy and global African liberation from over a hundred years ago. Now say it with me, fam: 'Africa for the Africans!'"

Everyone shouts the words in unison.

Then I pause to take breaths between each invocation. I look out over the members, wishing I could see my mother's smiling face out in the crowd.

"Take your time, sister!" an auntie calls out. "Take your time."

"We acknowledge," I begin again, my voice shaking, my eyes on the front door. Kamau is across the room and nods slowly, as if to say, *You got this.* "That the lands on which we gather are the ancestral lands of the Lenni-Lenape people, whose presence and resilience in Pennsylvania continue to this day. We take this opportunity to honor the original caretakers of this land and recognize the histories of land theft, violence, erasure, and oppression that have brought our movement and ourselves here."

With that, everything is organized chaos again. One of the elders comes up to pour libation for the ancestors as the aunties in the room start with their rhythmic clapping to "Lift Every Voice." Danika and Nailah join me in the front. Some of the little kids run up to help us sing, too, even though they don't know all the verses yet. The members stand, and this is our national anthem. From the outside looking in, people must think we're a church, that we really go hard for having service on Independence Day. But the truth is, because we're not all free, we don't rest. My father doesn't rest. I don't rest. But Mama . . . Maybe she wanted to rest.

The singing stops, and my father picks up the mic again. He had passed Freedom over to Auntie Fola, who then handed him off to other aunties and uncles and almost half the members in the room.

After a moment of silence for the members who have passed away, after some of the younger kids read quotes from the Douglass speech, after my father goes on and on about our duty to our ancestors who were still enslaved on this day in 1776 and are mentally enslaved almost two hundred and fifty years later, after the slide presentation for next year's trip to Ghana, after the info session for the Freedom School that's starting in September, and after my father says a few long words about his firstborn son carrying the Movement forward, Mama still isn't here. Some people are looking back at the door, too. Some elders and aunties shake their heads, pitying baby Freedom and me.

More members are looking back now, as if there's a commotion in front of the community center. *Mama!* I look over at my father, and for the first time in a long while, I see something new and different in his eyes—hope or happiness or excitement, maybe. Some of the uncles get up to walk to the front door, and I search the room for Freedom to make sure that I'm holding him when Mama comes in. One of the aunties had let him crawl on the floor, and I'm mad that his clothes are messed up before Mama sees him. So I let the aunties keep him and rush to the front door to greet my mother. The elders will side-eye her, mumble under their breath, or straight up tell her to her face that she was wrong for leaving them, her husband, and her children (in that exact order). But I'll give her a big, tight hug and apologize, and tell her that I promise to help out more around the house, to babysit Freedom whenever she needs me to, to read and study more, to be the best . . .

A lady at the front door wants to come in, but they won't let her. I freeze where I'm standing. Two uncles stand guard at the front door with their arms crossed, and I know for sure that they won't let that lady in. She's white. Even though she's Mama's friend, my father won't allow it. It doesn't matter that she helped bring me and my baby brother into the world.

"KD!" I call out.

"Geri!" KD responds, tiptoeing to try to see me over the uncles' broad shoulders. "I don't know what the big deal is. I just want to wish the baby a happy birthday and drop off this gift."

I push the uncles aside to get to KD, who with her long brown hair, sweaty forehead, and nearly damp tank top looks as if she's come here straight from delivering a baby.

"You good, Gigi?" Uncle Rasheed asks me while keeping his eyes on KD.

"We're good," I say, annoyed at him and the fact that it's KD and not my mother who's out here. "Y'all can go back inside."

The uncles just stand there, and I peek into KD's green minivan parked at the curb. I spot her daughter, Sage, in the passenger seat. Her light brown curly afro is pulled up high on top of her head, and she averts her hazel eyes. So I drop mine. I wasn't ready to see her just yet, and I'm glad she's still in the minivan. But Mama isn't in there. I look all up and down the block. Behind KD. Back into the minivan while avoiding Sage. Across the street. And for some reason, up at the sky.

"It's so good to see you!" KD starts. "And where is the little man? A year ago today, his little head was—"

"Where is she?" I cut her off.

"Oh, honey" is all she says as she examines my face the same way she does when she holds a brand-new baby in her arms, looking for signs of life and health. Her voice is like tap water—flat and smooth. Her accent only comes out when she's pissed or nervous. KD isn't from Philly or Jersey or Brooklyn like most people I know. She claims Charleston, West Virginia, by way of Lexington, Kentucky, and always talks about her Appalachian roots. She hands me a small gift bag and says, "This is for you. Please, don't let anyone else see it."

I immediately dig into it as if I'll find my mother in there. But it's just an envelope.

"Did you see her?" I ask KD straight up.

"Geri . . . No. I wanted you to have this on Freedom's first birthday," she says. "And after you open it, find some way to come see me. I have another package for you. Or we can meet somewhere."

"When did you see her?" I ask.

She doesn't answer. KD is at a loss for words, and I am, too. So I turn away, go back into the community center, where Kamau is trying to get Freedom to walk on his own.

"Was that Sage?" Kamau asks. "Did you invite her?"

"She wasn't invited," I tell him, and rush straight into a bathroom. I hold the envelope with both hands and turn it over and over again. It's a letter or a note with empty words, maybe. Everything that had come alive inside of me when I thought she'd come back to us today has wilted and withered and become lifeless, a feeling I thought I'd tucked away these past few months just to make room for a little bit of hope.

I don't open the envelope, and hide it inside of Freedom's baby bag. Back in the community center, my eyes meet my father's, and they're blank now, like they've been for a while. Maybe he was hoping it was her, too. But he keeps going.

After we sing baby Freedom's birthday song (the Stevie Wonder version, of course); after the aunties serve food (large aluminum trays of salad, barbecue tofu, collard greens, and rice and peas), and the music comes on (old school R&B, conscious hip-hop, and reggae); after the drummers open up the space for the members to dance; after all the kids in the Youth Group fold the chairs, take down the fabric and posters, and roll up the Black Liberation flag; after my father turns off the AC and shuts off the lights; and just as the fireworks in the neighborhood start lighting up the sky and it sounds like a war outside, Mama didn't come back.

ARTICLE II
BLACK AUGUST

"We are black, it is true, but tell us, gentlemen,
you who are so judicious, what is the law that
says that the black ~~man~~ [girl] must belong to and
be the property of the white [and black] man?"

—*Toussaint Louverture, leader of the*
Haitian Revolution, 1792

(Fixed it for you, King.)

SECTION 1

Mama is Haitian, so she insisted that I know about the Haitian Revolution the way white kids know about the American Revolution and the Civil War. I can name everyone involved from Dutty Boukman and Jean-Jacques Dessalines to Toussaint Louverture. And let's not forget the queen Cécile Fatiman, a Vodou high priestess who on that hot August night in 1791 summoned the African spirits to help my ancestors decapitate their French masters and burn down sugarcane plantations.

But even though there is no real war outside (at least not like the revolutions that created whole new countries), I was raised to know how to fight and defend my way of life. Not with fists or smart words or anything like that, but with the weapon that has killed and traumatized our people since the founding of this nation.

The first time I held a rifle in my hands, I was thirteen and my mother and father were by my side. I had already learned the history of firearms and gunpowder dating back to ninth-century China. My parents insisted that I know the origins of violence and war. Before that, they'd been arguing about guns for as long as I could remember. Not about me learning how to shoot one, but about Baba keeping one in the house. My father went around letting everybody know that he was legally strapped. It wasn't about being a gang member or selling drugs or any of those stereotypical things. It was because of these words that I had to memorize since I was five: *A well-regulated Militia, being necessary to the security of a free State, the right of the people to keep and bear Arms, shall not be infringed.*

My father drilled it into my head that it was my Second Amendment right.

He bought himself a Remington 870 and kept it under lock and key. And since I was his only child at the time, he insisted that I learn how to use it and use it well. When Freedom is old enough, he'll learn how to use it, too.

So now, every few months, and in August especially, my father takes me to the shooting range. It's a controversial topic for members of the Movement. We've had debates, fights, arguments about our Second Amendment right versus gun violence in our community, our Second Amendment right versus mass murders in public spaces, our Second Amendment right versus police shooting us dead in the streets. It never ends. But none of that matters because I'm still my father's daughter and there are way too many people coming for his neck.

It's a Saturday in the second week of August. At six o'clock in the morning, the sun is only a whispered promise at the edge of the dark sky. That's how early we have to get up. Our house is filled with strangers who are supposed to be like family. So my father calls this the Village House.

People who don't know what we're all about call us a commune.

So I once asked Mama if that was true. She said what we do is called communal living or an intentional community. Because capitalism and white supremacy want to keep us separated and isolated. But sometimes, isolation doesn't sound so bad. It's hard to be alone in this house.

My room is on the second floor, and I'm careful when I walk across the creaking hardwood floors so I don't wake up the other members, especially Jasmine, who shares the room with me. She's curled up on the twin bed against the opposite wall from mine. Sometimes, there's an air mattress on the floor for either Nailah or Danika or any other girl from the Youth Group who needs a place to stay, or for a sleepover.

Three of our six bedrooms are on the second floor, including my parents' room. There's a new woman in one of those rooms. She came right before Mama left, and I don't know much about her other than she loves helping me take care of Freedom. Two bedrooms are in the basement with some exercise equipment, a huge couch, and a TV with gaming consoles. Makai and his father, Uncle Rasheed, stay down there, along with Uncle Kyle, who's been here for too long. My father's office is on the first floor and it could've been another bedroom, but he needs somewhere to work. No one pays us rent, but they barter their time to raise money for the Movement and help spread our message. If we need more space for people to squeeze into this house, we have air mattresses, foldout couches, floor pillows, blankets, and a whole lot of love. At least that's what Mama believes; that's what she gives out. Love. And hugs. And food. And healing. But with each day Mama has been gone, a little bit of that love seeps out through tiny holes I can't even see.

After I'm dressed and my father is downstairs doing his morning workout and meditation, I grab my bag and step into my parents' bedroom to check on Freedom while he sleeps. His crib is pushed up against Mama's side of the bed. I lean over to stroke his soft, curly afro and kiss him on his plump cheek. I wish I didn't have to leave him here with the members, but I need a break.

My mother's altar is beneath a set of bay windows a few feet from their bed. It's covered with two white seven-day candles whose wicks are near the bottom, crystal stones in all shapes and sizes, an African violet plant that's almost dead, a glass of almost-evaporated water, the envelope that KD dropped off on Freedom's birthday, and a black-and-white printout of a photo of my mother that's curling inward along the edges. The photo is the one I took of her as she stood in front of a window just when the sun was rising. The sunbeam hit her at just the right angle, making her eyes look brighter, making her look happier. She was pregnant with Freedom, and she asked me not to show her round belly. It was the last photo she let me take of her before she left.

I sit in lotus position on the lavender velvet pillow in front of it, exactly the way she would, then inhale deep and exhale while pulling in my belly button toward my solar plexus chakra. It's starting to smell less like her. I wish my father would keep the windows closed so her lingering scent doesn't leave this room. But we would all suffocate from the heat. I remember her saying something about needing fresh air, hearing her pray and asking for guidance from the universe. I remember her talking to things that she can't see. So I pick up the envelope and do the same.

"Mama, where are you?" I whisper. "Why'd you leave us?"

Maybe it's the sound of my own hushed words that sends a chill up my spine. Maybe it's the truth of all those questions. I wait to feel something else, but all I hear is my father shuffling about downstairs and more people around the house waking up to do their meditations and morning rituals. I turn the envelope in my hand.

But curiosity is a giant magnet pulling me toward all the undiscovered truths the universe is trying to hide. And maybe, in this letter is a big world of truths. So slowly, slowly, I slide my finger under the glued flap and open it to find a letter. I unfold it and read the typed words.

To the Philadelphia Friends School Admissions Committee:

I am writing this letter in hopes that you would consider my daughter, Nigeria Jones, for admission into your school. She's been homeschooled her entire life, and as you can see, she received a nearly perfect score on her entrance exam. We don't have any grades or report cards for you to determine her ability to keep up with the academic rigor, but I hope an interview combined with her test scores can convey her intellectual prowess. I am her mother, and I've been teaching her how to read since she could talk. We run our school where we've hired math and science teachers. But I truly believe Nigeria needs more of a challenge so she can reach her full academic, social, and emotional potential. I know it's late in the year, but I'd love to come in with my daughter for an interview.

Sincerely,
Natalie Pierre

I read my mother's letter over and over again—holding my breath, digging into the spaces between the words for any more clues. She wanted me to go to school? After all she and my father have done to start their own school? The letter is dated May of last year, two months before Freedom was born, which meant she wanted me to start school that September. Part of me wants to tear this letter into pieces. The other part of me lights up with some glimmer of hope, a spark of a dream, maybe. Did Mama ever hear me and Kamau talking about his school? Did she ever catch me googling Philly Friends and sensing a little bit of envy for my cousin? And even though I couldn't hear their exact words, maybe this was what my parents had been arguing about before Mama left.

My father would never let me go to *their* schools, especially when he's starting his own. It's part of the system that he wants us to divest from—schools, corporations, prisons, and even hospitals. All these institutions that were built on Black labor while oppressing Black people. But why would KD even have this? Especially after what happened last year. My father said that KD was getting into Mama's head and he wouldn't let no tree-hugging, cultural-appropriating white woman get between him and his queen. And if he finds out about this, especially after what KD did to him, it'll break his heart all over again. I shouldn't have left the envelope here in the first place.

I fold the letter and stuff it into the pocket of my jeans. Then I focus on each of the crystal stones sitting on her altar—a clear quartz obelisk, citrine, a heart-shaped rose quartz, and an amethyst cluster. KD said there's more to this letter. But part of me doesn't want to go digging up what feels like a grave, or picking at what feels like an almost-healed wound.

The bedroom door opens behind me, and it's my father.

"What are you doing in here?" he says as he stands in the doorway. "Leave that baby alone. He'll be fine. It's time to go."

Freedom turns over, but he doesn't wake up, thank goodness.

As I start to leave my parents' bedroom, I notice the spot where my mother sleeps. Ruffled sheets and dents in the mattress make it look as if someone was in her place. I reach over to touch the spot, remembering the last time I saw my mother here. My insides twist. But I untangle the knot inside me with a simple explanation: Freedom was crying last night, and Baba rolled over to Mama's side of the bed to soothe him.

I kiss my baby brother one more time, grab my stuff, and head downstairs.

"It'll be just me and you driving out there," my father says as he grabs his keys and checks his beard in the tall mirror in the parlor. We're both wearing army fatigue pants with T-shirts and he's holding his rifle's carrying case as if his life depends on it. It does.

A woman is coming from the kitchen, and she's wearing a silk robe as if she's on vacation and this is some kind of bed-and-breakfast. Her name is Camille. She'll be the one watching Freedom. That was my father's idea. "Y'all stay safe out there," she says with a low, sweet voice.

"Thank you," I say, eyeing her up and down and trying to feel out her vibe.

"Will do," my father says. "We'll be back in a couple of hours, Nubia."

Nubia? I'm not even gonna ask.

"Next time, I wanna come with y'all," Camille or Nubia says, and I'm not sure I like her.

"It's a father-daughter trip," I say, and I walk out the front door behind my father like a soldier and her captain marching into war.

The shooting range is in Fairmount and we live in West Philly, so it'll take about twenty minutes to get there. Instead of his usual Miles-Coltrane-Monch-Sanders jazz playlist, or some new rapper spitting bars about government conspiracy theories, or even NPR, my father puts on an old Malcolm X speech. It's to prepare for his live podcast episodes this week. "Message to the Grassroots" blasts throughout the truck, and all I want to do is curl into myself and disappear.

He has so much to say to the world, but when it's just me and him, he lets other people's words fill the empty space between us. Mama used to be in that space.

I can't hold this in any longer, so the words fly out of me like birds let out of cages. "What did you and Mama used to argue about?" I ask over Malcolm X's voice preaching something about friends and enemies.

He sighs and responds, "We were arguing about what every other married couple argues about."

I sigh, too, because he's said this before. "Baba, can you please turn that down so we can talk? Radical honesty, right?"

"Radical honesty is something your mother says. Not me. Just keep it one hundred, Gigi." He turns down the volume only a little bit. Malcolm X's voice is something he wants to keep between us for whatever reason. Mama would've been annoyed, and she would've turned it off.

I want there to be silence so that the absence of words can swell and almost suffocate us to the point where we'll have nothing left but the truth. "Do you regret having those arguments with her?"

In between Malcolm X defining revolution, my father's breaths are loud and hot. "One of the last things your mother said to me was that I don't own her. That I didn't buy her at some trophy-wife store, and I'm not making monthly payments on her life."

I've heard her say those things. Mama doesn't yell. Her words are smooth and sharp-edged, as if she wields a sword for a tongue. "But what about us?" I ask, almost whispering. Malcolm X's voice is louder than mine. He's talking about the American and French Revolutions. I've heard that speech before, and he never mentions the Haitian Revolution. "What about me and Freedom?" I repeat louder.

My father finally turns down the volume. We're driving down Chestnut Street now, and I watch the passing frame houses, empty lots, and short buildings as if Mama will step out of one of them. Or maybe her face will be in one of the windows. "You remember all those things she said when she was in labor with Freedom?" he asks.

"After I begged her to stay home and she up and left with KD?"

I do. I will never forget that day.

"She didn't want me around," he continues. "She didn't want anyone of us around—said we were being ridiculous and I was getting too extreme. She knows what we're all about, and she goes ahead and lets that woman deliver the baby king? It was her idea to name him Freedom, you know."

"I know" is all I say, and his words don't reveal any of the truths I'm looking for. He turns up the volume just as Malcolm X says "Uhuru," the Kenyan word for "freedom," the rallying cry of the Mau Mau during their revolution against the British. My father taught me that.

SECTION 2

The big red sign that says RANGE is visible from a few blocks away. The main entrance faces the parking lot, so my father pulls into a spot as far away from the door as possible. Eight men and boys are huddled around another truck like his, and I immediately recognize them. They're new members of the Movement. Some of the boys are around my age. That's a good thing. That means our numbers are going up. I look around for any girls or anyone I could vibe with, but no. That's a bad thing. That means that the Movement can easily become my father's little army. This was another thing Mama didn't like—being surrounded by my father's followers, men who take everything he says as fact. Mama stopped coming to the range before she got pregnant with Freedom. She didn't believe anymore what my father believed about our Second Amendment right. "There's already too much violence in the world," she'd said. "I don't want that kind of energy around us, Keith."

I remember that argument from a couple of years ago. My father responded with his booming voice, "We live in America, Natalie. We're steeped in that kind of violence. This entire country will kill you and will even blame you for it. Your incense and crystals are not going to save you or our daughter."

My mother became livid and unleashed an inferno on my father. I had to walk away and force myself not to hear any of it. Mama fought back with deadly, puncturing words I couldn't hear. Later, she said to me, "Your ancestors will have your back, baby. Always. Nothing is trying to kill you as long as they have your back. They gave you wings, honey. *Wings!*"

I wish I'd listened to what she had to say to my father. I wish I'd rescued her.

This isn't a father-daughter trip to the range, after all. I don't know these men, but I have to call them my uncles.

"Nigeria, this is Uncle Kojo, Uncle Devin, Uncle Nate . . ." my father says, and I won't remember their names unless they keep coming around. Some stay; some go.

The uncles shake my hand and crack jokes about how I look just like my father; that he spit me out; that if I had a beard, I'd be his twin; that I'm built like him, too—broad shouldered and hard-bodied; that basically, I am my father in a girl's body. Their words ignite a flame in the middle of me, and I actually do become like my father and his rage. But I don't say anything, and force a tiny smile, just like Mama does. Then, as they laugh and give each other hard daps, we march into the building like an infantry, and I am the only female soldier.

A boy holds the door open for me. "Ladies first," he says.

Oh, shut up! I want to say. "Thank you," I actually say.

"Nigeria Jones, right?"

I glance at him, give him a once-over. I recognize him from one of the Movement's meetings, but then again, a lot of cute guys come through the Youth Group, and most times, they never come back. His eyes are intense, as if he's studying me. But I didn't give him permission to. "Who else would I be? I'm the only sister here," I say.

"You sometimes come on your father's videos. I like what you had to say about the Freedom School. I'm gonna come check it out. Your father came to my school to tell us about it. I stayed back to chop it up with him for a minute. Reached out a few days later, and now I'm here." His brow is furrowed deep, as if saying those words was hard work. Then he pulls out his phone to show me a photo. It's a selfie of him and my father. He smiles wide, as if that picture is his claim to fame.

"Oh," I say. "So you're a fan? You don't feel some type of way about him coming to your school to get you out of school?" That's the complaint going around on the internet—that my father is stealing kids from the public school system to be part of his little experiment.

"Hell no! I feel like schools don't prepare you for the real shit that's out there. I mean, look where we at. Why can't this be a class if it's our Second Amendment right?"

He's new to this, wet behind the ears. So every word he's spitting is a truth that's unlocking the shackles around his mind, and I'm here for it. "Yeah, but my father doesn't do this for everybody. You must've really impressed him."

He shrugs and licks his lips as if I just complimented him on his looks. I could say something about those eyes, high cheekbones, thick lips, and broad shoulders. But I'm not trying to look thirsty, and I don't know how long he'll be around.

"I've been reading his books" is all he says. Then he fixes his eyes on me, taking in my hair, face, and body.

"I'm not a book," I say, and walk away. But there is no walking away when I'm surrounded by all these uncles and brothers. My father motions for me to join him in front of our group, next to the registration desk, so I stand beside him ready to lead.

"All right, kings and young warriors," he begins. "Some of y'all are new to this. Some of y'all have experienced this under criminal circumstances, unfortunately. Some of y'all have been on either side of one of man's deadliest inventions."

"Hey, buddy!" the white man behind the counter calls out. "Keep it down."

And the air in the place becomes hard metal. The uncles make their bodies and faces like stone. But there's enough ammunition in this building to take down my father's tiny army, if it comes down to it. This white man, whose graying red beard reaches down to his chest, clearly is new here and doesn't know that my father is the leader of the most radical, militant movement to come out of Philadelphia (or it's trying to be). So because I am my father's daughter, I pick up where he left off.

"We're good here," I say to the white man while looking him dead in his face, and he didn't expect it. "We'll be paying for your services and renting firearms and buying ammunition. If you don't want our business, we'll go elsewhere."

The uncles and brothers start to quietly cheer, but my father shushes them.

I'm in a staring match with the white man, and my father won't step in. He has my back though, but he expects me to hold my own. So I do. "Do we have a problem here?" I say to the white man.

He finally looks away and glances at the uncles behind me. "You're good," he says. "Let me know if you need anything."

My father tries to calm the uncles down. This performance is not to get them all hype about me, a sixteen-year-old girl, defending a bunch of grown men. But my father raised me to be his secret weapon. When the enemy is expecting an AK-47 rifle, he pulls out a concealed pistol or a revolver. I'm his Smith & Wesson pistol from the back of his belt, his Colt revolver from his sock.

My father nods and winks to let me know that I did good. "All right, warrior princess," he says. "Tell 'em what time it is."

The brothers my age are looking around like kids in a candy store. Rifles, revolvers, and ammunition are secured on the walls and locked behind glass cases. A huge sign highlighting the Second Amendment of the U.S. Constitution hangs above the glass counters. The range officer starts to read the safety guidelines to us, but my father holds his hand up. Then he nods toward me, as if to say that I got this. So that's where I start.

"Please focus your attention here," I say, pointing to the blackboard. I read everything out loud, just like my father used to before he passed this job over to Mama. And just like Mama used to before she passed this job over to me, and then she just stopped coming with us. She wanted me to stop coming, too, but my father was not trying to hear it. I look around to make sure no white people are eavesdropping, motion for the men to get closer, and lower my voice. "Uncles. Brothers. Y'all have to watch everything with your third eye. Use your instincts, and be mentally prepared at all times. Y'all already know they don't want us here."

"All right, now, Kofi Sankofa *Jr.*," one of the uncles says, and they start to laugh.

My father laughs, too, and he's not supposed to. His whole thing is to make sure that the members respect me and my mother just as much as they respect him. Easier said than done.

"And I'll add one more thing," my father says, gently pushing me aside. "Following the rules here will prepare you for navigating gun ownership within the parameters of the law. Remember, we have a legal right to defend ourselves. And I didn't bring you out here so you can use these weapons against your own people over some petty beef. It's to protect yourselves and your families. Don't be stupid and reckless."

They're quiet when my father speaks.

The men either brought their own weapons or rented them from the front desk. If we have pistols or revolvers, we carry them in plastic bins into the hot range. Rifles are held in their carrying cases. Before we enter the range, I take all the precautions my father taught me. I have my own goggles, earplugs, and headphones. My locs are tied into a high bun, and I have on a long-sleeve shirt even though it's hot outside. Then I catch that boy staring at me. He doesn't realize that he's not prepared, and I'm mad that my father keeps picking up random kids from off the streets to bring them here.

"You should've worn a long-sleeve shirt," I tell him, eyeing the tattoos all up and down his arms. "Hot brass from the ejected cartridges hurts like hell. And don't do anything without someone more experienced helping you. Weren't you paying attention when I was reading the safety guidelines?"

"Not really," he says without looking away. "I'm good. I'm experienced. But I'll let you help me if you want."

I give him a smirk, like, *Negro, please!* He's brave enough to shoot his shot with my father standing right there and all these uncles around. But still, I make sure to keep an eye on him 'cause he looks like a loose cannon, as my father would say. Ready to use his new shooting skills out on the streets if we don't school him. "Just to add to what my father was saying," I tell him, "violence against our own is the oppressor's tool to eradicate us. We need soldiers to fight *for* our people, not *against* our people."

"I'm clear," he says, furrowing his thick eyebrows. "What's the sense of going to war with my brother when the real enemy is keeping us trapped in the hood with no other option than to turn against each other. I get it, sis. That's why I'm here."

I just look at him, and he stares back with intense eyes and his short fro is a hot mess, like he needs a haircut bad. I take a quick glance down at him—beat-up Air Force 1s with those army fatigue pants. He's like every other brother my father brings into the Movement. "Well, stick around, then," I say. "Especially when it starts getting tough. Just . . . come to one of the Youth Group meetings."

His whole face lights up, as if this is an invitation for something else. But I shut it down by turning away and not giving him any more of my energy.

Near the welcome desk, range safety officers are watching the uncles and brothers like hawks, but some of them know my father here. They greet him with smiles and pats on the back. They make small talk about the latest weapons out on the market or some new shit stirring up between the government and the NRA, of which my father is a card-carrying member, but he's also part of a national group of Black gun owners.

I'm used to being invisible here. I'm also used to the loud banging, whether it's in the range or on the streets of Philly. But here, the targets are cardboard and paper, not living bodies. My headphones mute all of that out, anyway, and all I'm left with are the sounds of my own thoughts.

I carry a rented Smith & Wesson pistol and ammunition inside the plastic bin into the stall—cased, unloaded, and with the muzzle pointed downrange. My father is always in the stall next to mine, but I can't see what he's doing. I've been coming here for three years, so he doesn't have to supervise me anymore.

"You all right over there, warrior princess?" he calls out.

"Yes, Baba," I say, and I want him to watch me. I want him to see how my aim has gotten better. I want him to correct my posture, lift my chin, and remind me that I'm shooting this pistol at everything that is trying to kill me. I want him to tell me why we keep coming here even when Mama started saying that this ain't right. These trips to the shooting range used to be just us, our little family—me, Mama, and Baba, our weapons, and our Second Amendment right. But he wanted this to be a whole movement. He brought other people to our monthly trips, and now he has a small army.

A screen to the left allows me to control the target system. A button eases the hanging cardboard toward me up the shooting lane. I unroll a large paper target and clip it onto the cardboard, and the whole thing glides back all the way to the one-hundred-yard line. Five black circles with red dots in the center are my aim. At other ranges, it's a black silhouette of a body, and my father said we won't go to those places. The black silhouettes are us, he said.

With my goggles, earplugs, and headphones on, I load the magazine and focus on every detail of the gun, every movement of my hands. My mind is blank. Except, I remember the very first time I did this. My father guided my hands, while Mama guided my thoughts.

"Brother Malcolm said that the most disrespected person in America is the Black woman," she'd said.

And that's enough reason to aim for the red dot in the circle. The loud bangs from the other weapons are a distraction, but I have to stay focused. Arms extended, my finger on the trigger, feet firmly planted, I pull. BANG! BANG! BANG! The recoil sends power down to every corner of my body, and for a moment, I feel invincible. I don't hit the red dot. I miss my aim.

The targets of the other shooters are gliding up and down the lanes. My father's voice is too loud, and that boy is asking him questions.

Stay focused. I aim for the other dots. If the red one in the center is America, then I think of what the others should be. *Who else is disrespecting me? What is trying to kill me?* Mama is a damn good shot. Rifles are her favorite. But one day, she said, "Too much killing going on in the world for me to be in here playing with fire."

That Mama-sized hole again—it begins to stretch wide and deepen inside of me.

Finger on the trigger, feet firmly planted, and shutting one eye while keeping the other on the red dot, I pull again. BANG! BANG! BANG! Then I remove the magazine from my pistol, place it down-range into the bin, step away from the firing line, and remove my headphones.

"Nice!" I hear someone say from behind me. It's that boy again. "You wanna aim just above your target, though. Your eyes can play tricks on you."

"Fall back, bruh. You just got here," I say.

"I don't need a shooting range to learn how to aim," he says.

"What? All you need is someone who looks like you, right? That's what they want you to do. Might as well aim it at your own head."

"Ouch. You wrong for that."

"I know. The truth hurts." I'm about to put my headphones back on, but I want to make sure that this boy knows what he's doing. He goes into the stall next to mine, headphones still around his neck, standing all wrong, aiming his weapon all wrong.

"Cover your ears and relax your shoulders," I tell him. "Firm stance and breathe. This isn't war; this is an art form." I repeat things my father has told me. He should be watching this boy.

He does what I say, and then, BANG! BANG! BANG! A hole. Another, and another. He hits his aim, and he keeps going with his eyes narrowed and lips pursed. He's emptying the whole round of his magazine onto that one target as if it's the thing that's trying to kill him, too.

"Cease fire!" someone yells. "*Cease fire!*" It's a white man on the other side of the boy's stall, and he's glaring at him as if he's ready to take the gun away.

"Clear your firearms!" the range safety officer immediately takes over. "Make them safe! Put them down and step away from the firing line!"

The boy fires a few more rounds, disobeying the safety officer, but I can't touch him while he's shooting, nor can the other man so he's not startled while holding the weapon.

"Hey! You're supposed to stop!" I say through clenched teeth.

"Cease fire!" the officer repeats.

The boy stops, thank goodness.

"Sir!" the range safety officer shouts from behind us.

The boy is holding on to the Smith & Wesson for life, and the target is laced with bullet holes, almost torn into pieces. He was supposed to change it before it got like that.

"Sir, please make your firearm safe, step away from the firing line, place your weapon on the table downrange!" the safety officer repeats.

The boy is frozen in his stance, and my heart starts to race. I hope he's not pulling some shit right now.

Then my father says firmly, "Son, I need you to follow directions. Don't put yourself or anyone else in danger."

Slowly, the boy seems to snap out of whatever rage he'd been in. My father comes over to him and gently guides his hand down, takes the weapon from the boy, makes it safe, and places it downrange. "He's just a little shaken up, that's all," my father says, pulling the boy away from the firing line and out of the stall. He takes the gun, removes the magazine and makes it safe, takes the boy's bin, and walks him out of the range.

The safety officer shouts, "The range is hot. You can now commence firing!"

I can't focus anymore, so I take off my goggles, remove my ear-plugs, leave the stall with my bin, and go over to the welcome desk. The uncles and brothers are surrounding the boy, making sure he's okay.

"Mind over matter, son," my father says, patting the boy on the back. "Mind over matter."

The boy's face is wound up into a knot like he's about to cry, so I turn away 'cause I know for sure he doesn't want me to see this. But this isn't new for me. My father brings boys from off the street into this shooting range and thinks that he can turn street soldiers into freedom fighters. Then they have a breakdown once they realize that shooting at cardboard is the only revenge they're going to get. The real enemy isn't anyone or anything that looks like them.

When the boy finally cools down, I return my weapon at the front desk and follow him to the water fountain. He's not my business, but I'm doing what Mama would've done in this situation. "You all right?" I ask.

"Nah," he says, "I'm fucked up."

I wasn't expecting that. "For real, though. Was that your first time holding or shooting a weapon?"

He takes long sips from the water fountain, stands, wipes his mouth with the back of his hand while looking over at the uncles and my father, and says, "Nah."

"I'm sorry," I say.

"Why are you sorry?" he asks. "I mean, it is what it is, right?"

"'Cause it's not supposed to be that way. We're the most impacted by gun violence. So, it's not really your fault if you had to stay strapped when you're only, like . . . what? Twenty?" I dig into my pocket for a granola bar I'd been saving for myself. But I hand it to him 'cause it's early and I'm sure he hasn't eaten, which will make him even more on edge.

"Eighteen. And I'm Chris," he says instead of "thank you."

"Nigeria, but you already know that," I say instead of "you're welcome."

He nods slowly. "It's like the country, right?"

"Like the nation. Like the motherland. Like Blackness. Like power. Like liberation. Like joy." I've been saying this most of my life, each time someone asks why I'm named after an African country. "And you? Like Jesus Christ or Columbus the colonizer?"

"You're funny," he mumbles, unwrapping and taking a bite from the bar, and then making a disgusted face. He stuffs it into his pocket and sips from the fountain again. Chris takes in a long breath, as if something is weighing heavy on his mind. He starts to say something else, but my father calls him over.

We all meet back at the welcome desk as my father announces the agenda for the day. "We're going to head over to Dunlap and offer our support to a family who just lost their son to gun violence," he says with his hands folded in front of him, head held high, eyes narrowed—his usual stance when directing the members. "A couple of us can stand guard in front of their house to let the community know that we're here for them. Maybe we can organize a 'stop the violence' rally."

I peep Chris shifting his weight, looking down and around as if avoiding my father's gaze.

"Nigeria!" my father calls out, startling me, and I quickly look away from the new boy. "I'll take you home so you can draft up some graphics for the rally. And I'm doing a live stream tonight, so you'll be moderating the chats."

"Huh?" is the only thing I can utter.

"If you can 'huh,' then you can hear" is always his response.

Protest is the air we breathe, but I feel myself choking on unspoken things, my lungs filling up with rage, my body welling up with a stew of feelings I can't name. But all I can manage to let out is "Yes, Baba."

SECTION 3

Every August, my father travels to penitentiaries around the country to talk about prison abolition and to honor the heroes of the San Quentin prison riot of August 1971. This is another reason why Black August is called Black August. My father says that while capitalism is profiting from Black History Month, radical revolutionaries like us still have Black August. Whenever my father goes on his book tours and spreads the message of the Movement, Mama is always home holding down the fort.

So I'm in his office where Mama has a desk pushed up against a far corner of the room. She didn't take anything with her: her computer, file folders, notebooks, and bills on top of bills. There's a thick stack of printed-out papers, and the first sheet is the title of my father's next book: *The Black Man's Constitution*. Mama helps my father edit his books, sends them out to the printer, ships boxes out to Black-owned bookstores, and organizes his book tours around the country. This is how we get most of our money, so she not only left a hole; she left the Movement hanging by a thin, weak thread. With her type A personality and organizational skills, Mama weaves an intricate, complex net for the Movement out of which all our programs run like clockwork. She handles the website, runs the Freedom School, applies for city permits for us to protest, manages the volunteers, and solicits donations from the members. And I'm always helping her out.

Every August, the Movement holds a celebration at Malcolm X Park to honor the heroes of the Haitian Revolution. Once, the local news station confused it with the American Revolution and thought that we'd get all dressed up in traditional African clothes and have Haitian drummers and dancers to honor *this* country. "Local organization commemorates the founding fathers of our nation" was what the reporter was saying into the mic and camera when the news station posted up in front of the park.

A kid from the Youth Group yelled out, "Fake news!"

The reporter was like, "Well, what other historical revolution could you be celebrating? This is Philadelphia." So of course, my father had to school the young reporter on live television. Anyway, the whole Haitian Revolution celebration thing was Mama's idea, and she's been organizing it since I was little.

My eyes are dancing all about her work space, and I gather a pile of papers and bills, and spot a black hardcover notebook hidden beneath everything. On the first page in Mama's handwriting is "Book Ideas." The top of the list is Baba's first book, *Black Families Matter.* Mama scribbled a bunch of notes about the breakdown of the family and how liberation starts in the home. She must've been writing down what my father was telling her. I flip the pages to see more notes and ideas about every single book my father published: highlighted words, titles of other books, questions, and answers. It's as if my father's books were all born out of the words in this notebook.

I sit back in the chair and let out a deep, long sigh. *Shit.* Has my mother been writing my father's books? I don't think I ever saw my father doing any of that. When I was little, he used to read more often, even sitting me on his lap as he tried to explain Marxist theory or African civilizations. He's always posting on social media, yelling at his haters, recording his podcasts and videos, and trying to lead a revolution. My mother was the one stuck behind this desk planning and organizing and . . . writing. Mama worked and worked and worked. And all I can do right now is lay my head down on her desk and rest and rest and rest.

Later that night, I'm holding the Movement's Youth Group meeting in the backyard, where Baba has just built a new deck with the help of some of the uncles. Mama's favorite spot is at the edge of the deck under the cascading leaves and branches of one of our tall elm trees, so I sit there cross-legged in a yellow papasan chair smoking a joint. The late-August heat wraps around us like a moist blanket, and the dancing smoke from the joint makes it feel even hotter. Weed is supposed to have a cooling effect, but it just makes me sweat, as if I'm sitting in warm, murky waters in the middle of a swamp. Still, the familiar earthy scent calms me and keeps me focused.

Only six of us are here from the Youth Group even though we're eighty-two members deep on paper. It's me, Kamau, Travis, Danika, Makai, and Jasmine. So I use the word "members" loosely. Still, about half of us are active. We attend the lectures, volunteer, help organize, and spread the word to schools and communities about who we are and what we do. I gave Freedom a bath and put him to sleep an hour ago, and I've got the baby monitor beside me.

"Feels like slavery out here," Kamau says as he takes a long pull from the shrinking joint. He came over earlier to hang out with me and Freedom since he's an only child and we're his only cousins and all. And since my father's not here, he's sticking around for the meeting and giving his two cents even though it doesn't count. His shirt is unbuttoned, and his long, skinny legs are spread out on the patio floor, taking up too much space.

"Well, you look emancipated the way you're sprawled out across this deck," I say. "Move, Kamau!" I nudge his leg with my bare foot, and he laughs.

Travis nudges Kamau's other leg.

Jasmine and Danika have to attend meetings because they're my vice president and secretary. We make up the ruling body of the Youth Group. Travis and Makai are here mainly because their parents insist that they practically give up their lives for the Movement. They believe that the Movement will keep them off the streets and out of trouble. And even though Kamau isn't technically part of the Movement 'cause his mother and my father had a falling-out, he comes just to hang with us.

"We need to email a reading list to the new members of the Youth Group," I say, trying to get everyone back on track as I flip through my notes and to-do lists on my iPad. "They can't just read my father's books, right?"

When no one responds, I look up and around. Everyone seems suddenly distracted, or they're trying to ignore me. Or maybe they're just high. "Hello? Are y'all even paying attention?"

Then, as if he's been holding on to these words for a minute, Kamau says quietly, "Your mother used to do all this." He passes the joint over to me, and I don't take it.

I pause for a long second. "I know. So now I'm doing it. Will y'all help me or not?" It's not until everyone's quiet that I realize I was yelling.

"Damn. My bad. I didn't mean to bring up your mother," Kamau says. He sits up to offer me the joint again.

I put it to my lips and pull, and pull, and pull. And inhale. The first time I ever smoked was with Kamau in Fairmount Park when we were thirteen and supposed to be in the library. He had promised me not to tell my mother 'cause I never kept secrets from her. But as soon as I'd gone back home, she knew. She always knew.

"Nigeria," Jasmine interrupts me. "You good? You want to pause for a second and talk about it?"

It's now that she asks me if I'm good, and not the night that my mother left? "I'm just chillin'," I say, taking my last pull and passing it over to Danika. "Far as I know, Mama is on a long vacation, that's all. Maybe she'll be in Africa waiting for us."

"You know what? You might be right," Kamau says dreamily with his eyes closed.

And everybody else starts talking again about the trip and being on a plane for the first time, and how we might not want to come back. Our voices are low and smooth, as if our words are clouds. I forget all about the meeting and lean my head back to look up at the night sky. It inches closer and closer, threatening to press its weight down over me and crush me until I'm nothing but stardust.

Someone slowly opens the screen door from the house, and the screeching jolts all of us back to reality. It's Camille—or Nubia—wearing new waist-length braids and her deep brown complexion in the moonlight makes her almost look like Mama. Almost.

"Y'all been keeping up with the news?" she asks, and it's weird how much she sounds like Mama, too, but I brush it off. "Kofi Sankofa said a few words."

"Are they burning down the city yet?" Kamau says while finally getting up from the floor. "Or else it's the same shit, different day."

I nudge Kamau with my foot because this lady is still new to the house and to the Movement, and she's not used to his sarcasm yet.

"Well, Kofi is bringing in someone new to the Village House," Nubia says. "He said to tell y'all to prepare the room with the double beds. And that weed smoke is coming into the house. Put those joints out before he gets here." She lets the screen door slam shut, and part of me doesn't like her telling us what to do.

Makai passes the joint over to Kamau, and he takes a last pull before he puts it out. We all look at each other as if we're brimming with questions we don't have the answers to. Leave it to Kamau to blurt out what we're afraid to say. "So your father is bringing in *another* stray? And where'd *she* come from?" he asks.

"Really, Kamau?" Jasmine says. "They're not strays, and I'm not a stray. They're our people, and they need help. Auntie Natalie wouldn't just have anybody up in her house like that."

I thought they were trying not to bring up Mama. But Jasmine is a huge fan of everything that we do, and she idolizes my mother. If there's some sort of scale that rates how devoted we are to the Movement, I'd put Kamau at a one and Jasmine at a nine point nine.

"She came here about two months ago. Mama was helping her out. You know what? That lady was the last person my mother brought in here," I tell Kamau. That was supposed to be a private thought. "All right, y'all. This meeting is adjourned. Who's gonna

59

help me fix the upstairs room?"

With that, Travis and Kamau get up to leave, but I know they'll end up staying. Dani doesn't move an inch. Jasmine and Makai have no choice because this is their house, too.

My father expanded the walls of our six-bedroom home to include an entire village, and it's for members who need a few days, weeks, or months to get their affairs in order. Mama is usually the one to hold open our front door for anyone who needed help. But she's also very careful about who she lets into the house. Clearing out the guest bedrooms is her job.

Back in the house and in the kitchen, I look around for the things Mama would use to cleanse the space: sage, Florida water, a brass bell, and maybe some garlic for the corners of the room in case the person was bringing in some bad vibes, especially if they'd been involved in something traumatic, which is often the case.

"I've seen her pray sometimes," Jasmine says as I rummage through the countertop drawers. "Speaking in tongues, or something, while she smudged the walls."

She's my shadow right now, staying too close and doing everything I tell her to do. "She wasn't speaking in tongues, Jasmine. She was praying in Creole."

"You really don't have to be as witchy as your mother, Nigeria," Dani says, who's not helping out, but going through our fridge as if she lives here. "She be OD'ing with that sage."

"That's 'cause my father pulls people from out the mud to bring them here," I say.

When we walk past one of the bedrooms on our way to the attic, Nubia is packing her things into a small suitcase and changing the sheets of the two queen-sized beds pushed up against each side of the room. Good. "Sorry to see you leave so soon, Nubia," I tell her.

"Oh, I'm not leaving. Just moving out of this room to make space for our brother in need," she says. "He can stay in here."

"Well, where are you going to stay? I can bring you a room divider from the basement so you can have your privacy," I tell her.

"Oh, I won't be in here" is all she says.

I furrow my brow wondering where else she could be staying. But that's not my problem.

Dani takes the Florida water along with a cloth to wipe down the furniture, Jasmine has a small hand vac, and we all start tidying up the room that's already spotless. We're still a little high, so we take our time to focus on what we're doing—scrubbing and wiping where it's clean, being paranoid about dust bunnies, and giggling along the way.

"You think he'll look good?" Danika asks. "I mean, Baba Kofi says that our future mates should be like-minded and all about liberation and nation-building."

"Yeah. But that takes a while, Dani," I tell her. "Whoever comes through here needs to detox, read all the books, know all the vocabulary words, and be about that revolutionary life before they shoot their shot with one of us."

When we're done, we don't even know how much time has passed, but as soon as we close the guest bedroom's door, the front door opens and I can feel the energy shift downstairs from the new guest.

When I reach the bottom of the steps, that new energy is someone I've already met. It's Chris from the shooting range.

He has a bandage around his head. His shirt is torn, and his hand is bruised. He stares at the floor so I can't see his face. His Jays are dirty, like he's been running through mud. They look new, so I know he's pissed, among other things. His presence feels as if he's sucked all the air out of the room, and maybe this house, because everyone is down here now, staring at him and wondering. *Wondering.*

"Son," my father says to the boy. "This is it. The Village House. This is what we're all about. We can't fight for liberation if we don't help each other heal. And this is where you can rest your head for now. Just remember, you chose us. You came to me."

My father's deep voice echoes throughout the house, and he's wearing a T-shirt with the Movement's logo—a Sankofa bird reaching back for a seed in the middle of a silhouette of Africa. His beard looks uneven and his diamond-encrusted Eye of Horus pendant hangs from a Cuban link chain against his chest, and when he dresses like this, he looks more like a rapper, so I get why brothers would want his help.

"Let me introduce you to everybody," my father continues.

We all gather around as Chris takes a seat on one of the old leather armchairs, and his face is lit up by the overhead lights—smooth brown skin, high cheekbones, and eyes that have seen more years than he's lived.

"You already know Brother Rasheed and Brother Kyle," my father begins, pointing to the uncles. "And you remember my daughter, Nigeria," my father continues, extending his arm out to me. "She'll help you with everything you need."

I quickly look over at Jasmine, Dani, and Kamau, who are all staring at the boy. I've never been the one to help. This is Mama's job. Jasmine remembers because she was in his position around this time last year—a runaway, broke, and without someone to look after her. But this may not be Chris's story. I walk over to my father, and he puts his arm around my shoulders. I lean against him, looking at Chris like he's a broken thing that needs fixing.

He's still quiet.

Nubia brings him a glass of water, and he takes it. She was also in this position.

My father sits on the couch opposite from the boy. Some of us sit, too, but I stand, ready to do whatever is asked of me. He leans in closer to Chris, looks him in the eye, and says, "Chris over here got into a fight. His mother has had enough of him. And this is the story of most young brothers out here on these streets. He's hurt, but he's come here to be with family. Chris, we're not asking anything of you for the first couple of weeks you're here, except for your loyalty and your passion for Black liberation.

"You'll have plenty of time to reclaim your African heritage through a name that's fit for a young king," my father continues with a wide grin. Then he turns to me. "Nigeria, get the stuff your mother uses to clean his wounds. Make him some peppermint tea to cool his head and a large salad. Then give him a fresh towel, a new toothbrush, show him to his room, and give him one of my books. He can pick one from my library."

"Yes, Baba," I say, and the first step I take after my father's commands is the one where I almost step into that Mama-sized hole and almost, *almost* fall.

"It's okay," Nubia says to me, touching my arm. "I got it."

ARTICLE III
LABOR DAY

"I never mean (unless some particular circumstances should compel me to it) to possess
another ~~slave~~ [enslaved girl named Oney Judge]
by purchase; it being among my first wishes to
see some plan adopted, by the legislature by which
slavery in this Country may be abolished by
slow, sure, & imperceptible degrees."

—*George Washington, Mount Vernon, VA.
September 9, 1786. Edited for clarity.*

Section 1

I keep myself distracted and busy by taking care of my baby brother. It's a routine—rhythmic and unpredictable, like jazz. Breakfast, bath, playtime; snack, story time, lunch; nap, snack, playground; dinner, bath, sleep.

And that boy, Chris, is always around, eating a lot, asking too many questions, reading, and following my father around like his shadow. He joins the brothers and uncles in the basement to play video games, debate politics, and be warriors or kings or whatever.

My father is finally home from his trips, and this morning, he wakes everyone up to get the day started on our liberation work. He knocks on my bedroom door while shouting, "Grand rising! A luta continua!"

It means "the struggle continues," and it was the rallying cry for the people of Mozambique and their fight for independence from the Portuguese, the first Europeans to enslave Africans and bring them to Jamestown, Virginia, in 1619. But it's just another Philly day in August, and we're all in this house *struggling* all right.

He bangs on the other bedroom doors, and the whole house is awake now.

Worry and fear are written all over Jasmine's face because this week she has to make up her mind about being a member: be fully devoted to the Movement by attending the Freedom School, or go back to her regular school and risk my father sending her home.

"Jas, you don't have to do anything except live free and die," I tell her. "But you do have to decide what your idea of living free is."

"Well, I'm not free if we're not all free," she says, standing on her feet as if she's proclaiming this to herself. "I mean, that's what I'm here for, right?"

"Right," I say, scooting off my bed. "You're gonna need that energy if you want to be a member."

Jas didn't come here with much, so she borrows some of my clothes, which are mostly thrifted. If she leaves . . . When she leaves, I'll let her take some outfits with her.

After a smoothie and a granola bar, we're all packed into the living room, where my father has T-shirts for everyone in the house. He added something new to the design in the back—the Movement's website and his name, his chosen name, Kofi Sankofa, instead of Keith Anthony Jones.

We form a circle and hold hands for morning affirmations and to pour libation. This is how we get ready for a day of spreading the message, doing the work, or studying the movements and freedom fighters who came before us.

When four-year-olds all over this country were starting preschool, I was learning the words to "Lift Every Voice" and Nina Simone's "To Be Young, Gifted and Black," and singing them to an audience of over a hundred of the Movement's members. On most days, I'd sing with whoever was staying at our house. So for us, Black national anthems are like how regular kids have to recite the Pledge of Allegiance and sing "My Country, 'Tis of Thee" every morning in school.

Each Youth Group member, including me and Jasmine, steps into the center of the circle while everyone claps or holds a fist in the air, and sings a song with the name of each child starting from the youngest to the oldest. Freedom is the first to go as he sits on the floor nibbling on a slice of apple. Then it's Makai, me, Jasmine, and Chris, in that order. Whenever Mama used to sing this song with the members when I was little, I'd turn all the way up and get hype. I would dance and laugh and become a shining light, just like I was taught to do. But now everything about me is dim; everything about the Movement is a blinking bulb about to go out. So I only smile and do a little shoulder bounce and two-step.

My face goes hot when I catch Chris smiling at me. I look away, but when he's distracted, I watch him carefully. His deep-set eyes are moving all over the place, as if he's trying to take it all in—the colorful African fabric on the couches and draped over the windows, the wooden masks and Black art covering nearly every inch of the house, and us, his people. Most new members who step into the Village House don't even know that a utopia like this can exist. Our eyes meet, and he smiles. My insides do something weird, and I smile back. He's still a stranger in this house, but he already caught up with the repetitive words to the song.

"Look at Nigeria! She's Black and beautiful!
Look at Nigeria! She's Black and beautiful!
Look at Nigeria! She's Black and beautiful!

Singing power to the people! Power to the people!
Power to the people! She's Black and beautiful! Hey!"

Something is missing. *Someone's* voice is missing from our collective chorus. This was Mama's idea for as long as I could remember. Even when the world was getting ready for the first day of school and I was just staying home, she made me feel like the smartest little girl in the world. I was going to be learning things from her, my father, my village, and the Movement. There'd only be about ten people gathered around telling me that the world belongs to me, but those ten or so people made it seem like the Movement was the entire universe. I never felt like I was missing out, that I wasn't learning important things, that all the kids who went to normal school would be smarter than me. The Movement makes me feel like I'm a genius, and sometimes I believe them.

Chris is awkward when it's his turn. "Look at Chris. He's Black and beautiful!" He doesn't know what to do with his hands or his face, so he rubs his chin, laughs a little, crosses his arms, laughs again. I'm embarrassed for him, so I don't look his way. This sort of thing is always weird for the new members my age—being put on the spot and told that you're Black and beautiful, an affirmation the world has denied us.

My father is standing next to Nubia, holding her hand. "Nigeria," he says. "Go 'head and start pouring the libation."

I follow his orders and grab the glass of water from the nearby ancestor altar, avoiding the photos and heirlooms on there, and walk over to the tall fig tree near the windows. I clear my throat, brace myself, and pour some water onto the soil. "For those whose shoulders we stand on, beginning with the ones whose blood runs through our veins and we call them by name. My maternal grandmother, Antoinette Pierre." I don't add any more of my ancestors and block out the names that are called out one by one by the members.

I pour out more water onto the plant. Chris is the only one who doesn't say anything. He must think this whole thing is strange. Then we summon the ancestors who belong to all of us—Queen Anacaona, Harriet Tubman, Toussaint Louverture, Marcus Garvey, Fannie Lou Hamer, and Malcolm X. My father asks Nubia to close us out with "Lift Every Voice," but she doesn't know the words. A lot of these members are new, so they don't know all four verses yet. I don't feel like singing, so my father does. He bellows the first verse off-key, clapping too loudly. Even as everybody tries not to laugh at his efforts, he keeps going. He smiles a little, and he glances at me. He forces the words and the melody as if he's invoking something that he doesn't actually believe.

My own singing voice is low, muted almost. Everyone sounds tired and off-beat. If Mama was here, she'd make everybody stop and start again. *Stony the road we trod* . . . She'd tell us to sing with our hearts. *Bitter the chastening rod* . . . I can almost hear her, as if she's directing the chorus with her own birdsong. I turn to the door to see if she had walked in and started singing with us. But no one is there. *Felt in the days when hope unborn had died* . . . The singing continues, and I swear I hear my mother's voice.

My father's eyes meet mine, and he furrows his brow as if to ask me what's wrong. He keeps singing and clapping, and I still hear my mother in the distance. I look down at Freedom, who is smiling and spitting out bits of his apple. Mama's voice is louder now, and I look at everyone trying to see her face somewhere, anywhere. But, nothing.

Then I run to the front door, open it, and step out into the warm September morning air with its overcast, low-hanging clouds. I can hear her singing voice everywhere.

"Mama?" I whisper, knowing that she won't answer, like all the other times she's haunted me like this.

"Nigeria?" Jasmine says from behind me. "You good?"

"I'm good," I lie, looking up and searching the sky for my mother as I exhale long and deep. "I'm good."

She just smirks at me, reading through my bullshit, and leaves me alone, thank goodness.

Back in the house and after the members have dispersed to do their own liberation work, I walk into my father's office to find out if he hears Mama's voice, too. He's sitting behind his three computer monitors and stacks and stacks of books. I don't think about what I'm going to say. The words just come. "Can we talk about Mama?"

"Not now, Nigeria," he mumbles, with his eyes glued to one of the screens. His beard is bushy, and he needs a haircut, bad.

Then I swallow a big gulp of air and release the thought that's been swirling around in my head all this time. "Did you see her?"

He jerks up. "Of course not."

"How do you know?" My voice is shaking now.

He folds his hands under his chin and narrows his eyes, the same way he's always done when he's about to drop some deep truth. "I miss her, too."

An opening. I step closer to his desk. "But Baba, you're not acting like you miss her."

He leans back in his chair and folds his arms across his chest. "Do you think I'm some kind of monster, like everybody else on the internet?"

"What? No. Of course not, Baba."

"Come see this," he says, motioning for me to step closer.

He pulls out his phone and shows me a photo. It's of Mama holding Freedom the night he was born. She's sitting up on a bed, and I'm on the right side of her looking down at my new baby brother with a crooked smile. KD is standing on the other side of her, and she's the only one looking up at the camera. I already know what this is about, and my father is probably pissed all over again.

"Who took this?" he asks.

"Sage," I tell him as the details of that night start to flood my memory. I don't want to remember.

"I didn't even know that your mother was still hanging tough with that woman."

"She's not just 'that woman,' Baba. That's Auntie KD," I say because it's the truth. But I bite my bottom lip because it's a truth he doesn't want to know.

"Your 'aunties' are the women who are part of this family. Your 'aunties' are the ones who helped raise you. Not *Katherine Dillon*. And what was she doing showing up at Free's party, anyway?"

"She wanted to drop off a gift."

Freedom toddles into the room. A bright smile spreads across my father's face, and he gets up out of his chair to sit on the dusty wooden floor to play with his son.

My father looks up at me, cocks his head, and asks, "Did you know she had wanted to go stay with KD? That she was planning on leaving me?"

That question, his words, almost takes my breath away. "What? No."

Freedom is on his lap now, playing with an old book. "She was my wife, and she wanted to just walk away from it all 'cause she wanted to be free—talking about she has a different idea of being free. Was I keeping her in chains? Huh? Was I?"

I let his words echo throughout the house. Then the quiet around us swells, filling up the space where Mama would've been—sitting at her desk pushed up against the corner like my father's secretary or something. And I wonder, with all the people that he knows, with all the places that he goes, if he ever asks for my mother. I wonder if the colors of her dresses and the scents of patchouli and lavender visit him, too, as if she's already a ghost, as if maybe she's not here and she's not there but somewhere in between. I wonder if he wants to crack open the universe to go find her.

"Did you know that Mama wanted me to go to school?" I ask.

"Not until Sharon brought it up," he says, too quickly. "My sister told me it was your mother's idea that Kamau go to a school—not just any school, a Quaker one called the Philadelphia Friends. Because it's *progressive*, whatever that means. She had brought it up when it was time for you to start kindergarten, saying that KD loved it for

Sage. But what do I look like sending my warrior princess to an all-white institution that calls themselves 'friends'? She could've at least brought up a public school like Central High. I get it, though. She wanted the best. But we're building our own . . . You got everything ready for the Freedom School info session?"

I'm still stuck on the fact that I could've been going to school with Sage since I was five. I could've had a regular life and still had time for liberation work, the same way Sage has time to help her mother deliver babies. "Yeah, but where are we going to have it? Mama used to book all the spaces."

He sighs deep and smooths down Freedom's curly afro. "We need to finish that book. Capitalism got people thinking that money is the only form of payment. Let's try to put out *The Black Man's Constitution* soon. It'll sell mad copies—a book that every Black man and boy in this country should have. The money from that will get us our own building. Might even be able to get some land in Ghana. That was your mother's dream, you know. To go back to Africa. Not even Haiti, but the motherland." He pauses for a second as Freedom starts babbling, and he kisses his cheek. "That's right, baby king. You're going to have your own constitution 'cause this country doesn't care about you. Nigeria, I need you to organize some of your mother's notes, go to the library to do some research. Look up who they call the founding fathers of this country, get some quotes, frame it within the U.S. Constitution, and remix everything for the Black man. Get Chris and Makai involved."

"Black men? But what about . . . ?" I start to ask, but someone calls my name.

Jasmine is coming down the stairs, and she peeks into his office looking for me.

"Grand rising, Baba Kofi," she says to my father. Then to me, she asks, "Nigeria, are you ready?"

"Ready for what?"

"Really, Nigeria? Market Street, remember? I want to go shopping for school."

I didn't remember. Shopping for school is not something I do, since I stay home to learn. "So you made up your mind about school?" I ask, glancing at my father and hoping he doesn't call Jasmine out on it now.

"We're not learning in our pajamas, right? We do get to leave the house, don't we?"

My father looks up and says, "Of course you do."

Jasmine and I exchange quiet, knowing looks, but I just say, "Can we go tomorrow?"

She doesn't respond and walks out of the office. I shrug, knowing that she wouldn't've wanted me to bring my baby brother, anyway.

"You need to leave your baby brother alone and go be around people your own age," my father says.

His words travel to every corner of this house. Our house is not our house. And for a second, I get why Mama would want to leave. People can be like walls, too.

My baby brother extends his chubby little hand out to me and says, "Mama."

SECTION 2

Mama never let me forget that the hardest work she ever had to do was to push me out. She was in labor for forty-eight *whole* hours. And KD was with her the entire time, ushering me into the world while my father was out saving the world. He wasn't there for me when I was born.

The night Freedom came into the world, Mama's contractions started just as a loud bang made us all jump. Fireworks. Since we live in Philly—America's birthplace—Independence Day sounds as if the people are waging war against the sky. Mama's baby wasn't due until the end of the month. Freedom was supposed to be a Leo. And you would never know that Mama was about to have a baby 'cause she was moving around like a tiny tornado. We were having our Black Liberation Cookout to replace Independence Day. So Mama was in the yard grilling veggies, giving out orders, and making sure volunteers brought plates to the elders in the neighborhood.

Then I saw her in the kitchen doubled over, holding her belly like it was about to explode. "It's okay, Gigi. Go back outside," she'd said in between deep fire breaths, waving me away.

So I told one of the aunties that my mother's belly was about to bust open.

Someone yelled, "Call the midwife!"

But the thing was, her new midwife, the one my father wanted to deliver his next child—the Black one instead of KD, who had delivered me—was all the way in New York delivering another baby. Freedom wasn't supposed to come that day.

My father wanted his firstborn son to be ushered into the world by one of our people. So when the baby king opens his eyes for the first time, he'll see the village that'll help raise him—us and only us. But KD showed up to our house when Mama's contractions were five minutes apart, the same way she showed up to our old house when I was born.

"No! Not again. Absolutely not!" my father had said when KD, wearing wooden mala beads and a loose-fitting caftan, stood in our living room. Next to her was Sage with her huge curly afro and bright hazel eyes. At that point, we hadn't seen each other since we were twelve, with Mama being busy with the Movement and all.

"It's not that my father hates white people," I had explained to Sage when she was wondering what the fuss was all about. The adults were yelling at each other as Mama tried her best to ride the waves of her contractions. "It's just that he doesn't want any white person delivering the baby. Our revolutionary ancestors won't approve."

"But my mother delivered you, and you're fine," Sage had said, as if it's me who changed. I didn't know how to tell her that it was my father who was coming up with all these new rules without making him look bad.

"We just want the baby to be surrounded by the people who'll love them no matter what," I told her. In the last few years, she and her mother couldn't come to my father's lectures, our Kwanzaa events, and even my own gratitude celebrations.

"But your mother and my mother are friends. We're already part of the baby's village," she said.

Sage wasn't wrong, and she wasn't right, either. The Movement has been what it is since we were both born. But this country and the world were changing, so my father and his revolution were changing, too. "Yeah, but . . . you're not part of the Movement" was all I could say.

Her shoulders dropped, and she looked at me as if I'd just put up a wall between us. And we couldn't see each other anymore. At least not like when we were kids.

I had turned to see KD massaging my mother's back as my father stayed on the phone trying to find another Black midwife in Philly.

"I need to get out of here," Mama said when some of the aunties surrounded her, rubbing her belly and feeding her ice chips. She wobbled up from an exercise ball and told me to pack everything into a duffel bag—all her birthing and baby stuff. I did what she said. Two aunties were telling her to stay put. My father was apologizing and trying to hug her and get her to stay home, but her contractions were giant ocean waves threatening to drown everyone in that house.

"Okay. I need you all to listen," KD had said. "If the mother is not feeling comfortable, it'll be worse for her and the baby. Her cervix is not dilating fast enough. We don't want any complications, now, do we?"

Everybody got quiet.

"Natalie?" KD asked my mother while placing a hand on her giant, round belly. "What do you want to do?"

In minutes, we were in KD's car, speeding to her house in

Chestnut Hill because the hospital was never an option. I was in the passenger seat while Sage was in the back seat with my mother because she was used to this—training to be a doula and all. I kept my eyes on Mama as Sage inhaled and exhaled along with her, and as KD coached her from the driver's seat, almost running red lights and all. I breathed in and out, too, trying to calm myself down, if not for my mother, then for my father.

He followed close behind in his truck, and I was glad he was coming alone and not with his usual entourage of uncles.

When we got to KD's house, which was also a birthing center, I remember not wanting to come in. But Sage held my wrist and walked me in, assuring me that I needed to be with my mother. I could count on one hand how many times I'd been in that house, so nothing in there was strange to me. Mama does Vodou, too. Mama prays to Buddha, too. Mama bows to the moon and makes offerings to Death, too. But something was off, as if by walking into that house with my mother about to give birth, everything would change. *Everything.*

My father had almost parked his truck on the sidewalk 'cause he was rushing to get to Mama. But as soon as he turned off the engine, sirens sounded and a police car pulled up behind him. He got out of the truck, ignoring everything around him and trying to get into KD's house. But both cops got out of their car, too.

"Natalie!" my father shouted from outside.

Mama was in pain, and KD walked her into the house and toward a back room where a king-sized bed was draped in bleached-white linen—the birthing room.

I followed them in, even as the two police officers called my father back to the truck. "Sir, you were going over the speed limit!" one of them shouted.

Behind me, the door to KD's house—the birthing center—closed shut, and Mama stopped halfway through the living room as another contraction made her double over and squeeze KD's hand. Sage was moving around the house getting everything prepared. And I was like a portal hanging in the balance between my father's world and my mother's world—stuck in the middle of peace and war like that space-time between a fresh cut wound and a fully healed scar. Maybe that was the first time a crack formed between my parents, and ever since then, there's been a widening chasm—this hole Mama left behind.

KD washed her hands, put on some scrubs with tiny baby ducks, and rolled a huge suitcase with her supplies into the birthing room.

Mama screamed, grunted, and cried as if she were the big bang that created the entire universe. She always told me that a Black woman birthed humanity, that everyone can trace their ancient ancestry to an African woman—the primordial mother, mitochondrial Eve.

A loud boom seemed to make the whole house shake, and I looked up thinking that the roof was being blown off. My heart stopped. "Baba!" I called out.

"It's okay, honey," KD had said to me while checking Mama's heartbeat with a stethoscope. "It's just the fireworks over at Pastorius Park. Could even see the gorgeous display from out the front window if you want."

But those fireworks were nothing compared to my mother's

screams. She was about to break in half. And me, I was splitting down the middle, too. Baba was still outside as fireworks made the sky a war. Mama was inside as this baby made her body a war. And I was just standing there like a border, both invisible and impenetrable.

In seconds, a baby's shrieking cry sliced through the sounds of bombs in the air. The small brown ball of a human in KD's hands, and the still-pulsing umbilical cord extending out of Mama had connected all three of them—my mother, her midwife, and this brand-new baby.

"It's a penis!" KD sang.

Sage applauded and smiled wide at me. "You're a big sister now! Hurry, come take a pic!"

I rushed over to stand next to Mama as she struggled to sit up in the bed. KD handed her the baby, and she looked down at him as if he was something she didn't understand—a hard puzzle of a baby whose arrival on this day made all the sense in the world. Mama started to cry, and Sage snapped the picture before I could even get a good smile in because my head was the universe spinning too fast, a whirl of chaos.

And that night, as fireworks lit up the sky, as my baby brother tested out his lungs in this new world, as my mother cried and cried and cried along with him, the sirens outside threatened to tear down this whole house.

So I ran out of the room and could see the confusion outside from the window. Police. Lights. Voices.

"Step away from the door, sir!" a man yelled.

"My wife is having my baby in there!" my father yelled back.

My insides sank. I went over to the front door and slowly reached for the knob and turned it. My eyes met my father's, and he pleaded while reaching out to me. For what? To say something? To rescue him? I didn't know. So I just said, "The baby's here!"

But before he could say a word, one of the police officers shouted with his hand on his holster, "License and registration, sir, or we'll have to detain you!"

"Nigeria, we need help in here!" Sage called out from inside the house.

And again, I was like a portal hanging in the balance between my father's world and my mother's world. In that moment, I chose both. So I rushed back in to say, "They're arresting my father!"

KD was holding the new baby, and Sage was fanning my mother.

"They're arresting my father!" I shouted again.

"What?" Mama asked groggily. She was sweaty and dazed, and her voice was scratchy and distant. "Tell him to come in. Tell him he finally has his son. He finally has his son."

"He's trying, but they won't let him!" I stepped closer, but I was afraid that I was leaving my father behind outside.

No one was listening to me as KD handed Sage the baby. Then she focused on Mama. The bleached-white sheets were quickly turning into the color of war. Mama's eyes became eclipsing moons, and KD kept calling out her name.

"Natalie, are you with me? Natalie, say something!" She placed two fingers on Mama's neck, inhaled deep, and shouted, "Sage, call the ambulance! We're taking her in!"

My head was on a swivel, watching Sage as she rocked the baby in her arms, then turning to the window and the front door as the whirling police car lights flooded the living room. "My father just wants to see the baby," I cried.

"Nigeria, sweetheart," KD said calmly. "I need you to focus on your mother right now. We have to take her to the hospital. She's bleeding too much."

"No," I said. "My father doesn't want that." Hospitals were never options because they were part of systems he wanted to dismantle.

"Well, it's not up to your father right now" was all KD said.

Then Sage came closer to me and whispered, "Hold your baby brother. I have to call nine-one-one."

He was wrapped in a soft white chunky-knit blanket that made him look like an angel nestled in clouds. His little face was both wrinkled and smooth, as if he was young and old like an ancestor in a tiny body.

I stared at my baby brother for what felt like an eternity, ignoring the chaos around me. In no time at all, the front door swung open, and two paramedics wheeled a stretcher into the bedroom. They lifted Mama from off the war-torn bed, and her face, her body, her whole being was someone I had never seen before—defeated and deflated.

"Mama?" I whispered, and let out a breath, as if a piece of my own life was leaving with her.

Then they finally let my father in. He rushed to Mama's side, crying out her name.

"Natalie! What'd they do to you?" My father's voice—the power-wielding Shango, that sea-parting thunderous sound—was small and fragmented, as if everything in that moment had broken him into a million pieces.

And Mama, barely here and barely there, whispered, "His name is Freedom. Freedom Sankofa Jones."

"Freedom," my father repeated, his voice shaking, glancing back at me and the baby, and I think I saw tears welling up in his eyes. "Okay, my love. We're going to call him Freedom."

I smiled, too, and repeated my new baby brother's name. *Freedom.*

As they rolled my mother out with my father beside her, holding her hand, KD came to take my baby brother from me.

"No! Where's he going?"

"To the hospital. We have to make sure he'll be okay," KD said.

"But they're systems," I whispered.

And this time, instead of my mother's cries piercing the night sky, it was my father's shouts. I couldn't make out his words; I could only feel his rage taking up the air like black smoke. They wouldn't let him onto the ambulance with my mother, his wife, and my baby brother, his son. So my father cursed everything and everyone around, even as fireworks lit up all of Philly celebrating America's birthday, which was also Freedom's birthday.

Before my father decides to go back to KD's, before he blames my mother for leaving us, before he finds her in that place where she's free, I go looking for her. I don't know what I'll find at KD's house, but at least I'll get some answers. Why did KD have that letter she wrote to the school? What's in the package? And maybe, just maybe,

I'll find out why Mama even left in the first place.

I text Sage to let her know I'm coming. No response.

I hoist Freedom onto my hip, grab his baby bag, and lie to my father about having to go to the grocery store and the baby needing some fresh air. I call a cab, and the twenty-minute ride up the I-76 and Lincoln Drive to Chestnut Hill is a quiet vacuum of unknowable things. Maybe I'm being pulled to where Mama might be, as if truth is a suctioning void. What am I even going to say to my mother after not seeing her all this time? What'll she do when she sees me and Freedom? Will Freedom even remember her? What will she think of him calling me Mama now?

Overgrown bushes, an uncut lawn, wildflowers, and a small oak tree are like a tiny forest around KD's house—an old wood-frame ranch on West Meade Street with chipping purple paint on the siding. The sign on the patchy lawn is for white people who want to tell the world that they're one of the good ones: IN THIS HOUSE WE BELIEVE THAT BLACK LIVES MATTER, WOMEN'S RIGHTS ARE HUMAN RIGHTS, LOVE IS LOVE, SCIENCE IS REAL, etc. Her business sign hangs over the green door.

Karma & Dharma Midwifery Services
Katherine Dillon, Certified Nurse Midwife (CNM)
Naturopathic Healer, Herbalist & Reiki Specialist

The front door unlocks, and it opens up to KD wearing a T-shirt with her business logo—a blossoming lotus that doubles as a uterus—and a big smile. "Nigeria!" she sings. "It's so good to see you and your brother. I'm so glad you both are here! Sage is inside working on her tinctures."

Sage comes to the door, and as my eyes meet hers, she narrows them with suspicion. She motions for me to follow her. On my way in, KD takes Freedom from my arms and showers him with kisses. She returns him when he starts crying and reaching for me, and rushes back to her office.

"My mother's here?" is the first thing I say when I step into their living room. For a moment, I'm frozen, not wanting to know the truth of whether or not she's in there, or what's inside the package she left with KD.

But Sage stares at me for a long time as if she wants to hug me, but if she does, I'll break. "Shit, Nigeria," she says. "I'm sorry, but your mother did leave something behind for you and she'll be really happy once you have it."

She grabs my arm, and I'm pulled into what feels like a portal, a time machine, or another dimension. I stand in the living room, which feels like the edge of a memory. So I don't move, not wanting to fall into that black hole. I search the space, instead, for any sign of Mama.

On the floor, right near the entrance, is an Elegua head—a triangular chunk of cement with cowrie shells for eyes, a nose, and lips surrounded by tea light candles. It's a West African symbol of protection, and I wonder if it belonged to Sage's father. Beneath the front window is a Buddha statue in the middle of small vases of fresh flowers, incense holders, a glass of water, and a singing bowl. KD is a Buddhist. In another corner is a small table covered with black fabric, black candles, a skull, and a crystal ball. KD also is a Wiccan— a straight-up witch. The walls in the living room are painted with affirmations and words like "bliss," "universe," "soul," "divine purpose," "Earth," and "mother." Macramé hangings, plants in all sizes, and paintings and illustrations of pregnant women cover every inch of this house, as well as statues and trinkets from every continent. The air is a mix of iron and eucalyptus, pain and magic. I scan the space for Mama's presence—her scent, her aura, her shadow. Anything. *Something.*

"Where's the package?" I finally ask.

But KD pokes her head out of her office, holding her phone in her hand, and says, "The mother is on her way. Contractions are five minutes apart. Get everything ready. She'll be here in twenty."

Sage grabs my hand again and pulls me into the kitchen. "You see those towels on the table? Put them in the oven to get them nice and warm."

I do what she says while keeping an eye on my brother. I'd done this before on the night he was born.

"We have to get a big pot of boiling herbs going—rose hips and red raspberry leaves. Put a separate pot out of blue and black cohosh just in case. The jars of herbs are on the counter under the bay window."

"Just in case what?"

"Just in case," Sage says. "Always just in case."

I do what she says.

Sage's curly afro is pulled back with a green bandanna, and she's wearing an off-white apron with an embroidered bee on the front—the same exact outfit she had on when Freedom was born. She was preparing tinctures and salves before I came in—pouring and mixing alcohol, distilled water, and herbs into glass measuring cups. I watch as she moves about the kitchen like a chemist.

My phone pings. It's my father texting and asking where I am. I ignore it.

"You like doing this?" I ask Sage. "If you can train to be a midwife, then why are you in school?"

"I still have to go to school to be a midwife, Nigeria. It's not the eighteen hundreds. And speaking of school . . ." She stops what she's doing, wipes her hands on her apron, and walks into her mother's office.

I'm alone in the kitchen, waiting and trying not to remember, trying not to hear the hushed echo of my mother's screams from the birthing room, trying not to see the muted colors and lights from the police cars flooding the living room. Houses have their own memories, too. Even when you're trying to forget, the walls are mirrors reflecting the past.

Then, for a moment, time stops. Something familiar and colorful and strange appears out of the corner of my eye. I quickly turn to the spot and blink and rub my eyes, making sure that what I saw is what I saw. I walk to the window, look outside, and see a dress that belongs to my mother—the blue-and-lavender tie-dye one that reaches down to her ankles. A gust of wind blows, and it looks as if she's floating midair. I swear, my heart skips a beat. *Mama!*

Here? Now? After all this time?

I rush to the door, unlock the locks, and turn the knob. I have to see her face, her eyes. She's standing there at the edge of the lawn, and she's inching closer and closer to the sidewalk, then the street.

And her feet . . . Her feet are not touching the ground. Mama glides, hovers, and when another wind blows, I swear, I swear she soars. *Mama.*

Another late-summer breeze blows, and what I thought was her dress is a plastic bag flying through the air like a parachute, and then it's a bird, and then it's a memory. I get a whiff of patchouli and lavender and I swear, I swear I saw her. I swear I can smell her. I swear I can feel her. She was here.

"Mama!" someone calls out, and I'm startled. I look down to see Freedom toddling over to me, reaching for my hand. I pick him up, kiss his cheek, and wonder if he saw her, too; smelled her, too; sensed her, too.

"What are you doing?" Sage asks as she returns from the office holding a thick manila envelope.

I look out at the street and up at the sky once more and say, "She comes here, doesn't she?"

Sage doesn't say anything, and when I turn back, she's holding the envelope toward me.

I don't take it and just stare at it as if Mama has folded her entire existence into that envelope, and maybe it holds the mysteries of her universe, or something. *Something.*

"I can keep this here for you so your father doesn't see it," Sage says, bringing the envelope to her chest. "But you gotta act fast. I wish you came to get this over the summer. I've been answering the emails and filling out the forms for you."

"What forms?"

Sage steps closer to me and looks into my eyes. "School," she says. "You got into my school."

"Philly Friends?" I ask. "Kamau's school? The one my mother wrote a letter to?"

"Yes, Philly Friends. Remember the test you took the February before last, when me and Kamau were both freshmen? You did really good, so they offered you a spot. But your father turned them down, and he didn't even tell you about it. Your mother wrote them that letter, but it was too late to accept any students for that year. Then this came in the mail a few months ago. Nigeria, they rolled out the red carpet for you this year."

Sage's words are a confusing stew of memory and possibility, hope and grief, dreams and reality. "School?" I ask again.

She sighs and rolls her eyes as if this is all too much work for her. "Yes, school. Nigeria, it's so messed up that me and my mother had to go behind your father's back, being all discreet, just to get you to go to school. We asked for your aunt's help, but she said she's not getting involved."

"They don't talk anymore, but me and Kamau still cool," I mumble, keeping my eyes on the envelope in her hand. I still don't take it.

"And this is the Movement that you don't want me to be a part of?"

"Family is different from the Movement," I say, not sure I believe that and mad that she's all in our family's business like this.

"Well, we're like family, Nigeria, whether you like it or not. We should've been there to celebrate Freedom's birthday. Your mother had some of her mail coming to our house, including all the stuff for your school. Did you know about your scores? Your scholarship?"

"What scholarship?"

"Holy shit. Mama! She doesn't know anything about this."

KD comes into the kitchen and walks straight to the windows and draws the curtains. She steps closer to me and says with pursed lips, "Your mother managed to keep this a secret all this time. Now it's up to you whether or not you let your father control your life."

"He's not controlling my life," I say.

She cocks her head and sighs, as if pitying me.

"Don't look at me like that," I say. "You don't know anything about us." I don't believe my own words. Mama had been spending a lot more time with KD since she got pregnant with Freedom. And I wonder if she wanted KD to deliver him all this time. I wonder how close they really were and what she'd been telling her about our family.

"Hey," Sage says, cutting through the tension between me and her mother. "Why don't you take a look at this, okay? Remember all those questions you had about my school? Well, all the answers are in here. They really want you, Nigeria. You're practically a genius."

I don't take the package from her. School. Genius. This is everything my mother wants for me. And everything my father wants to keep me away from. So I hang in the balance somewhere between African memories and American dreams. "She should've told me," I say, really low. "She should've told me she wanted me there."

"I heard your father doesn't want you to leave" is all Sage says.

"I gotta go," I say, ready to rush out the door as if the walls to the house are about to close in on me.

"Wait!" Sage says. "School starts on Wednesday. Orientation for new students was last week, and I had to lie and tell them that you were out of town. I'm doing this for your mother, but if you're not going . . ."

"I'm not going," I say.

KD comes over with a reusable bag and stuffs the envelope into it. "Look, Nigeria. This is what your mother wants, and if this comes between you and your father, my door is always open. You know that. You are brilliant. You got into that school as a junior. They want you there, and I know deep down in your heart, you want to be there, too. Your mother wants you there, honey."

I take the bag and stare at the both of them for a long second before I leave that house for good. I pick Freedom up from a floor pillow he had climbed onto, and call a cab on my phone.

"Oh, honey, I'd drive you home, but—" KD's phone pings. "Oh, shit! The mother is here!"

She runs to the door as Sage rushes back to the kitchen. A pregnant woman comes in with her partner and an older woman. KD's birthing house becomes a portal for life again.

Part of me wants to rip whatever's inside this envelope to pieces because it's already torn my family apart. The other part of me, which is all of me, is still chaos and confusion. I'm trying to make an ordered universe out of this wrinkle in time when my mother decided that she could just leave, that she could just fold into some secret part of herself and become a mystery. Maybe she wants me there with her, and she's reaching for me from across time and space, or some faraway place where she's actually, *actually* free.

SECTION 3

Sleep and rest are my birthright, but everything about my life right now breaks that promise over and over again. Jasmine is restless, too, but it's for a whole other reason.

She's made a storm out of my room, and she was supposed to go home over the summer. But she's still here. We don't pressure members to leave, but when it looks like they're really taking advantage, we hold a meeting with the elders. So it's a good thing that Jasmine is pulling her weight. But she can't stay here forever because we need to be always making room for new members. Her real family probably misses her, even though she says they're messed up. And besides, the point of being a member of the Movement is to gain enough knowledge and wisdom to pass it on. Each one teach one. I'm lying on my bed as I watch her rummage through a bag of clothes she'd thrifted earlier today.

"Some people already think I'm homeless, so buying clothes from a thrift store isn't a good look," she says while holding up a pair of old jeans. "The kids from around my way know that I'm not staying with my mama no more."

"It doesn't matter what they think," I tell her, hoping that she'd turn off the lights and go to sleep. My head is still spinning from today. "You're here with us, safe, warm, and getting healthier from all this vegan food!"

She laughs and throws a T-shirt at me. I throw it back only cracking a smile 'cause I'm trying to cheer her up when I don't even have energy for myself.

Jasmine is quiet for a hot minute, and I'm hoping that she's getting tired. But then she says, "I'm not going back to my school. That's one of the rules for living here, right? Decolonize, divest, and indigenize."

I sit up on the bed now. My world feels like it's peeling away to reveal some seed of truth nestled deep inside me, and maybe Jasmine can help dig it out. Even though she's slowly becoming a poster child for what the Movement can do for lost souls, I need her to really think about what she wants for her life, and I need to do the same. "Look, Jasmine. You already know that if you're a member and you live in the Village House, you have to give a hundred percent to the Movement. Which means helping us start our own school. You know what my father's trying to build here. You have to live and breathe the Movement. But at the same time, you gotta think about if that's what you really want."

She exhales deep and plops down on her bed. "My school will be up in my business if I don't show up on the first day of senior year," she says, folding back the pair of jeans into the bag. "They didn't even send a guidance counselor or a social worker out to my house. I mean, what used to be my house."

"Well, it's not like you're in danger here. You're actually doing good, and I think your mother knows that. Look at you reading big books! Everybody knows that we save lives, and you're an example of that. But . . . maybe . . ." I pause for a second and think carefully about my words because I'm also speaking to myself. "The Movement should be like a stepping stone and not your entire life."

"Nigeria, I can't go back to my old life. I feel like I was in some kind of deep sleep not knowing my history. But here . . . I need to go out there and tell my story. I need to tell all these kids how my life has changed because of y'all. And maybe when I'm older, I can start my own Village House," she says.

I take in a deep breath, preparing myself for what I'm about to say to her. "You can do all those things without being in the Village House, without being part of the Movement, even."

She freezes and looks at me with narrowed eyes.

"I'm telling you that this place saved my life and you telling me that I don't have to be here?" she asks. "What you trying to say, Sister Nigeria?"

I put my hands together and bring them to my lips as if praying, and I count down in my head from five. "My bad, Jasmine. I didn't mean it like that. It's just . . . I've seen members get caught up in the Movement, and once they see my father mess up and they lose trust in us, they turn their backs and forget what they've learned here."

"I know y'all are not perfect," she says. "I heard some of the Youth Group members call this a Blacktopia, so y'all damn near close."

I want to say more, but Freedom starts to cry in my parents' room. I'm glad I have a reason to step away from Jasmine.

It's almost midnight, and my father had left to do his usual errands around the community—checking up on the uncles, being a guest on somebody's podcast, and stirring up shit with the oppressors. He hadn't come home yet by the time Freedom fell asleep. I wish I could keep my baby brother in my room, but he just got used to sleeping in his own bed in my parents' room. Some people are moving about downstairs in the kitchen, and I'm mad that there can never be real peace and quiet in this house. Mama used to impose a curfew, and after a certain time, no one was allowed into her kitchen. But now this whole house is a free-for-all.

There's light coming from under my parents' bedroom door. My father must've come back. So I knock. "Baba, is Freedom all right? I can help put him back to sleep."

He doesn't answer.

"Is it okay to come in?"

Nothing.

"Baba?" I ask one more time before I open the door.

And when I do, my whole body becomes stone. I blink a few times to make sure that who I'm seeing is who I'm seeing, that the woman on Mama's side of the bed is not actually Mama.

So I take in a deep, cooling breath to calm myself down and ask, "What are you doing in here?"

She's wearing a sheer white nightgown and patting Freedom's back as he lies on a pillow, and all I want to do is yank her off that bed and drag her out of this room and, maybe, out of this house. Her eyes are wide, like she just got busted, and she's probably trying to come up with some bullshit.

"What are you doing in here?" I shout this time.

Freedom starts to cry again.

"Nigeria, I need you to calm down," Nubia says.

"I am calm. I asked you a question, that's all."

"Nigeria. Your father and I . . ."

"My father and you?"

"He should've spoken with you. . . . If not, I should've told you . . ."

"Told me what?" I shout even louder because there's never been another woman on this bed besides Mama.

"Please lower your voice. There's no need to get everyone else involved."

"Nigeria, what's the matter?" Jasmine calls out from down the hall.

Other people are coming up the stairs, and I swear to my ancestors that it better be my father so he can tell me what the fuck is going on in here. I rush toward Freedom, pick him up, and hold him close as he cries. I step as far away from that lady as fast as possible because if I don't . . .

"All right, y'all. Let's calm down," Uncle Ra says from the doorway.

Jasmine and Makai are behind him, watching.

"Nigeria . . ." Nubia calls out, but she doesn't say anything else.

I stomp out of the room with Freedom in my arms. Everybody makes a path for me in the hallway as I aim for my bedroom. But Jasmine will be in there and I need my space. So I turn around to head downstairs, but there are too many people in this house and I need my space. Freedom is crying louder now and rubbing his eyes and I need my space. I hold him tight trying to shush him.

"Nigeria, put the baby down and let us talk to you," Uncle Ra says from behind me.

But I keep turning and turning, looking for a quiet place to calm my baby brother and myself down.

Nubia comes out of the bedroom and is walking toward me. So I go down the stairs just as my father is coming in through the front door. Our eyes meet. Then he looks up at the top of the stairs, where everybody is watching. Then he looks down at me.

"Nigeria, bring Freedom back to his bed and let's talk," he says.

I ignore him. The living room is empty and dark. That's where I find my space—on an armchair where Mama used to sit when she was pregnant with Freedom. My baby brother curls himself on my lap, and in seconds, he's asleep again, and everybody leaves me alone.

My mind spins in circles. All I have are questions that I don't even want to ask. *Why didn't anyone tell me that he was ready to move on with his life?* I don't know how much time has passed when my father comes to take Freedom from me. "Get to bed, Ni. We'll talk in the morning," he says.

I let go of my baby brother only because my arms are tired. I am tired. The walls to this house are inching closer and closer, and there's a scream lodged in the back of my throat. My whole body is a rock with tiny cracks forming on its surface. When my father leaves, I get up and walk past the kitchen with its dirty dishes and lights still on, through the back door, and onto the patio in the backyard. I sit in Mama's spot and remember all the things she's taught me about staying calm and centered, about tapping into my goddess consciousness and not letting the world throw me off-balance. She taught me how to take deep pranayama breaths, but instead, I hold my breath and wonder what will happen if I just . . . stop. She taught me how to ground myself by naming all the things I see and feel. But instead, I close my eyes and wonder what will happen if I just . . . stop.

Someone turns off the lights in the kitchen. Then it's quiet, except for the passing cars and crickets and the humming sounds of nearby air conditioners. I let myself merge with the darkness and wonder about all the places my mother could be right now. I can't imagine her sleeping soundly, being at peace knowing that she left us behind, away from us. So I don't want to think about her. But it's like she doesn't want me to forget her, so she haunts me in the strangest places—at KD's house and in my dreams. I don't have an answer to *Why'd she leave? Is this why? Does she even know about this new woman?*

I don't know. I don't know.

The smell of weed makes me think that she's probably here. This is where she'd come out and smoke a joint by herself while sipping on a mug of herbal tea. She'd also have a bundle of sage beside her, or a stick of incense. The sweet, bitter, and earthy scents would dance around each other and intertwine like vines and rise up to reach me through my bedroom window.

I sniff and sit up on the chair. The smell is close. Too close. Maybe she's haunting me again, and the thought of her presence sends chills all over my body.

"Sorry. Is it bothering you?" a voice in the dark asks.

"Who's there?" No response. Then I ask, "Chris?"

Still, nothing. Then, after a long second, he says, "I'm thinking that I might not want to answer to that name no more. King Kofi was right," he says, and his voice is like smoke, too.

"How do you know? You haven't been around the world yet," I say. There's a small bench at the edge of my mother's vegetable garden, and he's probably sitting there. That was her other spot, but the garden is overgrown with weeds and the mosquitos are ruthless.

"My world is Philly," he says. "North Philly, West Philly. Each hood is like a different continent."

This is the most he's spoken since he got here last month, and I wonder who fixed him. "Whatever, globe-trotter. I hope you have on a long-sleeve shirt and some pants 'cause the mosquitos are gonna tear you up over there."

"You *stay* warning me about shit that's gonna tear me up. First, it's the bullet casings, and now it's the mosquitos."

He's right. Why do I care anyway? But that smoke—both from the weed and his voice. "Can I get a hit?" I ask.

I hear the twigs and dried leaves under his shoes. Then he's barely visible in the moonlight at the bottom of the patio steps. I make out a black T-shirt and his short braids hanging over his forehead and ears. He brings the joint to his lips and pulls, releasing the smoke into the moonlit air. "Meet me halfway," he says.

"You sure are chatty all of a sudden," I say, not moving from the patio.

"And you sure sounded like you was ready to throw hands in there."

"Let me get that hit so I can just . . . disappear . . ." I say, letting my voice trail off with that last word.

"Then come over here where it's dark."

"Meet me halfway," I say, almost whispering. I get up from the chair and sit on the patio steps, where the light is just dim enough for both of us to look like ghosts.

He sits next to me while holding the joint that's now a roach—small, black, and burnt, and barely the size of his fingertips.

"Clearly you've been nursing this for a while," I say.

"My bad. That's rude of me. It's like I'm offering you crumbs," he says.

"You didn't offer. I asked. Keep smoking so I can get that contact high."

"I got a better idea." He takes a long pull and motions for me to face him.

I know exactly what to do. He exhales long and deep, releases the smoke, and it's like a ghost is escaping his body. And I open my mouth wide, wide and take in everything that he is, that he was. The smoke moves between us as easy as breath. I didn't realize that he was pulling me in closer and closer with smoke for hands, the night air for a body, and deep, deep sorrow for something like desire.

My head is lit up with a thousand fireflies, and maybe I'm glowing right now. I'm inches from his face when I ask, "Where'd you come from?"

He licks his lips and says, "I come from your father's worst nightmare."

"What's that supposed to mean?" I pull away, and if it wasn't for the smoke, I'd walk away, too, 'cause I don't want to even think about my father right now.

"That's what he told me. That I'm his worst nightmare. No home. No family. No goals. And I don't give a fuck about anything. America's worst nightmare."

"My father tends to exaggerate shit. And *he's* America's worst nightmare, not you. That is, if he manages to dismantle white supremacy and start a race war like they accuse him of doing. You're America's wet dream. If you don't give a fuck about anything, that'll be a reason to lock you up or shoot you dead in the streets. You and everything that you stand for justifies their injustice."

"That's fucked up," he says, taking another pull, and the joint is so tiny now it looks like he's smoking hopes and dreams.

"You're acting like you don't know."

"I didn't know. Your father is helping me see the world with new eyes. I mean, when you grow up the way I did, you ain't thinking about no fucking . . . *white supremacy*. At least not like that."

I keep my eyes ahead, staring into the dark backyard. There are so many memories here. But this moment feels like it's all been painted over with one giant brushstroke. The sight of Nubia on Mama's bed creeps in like a shadow, and I should be pissed all over again. But I don't let it take over this moment—this distraction with this boy I hardly know who lives in my house. "Who fixed you?" I ask. My words and thoughts are a muddy mix of exhaustion, rage, curiosity, and something hot stirring in the middle of me that I can't name.

"What you mean 'who fixed me'? I'm not broken."

"People come here to get fixed. You're already talking about changing your name. And that's the problem. When you're broken, you don't even recognize the tiny, fractured pieces of yourself orbiting around your soul like dust. You think the dust belongs to the world, but really, it's all part of your broken self."

He doesn't say anything for a hot minute. Then he asks, "Who broke me?"

"You mean who broke *us*?"

"Let me guess. The white man?" He chuckles and flicks the roach onto the ground.

"That's not funny. If you're not gonna take this seriously, then you don't need to be here." I get up from the steps to look for the end of the joint he just threw away. "Don't toss your shit out over here. This is sacred ground," I say. It's too dark to find it, but I keep looking anyway.

"If y'all are so perfect, then why'd you come at Nubia like that? If there's one person who *fixed* me, it's her. I remember how you just gave me a Band-Aid and left me there bleeding on your kitchen counter. It was Nubia who came and cleaned me up."

"Her name is Camille" is the only thing I can say because he's right and I won't admit it. I sit back down next to him on the steps, closer this time.

"Oooh," he sings, bringing his fist up to his mouth and leaning away from me. "Is that shade I detect? You're not feeling this Nubia chick, huh?"

"No shade," I say, shaking my head. "It is what it is."

"A'ight. So, you don't agree with what your father says in his books about preserving the Black family?"

A stone sinks in my belly, and time stops. And maybe the dark night air becomes a blazing red color and everything is up in flames right now. I wish. I don't have a thing to say about this, but I have all the feelings.

"There's this chapter in *Black Families Matter*, the first one, where he says the revolution starts in the home," Chris continues. "Mother, father, child. Aunties, uncles, cousins. Grandparents. Elders. All under one roof. And what white supremacy does is separate the king from his queen. So the foundation is broken from the jump. And for Black people in this country, with all these brothers locked up and getting murked . . . With all these sisters out here being single mothers . . . If we want to be free, let's put the queen first, feel me?" He rubs his hands together while looking at me sideways, as if he just dropped some science I've never heard of.

"So you've been reading my father's books, huh?" is all I can say, remembering the notes my mother had written.

"Ain't that one of the requirements for living here? Just finished *Black Families Matter, Volume I*, and I'm about to start *Flip the Table*. He promised to let me read a draft of *The Black Man's Constitution*. I've been a fan ever since King Kofi came to my school when I was a sophomore. Got a selfie with him, too. Your mother, the queen Natalie Sankofa, was mad cool. From that point on, I knew I wanted to know everything about what y'all do here."

"Natalie Pierre," I quickly correct him. "She never changed her name."

He pulls out his phone, and in seconds, he's showing me pictures of the Kwanzaa celebration in the basement of Allen Church from two years ago. Mama had made a whole vegan spread with baked cauliflower in the shape of a turkey, mac 'n' cashew cheese, and deep-fried mushrooms that looked like chicken. "I thought I'd be eating all this shit while living here."

"She'll be back," I tell him.

"You for real?" is all he says as he pulls out a lighter and another joint from his pocket.

"Yeah, I'm for real," I whisper.

"The only thing I don't like, though, is this plant-based shit your father got everybody on. I stay hungry up in this house. Nubia tried to make some tofu shit the other day, but it was nasty," Chris says, and it's music to my ears.

The fridge in our kitchen has been empty. Everybody is supposed to contribute something to groceries, and Mama would go to the farmers market and get fresh fruits and veggies to feed everyone living in the house. But since she left, everybody's been on their own, including me and Freedom. I cook for both of us and not the whole house. "She can't take my mother's place," I mumble, more to myself than to Chris.

"She's not supposed to take your mother's place. She's queen mother number two. Two queens can't occupy the same throne. That's how they did it back in Africa. All the king's wives had their own compound."

"Who told you that?"

"Where you been, Queen? In the few weeks I've been here, I know more about the Movement than you do."

He *thinks* he knows. "I gotta get outta here," I whisper.

"Why would you want to leave, though? Being here is the best thing that's ever happened to me. I wasn't feeling it at first, and I still don't understand some shit y'all be doing. But I was ready to murk some kid, and your father took me to the range so I could be humble and respect the weapon. But my dumb ass still didn't get it and King Kofi showed up right on time to save my life. Queen, your father saved my life! The Movement saved my life!"

But who's saving me? I want to ask. "That's what we do. Save Black lives" is all I say.

"That's what I'm talking about! Black lives matter in the Sankofa Movement all day, every day. I'm living proof that y'all don't just talk that shit; y'all walk that shit, Queen!"

Please stop calling me Queen, I also want to say. I'm the ruler of no one and nothing. My house is his house. My family is everybody's family. And all I want to do right now is hold Freedom in my arms because my baby brother is mine and only mine.

Then Chris says, "Yo, I got the munchies, and I wanna get some fried chicken or a burger or something, 'cause I'm starvin' up in here!"

So now it's midnight and I'm in the kitchen making Chris a meatless burger because he needs to know that it tastes just like the real thing, even though *I've* never had the real thing. He's sitting at the counter watching me and smiling and insisting that a burger made out of plant protein won't taste like beef.

"Can I get some fries with that shake?" Chris asks.

I dig into the freezer looking for a bag of sweet potato fries. "It's called a smoothie, not a shake."

"It was a joke," Chris continues. "Get it? *Your* milkshake."

I roll my eyes, not wanting to play any games with this boy. My head is somewhere in that manila envelope I got from KD's house.

"It was a joke," he says again.

I ignore whatever joke that was, and I pull out the blender to get started on his smoothie. I'm focused on taking over where Mama left off. She would've done this for anyone. I've seen her stay up all night preparing meals for members or the Movement's events.

"Nice," Chris says when I place the burger and fries in front of him.

"Thank you" is all I say.

"You're too serious," he says.

"This is serious work," I say.

"Yeah, but you need to smile and laugh a little. Joy is a revolution, too, you know."

And maybe I'm disarmed for a minute. Only a minute.

As he chomps down on his food, I keep myself focused and distracted by loading the dishwasher, cleaning the stove and countertops, sweeping, and mopping. By the time I'm done, Chris has already told me good night after trying to get my attention and cracking corny jokes or whatever, and my eyes are burning from lack of sleep.

Mama never let me forget that since the kitchen is the heart of the house, a clean kitchen is like a light heart. And I wonder if wherever she is, wherever she found that freedom she was looking for, she has a light heart.

Someone is coming down the steps. Nubia shows up in the kitchen holding Freedom in her arms as he rubs his eyes and pouts. "Does he usually ask for milk in the middle of the night?" she asks.

And that's when I know that people can be like prison bars, and I have to break myself down to the very smallest thing in the universe so I can slip through the cracks of this perfect thing my father created—this Movement, this Blacktopia—and fly and fly and fly. Like Mama, maybe.

I used to wake up in the middle of the night and be hungry, too. I can still remember when my toddler bed was in my parents' room when we used to live in a small apartment near Temple. Mama would take me to the kitchen for some cookies and almond milk. She'd sit on her favorite papasan chair, and I'd climb onto her lap for story time. There was one book she would read to me over and over again: *The People Could Fly* by Virginia Hamilton. Some nights, she would read the whole book from cover to cover. Other nights, she would only read the last story, where the people flew away to be free. Most nights, and when I got older as she twisted my locs, she would tell her own story of flying, of the wind taking her by the arms and holding her up to the sky so she could ride the clouds—just like the people in the book, the enslaved Africans who couldn't have freedom on the ground, so they looked for it in the sky, where the wind carried them home, back to the motherland, back to Africa.

I take Freedom to my room because he was reaching for me while Nubia held him. He's not used to her, and I don't want him to be. Jasmine is asleep, so I put my baby brother down on my bed. He wakes up, whimpering a little, and climbs onto my lap. So I pull out my copy of *The People Could Fly* from a nearby shelf and start quietly reading the last story to him. "They say the people could fly," I start. "Say that long ago in Africa, some of the people knew magic."

I read to myself mostly, because Freedom falls asleep immediately. And maybe I don't want him to know about slaves and ships, and masters and whips. Would Mama be reading this story to him the way she did for me? She wanted me to know where we came from and why we were building a Movement. And after everything, after reading this story to me over and over again, she leaves us? She leaves me?

What if I want to fly, too?

I put Freedom down, find that bag from KD's house, pull out the package, and place the navy-blue folder thick with what feels like an undiscovered universe on my lap. The name of the school is embossed in fancy silver letters. I trace each line and curve with my finger and whisper the words as if I'm praying to the ancestors. "The Philadelphia Friends School."

And Mama's voice inhabits the room like an old song coming from faraway speakers. "You are so smart, Nigeria. You can do anything you want in the world," she had said to me one day.

"She's more than smart. She's a genius," my father had responded. "We raised a prodigy. She should take all the tests in the world just to let those white folks know that we don't need their education."

"Keith, you forgot where we met?" Mama had asked.

And I remember that night when she announced that she was having a baby, I climbed into the bed with her, curled into her arms as she told me a new story. "Did I ever tell you how I met your father?" she started.

I shook my head, and her voice . . . Her voice, her warm honey lilt, is all the story, all the dreaming, I need right now.

"He was *fine*. He was so fine. But he was young. Just *young*. But so old. Reminds me of you, how your soul seems like it's been through lifetimes of pain, lifetimes of joy, when you've only been here for fourteen years. Your father can't fly and travel like we do. He's too wound up in this world to even think about finding peace somewhere else.

"He was a sophomore at Temple, and I was in my first year of grad school. The PhD program in African American Studies. I decided on Temple because I learned that Philadelphia had America's first refugee crises—French plantation owners and enslaved Africans from Saint-Domingue, what would become Haiti. I felt a connection to Philly, you know. Like, maybe one of my Haitian ancestors came to this country in 1793 and lived and thrived and I am just as connected to this place as I am to Haiti . . . And maybe your father. Well, he loved that I was Haitian—that I have revolution in my bones. He was a whole five years younger, and he was so proud to be with an 'older woman.'" Mama chuckled and wiped tears from her eyes. "He'd written a paper about the Haitian Revolution, and he wanted to impress me. He did. He really did. Your father had so much passion. Still does, clearly. By the time I met him, he was already president of the Black Student Union, organizing protests, shut-ins, sleep-ins, read-ins, fighting people online, yelling and carrying on every time there was some injustice, you name it. People were calling him Fred Hampton or Malcolm X reincarnate. He changed his name from Keith Jones to Kofi Sankofa and thought he was teaching me something about Africa and African words. He proposed when he graduated. Got down on one knee and asked me to be his warrior queen. But I didn't really know what I was saying yes to. What started out as protests and social justice work became nation-building and decolonizing and dismantling everything. In trying to make things better, he was making my life worse. He wanted us to have our own little army . . . A bunch of kids to make up for all the absentee fathers out there, he said. But all I could give him was one little girl that he tried to make an army out of. Baby, I'm sorry I couldn't give you any more siblings. But Gigi? I'm finally going to have another baby. And I'm praying to the ancestors that they come back as a boy. That's what your father wants. A warrior prince, a baby king.

"You're so smart," she continued. "So, so smart. The tests can tell it. Your father loves you. And he wants the world to know how much of a genius you are."

So that's why my father made it like a game, or part of my home-schooling. Sign up for a test, practice and study, take it, and ace it. We ignored the congratulatory letters, the scholarship offers, the acceptances to this and that fancy school. Or better yet, my father bragged about my high scores and the schools' letters in his videos and told his followers that these white folks need us more than we need them. That's how he got a bunch of people to sign up for the Freedom School and his promises to have our own building.

I didn't know. I didn't know that all this time, Mama was dreaming for me. And I was too busy, too caught up in my father's world to even notice, to even dream for myself.

PART TWO
THE DIVIDED STATES OF NIGERIA JONES

MY BODY AS LAND ACKNOWLEDGMENT

I acknowledge that here on my body on which you gather are the ancestral bodies of all Native and African people, whose presence and resilience in this country continue to this day. I take this opportunity to honor the original caretakers of this body and recognize the histories of body theft, violence, erasure, and oppression that has brought your institution and yourselves here.

ARTICLE IV
BLACK TO [FREEDOM] SCHOOL

"A woman is free if she lives by her own standards and creates her own destiny if she prizes her individuality and puts no boundaries on her hopes for tomorrow."

—*attributed to Mary McLeod Bethune, aka The First Lady of the Struggle, master teacher, educator extraordinaire, 1875–1955*

"Quakers almost as good as colored. They call themselves friends and you can trust them every time."

—*attributed to Harriet Tubman (but did she really?), the abolitionist queen to whom all freedom-loving people bow down, c. 1822–1913*

GRIEVANCE 1

A wide green sprawling lawn separates the school from the sidewalk where the cab drops me off in East Falls. A brick structure with white lettering lets everyone know that this is the Philadelphia Friends School and it was founded in 1689. It's been raining hard all morning, and the dark gray clouds cast a shadow over the school building with its clock tower and white-framed windows. Loud thunder rolls high above Philly, and the pounding on umbrellas and on the pavement makes everything ominous and dreary—as if this is the end of the world. Maybe it's just the end of *my* world, the one I used to know.

On the other side of that lawn, a long line of cars are dropping off white kids near the entrance with quiet, controlled uniformity. This school is like walking into a whole other world—the real world—and that lawn lets me know that traveling between spaces is not as easy as it seems.

I'm here, I text Sage.

And I can't believe that I am actually here. Last night, I went to bed not knowing what I'd do about this dream of mine. And this morning, it's as if the pounding rain were drumbeat rhythms making a path for me. I don't have an umbrella, so my locs soak up all the rainwater, and everything about me today will be a sponge.

Less than a half hour ago, I was in the Village House, the place I called school for most of my life, and now I'm walking through the red double doors of a mostly white private school. My heart is a djembe drum, and every cell in my body wants to run down those halls and into those classrooms to just sit there and be . . . free.

I think of texting Kamau, too. But this whole thing is supposed to be a secret from my father, and I don't want Aunt Sharon to find out, either, even though they're not talking. Mama trusted KD with this as if she and her daughter are some sort of lifeline.

Go to the security desk, Sage texts back. It's too late to see Diane in the admissions office, so you'll have to go straight to the meeting.

I'm here to see you! I text.

I'll meet you in the lobby.

I've been here before. Kamau had asked me to tour the school with him and his mother, Aunt Sharon, when he'd decided that he didn't want to homeschool anymore. "It's the best in Philly," he had said with a proud smile.

"But it's rich and white," I had told him. "Is that why it's the best?"

"If we want to change the world, don't we have to be in the same room with the people who run it?" Kamau had responded, and something lit up in me. This was different from what my father had always said about divesting and decolonizing. My father doesn't want to change the world; he wants to create his own world—a world that I'm not sure I want to be a part of anymore.

In that moment, I looked up everything I needed to know about my cousin's school and started dreaming of a different life for myself—one where I could change *my* world.

But I was still in my feelings about Kamau leaving me behind. We were both thirteen going on fourteen and were supposed to be starting high school like everyone else our age. But we were never like everyone else. Then, after Aunt Sharon started questioning my father's new ideas, he and his mother just up and decided that they did, in fact, want to be like everybody else, but only a little bit since this was an independent school founded by Quakers and all. A lot of the kids who go here, including Sage, are basically hippies and free-spirited artists—if they're on scholarship. So maybe I'll fit in. I hope.

"It's kinda like us, but for white people with money," Kamau had told me. "Did you know that Quakers were the first abolitionists?"

I remember the short speech a Black lady had given on the tour and thinking that Kamau must've been one special snowflake to have gotten into this school. "We have a thirteen percent acceptance rate," the lady had told the group. A few of those kids and their parents glanced back at us. "We are one of the oldest schools in this country and are part of a long legacy of Quakers, or the Religious Society of Friends, who were prohibited from owning slaves and were the country's first abolitionists, many of whom were essential to the Underground Railroad."

"If they were abolitionists, then how come there aren't more Black kids here?" I had whispered to Kamau. "The website says there are only six percent."

Aunt Sharon had shushed us as she smiled and nodded, doing all the things, it seemed, to make sure that Kamau got into that school. And he did, with a full ride.

I had walked through this lobby, and there was some kind of church in their courtyard that they call a meetinghouse. But all of that was overshadowed by another huge argument between my father and his big sister afterward.

"So you want to be a Quaker now?" my father had said when Kamau and Aunt Sharon dropped me off.

Kamau said, "No, Uncle Keith, you don't have to be a Quaker to go there."

But my father was only talking to his sister. "You're trying to make him a token Black boy in that school? After all he learned in the Movement? After all I've done for him? Quakers owned slaves, too, you know."

Aunt Sharon, who has a temper just like my father, went all the way off. She said, "You think you know everything. They didn't own slaves. And I'm getting sick and tired of all this racist bullshit, Keith! White people are not the devil, and you're starting to act like one!"

Then they went back and forth on whether or not Black people can be racist, and Aunt Sharon had a few choice words for my father, and my father had several choice words for Aunt Sharon. But the worst part was when Mama stepped in to defend my father. Wrong move. Mama should've stayed out of it. But the good thing is, me and Kamau are still cool. Though not enough for my mother to trust his mother with something like this. Maybe Mama didn't want Aunt Sharon to be like, "I told you so," and tell my father that she'd been right all along about getting me into a good school because I was so smart. The beef between his mother and my father had been going on for years, but it got worse when my father found out about Kamau. It's affecting how I deal with my favorite person in the world. Kamau should've known about my mother wanting me to come here. He should be the one helping me and not Sage.

So I text him. You're not gonna believe where I am now.

I keep my eyes glued to my phone as kids walk past me. The school's lobby reminds me of oppression and white supremacy with its giant portraits of the school's founder, William Penn. Mental note to research everything about him. Philly Friends is like a whole college campus, with school buildings that look like churches. My father calls places like this the bowels of white supremacy. It's where oppressive ideas are born and incubated to maintain white male dominance all over the world, and the portrait of William Penn staring down at me like that reminds me of everything my father says, everything the Movement wants to destroy.

A flash of regret passes through me like an electric shock, jolting me back to reality. What in the world am I doing? I don't belong here.

A text comes in from Jasmine. Where are you?

"Turn off the location on your phone," someone whispers behind me. I almost kiss Kamau when I turn around, his face is so close. I hug him so tight and for so long, the kids around us must think that we're together.

"Please, girl, I have a reputation to maintain," he says, gently pushing me off him. But his smile is sunshine on this rainy day. "And you are soaking wet!"

I hug him again and bury my face in his neck. This isn't the place or the time, but I didn't know that I'd been holding back a deluge of tears.

"Nigeria, no, no, no!" he says, pulling my arms away from him. "Get it together, girl. You're here. Now we have to make sure you stay."

"I thought you weren't supposed to know about this." My voice is a fault line and I am the earth breaking into pieces, entire continents adrift. I feel like a whole natural disaster right now, so I hide my face from the sky.

Kamau takes my hand and walks me away from the entrance and to a corner of the lobby with a bench and sits me down. I keep my face covered because there is a storm there. An avalanche of all the stones I'd been swallowing back comes tumbling out of my throat, and I sob. Worse than my baby brother. Worse than after Mama argues with my father. Worse than when Mama left. Worse than every time I ever had to shed tears over something I couldn't control—which is everything. *Everything.*

"Nigeria, do you even cry in your own house?" Kamau says. "You can't let it all out here, either. We should be in Diane's office."

"Who's Diane?" I ask, sniffing back my joy, my relief, and all the emotions I can't let out right now.

"Diane Hutchinson, head of DEI. We've been helping her get you registered. You're here. You finally made it, girl!"

"Did you know that my mother tried to get me in this school, too?"

"Yeah, because my mother was trying to convince her, and your mother was trying to convince your father. And we all knew that was a lost cause. But this little stunt your mother pulled . . . I'm mad that I had to find out from Sage."

Then someone's hand is in my face, holding out a tissue. I take it and don't look up.

"It's sprinkled with a few drops of ylang-ylang oil. It should calm you down." It's Sage, of course.

My phone pings again. A text from Jasmine. Nigeria WYA??? You left me out here with these boys and Chris is driving your father's truck picking up his friends.

Before I text her back, Kamau grabs my phone, presses a few buttons, and returns it to me.

"Turn off your location!" he says through clenched teeth. "He's going to find out at some point, but for now, you're here. We'll deal with your father later."

My teary eyes meet Sage's. Her wild, curly hair is a shadow around her face, and she's looking down at me. So I pull myself together, wipe my face, and swallow back the stones just as a Black woman walks toward us with a huge smile. I've seen her before. She was the same woman from when we first toured the school. Wearing a brown suit and short cropped hair, she holds out a mug covered with a napkin when she reaches us.

"Peppermint," she says to me with a deep, powerful voice. "I'm sure it feels like a breath of fresh air here."

And I exhale. I take it and hold it as if it's everything safe and familiar.

"Welcome to the Philadelphia Friends School, Nigeria Jones," the woman continues. "We've been expecting you. I'm so glad you're finally here."

I glance at both Kamau and Sage, and look all around the lobby half expecting my mother to come out from behind a door to tell me that this is the freedom she wanted for me. My mouth can't form the right words or any cohesive thought. So I just wrap my hand around the warm mug, watch the white kids walk into the school past a security desk where a Black man is signing them in, and sip on the tea.

"I'm Diane Hutchinson, the head of Diversity, Equity, and Inclusion," she says. "And please, just call me Diane. We're on a first-name basis here at Philly Friends. Your application was complete since spring of last year, but we didn't have any openings for the tenth grade. So, we deferred your acceptance and offered you a seat for this year. I'm so glad you accepted. Let's get your paperwork in order so you can have a smooth transition. I'm well aware of your situation, and Sage and her mom have been a tremendous help."

What situation? I think, but I just keep sipping. And I can't look away from the portrait of William Penn with his Quaker hat and his Quaker face and his Quaker ideas and his Quaker oats in his fat belly, and wonder if he, like the founding fathers George Washington and Thomas Jefferson, owned a Black girl who was my age and looked like me and did whatever he wanted to do with her. So I remember who I am and where I come from. "My father doesn't want me to come to this white supremacist school." It's a truth I need to say out loud because I'm risking everything to be here.

"I understand that, Nigeria," Diane says. "But what do *you* want?"

I don't say anything to her and keep my truth in that quiet, invisible space between my dreams and my memories, what I see for myself and what I remember of myself. I can't speak that reality into existence just yet. The Village House, the Movement, and my father are doors I haven't really closed. Neither is Mama's absence.

GRIEVANCE 2

I can count on both hands how many times I've been around this many white people. A few of those times were in museums in Center City, and in New York. That's it. Not counting the times I've been in KD's car and her being one of my mother's best friends and the only white person in my life. My parents have always kept me in a Black bubble for my own protection.

So if I do go to this school for the next two years (I still can't believe that this is even an option), I'll be coming into this meetinghouse every week to attend *meeting for worship*, they call it. It's supposed to be like Mama's silent retreats, where she listens to the ancestors and gets downloads from the universe. Except here, I'm sitting on meetinghouse pews with hundreds of other kids, almost all of them white, so my mind automatically starts to count the brown faces.

Sage is in the front somewhere, sitting with her friends, and Kamau is way on the other side of the room. I had come in late after I went to Diane's office so I could pull myself together. She gave me a temporary ID for the day and my class schedule. I'd been wearing a gray The Free Black Women's Library T-shirt that had gotten soaked, so she gave me a new, dry Philly Friends navy-blue T-shirt to change into. Wearing that logo and the school's colors, I already feel branded and owned.

Diane also showed me the papers Mama signed back in April and May of last year, when she was pregnant with Freedom, and she never said a word to me. "Did she sign anything recently?" I had asked Diane.

"Recently? Well, of course not. I've been communicating with Katherine Dillon since the start of this year, to follow up on your deferred acceptance." She spoke softly and slowly as if I'm made of fragile glass. "Again, I understand your situation. But if you can let me know what you decide by the end of the week, that'd be great."

"If my mother really wants me to be here, then she'd be here, too. She'd drop me off. She'd be in this office talking to you instead of me," I said.

She shook her head, pitying me. Then she showed me all the email exchanges she and my mother had, going back to early last year after I'd taken the test. So Mama had been planning this before Freedom was born, before she left us. And she didn't tell me? *She didn't tell me!*

"You were one of the highest scorers," Diane said. "We reached out to Mr. Jones first, but he made it clear that he was not interested. Then your mother called back and pleaded for us to reconsider. Nigeria, you will thrive here. You are so, so special. Your mother sent us the essays you'd written and videos of your speeches. The world needs your voice, and this is exactly where you need to be in order to cultivate it."

I stopped her from saying more. She was about to gas me up and tell me that this is the best and only place for me. We do the same thing to get kids into the Youth Group. "Can I still come here even if my father disapproves?"

"Nigeria, we will try our best to talk to him. It's no cost to your family. Everything you need will be provided for. This is where future leaders are shaped and molded. There's no denying that your father wants you to be a change-maker, just like him." Then she went on to tell me that she started out in public school, and she came here in the seventh grade through some program for Black kids, and that this school exposed her to the world and she learned more about Black history and culture than she ever would going to a public school.

I wasn't impressed, but I said, "Challenge accepted." I agreed to attend the meeting for worship and take it from there.

So here I am in this church (that they're not calling a church) with my dark brown skin, rain-kissed locs tied up above my head, and a Philly Friends T-shirt, letting this little part of the world know somebody thinks I belong here.

My phone is off, and no one in my family or in the Movement knows where I am. Except Kamau and Mama. I hope she's happy right now. I make eye contact with Kamau. He smiles and nods. I wish I found a seat next to him, but I'm in the back row at the very end of the pew where I can just disappear into the shadows.

"Welcome to a new school year here at Philadelphia Friends," a man standing at the podium says as the entire upper school sits in silence in the meetinghouse. "I would like our friends to reflect on what new beginnings and forgiveness mean in your life and how you extend grace to others—both strangers and loved ones, friends and family. Let us reflect on fresh starts for this first meeting for worship of the school year."

This sounds like a church. *What am I doing here?* Even as my mind races with doubt, I try to fold myself into the tight corner of the pew where the armrest meets the seat. An empty aisle and a stained-glass window is to the left of me. To the right of me, a white boy only scoots a little bit to make space for me. He's too close. I don't want his leg to touch my leg, and he doesn't even look my way to see who he's about to rub up against. In that moment, I second-guess everything again. My father's words to Kamau echo in my mind. *After all that you learned in the Movement, this is where you want to be?*

Then the memory comes to me as if a stone just hit my head. "She's not going to their schools, Natalie," my father had said. I was little—four or five, maybe. Mama had wanted me to start school. Was it this school? But my father talked her out of it. They'd argued about it for a few days, and then it was over.

Mama's voice slips into this memory, distant and small, as if she's slowly fading away from everything that I remember. "What do you want to be when you grow up, Ni?"

"A revolutionary!" I had said with all the confidence in the world. Again, I was little and had only known the world my father built.

But now I realize that revolutions belong to my father. He'd always tell me what I was supposed to be when I grow up, as if he made me with his own hands, shaped and molded me like some god creating an army, Shango and his children, a soldier for his people. His little warrior princess. A revolutionary.

That white boy is still too close, and all I want to do right now is push him away and tell him to back up off me. So I bump his leg really hard with my leg to force him to move over.

He just looks at me.

"Can you please move over?" I whisper. But we're supposed to be dead quiet during this *meeting of friends*. We're not friends, of course.

"Sorry," he whispers. Then he turns away and he still doesn't move.

I catch Kamau looking in my direction, and he raises his brow. I shake my head to let him know that I'm good, but I'm really not. My hands are sweaty, and I wipe them on my jeans. My heart beats in my ears. It's supposed to be quiet, but I am making a loud sound with every cell in my body.

Mama taught me how to take an inventory of my soul. She said to name all my senses and describe what I see, hear, smell, taste, and touch when things don't seem right, when I'm nervous, anxious, or feel out of place.

What do you hear? she would ask, and her soft voice echoes in my head. And I all hear is *them*, my father's *them*. That's all he talks about: *they, them, they, them*. *Those* white folks and *their* supremacy and what *they* did to us.

What do you see? Sometimes, I don't see white. I see faces with much, much lighter skin than mine. Their hair is black, brown, and blond, light and dark, long, short and straight. Their clothes are in all colors. But I don't see white. White is what I wear to block out negative energy. White makes me feel calm and peaceful and safe. White is what reflects light. White is colorless and represents the purest pure. So I don't see white, even though they're supposed to be *white* people.

But then, the more I really look at them, I see the color red. Red makes my heart beat fast and makes me want to run far, far away. Red is screams and shouts. Red is the smell of copper and the taste of salt. Red is the spilt blood of my ancestors tainting the ocean and blending with the clay earth on this side of the Atlantic. I look around at all those faces, and it feels like the whole room is squeezing in on me, and this boy won't move, and I swear he is inching closer and closer trying to crush me. And red is hot, too, because the heat from his body is fiery flames and I want him, *need* him to move.

My body is shaking with some kind of rage I didn't know I had, so I get up from the pew, take my bag, and walk out of the meetinghouse.

The humid air outside is like warm, crashing ocean waves against my body. I reach into my bag for my water bottle and take a long sip. Then I inhale and exhale deep, and I am free again.

The meeting for worship is supposed to be forty-five minutes. I only lasted ten.

The redbrick meetinghouse, with its white shutters and its triangular roof, sits in the middle of the courtyard behind the upper school building. On the other side of it is the lower school and a colorful playground for the younger kids. That building was built in the late 1600s, and I wonder what my ancestors were doing at that time. Were my father's people part of the first Africans to arrive in Philadelphia as early as 1684 on the ship called *Isabella*? Were my mother's people already in Saint-Domingue before it was called

Haiti? Or were they all living free in Africa not knowing that the world was about to turn upside down? I wonder if William Penn, the founding father of this school, as well as Philadelphia and all of Pennsylvania, believed that a girl like me would be here.

I walk over to a nearby bench and just sit there catching my breath for a moment. The meetinghouse doors open, and Sage walks out. She looks around the courtyard until her eyes land on me, and I quickly look down, trying to be invisible. In a few short seconds, she's standing in front of me. I stare at her feet. We're wearing the same beat-up Birkenstocks with exposed, unpolished toes.

"I wanted to see if you're okay," she says.

"How do you do it?" I ask, looking up, not wanting to waste any time with small talk. "How do you just sit there in silence with all those white people? I know your mother is white, but still . . ."

She looks at me like she's confused, shrugs, shakes her head, and says, "They're just people, Nigeria. Look, when it gets quiet, just think about things that make you happy, or do your homework. I write a whole essay in my head. Or maybe you can talk to God in your head and wait to hear what he has to say."

"That's easy for you, Sage. You grew up in this school. What'd you call it? A *lifer*?"

She sits down next to me as the little kids pour into the courtyard. This school is way different from what I know of public schools, 'cause here, they mix the little kids with the bigs like it's a village—a tiny Quaker town in a big, white city.

"Nigeria, do you really hate white people that much?" she asks.

We get that question all the time, so I always have an answer ready. "I think white people hate us way more than we could ever hate them."

"How could you say that? My mother—"

"Don't confuse the noble actions of one person for the atrocities of an entire people." I had that response in my back pocket, too. Whataboutism always comes up in these conversations.

She's quiet for a second; then she says, "So maybe you won't like it here if you keep thinking like that."

"It's not just what I'm thinking, Sage. It's the truth. It's reality." I'm looking at her now, as she stares out at the courtyard. Five different crystals hang from leather strands around her neck. She wears wooden mala beads on each wrist, and she must think she's the perfect manifestation of love and light, as I've heard her mother say. We used to be closer, until one of our arguments ended with her saying that I can't stop talking about race, and I told her that I can't stop being Black.

"It doesn't have to be that way, Nigeria. That's why your mother wanted you here. You don't have to go through life—"

"What's it like not having a lot of Black people around in this school?" I ask. "Being that your father is actually from Africa and all. And is he ever coming back from Senegal?" I know that question is a dig, but I'll keep cutting her off as long as she keeps telling me that what we believe and what we stand for is wrong.

"Well, my father prefers to stay there. You should come with us next time we go to Dakar, where there's, like, no racism. I bet if the Movement does go to Africa next year, you will change your minds about a lot of things. Everybody's so open and accepting there, like in Haiti, where Aunt Natalie is from."

I have to bite my tongue. This is how we ended things last time. KD and Sage have been to different countries, teaching girls and women about their reproductive rights, so she thinks she understands how the world works.

"So we try to do the same here," she continues. "We have some affinity groups like Black Girl Magic poetry and Black Lives Matter activism and Black at Philly Friends, where we try to address how we're treated here. Those are cool, but I like to be friends with everybody. It's more reflective of the world we live in."

I look at her with the same raised eyebrow my father gives me and say, "Really?"

"Yeah, really. Look, Nigeria. I want you to be here. You know, I once overheard your mother telling my mother that she wanted you to see the world differently than what your father was teaching you." She's facing me now. "He's raised you to believe that white people are evil and you have to separate yourself from everything. That's dangerous, Nigeria."

I know that look, as if I need saving from my own family and my own village. "Is that what Diane thinks when she said she knows my situation?"

"I mean, why else would your mother hide this from your father?" is all she says.

And she should've just punched me in the gut instead. It would've hurt less.

Even as the meetinghouse doors swing open and more kids come into the courtyard, even as Kamau approaches us and looks at me as if he's throwing me a lifeline, even as Diane comes over with a wide smile, I feel as if the still gray sky is slowly pressing down on me and I am a storm cloud about to burst with lightning and thunder and rage.

"Gigi, you good?" Kamau asks as he sits on the bench on the other side of me.

I want to tell him no, to get me out of here, to take me home because my being here is something my mother kept from my father; it's another thing that pulled them apart.

But that white boy who'd been next to me in the meetinghouse is standing in front of us, looking down at me. Just looking down at me. And more kids come around trying to get Kamau's attention for some reason, and there are too many eyes on me right now. So I become a passing rain cloud and smile like the late-morning sun because my father always says to never let them see you sweat. Never give them the satisfaction of knowing that they are winning over and over again. Because there's no crying on the battlefield.

"Nigeria, would you like to come back into my office?" Diane asks.

So I smile wide and say, "I'm good. I'm just not used to all these white kids, that's all."

From the look on their faces, I've offended some of them. But it's the truth.

That white boy steps closer to me and extends a hand. "Hi, welcome to Philly Friends," he says, with his voice cracking. "I just want to apologize for what happened in there. I didn't realize that you were uncomfortable."

And I am disarmed.

"Nigeria, this is Liam," Kamau says. "He's cool, I promise."

Liam still has his hand out for me to shake. I don't take it.

So Diane says with her soft but firm voice, "Did you know that the Quakers introduced the handshake as we know it today? They were against bowing and removing their hats as a greeting and wanted to dismantle hierarchies among men. In their minds, we're all equal in the eyes of God. It's a kind gesture toward our friends."

And I am on a different planet.

Sage leans over and whispers, "Don't worry, he's not the devil."

And maybe Liam heard her. He quickly drops his hand and steps back. Then he awkwardly turns around and walks away. So do some of the other kids, and I'm left with Sage, Kamau, and Diane surrounding me again.

"We have to work on this," Kamau says, sighing and shaking his head. "I'm not letting you go anywhere. You're staying, and you're coming back tomorrow, and the day after, and the day after that. I'm telling my mother, and she and your father are gonna have to fight each other on this."

And I wonder in that moment, if Mama would be fighting for me to stay here, even though this doesn't feel like freedom. This doesn't feel like the world is opening up to me. Instead, it's closing in, and I will be making myself small, small, just to be able to fit.

Hours later, I am still here. We go from class to class, and Diane is at the beginning and end of each one to make sure that I'm doing okay. I can quickly become the only Black kid in a particular corner of the school at any given moment. If us Black kids are all spread out, at different ends of halls or in different classes, we become lone brown spots in seas of white.

If I do come here, I don't think I'll ever get used to this.

And maybe they won't get used to me—my matted locs like tree branches, my deep brown skin, my thrifted clothes, my many crystal pendants, beaded bracelets, and silver rings. I feel loud here and big, as if I'm taking up too much space and too much time. Sometimes I wonder if they'll be able to hear my thoughts even when I don't speak a word. And maybe those unspoken thoughts are my father's shouts.

They'll think I hate them.

I went back to Diane's office where she let me look through old yearbooks and I counted the brown faces again. Time went by way too fast, and not once did I turn on my phone to check on my baby brother, Jasmine, Makai, and Chris. I didn't know that this little detour in my life is the break that I wanted, the little bit of fresh air that I didn't know I needed. Still, I don't get too comfortable with that idea because I am still my father's daughter, president of the Youth Group, warrior-queen-in-the-making.

"If there's a class you're not feeling, just let me know. Your schedule is flexible for now. And there are some people I'd like you to meet—the head of school, our psychologist . . . But one step at a time, okay?" Diane says to me as we walk to my next class.

"Psychologists?" I ask. "Why are psychologists here?"

"Because we take mental health very seriously at Philly Friends."

I hear my father's voice saying that the systems in this country can really be a mind fuck, and maybe seeing a psychologist wouldn't be a bad idea.

I have two Black teachers, one for math and one for dance, and this is something I want to tell my father, but he won't care. Kamau is in my dance class, and the teacher, Alisha Duncan, was a world-renowned dancer who stands like a tall elm tree and moves like the wind.

"This year, we'll continue the history of dance in America, starting with the vaudeville performers of the late eighteen hundreds," she says as we all sit on the floor of a real dance studio complete with wall-to-wall mirrors, barres, and a baby grand piano.

I settle into my skin a little more because the teacher looks like me. I hang on to her every word, and I want to make eye contact. And we do. She sees me and smiles and says, "Love your hair!"

I smile back at her big and bright.

The white kids still outnumber the Black kids in this class, but here they are learning from a teacher whose dark skin and close-cropped hair is a sign of mastery and regality. So I know that the kids at Philly Friends get to have the best of the best, no matter what they look like.

"Can anyone name some pioneers in Black dance?" Alisha asks, stretching her long, graceful neck as she looks out over the students.

I'm the only one raising my hand. "Pearl Primus, Katherine Dunham, the Nicholas Brothers, Alvin Ailey . . ."

"Excellent. Thank you," she says, because I could keep going.

A few men walk into the class carrying djembe and conga drums and we start our warm-up exercises to African rhythms, and even the white kids have to bend their bodies to the sounds of the motherland. Alisha asks both me and Kamau to come to the front as the other kids follow our lead.

And I am full.

Until I get to my math class, where the teacher is actually from Nigeria who insists on not being called by his first name. He looks up when he sees my name on the roster, and Mr. Egwu says with a thick accent and without smiling, "You are named after my country."

"I know" is all I say as all the kids turn to me.

Other than Mr. Egwu, I'm the only Black person in the room, and I try to make eye contact, but he looks past me only speaking in numbers and equations with the other students. So I shrink into the background while holding on to the secrets I know about how Pythagoras learned his theorem in Africa and how the ancient Egyptian pyramids were built from the knowledge of advanced mathematics and physics. But he never asks about that, and I don't think he ever will. Either way, I keep my head down and copy and solve equations the way I was taught to do since I was three. A few minutes before the end of the class, Mr. Egwu asks someone to come to the smart board and solve an equation using sine, cosine, and tangent in a trigonometry function.

A white boy gets it wrong.

I get up right behind him and solve it in half the time, and my universe expands because here, I get to really shine and flex, and I want to tell my father this, but he won't care.

"Very good, Ms. Nigeria," Mr. Egwu says. Then he asks, "Why are you named after my country?"

"Because my father believes that we are descendants of the great Yoruba people, who will one day rise to become a global super-power," I say, and it's a question I've had to answer a million times.

"Well, I think your father is a very wise man," he says with a chuckle.

I hope he never finds out who my father is.

At lunch, there's a salad bar that seems to have every kind of vegetable on earth. The food options are up on a screen indicating plant-based, gluten-free, and keto written in fancy letters. I nod to some of the aunties and uncles serving the food, hoping that they're being treated right. And everyone just grabs whatever they want without paying.

"Stop acting like you ain't never seen this much food," Kamau whispers behind me, holding a tray with grilled salmon and brown rice. "That's what they expect you to do."

So I grab a rice bowl and a fresh green juice and pretend this is my new normal and follow him to a table full of his fans. "How'd you get to be so popular?" I ask him, 'cause he only started school in the ninth grade and had two years to learn how to navigate this world.

"Honestly, Gigi, I wasn't even trying that hard," he says non-chalantly.

"Must be nice," I mumble as we approach a round table with wooden chairs, and some of his friends can't stop staring at my hair.

My last class for the day is an elective called The Constitution and You, and this is something I want to tell my father, too, but he won't care. This school is not where he wants me to lead his revolution. Diane said I can just come back to her office afterward and let her know what I think. Since I'm on the fence about all this, sitting in on these classes is like a tryout. That white boy from the meeting-house is in here, and so is Sage. She starts introducing me to some of the other kids, but I stop her. "I'm good, really," I tell her. I didn't come here to make friends, despite everyone here calling each other "friends."

Classes at Philly Friends are not made up of rows of desks and chairs. Instead, we sit around oval tables and have an open discussion about what we're learning. In the classes I've been to, nothing the teacher said was a hard truth because everyone has a voice, everybody has a perspective. And the kids in these classes act and speak like they already know everything.

Liam waves at me, but I turn away. Out of the corner of my eye, I notice that he makes it look as if he was just twirling his pen around his fingers. He's embarrassed. And I feel a little bad. So I wave back and smile. I think this white boy really wants to be friends. I'm try-ing. I let my guard down and push my father out of my head. I'll have to go along to get along for these next two years. If I decide to come here. And that thought is sinking deeper and deeper into my soul to become my reality, my truth, my new life.

I wear a pleasant smile like a mask.

"Constitutional law is, quite frankly, redundant," the teacher says as he takes a seat around the table. He doesn't stand in front of the classroom, and he's not even at the head of the table. Henry is his name and he's a small white man with a headful of curly brown hair and he wears thick black eyeglass frames that make him look more like a scientist than a recent law school grad. He studied at Princeton undergrad and law, according to all the paraphernalia around the room.

"Because the Constitution is already the supreme law of the land," a boy says.

Three other brown faces are in the class besides me and Sage, out of twelve. And I remember all those times my father told me that we as Black people are not a minority in the world. We are the global majority. He tells his followers not to believe those lies about us, that even if we find ourselves in spaces that are as white as Scandinavia, we have an army of brothers and sisters from Harlem, New York, to Nairobi, Kenya, taking up space on this planet. This is one of the few of my father's teachings that I hold on to right now. There are two Black girls, one Black boy, and a South Asian boy, and I want to believe that our presence in this classroom is like ink spreading over paper.

"Yes, the U.S. Constitution is the supreme law of the land," Henry says. "It's a good thing it wasn't written in stone."

"The supreme law of the land? Is it, though?" I ask. My heart races as the words fall from my mouth. I've done this before, but not in any place like this.

"Ah, Nigeria, correct?" Henry sings as if he's been waiting for me to speak. "Care to elaborate?"

I don't skip a beat. If nothing else, my father has prepared me for this. "What makes it the supreme law of the land if its rules are constantly broken?" Even though I've been having these kinds of debates since I could talk, I'm not going to be like my father in this classroom. While he makes finite, not-up-for-debate statements, I will only ask questions.

"They're called amendments," Liam says.

And I'm caught off guard. It sounds like a dig, as if he's trying to embarrass me the way I had embarrassed him.

"That's right. The United States Constitution is a living and breathing document because it can be amended," Henry adds.

This is where I shut up, even though Sage smiles and nods as if telling me that I'm doing good. The other Black kid is just sitting there listening. Liam and the other white kids take over the conversation.

So I fall back and listen to Henry talk about the type of paper the United States Constitution was written on—parchment and not hemp.

"But Henry, what if the Constitution *was* written on hemp?" a boy asks.

And everybody laughs. My mind swirls with too much knowing. I'm sure my father has told me this already, maybe during a lesson on the Egyptian papyrus.

"Were the founding fathers high when they wrote the Constitution?" another boy asks.

Everybody laughs again, and I don't know how serious this class is supposed to be. More jokes about marijuana and the building of this country are bounced around by the white boys like a ball game. Again, my thoughts are weighed down with too much information because I could say something about marijuana and mass incarceration, or the Rockefeller Drug Laws and the criminalization of addiction. All these things I've heard my father talk about and he's made me read and write papers about.

But I keep quiet because here there is no war. I force myself not to see the color red anymore, or even black and white. I want to be color-blind like everybody else.

"This was such a lively discussion," Henry says at the end of the class. "I hope you all know by taking this class, you have the opportunity to join LD debate this year. I mean, we're not forcing you. But give it a try. I'm sure you'll want a head start on the new resolution."

The class shuffles about with excitement. I glance at Sage, who is all smiles and seemingly hanging on to Henry's every word.

But then he looks at me. "Oh, Nigeria. In case no one has told you, this class also prepares you to be on the debate team if you choose— Lincoln-Douglas style, named for the infamous Great Debates of 1858 between Abraham Lincoln and Illinois senator Stephen Douglas. We've won some statewide championships in the past, so we're pretty good."

"I know what a debate is," I quickly say.

"Yes, I'm sure you do. But Lincoln-Douglas is a specific style of debate. There are rules and a timer. I'm sure you've seen the recent presidential debates. Something like that," Henry says.

"I know what a debate is," I say again, firmer this time because clearly he didn't hear me.

Henry smiles, nods, and looks away. "So are you all ready to hear this new resolution?"

I catch Sage glaring at me, so I glare back.

Henry clears his throat and reads from his phone. "Resolved: When in conflict, community standards are of greater value than individual liberty." Then he writes it on the smart board.

The class is quiet for a long second; then everyone starts talking all at once. I repeat the resolution in my head, trying to make sense of every word. *When in conflict, community standards are of greater value than individual liberty.*

I look around at all the lit-up faces in the classroom. It's as if Henry just announced some new song that just dropped. And for a hot second, I start to wonder if these are my people—Black, white, and everything in between—nerds who get excited over a new debate topic. And I want to tell my father this, too, but he won't care. Or worse, he'll make me stop coming.

GRIEVANCE 3

Maybe, just maybe, my first day at this school was like Mama's healing Reiki hands, a warm cup of herbal tea, a full-moon-charged crystal that radiates in my palm after a long stretch of deep meditation. It was time away from my father and the Movement (my baby brother, too, but I hate to admit it), and it was exactly what my soul needed. My insides are playing tug-of-war with my mind. I'm not supposed to feel this way. My world has opened up, and I can't believe that, if I decide, this will be my life from now on. The thought of going back to my house and back to the Movement leaves me with a sinking feeling that is the opposite of flying. I'd be stuck to muddy ground. I'd be stone. This is how Mama must've felt.

My mind is swirling with the weight of what tomorrow will bring, or the next minute when I finally turn on my phone. I'm standing outside the school next to the front gate as fancy cars line the curb picking up kids. I'm not drowning anymore in this sea of white. Maybe I'm floating.

"If you need my mother to have your back, we're a text and phone call away," Sage had said before she ran off to some after-school meeting. She leaves me here after practically begging me to come this morning.

And this morning, I left Jasmine to deal with those boys. I left my baby brother with a strange woman who sleeps in my parents' bed. I left all the planning and organizing for the Freedom School. Maybe I left whatever dreams my ancestors had for me, whatever life I had decided to be born into. But this is Mama's dream. Is it mine, too?

I finally turn on my phone to see a deluge of texts and voice messages, and something heavy sits on my chest and there's not enough air out here. Even though the rain clouds have parted, I still feel the sky pressing down on me.

"Nigeria!" Kamau calls out as he walks toward me, and my chest is still tight. He grabs me by the shoulders and says, "You look like you're having a panic attack. Breathe, girl, breathe."

He inhales and exhales deep pranayama breaths. Smell the flower, blow out the candle, Mama used to whisper. And I swear I can hear her now. Kamau with his light brown face, deep-set eyes, and peach fuzz above his lips stays focused on me as I breathe in and out, too, and my eyes well up with tears. I hate that about myself. I'm always a river flooding and muddying everything around me. Kamau's presence calms me, even as kids walk by and do a double take. He lets go and takes both my hands.

"You good?" he asks.

"Sorry I'm messing up your reputation," I say, my voice shaking. "It's just that—"

"We're staying out of it until you deal with your father," he says, cutting me off.

"What? Staying out of it?"

He sighs and says, "Did you read the texts from your father?"

My insides twist. I take a moment to let it all sink in, and then I ask, "How'd he find out?"

"Hell if I know," Kamau says. "My mother texted me that Uncle Keith is looking for you."

I swallow a big gulp of air. *Shit.*

"Gigi, I want you to come to this school and I know it's gonna start a whole lot of family drama," he continues. "Everybody in the Movement is going to have something to say. But what's worse is that your mother is not even here to have your back."

And with that, he's punched me in the gut. I shake my head to stop him from saying more. I'm flooding again, but I swallow back the river. I peep all the kids who'd been looking at us this whole time, including Liam. "Your fans are all up in our business," I say, changing the subject because whatever happens from this point on, it'll be my mother's fault.

"I have to meet up with somebody," he says. "But I really do hope you come back tomorrow."

"Let me come to your house," I say, grabbing his hand. "It'll give us time to talk and plan, and tell your mother about everything. I know there'll be a lot of drama. But . . . if you want me to come here, then help me."

"Kamau! You ready, bro?" A boy calls out in the distance.

"I gotta go. See you tomorrow, cuz! Hopefully. Praying for you, girl," Kamau says, and my cousin slips from me when I need him the most. I can't believe how Kamau eases from the super-Black world of the Movement to this private school in East Falls like it's nothing. Even from where I'm standing, I see these kids swarm around him like he's a queen bee. He moves through them like royalty—shoulders back and chin up as if he's wearing a crown. And according to my father, I'm supposed to move through this world like a queen, too.

There are fewer kids around now, and I still don't know which way I'm supposed to go. Back home to the Movement, or forward to some new life I can't even imagine.

"Hey, what'd you think of the new resolution?" someone says behind me, and I turn around to see Liam. I didn't mean to, but I sigh and roll my eyes.

"Oh, sorry to bother you," he says, and starts to walk away.

"Wait," I say, not really wanting to be rude. "I actually think it's interesting. So you're on the debate team?"

"No, but I will be, I guess. It looks good on my college applications."

"Oh, yeah. *College.*" Another thing that separates me from the rest of the kids my age. I was never planning on going.

"Do you have your list already?" Liam asks.

"Oh, um . . . College is a capitalist scam. If this country wants its people to work and contribute to society in meaningful ways, then higher education should be free across the board." I've heard my father say something like this a million times, and Mama mentioned college only once—even though they both got their degrees.

Liam nods as if what I just said is a hill he'll die on. "I know, right? I mean, with the shrinking middle class and college debt at an all-time high, this country has no future. We'll be a third-world nation if we keep going at this rate!"

"We? Oh, no, I'm not going down with this sinking ship. It's you and your people."

"What's that supposed to mean?" he says. "You're not from here?"

"Unfortunately, I was born in this settler colonialist experiment. But I was raised to divest, decolonize, and indigenize. My people are finding ways to separate ourselves from the white supremacist agenda. So while *y'all* become a third-world country, we'll be thriving and living according to the ways of our ancestors." I think this is the longest conversation I've ever had with a white boy, and already he starts with the assumptions and microaggressions.

He looks stunned and is probably finding the right words to offend me. But he says, "That's . . . amazing! Wow. Like, that's exactly what they should be teaching us at this school. I mean, look at the Quakers. They were badass. I've been going to this school my whole life, and they're not really teaching us how to dismantle white supremacy and tear down the system." He's all excited and looks like he's ready to jump out of his skin and burn his own whiteness down to ashes.

"Did you just say 'dismantle white supremacy'?" I ask. My mind is doing summersaults trying to figure out what he really means. It's easy for us to completely misunderstand each other even though we're both speaking English.

"Yeah," he says, then relaxes his shoulders. "I know what you're thinking. I'm white."

"Yeah, you are" is all I say.

He tosses his hair back. It's a light brown disheveled mess that falls right over his face. A plain blue T-shirt, black cargo pants, black Converse sneakers, a silver chain tucked inside his T-shirt, and an assortment of stone rings on his fingers—onyx, tiger's eye, and lapis lazuli—lets me know that he's more than a little basic, and he's probably rich.

So I say, "Cool rings."

"Yeah, you too," he says, looking down at my hands.

For a long minute, I'm just standing there and he's just standing there. Kids walk past us, some say hi to him, no one says a word to me.

"Nigeria, right?" he finally says. "Look, I'm sorry about what happened at the meetinghouse this morning. I tried to move, but the kid next to me wouldn't budge."

"Oh, so you did get the hint?" I say.

"I mean, that was low-key a hard nudge."

"Yeah, I don't like people up on me like that, especially white people." I have no filter. I can't help it; I was raised that way. Mama calls it radical honesty. But again, I'm *trying*.

He just gives me a nervous laugh as if he's both confused and amused by what I just said. Then he quickly sniffs his armpits. "I swear I'm not usually musty. I like to take showers, I promise," he says, smiling.

"I'm sure you do, but you can't wash off that whiteness," I say, and I quickly bite my bottom lip. I shouldn't've said that, but the words just came out.

He chuckles, crosses his arms over his chest and looks down, his hair dropping to form a shield around his eyes. I can't tell if they're blue, green, or gray. Then he looks at me with that smile. I don't really mean to, but I smile back only because his face opens up and invites me in. "I'm not racist," he says.

"I didn't say you were."

"I'm learning. We're all learning here. We have discourse, we read the books, we have the most diverse teaching staff. . . ."

"Um, a handful of teachers of color is not diverse. So again, I didn't say you were racist." I don't add that this school and whatever they do here has nothing to do with him being racist or not.

He rubs his chin, where there's barely peach fuzz, and nods. "Okay. Nice . . . chatting with you, Nigeria." He taps his foot on the ground and takes a step back, probably thinking he should leave me alone now, but there's something else keeping him there.

And then it starts to drizzle. We both look up as if rainfall is something new we're experiencing for the first time. Then he glances at my hair and down at my sandals. But he doesn't say anything.

So I help him out. "Bye, Liam. Nice chatting with you, too." Conversations with white people are going to be work. I don't know how to do it with ease. Why after only a minute of talking to this boy do I bring up racism? I can't separate the two—whiteness and racism, whiteness and oppression, whiteness and history. I blame my father and his Movement.

"Okay, bye, Nigeria." He holds out his hand.

I take it this time and say, "The Quaker handshake, right?"

"Right. Nice to meet you, friend."

I'm still holding Liam's hand when a loud bass coming from a car's speakers reaches my bones. It's down the block, and I know the sound of my father's truck. It's like his voice, commanding and omnipresent. I quickly let go of Liam's hand and turn to see the black Escalade inching toward the curb, near the school's entrance, along with all the other cars with parents or chauffeurs or whatever.

My insides become a tight knot. "Shit," I say out loud, and turn back around to see Liam still standing there. "Bye!"

"Oh, here. I think you could use this," he says, handing me an umbrella from his bag.

I take it, only 'cause I want him to get away from me. The rain is coming down hard now, so I make my way to my father's truck. My world is about to fall apart.

When I open the passenger-side door, Chris is sitting there and my father is in the driver's seat. Chris points his thumb to the back. *Why is he here?*

"They're giving out free umbrellas?" is the first thing my father says to me when I'm in the back seat. It's not until I close the umbrella that I notice the school's logo. "And you repping hard for that school, huh?"

My father turns around and points to my chest. I still have on the Philly Friends T-shirt Diane gave me. *Shit.* The swishing of the windshield wipers is the only sound in the truck for a hot second. And Chris is here. He's sitting in Mama's seat. He's sitting in my seat.

"I went to see Kamau," I finally say.

"I don't care what you did in there or why you were there. You abandoned your post. You left your brothers and sister hanging. Y'all are supposed to move as one unit when I send you out. But you're over there chasing after some dream your mother had. What is it about that place that makes you think you belong, huh, Nigeria? Your mother and I were on a completely different page when it came to this. You know what I told her? I said that you'll be going to that school, or any other school like it, over my dead body. Am I dead, Nigeria? Huh? Am I dead?"

He turns back to me for a second, waiting for an answer.

"No, Baba," I say, dropping my head.

"Look up and face me when I'm talking to you."

I do as he says.

"Defend yourself, Nigeria! I didn't raise you to be submissive!"

I search my mind for the right words. "They contacted Mama because I aced that test," I say. At the very least, I have to defend my mother.

"No, they contacted me first and I told them to kiss my Black ass. Of course they want you in there. You'll make *them* look good," he says, driving off the campus and practically speeding down Ben Franklin Parkway in the pouring rain. "No matter what they say about diversity and inclusion, these schools were built for kids like that white boy you were talking to. He probably has parents paying for tutors, a trust fund, and all these privileges that'll secure his spot at the top of the food chain. But you know what? All the money in the world won't make him anywhere near as brilliant as you. He can't even begin to touch your intelligence and the amount of things that I've taught you. That's why they want you in there, so they can take credit for my work. My work, Nigeria. I made you! Your ancestors made you! Your genius is inherited. They do not deserve you!"

His words and voice take up all the space in the truck, and there isn't even enough room for me to form my own thoughts, to come up with my own words. I want to roll down the window and let the rain come in. I want to open the back seat door and jump out. I want to open the sunroof and just fly toward the gray sky. But I don't even move one inch. Chris is staring at me in the side-view mirror. Our eyes meet. I look away. "Can we talk about this when we get home?" I ask my father, and my voice is shaking.

"I'll be going live on my channel this evening. Whatever you have to say about spending a day at the *prestigious* Philadelphia Friends School, you can tell it to the members. I'm sure they'd love to hear how it compares to the Sankofa Freedom School."

"That'll be dope!" Chris adds. "It'll be like you were a spy or something."

"Chris, you should read *The Spook Who Sat by the Door* by Sam Greenlee," my father says. "I'll give you my copy, and then watch the movie. It's about a Black man who infiltrates the CIA in order to help his own people. Now, if that's your plan, Nigeria, then we can discuss. But I don't know what you'll be learning from them that you can't learn from us."

I remember that movie. My father made me watch it when I was eleven. Infiltrating a Quaker school wasn't my plan, but maybe if I let him think that, he'll change his mind. So I say, "There's a debate team. They've won national championships. I think they give cash prizes."

"Yeah, Sharon told me about their team when she was trying to convince me a while back to let you start with Kamau, but you know I wasn't hearing it. Besides, you would wipe out any competition."

"Well, that's why Mama was even thinking about Philly Friends.

We could replicate what they do at the Freedom School. Train everybody. Go national. Win money. It's called the Lincoln-Douglas style based on the Great Debates of 1858."

"Right. Abraham Lincoln and Frederick Douglass. Okay. So, say you do go to that school and join that team. Who will you be competing for?"

What? I don't dare correct my father. "The school" is all I say.

"Wrong answer."

Wrong Douglas, I say in my head. "Myself?" I say out loud, wishing that I never brought up the debate in the first place.

"Is that a question or an answer?" my father asks.

"Myself," I say, lowering my voice.

"Wrong answer."

I swallow hard as my mind searches for something my father wants to hear. So I ask, "If not me, then who?"

"Us, Nigeria. Us! We the people. Our people. So if you go to this Quaker school that costs more than what most of our people make in one year and you join the debate team, who . . . are you . . . competing for?"

"My people," I say. My voice trembles, and for my father, this is a sign of weakness.

"Say it like you mean it!"

I clear my throat, swallow back defeat, and say much louder, "My people!"

He shakes his head as we merge onto the highway. "If I have to remind you of that, then you're not ready. You're simply not ready," he says. "See, in *The Spook Who Sat by the Door,* he had an agenda.

He knew exactly what he was going in there for. We have our classics, too, you know. In fact, Chris, I'll get you your own copy so Nigeria can read it first. She clearly needs a refresher."

I try to hide my face from Chris, but he doesn't even look into the sideview mirror again. He shouldn't have heard all of this. He's still a stranger. He doesn't know what we're all about, and in this moment, he gets to watch this war between father and daughter; he gets to see my wounds. So my entire soul folds in on itself when my father says that I am not ready. The silence stretches thin around us, and if I say one word, it will snap. I will snap. But I don't cry. I should know better than to let his words open me up like this. But he's my father.

"I still love you, though," he says after a long minute.

And there he goes with that word "love" again.

My father turns up the volume to that new underground rapper out of North Philly he's been mentoring. I know he wants me to hear the lyrics about the shady government and brothers locked up and sisters needing to reclaim their thrones, but I'm not trying to go there with him right now. So I lean my head back to ignore the words and absorb only the music.

My phone pings in my bag. I immediately think of Kamau. But it says, *Maybe: William Fisher.* And the text reads: Hey. I didn't find you on social media. So I got your number from Kamau. I hope you don't mind.

I do mind. I can't believe Kamau has this white boy texting me on my father's phone. It's his phone because he pays the bill and he will keep reminding me of that. I read the words in the text over and over again as the rapper says something about Black bodies in jails, lab-made viruses in our cells, and the air filled with chemtrails.

So I text back: Hey. Liam?

He immediately sends a smiley face, and I leave it at that.

I quickly hide the screen, even though my father won't be able to see who I'm texting. He's bopping his head to the beat as if this is the best joint he's ever heard. Chris is looking at me in the side-view mirror again, and I ignore him. He knows too much about me now.

Then the beat changes to something heavier and darker. My father raps along to the words: "We ready for war! We ready for war! Raising Black consciousness and defending the poor . . ."

And all I can think about is a smiley-face emoji from a white boy named William Fisher.

GRIEVANCE 4

"Oh, is this what we're doing now?" Makai asks when I step into the kitchen after we get back to the Village House. "The Philadelphia Friends School? Founded in 1689?"

I cover the logo on my T-shirt with my hand, but it's too late. I'm mad that I'm still wearing it.

"So, let me get this straight," Jasmine says, and I know she couldn't *wait* to get on my case about this. She and Makai are in the kitchen making dinner, and my father went into his office to prep for his live stream. Chris went to his room, avoiding us as usual. Or just avoiding me. "You had us thinking you were at the Free Library all this time, when you were sitting up in some white private school?" She pounds her fist into her palm as if she's ready to fight me.

And I'm ready to fight for my decision, even after my father just clowned me in his truck.

"I know I should've been straight up with y'all, but my bad. I had some things I needed to do."

"Things to do like what?" Makai asks, looking really disappointed. "Your father wanted to know where you were, and we couldn't tell him shit. We're supposed to be looking out for each other. We need to have an emergency meeting."

"We don't need a meeting for this," I say, climbing onto a tall seat near the counter. "It's all part of my research for my father's next book, *The Black Man's Constitution*." I'm getting my story straight right in that moment because the truth won't make sense to them. The truth doesn't even make sense to me.

"What does a private school have to do with that book?" Makai asks.

"Well . . . The Quakers were the first abolitionists; they were nonviolent and opposed the American Revolution."

"And? They were still colonizers."

"Yeah, but what if they had drafted the Constitution? What if they included . . . Black men? I was just doing my research like my father asked me to, that's all."

"That's cap!" Jasmine says. "I *been* heard you and Kamau talking about his school, and you were a thirst bucket wanting to party with his rich white friends."

"You really think I'm out here wanting to party with rich white kids?"

"I mean . . ." Jasmine says, smirking.

"It's true," Makai adds. "Every time Kamau is around and he talks about Philly Friends, you were there soaking it all up."

I take a good look at my brother and sister. Neither of them will really understand what it's been like to be me, to be in this house, to be abandoned by my mother, to be my father's daughter, and until last year, his only child. "If I'm being honest . . ."

"Radical honesty. That's what we're all about. Radical every-thing," Makai says 'cause he lives and breathes the Movement.

So I take in a deep pranayama breath, exhale, relax my shoulders, and close my eyes for a hot second. I owe them the truth, at least a little bit of it. "I was curious. Two of my faves—Kamau and Sage—go to this school where they meditate and learn about Africa. Can you imagine a bunch of white kids doing African dance? I saw it with my own two eyes. Kamau *been* telling me, but I had to see it for myself. Y'all. Those kids have the best of the best. Their cafeteria looks like a restaurant."

They just stare at me without saying a word. Then all Jasmine says is "I don't think I wanna see white kids do African dance."

"Neither do I, but can we all go to this Philly Friends?" Makai asks. "Can they bus kids from the hood like they did back in the day? Can we *integrate*?"

"Of course not; I got in. You know how my father had us take those tests . . ."

"Yeah, they sent me acceptance letters and scholarships, too," Makai says. "But I wasn't trying to be, like, the smartest kid up in that jawn and think that I could run the world. They wanna let in, like, two, three smart Black kids just so they can pat themselves on the back? Bait and switch, like your father says. And you fell for their Jedi mind tricks."

"Come on, Makai. Now you're sounding just like him." I grab a tortilla chip from a nearby wooden bowl.

"It's because of your mother, isn't it?" Jasmine says, reaching for my hand.

I stop mid-chew. Then I just nod. Slowly.

"I'm saying, though . . . Auntie Nat was working hard to get the Freedom School up and running. Why would she want you to be in some private school, anyway?" Makai asks.

Jasmine nudges Makai. "Shut up!"

I get up from the stool, stare Makai down, and say, "You don't know my mother to be talking about her like that."

Then they both get real quiet. I get it. Makai doesn't live with his own mother. Him and his father live in the basement, and they're part of my father's foot soldiers. But with each year Makai stays with us, the more he starts to sound like my father. I only glance at Jasmine because she's still trying to figure all this out, and she's looking to me for all the answers.

Chris comes into the kitchen and says, "King Kofi is ready to go live. Y'all need to be quiet."

And the tension in the kitchen breaks, thank goodness. Chris doesn't even look in my direction.

My father talks to his followers as if they're family, as if they're all sitting here in our living room and he's lecturing them on how to break away from corrupt systems to achieve true liberation. But he also knows the enemy is watching and recording everything he's saying. I think of Diane from the school or anyone else who knows that Kofi Sankofa is my father. If they don't, it's a secret I'm ready to bury and hide.

He tells the listeners that he's postponing the interest meeting for the Freedom School, and says the Movement will be starting a big fundraiser, instead, to get our own building so we don't have to rely on local church leaders who don't really like us, and city officials who think we're troublemakers.

Then he invites Chris to come talk about his experiences in what the media calls one of the worst schools in Philadelphia and in the country—the fights, the teachers who keep leaving, the kids who don't graduate. My father goes on and on about the messed-up American education system, and how we need our own way of teaching our children. Chris takes my job of moderating the chats and blocking any trolls. He's taking it all in and adding his two cents by saying "Facts!" over and over again. And I hate that for him.

After my father ends his live stream, after the members have gone off to their corners of the Village House, and after Chris and I make eye contact without saying a word, I feed, bathe, and put my baby brother to sleep in my bed. I finally change out of that Philly Friends T-shirt and fold it into my bag. I'm not getting rid of it. Jasmine comes into the room, so I go back down to the kitchen to clean up and wait for her to fall asleep.

I just need a corner to myself where I can be alone.

As I scrub pots and put dishes away, I plot my next move. I need to go back to Philly Friends. I need to start living the life Mama dreamed for me, the life that I dreamed for myself, too. But my father, and even the Youth Group members, has placed invisible shackles around my body and I can't spread my wings to fly.

Someone comes down, and I ignore the footsteps. This house is full of family, full of strangers. Then a weird sound makes me turn to see Mama covering her mouth. And I drop a plate. It crashes on the floor and shatters into pieces. "Mama?"

Her face is all twisted up as if she ate something sour. She looks sick.

"Any milk in there?" she mumbles.

I don't say a word for a long minute, blinking a billion times to make sure that what I'm seeing is what I'm seeing. Then I ask, "Oat or almond?"

"Cow! Real milk!" she shouts while rushing to the trash can. She throws up.

I don't move. I just watch her. She came back. She came back?

But those braids are not her waist-length locs. That curvy body is not her thin, graceful frame. That raspy voice doesn't belong to my mother. My eyes keep deceiving me. My memory is a maze full of twists and turns and walls that I keep bumping into over and over again.

The realization settles in my bones. *Shit.* That's not my mother. But I'd seen her do this too many times when she was pregnant with Freedom.

So when Nubia moves over to the sink to wash her face and pull herself together, I ask straight up, "Are you having a baby?"

She freezes, clutching the edge of the sink as if it's the only thing keeping her on her feet. Then she nods. "I'm so sorry, Nigeria. Your father wanted to tell you himself. I'll take whatever milk you got," she says, panting, then rubbing her belly.

So I go into the fridge, pour out a glass of oat milk, and ask her, "Is it my father's?"

She takes a big gulp and looks at me. "I can never take your mother's place, Nigeria. Your father doesn't want that."

"She's coming back. She's coming back for me and Freedom, and we're leaving. So you can stay in this house all you want."

"Oh, Nigeria. Look, I'm so, so sorry," she says. "I want you to know that I love your father and he—"

"Are you the reason my mother left?"

She finishes the glass of oat milk and wipes her mouth. "Heartburn," she says. "Nothing stays in my belly these days."

"Camille! Did you already know Mama?" I call her by her real name 'cause I'm not playing with her right now. I need answers.

"I met your mother at one of the seminars before she was pregnant with Freedom, and . . . the idea of me moving in came up," she says. "If your father could've provided for me and your mother, then we should've been able to get past our egos and bring beautiful Black children into the world. Raise them like a village. An ancestor chose us, Nigeria." She keeps rubbing her flat belly. "An ancestor chose me and your father."

A red-hot burn crawls up my body. I don't like her. I want her out of this house. But I don't say a word and just look at her face—her dark brown skin, her curious eyes, her long braids—and wonder if my father wanted another version of Mama, one who would give him the little army he always wanted.

"Please don't tell your father I told you," Nubia says.

"We don't keep secrets in this family," I hiss.

"But your mother kept secrets."

"Don't you dare mention my mother!" I say through clenched teeth.

"I'm sorry. Again. I didn't come here to bring mess."

162

And the only thing that keeps me from cursing her out is another set of feet coming down the stairs. We both move away from each other and pretend to be doing something else.

"What's going on here?" my father asks with his drumbeat voice.

Because we're all about radical honesty and it's a truth that's taking up space in this house, I say, "She's having a baby."

Nubia drops her shoulders and looks at me as if she's ready to jump down my throat. I dare her.

"That's right," my father says. "I meant to call a meeting with the elders—"

"A meeting with the elders?" I ask, cutting him off. "You were going to tell the members before you told me?"

"Wait a minute, little girl . . ."

"Oh, I'm a little girl now? Baba, I've been taking care of Freedom all this time—feeding him, changing his diapers, putting him to sleep . . . And I'm a little girl?" My heart races, and the words are spilling out of me like an avalanche.

"Well, you're acting like a little girl by disrespecting me and Nubia like this. You have a question, ask me. But you do not question my choices."

I look down at the tiled floor, my bare feet, the shredded bottom of my jeans. . . . Anywhere except at my father because I've heard those words before. He used to say them to Mama almost every other day while she was pregnant with Freedom.

"Nigeria, look at me," he says.

And I do. I avoid Nubia, who's made herself small sitting on a stool near the counter. She folds her hands and looks down.

"Yes, you're still a little girl because you're only sixteen. But you're also my warrior princess. The operative word is 'princess,' not yet a queen. You shouldn't be up in the house taking care of no baby. Freedom is my responsibility, and I appreciate everything you've done in the past year. But . . ." He extends his hand out to Nubia, and she takes it, still with her head down. "I love this woman, she's living here now, and she's the queen. And yes, you're going to have another sibling."

"But what about Mama?" I ask, and my voice cracks. My insides are an ocean tide rising and rising.

"I will always, always hold space for your mother," he says, and I catch Nubia trying to pull away, but he gently squeezes her hand.

So with that, I can't keep it in anymore. "Mama wants me to go to school."

"We're not having this conversation again, Nigeria."

"You holding space for Mama means that you should honor her wishes. She did all this paperwork to get me into Philly Friends. You're moving on with your life, why can't I? What are you going to tell Mama when she comes back?"

He lets go of Nubia's hand and steps closer to me. "Well, it's clear you're not living in the real world."

"When have we ever lived in the real world, Baba?" I step back away from him.

But he extends his arms out to me for a hug. "Come here, baby girl. I'm not trying to fight you. I'm not trying to be your enemy. We're definitely fighting a war, but this right here . . ." He points to himself and then to me. "Me and you? Father and daughter? This ain't it. The Village House is not a battlefield. We're all about peace, Nigeria. Peace, love, and understanding. You know that."

I don't know that. And if that were true, Mama would still be here. Where was her peace? Where was her love and understanding? So for the first time in my life, I don't walk into my father's embrace. When he last held me in his arms, I was a rainstorm of tears and a tsunami of sadness. But not now and not here, especially in front of this new woman of his. "I'm going to school tomorrow" is all I say, and he drops his arms.

"No, you're going to the library to do research for the next book. We need to have it ready for the printer by early November, so I should have a draft in a couple of weeks. That's all the school you need right now. Unless you tell me you're trying to become a brain surgeon or a rocket scientist so you can launch Black people into space when shit hits the fan. And don't you ever enter any of those institutions without my permission. They aren't for us. They were never meant for us. Do you hear me, Nigeria?"

I hear my father loud and clear, but I'm not listening to him. In my heart, I'm still going to school. But how do I move this body to somewhere I'm not supposed to be? How do I break free from these invisible chains to fly toward the sky? How am I supposed to soar when even home feels like a cage?

Then, right in front of me, my father takes Nubia's hand again and says, "Good night, warrior princess. We'll let Freedom sleep in your bed, but this'll be the last time. You have work to do, and I got something planned for tomorrow."

When they're upstairs, I glance at the front door. It was so easy to just walk out this morning, to have my bag packed with blank notebooks and my Philly Friends folder, to have a whole new life ahead of me. But now the front door to the Village House might as well be locked and dead-bolted.

GRIEVANCE 5

I slept like a rock, even though Freedom's little warm body was pressed against mine all night. I'm used to it by now. He didn't even cry. He sleeps better with me.

The whole house is awake by the time I open my eyes, and I'm mad I didn't give myself enough time to plan. Yesterday, I was up at four thirty in the morning with all the steps to how I'd be starting school already laid out in my mind. My father was feeding and dressing Freedom, and I made up the lie that I needed to be at the Parkway Central Library right when it opens. No one was paying attention to me, so I slipped out the front door and sprinted down Osage Avenue to the corner of S. 51st Street across from Malcolm X Park, where I caught a cab. Easy.

But I got busted yesterday. And it feels like my whole life is falling apart.

"Your phone was blowing up last night when you were downstairs," Jasmine says from her side of the room.

Her voice wakes up Freedom, and he smiles before he even opens his eyes. I kiss his forehead and whisper, "Good morning, Sunshine." I ignore whatever texts or calls came on my phone because I already know who they're from and what they're about. I had kept it in my bag yesterday, avoiding that other life that's waiting for me.

"I guess you're stuck with us now," Jasmine continues. "I saw when you left yesterday, but I didn't say anything."

Freedom opens his eyes and pulls himself up on his chubby little hands.

"What you getting ready to do, young king?" I say to him, ignoring Jasmine's comment. "Going to work?"

"King Kofi won't let him work for corporations," Jasmine says, crawling out of bed.

"If he wants to work for a corporation, he can." I scoop my baby brother and hold him up high above me. He laughs and drools onto my face.

"You serious? You wouldn't stop him? That'll be like prison. Your father wouldn't let that happen."

It's way too early for her to get on my nerves. We've been cool for the eighteen months she's been here. But I swear, with each day, she sounds more and more like Makai, who sounds exactly like my father. "He can do whatever. If he wants to be a little worker bee, run his own company, drive a bus . . . it's his choice."

"But don't you have dreams for him?"

I pause for a second. "My dream for my baby brother is for him to live up to his name" is all I say.

"But he has to know what that is first. Like, I didn't really know what freedom was until I became a member."

"It's different for me, Jas. This house and this movement are all I've ever known. And this is the kind of freedom where a bird flies into a glass door."

She stands in front of her bed stretching and yawning. "Is that why you wanted to go to that school so bad? You wanted to see what it's like?"

"Yeah. Kind of," I tell her. I'm careful not to say too much. Jasmine might snitch if I tell her that I'm still going. I just don't have a plan yet. I end the conversation by getting out of bed with Freedom to start the day. I shower with him, get us both dressed, and go down to the kitchen for bowls of oatmeal and fruit. I do everything as normal until Nubia comes over with a smile on her face. I squeeze my baby brother tight before putting him in his high chair without saying a word to her.

Jasmine, Makai, and Chris are standing in the living room waiting for directions. My father had called everyone to order with his "a luta continua," and this is the start of the Freedom School, where we'll learn at home, in the library, at museums, and even on the streets. All of Philly is our classroom, and with so much history in this city, we probably know more than the average kid sitting up in a public school. At least that's what my father tells the Youth Group members. But these past few months without Mama was just us going to the library and coming up with ideas for my father's books.

He comes in and throws us each a brand-new black T-shirt with the Movement's logo. "Let them know who you are and where you come from. Truancy cops try to pick you up, they'll know who to call."

Everybody else is happy to change out of whatever they were wearing to put them on. I throw mine over an African print top. In seconds, we're all in uniform—each of us a walking advertisement for my father's revolution. He even gives me a tiny one to put on Freedom. It's too small for him. My baby brother is growing so fast, and part of me wants him to stay a baby forever so I can always scoop him up into my arms. I give him one last kiss.

"Nubia's got him. I need you to be focused today," my father says to me before we leave.

I freeze in the doorway as I watch Nubia pick my baby brother up from out of his high chair. There's nothing else to do but to surrender to this new reality, and it feels like walls are coming up around me. She lives here. Freedom is also my father's son. I don't really want to be a second mama right now because I have my own life to live. So I surrender and let Nubia know what foods he likes and his favorite books and that he needs to be engaged and sang to and spoken to. She hears me. I hope.

"Let's go, Nigeria!" my father shouts from outside. "There's work to do. There's people to free. There are systems to dismantle. A luta continua!"

I swallow down the scream lodged in my throat, hoist my bag onto my back, and step out of the Village House. I wonder how many times I'll have to play this game of coming home, feeling trapped, and trying to escape.

My heart stops when I see what's parked in front of our town house.

Mama's car. Her silver Prius. The one she didn't take with her, the one that she was starting to teach me how to drive in, the one she said I could take with me to college and that was the first time she let me know that I didn't have to stay in the Village House forever.

"What's that doing here?" I ask no one in particular.

"It'll be yours as soon as you get your license," my father says, walking past me to get to the car. "But for now, some of the members are using it. Your mother would've wanted to put it to good use."

I let his words sit in the warm September morning air for a minute. I don't want to believe him. I don't want to think that Mama wants just anybody driving her car. I walk toward what feels like a ghost—if ghosts can be cars. The last time I was in here with Mama was when her belly was just starting to get big and she went out to see a midwife for a checkup—the one who was supposed to deliver Freedom. After that, my father wouldn't let her drive herself while she was pregnant with the baby king.

I remember the long rides with Mama to the Lancaster Central Market to visit the Amish farms out there. She would talk about how free the Amish are, not investing in capitalism and technology, living according to the land, and making a commitment to their God and their free will. "Imagine Black people in this country living like the Amish," Mama had once said. "With all that land and the police and government leaving us the hell alone. Now *that's* the American dream."

"As long as we don't have to wear those outfits," I remember telling her. And we laughed, and she hugged me, and I sniffed her locs and wished that those days would last forever.

We would fill mesh bags and cardboard boxes with seasonal fruits and vegetables. She'd get her pure wildflower honey, fresh herbs, lavender and eucalyptus bundles, and her car would smell like a garden after a rainstorm.

On some of the Saturdays before Freedom was born, me, Mama, KD, and Sage packed into that Prius and drove all the way out to Brooklyn to sell crochet hats and scarves, crystal stones, give tarot card readings, and hand out business cards for KD's midwifery services at an outdoor farmers market. Mama gave out flyers about the Movement and my father's books. Me and Sage walked up and down Brooklyn streets sneaking around eating non-vegan ice cream and pizza, making Sage promise not to mention it to my mother, and checking out Brooklyn boys in the skate park and at the basketball courts.

So I climb into the back seat and into what feels like a time capsule. It's been over a year since Mama left without her car, and patchouli and lavender still fills the air. I avoid the passenger seat because it feels too close to her absence, too close to the hole she left behind.

Jasmine touches my hand. "You good? I didn't think we'd be in here."

"I mean . . . We can't just let it sit there," I say, half lying. "I'm glad my father didn't sell it just in case she comes back. But somebody's gotta drive it in the meantime. I guess."

"Nigeria? Your mother . . ." she starts to say.

But Makai hops into the passenger seat and starts running his mouth, as usual. "It's the first week of school for all these people. I call them sheeple. Sheep. People. Get it? So, by not attending their institutions, we're breaking free from the shackles of mental slavery," he says. "The American education system is founded on white supremacist ideas of indoctrination and groupthink mentality." He's repeating my father's exact words, and soon, Jasmine will probably be saying the same things, too.

I want her to finish her thought about my mother, but she's staring at Makai lost in her own revolutionary thoughts. Chris hasn't come in yet, and he's standing outside talking to my father. I narrow my eyes at them, wishing I could hear their conversation.

"Is he trying to be the next Youth Group president?" Makai asks, and he must've read my mind.

Makai's been around much longer than Jasmine, so he's like my actual brother at this point. But I mostly keep my distance from him because his father, Uncle Ra, is like my father's bodyguard, and by extension, Makai will protect King Kofi Sankofa by any means necessary, even though he's only five feet tall at fifteen years old. His bark is worse than his bite, as Uncle Ra says. It makes sense that he would notice how Chris is quickly climbing up the ranks.

"Don't pay him any mind, Makai," I tell him. "He won't be here for too long. You're fam. He's still a stranger."

My father is motioning toward the car, and Chris is nodding as if taking orders. Before I can connect the dots to understand what's happening, Chris starts to make his way to us, and then he's in the driver's seat. Mama's seat. I clench my hand into a fist. *No.*

My father walks to my side of the car and motions for me to put down my window. "Chris'll be taking y'all to the library. I'll be at a rally in front of city hall for another kid who got shot in Dunlap. Y'all can tune in at noon for the live stream."

I watch my father get into his black Escalade with a couple of the uncles and he drives off. Us Youth Group members are left alone, packed into my mother's car, and I'm supposed to be their leader. But Chris is still brand-new and my father already trusts him to drive us around?

He fidgets with all the nobs and buttons before turning on the engine.

"Y'all know this was the queen's car, right?" Jasmine says. "Respect the ride."

"Is," I correct her. "And she doesn't like being called a queen."

Chris lets go of the steering wheel and turns back to look at me. "My bad. Then you should be driving."

"I don't have my license."

"Then at least sit up front with me."

"Yeah, I'll move," Makai says, opening his door.

"No, I'm good back here," I tell them. Then I ask Chris, "You got your license?"

"Yep. I already drove this car. Your father had me behind the wheel since the first week I got here," he says, adjusting his seat and the rearview mirror. "You good, though?"

"Just . . . be careful. My mother will be pissed if there's a scratch on her car."

They all look at me funny, but they don't say a word.

Chris starts the car and pulls away from the curb, drives down our block with its row houses lining the narrow street. He makes a right turn on S. 51st and drives along Malcolm X Park and down a few blocks until he reaches Walnut Street and makes another right. I'm still stuck on the fact that this new boy is allowed to handle my mother's car.

"We're supposed to go to the library, but it's not open yet," Makai says.

We don't say anything as I glance over at Jasmine, who's scrolling through her phone now. Chris clutches the wheel and drives as if he owns these Philly streets. I wonder if he'd been watching my father all this time, mimicking his every move, even how he holds the steering wheel. I peep his profile—his smooth, sharp jawline and intense eyes hidden behind round wire-framed glasses I haven't seen before. So I ask, "When did you start wearing glasses?"

"Since I started reading all your father's books" is all he says with a half smile.

And Jasmine bumps my leg because I'm staring too hard. "Aren't you going to answer your texts? Your phone keeps dinging," she says.

I've been purposely ignoring them. So I reach into my bag for my phone and scroll past a bunch of unread text messages hoping to see my mother's number. But they're all either from Auntie Fola, Kamau, and lots and lots are from Sage. I don't read any of them. I need to think of how I'll get from the library to Philly Friends in time for my first class.

Chris turns up the volume to that underground rapper who's spitting bars about the government conspiracy theories over a dope beat and a sample of an old love song I recognize. Makai is the only one who starts bopping his head and rapping to the lyrics.

"Y'all know him?" Chris asks.

"Yeah, we know him," Makai says, all proud.

"I think he's corny, respectfully," Chris says with a smile, and I know he's just clowning Makai.

"Man, you bugging. He's dope," Makai says. "I mean, who else is dropping truth like this? It's messed up how we got rappers out here talking about guns, bitches, money, and getting high. But when somebody exposes the government, people think it's corny."

"I didn't say anything about his content," Chris says, driving way too slowly down Walnut Street, and it's clear that he probably just got his license. He turns down the volume and continues, "His flow is off. He needs to work on his delivery, his breath, and his stamina. He don't have to say everything in one bar. The truth hurts, and not everybody will hear his message if he mumbles."

"I respectfully disagree," Makai says. "Not every Philly rapper needs to sound like Meek Mill. No disrespect."

"We can agree to disagree, brother," Chris says. "But keep Meek's name out of this conversation."

"I'm saying, though," Jasmine adds her two cents. "With all the rich rappers out there, how come none of them are helping the people? Instead, they just tell us that we could be rich and famous, too. And that's cap."

"Yeah, that's cap and that's capitalism," says Makai. "Or else there wouldn't be any hoods in the first place. That's why we gotta sell all of King Kofi's books. Hey, Gigi. How far did you get with the new one?"

I don't answer him, and only the rapper's voice fills the car for a long minute. It starts to drizzle, enough for Chris to use the windshield wipers. He narrows his eyes, focusing on the road, and then he turns up the music again. Makai looks back at me, waiting for an answer. Jasmine is biting her nails down to the nub. The morning sky turns even grayer, just like yesterday. I know what we're supposed to do, and I know why we're supposed to be doing it. But tiny cracks are forming on the surface of us, or maybe it's just me.

My phone vibrates in my hand. It's Sage. I know what she wants.

I ignore it to give myself more time to think and plan. If Mama really wants this for me, the universe and the ancestors will guide me.

The rain is slow and steady, as if the entire sky is crying. I watch the Philly streets go by from my mother's car with its Black Liberation flag hanging from the rearview mirror. Whenever we drive through one of these narrow blocks lined with dilapidated row houses, people break their necks trying to see who all is in here. The thing about Philly is that its neighborhoods have borders. They're not invisible. You see where poverty ends and where opportunities begin. It's like driving down a smooth road, and when it gets bumpy all of a sudden, you know it's the hood. Someone drew that line in the exact spot where things like smooth roads stop being free. This is what my parents and everyone else in the Movement forced me to see. And it wasn't just about seeing the difference; it was about understanding why it's that way.

Sometimes, when my father drives his Escalade, he'll pull up to a corner where a bunch of brothers are hanging out, or he'd stop and talk to some of the men his age or older walking with a limp, or dragging their feet as if there's a heavy weight across their shoulders. The women and elders stand at bus stops or push shopping carts down broken concrete or hold children's small hands as they walk to the end of sidewalks. The kids my age are all over the place before the school doors open to West Philly High. They're acting a fool and having fun, and maybe they don't notice the dark clouds over their heads called oppression and racism and disenfranchisement—words that I learned along with my ABCs and 123s. I was taught that poor, Black neighborhoods can be like cages, and as a member of the Movement, I'm supposed to spend the rest of my life making everyone else see the metal bars and locked doors for what they really are. Except, I don't have the key to let us all out. My father thinks he does, but he's still in here.

"Drop me off at Philly Friends," I say flat out.

Jasmine's mouth hangs open. Makai and Chris are dead quiet.

"We're in my mother's car, and she wants me to go to that school. Now take me over to East Falls. I don't care if you snitch. I just need to start my second day."

They glance at each other as if I'm the butt of some inside joke.

"We have direct orders from Uncle Kofi," Makai says.

"Sister Nigeria, I don't think that's a good idea," Jasmine adds.

I don't know how to drive. If I did, I'd jack this whole ride.

"I know how to get there. I remember the route King Kofi took yesterday," Chris says.

"No, we're not doing this. We have to go to the library," Makai says.

"It's on the way," I lie. "Put it in the GPS."

"You're going to abandon us again? If you leave, then we'll all get in trouble," Makai adds.

My phone vibrates in my bag. I only pick it up because it's probably a sign—a way out of this car and into the school building. It's Sage. "Yeah," I answer.

"Are you coming? Please tell me you're coming," she says, sounding out of breath, as if she'll only take in a gulp of air if I tell her what she wants to hear.

So I say, "Yeah. I'm coming." And hang up.

"You're, like, voluntarily choosing to be mentally enslaved?"

Makai asks, and he's turned his whole body to me, removing his seat belt and all.

So Chris pulls up to a curb and parks the car, and in that same moment, my phone rings again. I look down at the screen and almost drop it when I see Mama's picture and her name.

I can't respond fast enough. I can't grip the phone tight enough. "Hello! Mama? Mama? Hello! Hi, Mama!" My voice is shaking. My whole body is the thunderous sky opening up to let it all pour out of my soul because my mother is finally, *finally* calling.

I wait to hear her voice. But there's silence. So I hop out of the car and press my fingers over my other ear. "Hello? Hello? Mama?"

Nothing.

I look at the phone. The caller is still on the line. "Mama? Is that you?"

Nothing.

"Mama!" I yell, and I want to jump into the phone and grab her, or hug her, or scream at her, or cry in her arms—any-and-everything all at once. I hold the phone to my ear wishing, *praying* for her voice to reach me from wherever she is. "Are you there, Mama?"

Still nothing. I look at the phone. The call has dropped.

I don't know when Chris and Jasmine had gotten out of the car. I didn't feel Makai's hand on my shoulder, nor see Jasmine holding a box of tissues. I didn't feel the tears streaming down my face. I didn't notice Chris looking at me as if I've lost my mind. I wipe my face and keep staring at the phone, expecting it to ring again.

"Why don't you call that number back?" Chris says with a voice I've never heard before—soft, almost whispering like a feather gliding across air. "Maybe it was a bad connection or a wrong number."

Jasmine nudges him and widens her eyes, as if Chris just said the wrong thing.

But it was the right thing. It was exactly what I want to hear right now. So I do call back. It goes straight to voice mail, which is just a long, sad, empty beep. Then I video call her. It doesn't go through. I don't know how many times I try and try again. But I find nothing. *Nothing.*

The light rain pounding on my head feels like djembe drums calling me to dance, to move, to go. So I get back into the car to grab my bag. I freeze when I see Mama's eyes in the rearview mirror as if she's sitting in the driver's seat. How do I reach for her through there? Through a phone? Through the clouds? I get out and walk away from the car, and I try to become one with the gray sky, hoping, *praying* that my wings will grow and fly me to that school in time for my first class.

"Why you want to leave us, Sister Nigeria?" Makai asks.

I don't answer him. I don't owe him anything. Mama called, and that was her way of letting me know that I can do this. I can disobey my father. I can start living my own life. I reach into my jeans pocket for my phone. I need to find a bus that'll get me to East Falls, or call a cab, or walk, or fly, or something. But it's not there.

Someone taps me, and it's Chris. "You dropped it," he says. "And it was ringing. It's someone named Sage."

So I grab the phone and put her on speaker. "Where is she?"

"That's exactly what Diane just asked me," Sage says. "So where are you?"

"I'm talking about my mother. She just called."

We're both quiet for a moment, trying to make sense of what I just said.

"You're getting wet," Jasmine whispers before she goes back into the car. I ignore her.

"Nigeria, if you don't show up again, you'll forfeit your scholarship and your spot," Sage says over the phone. "Look, your first class is at eight forty-five, but you have to meet with Diane before that. This whole thing was not my idea or my mother's. It's *your* mother who wants you to do this, Nigeria. We're helping her out." She hangs up.

My locs are usually a sponge absorbing all the rain before it reaches my face. But this time, everything is an avalanche of rainwater and I'm drenched. My T-shirt is sticking to my skin, my exposed toes and wet sandals make it feel like I'm standing in mud. My soaked jeans are extra weight around my legs, and I'm in a sinkhole.

Chris takes my hand and says, "Let's go. I'll take you. This was your mother's car anyway."

"Is," I correct him. "*Is* my mother's car." I look down at my phone again. My mind is racing, thinking of what just happened on that phone. But I don't question the universe or the ancestors.

With that, I hop back into the passenger seat this time, and Chris and I exchange quiet, knowing looks, and I wonder if he heard everything last night, too. And maybe he's not so Team King Kofi, after all.

"What do we say to your father?" Jasmine asks.

"Tell him the truth. Radical honesty."

"Radical honesty?" Makai asks. "So we're doing radical honesty now? Cool, cool. I know ain't that many kids out here pressed about getting to school on time. So there must be something special about this place. They must make you feel like they about to crown you the queen of the world or something. I know that's how Kamau be talking about that school. They treat him like royalty 'cause he makes *them* look good."

I turn my whole body to face him in the back seat. "Makai? Aren't you tired of all of this? Of having to read my father's books? Of listening to all those live streams and podcasts? It's the same thing every single day. Over and over again. I get it by now. We're oppressed. Racism is fucked up. Black people are messed up because of it. White people are evil because of it. And then what? What are we supposed to do with all that when nothing changes?"

I didn't realize how much I'd bottled up those truths. And with each word I spoke, my heart beats faster and faster because Makai is the last person I want to challenge right now. Whatever he has to say, he'll sound just like my father and he won't shut up about it.

He starts, "I could never get tired of fighting for liberation. But you don't think *you'll* get tired of being in that school? It's called tokenism, Sister Nigeria. They'll make you feel special when all it really does is make them . . ."

And I block him out as Chris drives down Black Road and up Martin Luther King Drive, and the way things are going right now, maybe that's a sign, too. The ride through Fairmount Park and along the Schuylkill River is always peaceful, so Makai eventually shuts up and we're quiet, thank goodness. I glance over at Chris, and I wonder why he's sticking up for me when it's my father who took him in and let him drive my mother's car. If anyone gets in trouble, it'll be him.

My phone dings again, and it's another text from Sage. Fifteen minutes until the meeting for worship. Go see Diane in the admissions office when you get here. She's trying to call your father. I hope he lets you stay.

It's not up to my father at this point. I have to walk through the doors of that school with its claims of being our *friends* and its progressive education on my own, without my father's permission. And if Philly Friends will be my life for the next two years, then maybe the sky will open up for me, the clouds will part, and the universe will expand.

"Nigeria," Jasmine says from behind me with a low, sad voice. "I think you should tell everybody about Nubia. They'll find out at some point. Maybe if you tell them, this will all make sense."

I don't even ask how she found out, because as my father always says, family business is the Movement's business. And the Village House has ears and eyes. "Nubia's trying to take my mother's place," I say. "So me and Freedom . . . we're leaving. Mama's coming for us."

"Don't say that, Nigeria," Jasmine whines, sounding as if she's about to cry.

"I don't want you to leave. I just got here," Chris says quietly.

And something warm and syrupy settles inside of me, and my whole body comes alive with . . . with *newness*. I quickly look over at him as he keeps his eyes on the road. I'm mad that he's saying this in front of Makai and Jasmine. I'm mad that other than my brother, someone else can keep me in that house for longer than I want to stay.

"Oh, we're catching feelings now?" Makai asks. "Cool, cool. At least we're keeping it in the village."

"Oh, shut up, *Brother* Makai!" I say, taking a tissue and throwing it back at him.

No one says anything for a second. Then Jasmine is the first to start laughing. And then Chris. And then I pop, bursting wide open with a belly-aching cackle. The car swerves a little because Chris is laughing so hard. I grab his leg. And I keep my hand there.

"So I'm a joke now?" Makai asks. "Okay. We'll see who has the last laugh. There's nothing funny about revolution, *Sister* Nigeria."

We all laugh even harder.

Even Makai starts to chuckle, realizing how ridiculous he sounds sometimes.

And I'm over here fighting for my life trying to get to some rich white private school way on the other side of our hood. I double over and start cough-laughing because I didn't know this much joy had been lodged in my throat and in my body.

GRIEVANCE 6

"It's like you're the spook who'll be sitting by the door," Chris says when he drops me off. I thought he was on my side, but he's bringing up what my father said yesterday, thinking that I was actually listening to him.

"Yeah," I lie. "A spook by the door." But being at this school is not some secret spy mission for the Movement. So I turn off my phone and walk through Philly Friends's red double doors without looking back at my mother's car and the Youth Group members.

Kamau and Sage are not around to greet me. So I do as I was told and head straight to the Diversity, Equity, and Inclusion office. The letters DEI are on the door beneath Diane Hutchinson's name. If the last two letters are flipped, it spells "die," and I wonder which part of me is dying by coming to this school, by adding to the diversity and being included.

"Do you need another T-shirt?" Diane asks. "It's supposed to rain all week, so if you'll be coming in wet, should I keep a few here for you if you come back?"

I nod because my own T-shirt is wet and ice cold against my skin. I also don't want anybody to know who I am and where I come from—with the Movement's logo on my chest and all.

In the bathroom near Diane's office, I change out of the Movement's T-shirt into the Philly Friends one. I'm swapping one brand for another, one skin for another—as if I'm switching allegiances.

Diane makes me sit at a round table in her office. A tray of cold cereal, a sesame bagel and cream cheese, a banana, yogurt, and tea were already waiting for me when I got here. It's served on real ceramic plates with the school's logo in the middle and with silverware, as if this is somebody's house. All this special treatment is making me feel like a charity case. In this school, maybe I am.

"Nigeria, I'm so glad you're back. Listen, I know a lot about your father. I'd spoken to your mother about all the things you learned at home and how naturally brilliant you are, and this is the kind of self-guided, independent learner we want here at Philly Friends," Diane says in almost one breath. "But we really need your father's permission. When we deferred your acceptance and offered you a seat as an incoming junior, we weren't aware that your mother—"

"My mother already did everything," I say, cutting her off. "You told me she filled out all the papers, I'm registered for classes, I got a scholarship, and I already have family here. That should be enough." I leave the breakfast untouched and get up from the table wearing my second Philly Friends T-shirt. "I don't want to be late for my first class. Can I go now?"

"Wait," she exhales, and motions for me to come over to her desktop computer. "I want you to read this so that you know what we're up against."

She points to the screen where the email's subject line in capital letters is: WARNING. It's from my father, and I brace myself before reading his message in bold letters.

REMOVE MY DAUGHTER FROM YOUR INSTITUTION NOW! I DO NOT WANT MY CHILD IN YOUR SYSTEM OF WHITE SUPREMACIST INDOCTRINATION!

A flame ignites in my belly, and I feel like punching that computer screen. I feel like shouting into the air.

"Have a seat and drink some tea," Diane says, noticing that I'm about to blow up.

I sit, close my eyes, inhale and exhale pranayama breaths to cool down. I activate Mama's face in my third eye—her bright smile, shining eyes, her glowing skin. She wants this for me. I want this for me. I let out a long, weighted breath and release a quiet moan. I take a sip of peppermint tea and I'm calm again, and ask, "Do Kamau and Sage know about this?"

"This isn't their concern. This has to involve a parent or guardian."

"Guardian? Then you should forward that email to KD. She's helping my mother with all of this."

Diane leans forward a little bit, examining me from her desk, and says, "Nigeria, why do you—"

"KD should know about this," I cut her off again, standing away from the table. "She can be my guardian."

"It has be a *legal* guardian. . . . Look, Nigeria. We can't keep you if your father doesn't want you to be here."

"My class is starting now." I grab my bag and start to walk out of her office. "Call Kamau's mom, my aunt Sharon. She's blood family. You can talk to her." I know better than to get Aunt Sharon involved because it'll be a civil war in our family. But I just have to get through this second day.

"Did Kamau tell you about our affinity group?" she asks. "We have our first meeting after school today. You should come. Nigeria, I'll do my best to keep you here. But just be prepared that this might be your last day. At the very least, you can have somewhat of a full Philly Friends experience before you leave."

I don't want to prepare for that. So I nod and swallow hard, not really knowing what power she'll have over what my father wants for me. Mama can't even get him to change his mind. But right now, he's a nonissue. What matters most is that I'm here. I'm actually here, and he couldn't stop me.

I missed the meeting for worship, thank goodness, and breeze through the next couple of classes until lunchtime where I see Kamau for the first time today. I spot him leaving the cafeteria and walking into the library, so I run to him and grab his arm. He doesn't even turn around, knowing that it's me.

"Really, cuz?" I say.

He glances back, then motions for me to follow him into the library and toward an empty spot on floor pillows near a set of tall windows. A group of kids are also making their way to that spot, so Kamau takes my hand and we speed walk, reaching the floor pillows before they get there. We plop down, a little out of breath. I'm laughing. He's not. I take his arm in mine and rest my head on his shoulder, like he usually does to me. He lets me be for a moment without saying a word.

Then he says, "Your father called my mother telling her to stay out of your life. That if she's going to be an auntie to you, she has to respect his boundaries."

I lift my head from his shoulder. I'm not surprised, but I act like I am. "Are you serious?"

"He thinks my mother had something to do with you coming to this school," Kamau continues. "Which is why she had to stay out of this."

I pull my arm out of his and lean forward, resting my chin in my hands. "Why did your mother change her mind, anyway? Why'd you stop homeschooling with me?"

"Come on, Gigi. You know what's up. Auntie Natalie was such a good teacher. My mama trusted her with my education. I mean, look where we at now. With the best of the best. But . . ." He looks down at his hands, examining his nails. His left pinkie finger is painted black, as if he was trying out the color against his light brown skin. "Did you ever actually read your father's books? Like *Black Families Matter*?"

I glance at him, hesitating a bit because I don't like talking bad about my father to anyone, not even my cousin. "No. I hear his mouth every day, I don't need to read his words, too. Trust."

He laughs that sunshine laugh of his. And I can't help but to giggle, too.

"That's real, cuz," he says, still laughing. Then he sighs. "Man, woman, and child. It's all about the Black family for him. Man, woman, and child."

I don't have to dig deeper to know what he means, to feel what he feels. "I'm sorry, Kamau," I whisper.

"I wish he would just come out and say it—that he doesn't want his nephew being gay. It's okay for everyone else, but not for his own blood? I mean, my mother got tired of him telling her that she needs a man in the house, and him steady trying to hook her up with one of the uncles because he thinks it'll set me straight. Literally. My daddy is just fine, and he loves me just the way I am. He even said I could come stay with him down in Atlanta. Might even apply to Morehouse. You know what? You should go to Spelman, cuz!"

I can't dream that far into the future yet. So I say, "Kamau, I'm just trying to make it to next week. Hey, listen. Since your mother and my father are not talking anyway, maybe Aunt Sharon can help me stay in this school. Like, I don't know. . . . She can be my guardian since we're actually related and all."

Kamau rolls his eyes as if I've asked too much of him. "You know that saying? Blood is thicker than water? We had to call all these random people uncle and auntie, but your father made his own sister a stranger just because she challenged him. And I challenged him just by being myself. And Aunt Natalie should've been a wake-up call, but—"

"Fine, then," I say, cutting him off because I don't want him to bring up my mother. "Kamau, I really do want to stay here. I want to graduate with you, and yes, you could go to Morehouse and I could be at Spelman or Yale or Harvard or . . . What's the whitest school out there?"

Kamau rubs his chin, seriously thinking about my question.

"Probably Oxford. The British Empire and shit . . . What your father calls the bowels of white supremacy."

"Yeah, Oxford or Cambridge . . ." I say, knowing my father would be *livid* if I went to any of those schools.

"But seriously, Gigi. I hope you're not doing all this just to get your father mad."

"Of course not! You think I want him yelling at me all day? I'm doing this for me. No matter what anybody says. But for real, though. Makai is the worst. He thinks I'm selling out. I can take my father, but *him*?"

Kamau laughs again, and he knows exactly what I'm talking about. "If I'm being honest, they would love Makai at this school."

"That's the problem, though. What's the point of being a revolutionary if places like this can claim the revolution for themselves? Nah. Makai is right where he belongs."

"How about you, though? Day two at Philly Friends. You feel like you belong here?"

I pause for a second and look around the library with its many lush plants and shelves upon shelves of books. The kids here are an oil-and-water mix of uptight and free-spirited. They work hard and play hard. Some kids are sitting alone with their laptops, others are in small groups whispering among themselves, and in a far corner is a crew of Black girls. They're all poring over some poster board project and I wonder if they're lifers like Sage. Maybe I want to be friends with them. "I belong wherever I am, Kamau. Wherever I decide to be."

❧

The Constitution and You is the class I was looking forward to. Sage is there, and I haven't seen her all morning. She smiles as if telling me that she's glad I'm here. But I give her a look letting her know that this is just the beginning. I'm going to need her help.

Liam waves to me from across the oval table, and I just smile. I'm supposed to be mad at Kamau for giving him my number, but I'm not. Maybe he'll be my first friend at this school. Maybe not.

"Abraham Lincoln was truly our first great president," Henry says as he leans back in his chair and folds his hands across his belly. "Why do you think that is?"

I wonder if he was ever actually a lawyer, as many times as he brags about his law degree from Princeton. He'd glanced at me when he added it was the same school Michelle Obama went to.

A white boy raises his hand, and I narrow my eyes at him, hoping he doesn't say anything stupid. Or else I'll have to speak up. Right now, I just want to sit back and listen and not have to teach anyone.

"He freed the slaves!" the boy says, a little too giddy.

I sigh and roll my eyes. I didn't mean to, but I want to avoid discussions about slavery, especially here.

Henry catches me. "Nigeria, do you think he's wrong?"

They're all watching me now, including Liam, who's been staring at me for whatever reason. How come Henry doesn't pick Sage or the other Black boy?

So I have to decide who I want to be in this moment. Never mind that my hair, my skin, and my body tell my story before I even speak. Do I confirm what they think they know about me? Or do I flip the script and put on a mask and become a whole other person? So I say,

"Yeah. Abe Lincoln freed the slaves, but it was a political move and not because he cared about human beings."

Liam focuses in on me. I look away from him because he's being weird and I don't want any white boy to question me right now, including Henry.

"That's right," he says. "Emancipation Proclamation in 1863, three years into the Civil War. He was a morally upstanding man of great stature and—"

"But didn't slavery end in 1865?" Liam asks, glancing at me.

I slide down in my chair. I want to disappear until they start talking about something else besides slavery. Sage doesn't say a word, and she usually has an opinion about everything.

"It was *legally* abolished in 1865," a Black boy says. "But many slaves didn't know that they were emancipated two years before that." Tyler is his name, and if I close my eyes and just listen to his voice, I won't even know he's Black.

Thank goodness someone else can carry this conversation. But I still add, "Enslaved. Our ancestors were not slaves, they were *enslaved*. Huge difference."

"You're absolutely right, Nigeria," Henry says. "Did you all know that the word 'slavery' does not appear in the Constitution? Yet, it is an institution that is foundational to all the ills and turmoil in this country."

"The word itself doesn't have to be written out for it to be enforced," Tyler adds.

Tyler and I seem to be tag-teaming on this, so I say, "Yeah, like how slavery continues today without it being called slavery. A loophole in the Thirteenth Amendment allows for mass incarceration and the growth of the prison industrial complex."

"Are you comparing criminals to slaves?" Liam asks.

"Again, not slaves but the enslaved. Enslaved. Imprisoned. In this country, it's the same thing."

"Please elaborate," Liam continues. "Are you saying that enslaved people were already criminals?"

I sigh because this is exactly what I didn't want to get into.

Henry sees my frustration and adds, "And these are the sorts of questions we should be asking ourselves and each other in this class, as well as when we start drafting our arguments for the debate. As a reminder, this month's resolution is 'Community standards are of greater value than individual liberty.'"

Liam keeps looking at me as if he's still waiting for an answer. But I won't give him that satisfaction. Sage is cleaning her nails, and I can't believe she didn't add anything to this discussion.

"But what do Abe Lincoln and slavery have to do with that resolution?" the South Asian boy named Hasan asks. "Are the community standards slavery and individual liberty . . . states' rights?"

"Excellent start, Hasan," says Henry. "As for the resolution, you make your own arguments for both the affirmative and negative sides. Use whatever examples you want. But the series of debates with incumbent senator Stephen Douglas in 1858 were where Lincoln solidified his ideas on slavery before he ran for the presidency. He was morally against it but didn't know how to change course. Which is why he didn't side with the abolitionists, who knew exactly how slavery should end in this country."

"Abolitionists were some of the first feminists," Sage finally says. "And *still* we don't have a woman president. So community standards is the patriarchy versus women's rights as individual liberty."

Henry furrows his brow, then holds his hands out asking if we disagree with Sage. No one offers a rebuttal, but Hasan changes the subject back to slavery.

I look around the small class as everyone thinks out loud and answers big questions even when they're wrong. I wonder if I'm in here with future politicians and CEOs. I wonder if they really understand what I'm saying, and if they do, will they change this country? Will they dismantle white supremacy and capitalism so that the whole world can be a utopia? My father doesn't think it's possible, which is why he wants to divest. But here, maybe new ideas are being born and shaped and tested out in this school first. Maybe.

Class ends, and Sage runs off to some other thing. So I have to find my own way around this school and not rely on her and Kamau. Tyler passes me, and I tap his shoulder. "Hey. Thanks."

"For what?" he asks.

"For saying all those things. I didn't want to be the only one correcting everybody."

He steps back from me a little bit. "Yeah, I'm just trying to get a good grade for class participation." And he walks away.

I shrug and make a mental note not to count on him too much whenever these discussions come up. I'm not sure I can depend on Sage, either.

Diane had given me the room number for the after-school affinity group called Black at Philly Friends. If it's anything like the

Movement, where we sit around and plan how to burn down the master's house while we're still living in it, then I'll pass. But still, I'm poking my head into every classroom and corner of this school. The more I learn in this place, the more my world will widen, the more land and sky I can conquer.

I pull my shoulders in when I'm walking through the halls, looking at almost every white kid. Do they see me? Like, really see me? Most just look up at my hair. Others look through me. Some smile. Others say hi. I only wave when I need to. I'm breathing hard because this is an ice-cold ocean and I'm treading water, barely staying afloat.

"Nigeria?" someone calls out. I turn around to see Liam. I almost turn back, but I have to be friendly. I have to fit in. Sort of.

"Good points in there," he says.

"Thanks," I say. "But I was just telling the truth."

"Of course, of course. Um, I was thinking . . . I know it's still early, but we should get started on the resolution."

"We? I didn't know this was a group project."

He nods. "Yeah. Wanna partner up? We need to have a team of two, and we have to argue both sides. We can even compete against each other."

Too many thoughts are going through my mind. What does he want from me? Partner up? With him? I'll join Sage or Tyler before I team up with him. But all I say is "Sure."

"Okay. Cool." He smiles with his whole face and just stands there.

I don't have a filter for all these intrusive thoughts and my father lives in my head, so I ask, "Do you have a trust fund?"

"What?" he laughs. "I wish."

I drop my head, a little embarrassed. It was a random question, so I follow up with "How do you pay for this school, then?"

He shrugs. "Financial aid."

I nod, looking him up and down and not really knowing what to do with that information.

"Maybe that could be one of our points for the debate," he says. "Community standards as overpriced and privatized education versus individual liberty as freedom to choose the quality of our education."

I'm looking dead at him now, trying to make sense of his words and his eyes. Part of me wants to examine him in that moment, pry him open to find out if everything I've learned about white people is true. But someone touches my shoulder and I'm pulled away from Liam's magnet.

It's Diane. She looks concerned. My stomach sinks because this is the end of the school day and I know what this is about. "My father's here?" I ask, not letting her tell me the bad news first.

"No. Someone else is at the front desk for you. Your brother, Chris," she says. "Is he in school, or . . . ?"

"Chris? He's here?" He's not supposed to be here. He's not supposed to be part of any of this because he's brand-new to the chaos called my life. Diane doesn't know that he's not my blood brother. Whether or not he's in school is none of her business. I turn every which way trying to remember where I am in these wide halls.

"Oh, I can take you there," Liam says.

"Would you please?" says Diane. "I have to moderate the affinity group. Nigeria, I'm sorry you can't join us."

"I'm coming back tomorrow," I tell her.

She nods slowly and says, "We'll hold out until the end of the week. We have to get your father on the phone. But after that, we have to respect his wishes."

Liam clears his throat. He wasn't supposed to hear any of that. Diane walks away, and I tell him, "Just point to the front desk."

"I'm going that way."

"Tell me where it is."

He points toward the end of the hall and starts walking beside me anyway. "You're leaving?" Liam asks. "It's only been two days."

"I'll be back," I say, wishing he would mind his business.

"I hope so," Liam says.

Then I spot Chris sitting on the set of fancy chairs beneath the portrait of William Penn. "What's good, Sister Nigeria?" he says.

"Bye, Nigeria," Liam calls behind me.

I feel like I'm standing on a fault line and my world is slowly splitting in two. "My father sent you?" I ask Chris.

"No. I need to get you back home before he finds out," he says. "Let's go. We got, like, an hour to get out of this part of Philly. If anything, we could just say you was rolling with me. Jas and Makai are at the library, and they'll take a bus back."

He motions for me to follow him out, and I do, only because he's keeping this secret for me. Even though he's brand-new to us, he's more of a lifeline right now than both Sage and Kamau. So I walk out of the Philly Friends double doors with a runaway boy who lives in my house.

I slide into the passenger seat—my seat—and Chris drives down the I-76 taking me to wherever I need to go. Mama must've sent him. She sent him for me.

"What if you get in trouble with my father?" I ask. "He might kick you out of the Village House."

He shrugs. "I'm not getting in trouble for looking out for his daughter. And besides, that's what he told me to do. To keep an eye on you."

"I don't need anybody to keep an eye on me. You just got here, Chris. Why does he trust you like that?"

"You and I just met, but King Kofi's been mentoring me for, like, three years now. Since I was fifteen—in the tenth grade at Strawberry Mansion. A bunch of us would meet up with him and some of the uncles after school for a workshop on manhood and Black history. Been listening to his live streams and reading his books since then."

"Damn. You're already in too deep."

"Is that a bad thing, though? I got my own mind, too, you know," he says as he makes a left on Belmont Avenue.

"I don't want to go home yet," I say.

"Nah. I'm taking you home. If you want to keep going to that school, you should lie low. Do what you're supposed to do. I'm just looking out for you."

"I keep telling you I don't need you to look out for me."

"I know. You're grown. But I respect your father, even if you don't."

"I do respect my father. I just don't always agree with him."

"Same. Which is why I think you should go to that school," Chris says. "He's right about you taking what you need from them to help us. We should do what they do, but flip it and make it Black and revolutionary. You should take notes so we could make our shit just like their shit. It should be called the Sankofa Friends School. Nah. More like a family. Yeah. The Sankofa Family Freedom School."

"They've been doing what they do for almost four hundred years," I tell him, not really feeling any of his ideas. "We can't catch up."

"But how many of our ancestors must've laid down those bricks, cleaned those floors, cooked that fancy cafeteria food?"

I think of the ones I saw serving our lunch, the security guards, and even the few Black teachers they have. "Yeah" is all I say because I'm not trying to go there with him. It's enough that I'm even sitting in that building. It's enough that I'm there, taking up space with my body and my voice. What I want and who I am should be enough.

"I wanna be in there with you. Go back to high school 'cause I was cutting half the time anyway. You think they'll let me in? I'll take over and turn that shit upside down," Chris says, laughing.

"Did you graduate, though?" I ask, already knowing the answer and avoiding his last question.

"Nah," he says. "I'm good, though. I'm here."

Whoever Chris is and whatever his dreams are must be enough for him right now. He has a way about him—like he's free and the world is his, even though he's driving my mother's car and living up in our house.

"How 'bout you? You good?" he asks, glancing over at me with a smile that makes my insides flutter.

I just nod and return a half smile, lean back in my seat to let the smooth ride pull me into a deep, deep rest. The day was heavy and the gray clouds have parted to give way to a late-afternoon sun.

"You need to take that Philly Friends T-shirt off before you get back to the house, though," he says.

"Shit," I say, sitting up, and my mind starts racing again. "I left the Movement's T-shirt at school."

"You got a jacket or something? Or you wanna risk it and just run into the house before he sees you?'"

I turn around to scan the back seat. Nothing is there, of course. But Mama keeps boxes of secondhand clothes in the trunk to deliver to shelters around the city. Would my father or anyone else have cleaned it out? I hope not. A lot of her stuff is still in her closet and dressers at home waiting for her to come back. "Pull up to the corner. There should be something in the trunk," I tell Chris.

There are more boxes than I thought—barely closed and unmarked. I open one to see some of Mama's clothes, shoes, and books—things that I didn't even notice were missing. My whole body goes numb, except where my hands are touching Mama's clothes. The soft fabrics beneath my fingers are the closest I've been to her in months. The blue-and-lavender tie-dye and African print dresses that she always wears are balled up and thrown in. I rummage through everything to find some clue, some note, something, *anything* that will let me know when she's coming back.

The cars are whizzing down Belmont, and the afternoon sun shouldn't be shining right now because everything about this moment is still dark clouds and rainstorm. I move the boxes around looking for whatever else they took from my mother.

I spot a purple suitcase that belonged to her. I quickly open up the suitcase to see more of Mama's clothes, except in here, they're rolled neatly into rows. Some of the clothes are mine—a few T-shirts and jeans I haven't seen in months, maybe in over a year. A small travel cube holds a few tiny onesies and diapers. Baby clothes for a newborn. Is this Freedom's old stuff? But the tags are still on. They're brand-new and were never worn. My heart sinks. Did Mama get these *before* Freedom was born?

I quickly run my hand beneath all the clothes, dig into the zippered pockets, feel along the corners of the suitcase. Nothing. Mama definitely did the packing because of how neat and organized everything is. She took her time rolling each dress. She bought newborn clothes. She put in some of my clothes. She got me registered for school. And now there's a packed suitcase that's been sitting in her trunk for over a year.

She knew she'd leave. She always knew. Right now, I love her even more for that. And I miss her even more.

The hole she left behind becomes a bright, endless sky, and if I leap toward it with my baby brother, I wonder if we'll be flying in some other alternative world where our wings are wide enough to claim the whole universe as ours.

Something in me opens wide, wide, and I slide back into the car feeling as if Mama's car and this boy are both a key and a door leading me down the winding road called my life.

"So this is how you want to roll? Sneaking behind my back again after I gave you clear directions? After I told that school to leave you alone?" My father's presence is a thunderstorm waiting for us as soon as we walk into the Village House.

Freedom is toddling toward me as I stand in the doorway with Chris behind me. He starts to cry. My father quickly scoops him up, and I'm glad he's holding my baby brother. He'll be less angry. Hopefully. But Freedom keeps crying, and I rush past my father and start heading up the stairs.

"My bad, King," Chris says as he comes into the house and closes the door behind him. "She needed something from that school, so I offered to take her. It was raining and—"

"I don't need you to lie for me, Chris," I say, standing in the middle of the staircase.

"And I don't need you to lie *to* me," my father says to him. "Golden rule for staying in the Village House: radical honesty. Golden rule for belonging to the Movement: Respect me and my vision."

I don't want my father to get on Chris for looking out for me, so I rush back down the stairs and say, "Baba, I'll keep going to that school, and you can't stop me. You can't stop me."

Freedom reaches for me, but I don't take him. My eyes are locked on my father's face—his narrowed eyes, bushy beard, sweaty forehead. He's a whole head taller than me, and he's not looking down at me as he bounces my brother in his arms. I stand my ground.

My father's eyes finally meet mine just as Chris walks past us and goes into the kitchen. Nubia comes from out of nowhere, it seems, and takes Freedom. He doesn't cry, and he rests his little head on her shoulder. That almost sends me over the edge. But I inhale and keep simmering.

My father releases a deep, warm breath and says, almost whispering, "Radical honesty? I don't want to lose you, too. I don't want to lose you to those systems and institutions, Nigeria."

And the flame that was ignited in me turns down. I don't simmer, but I'm still heated. Tears well up in my eyes, but I don't cry. Not now, not in front of my father. His eyes become wet, too, but he holds in his avalanche. Or else we will both drown.

He's the first to walk away.

That night, the house is quiet. There's no live stream or podcast recording. There's no family dinner or communal affirmations. Jasmine is lost in a book about mass incarceration. Makai is down in the basement with his father. Nubia put Freedom to sleep early in my bed, and I'm grateful.

But still, my mind needs to quiet down. The voices and faces of the kids at Philly Friends crowd my thoughts and I don't know if there's enough room for my own imagination. It's midnight, and I'm in the kitchen searching for something to eat, anything that will fill me up until I'm numb. I was way too anxious today to think about food. I hear someone coming down, so I quickly close the fridge door.

I pretend not to care as Chris walks past me, nods, and heads into the backyard. I put some dishes away and join him out on the deck, where he's lighting a joint and staring into the darkness spread across what used to be my mother's garden. It would've been harvest time now—onions, garlic, tomatoes, and potatoes mostly.

I sit next to him, purposely grazing my arm against his, and he feels liquid. Or maybe I've melted a little. He passes the joint to me, and I hold it between my fingers until I gather myself into something solid and unmoving. I'm mad that he has that effect on me.

Then I put it to my lips and pull and pull and pull until the fireflies in my head quiet my racing thoughts. I shut out Nubia. I shut out my father. I shut out the school. I shut out the world.

"Every family got their shit," he says, taking the joint back. "Even the ones that think they got all the answers."

"So you heard everything," I say.

"I didn't have to hear anything. I'm just stating facts." He starts bopping to some beat in his head and exhales a long string of smoke that dances up into the air. "If I'm being honest," he starts, "the Movement should have a whole music department. Like, positive vibes only. No curses, no street shit, just elevating the consciousness of the people. Music that makes them feel like . . . like this."

I want to tell him that I love how he just starts off our conversations from some whole other place, like he's already with the moon and stars. But I just say, "That'll be dope."

I keep my responses short 'cause I don't want him to ask me anything about that school. Or about what's happening in our family. I just want to be up there in the night sky with him, floating.

"King Kofi said I could run the music department," he continues.

And with the mention of my father, I come back down to earth. "You don't have to call him 'King' you know."

"It's a sign of respect." He shrugs as if it's no big deal. "And the kids in the Freedom School could learn music and maybe we can even have our own music distribution company. Like a Berry Gordy or Quincy Jones, but super Black. Know what I mean?"

"Word" is all I say.

He turns to me as if he's just seeing me for the first time. "Where you been all my life?"

"I've been here."

"I mean, you know how much shit I could've avoided if I knew about your father, the Movement, this house . . . and you . . . when I was, like, five?"

"Would your mother have become a member?" I ask point-blank.

"Probably not. She wouldn't like all this Africa shit. She goes to church and prays for me to come home to Jesus. But I dropped out of school. Got into some trouble. So she kicked me out."

"I hate that for you."

"I hate that for us." He takes another hit from the joint and furrows his brow as if this moment is a complex game he's trying to figure out. He studies everything, even the smoke that he exhales. Then he turns to me again and studies my face. With his free hand, he takes my chin, leans in, and kisses my lips. He pulls back and looks into my eyes as if I'm something he doesn't understand yet. "I feel free," he says.

"You are free," I whisper, and this is truer for him than it is for me. He still has my chin in his hand.

The phone buzzing in my back pocket is the only thing that makes me pull away. I hold it away from Chris's view. It's a series of texts from William Fisher.

I want us to be a team. Like an odd couple. Both sides of the argument. Affirmative and negative. Pro and con. Do-over for the next meeting? You can get all the space you need. No one will sit in our row. I'll stay way on the other side.

I don't mean to smile. But this moment feels like I'm nestled between sunshine and ocean—this text from a white boy, and a kiss from a Black boy.

Chris holds the joint out to me again, then brings it closer to my lips, and I pull and pull and pull again and inhale until my head fills with starlight and stardust. Then I exhale as he opens wide and swallows my smoky breath, and we exchange hopes and dreams for a free world and a free life. I don't know if his version of being free is the same as mine, though.

My phone pings again, and it's a smiley face from Liam. I put it facedown on the deck, because I'm here now, with this runaway boy who is stretching my world wide open.

Chris takes my chin and kisses me again. I close my eyes, and we are both soft clouds. I let go of everything, swing my leg across his lap, and straddle him. He pulls me in closer, wraps his whole self around me, and swallows my soul. I become moonlight and he is the night sky, and this is a freedom I didn't know I wanted, didn't know I needed.

That night, I curl into bed next to my sleeping baby brother, pull his warm little body against mine, and reach for my beat-up copy of *The People Could Fly*. Freedom never got to hear Mama's honey-sweet voice read those words, as hard as they were to listen to. So I'll take my mother's place and retell our history of enslaved ancestors and brutal masters, conjuring magic and blackbird wings. Mama would read these stories to me almost every night. And maybe these stories were not just history, but a roadmap for tomorrow, like a Sankofa bird. So, maybe she was reading me a sky map—charting our journey across the sky, back to home, back to ourselves. Maybe.

INDIGENOUS PEOPLES' DAY

Areyto of Anacaona:
"Aia, bombaia, bombe
Lamma samana quana
Aia, bombaia, bombe
Lamma samana quana"

—Anacaona. "Golden Flower." The Taino queen
from what is now Haiti and the Dominican
Republic, poet, dancer, and avenger of her people.
No explorer, colonizer, linguist, or historian
has ever been able to translate these words.

But if you know, you know.

1. MY BODY IS NOT A NATION.

"Why do you want to keep going to that school?" Chris asks me while I twist his hair. "Your father says you can't. And he's family." He'd taken out his braids and had decided to grow locs, like me. Like my father. Like most of the members in the Movement. Like Bob Marley and the Rastafarians. Like revolutionaries who don't subscribe to Eurocentric beauty standards. Chris is becoming conscious now, and this is what happens to anyone who lives in the Village House.

"I'm spreading my wings," I tell him.

I'm sitting on the couch while he sits on a floor pillow between my legs. His arms are over each of my thighs, and he kisses my bare knee poking out of my torn jeans. He must've bathed in Egyptian musk and discovered the super-Black world of natural fragrance oils, shea butter, black soap, and incense. We're in the living room, and most of the members are out running errands or working or whatever. It's the end of September, and Philly Friends is closed today for Rosh Hashanah. I'm still going to school behind my father's back, using the library or museums as an excuse. I'm supposed to be helping him with his new book, but I'm going to school instead. Chris keeps my secret, dropping me off and picking me up in my mother's car.

That's one of the reasons why I'm doing his hair that day. We have a deal. Or maybe it's more than that. I can't front. I'm starting to catch feelings. Bad. And that's not a good thing. At least not in the Village House.

It's one of those rare days when we almost have the house to ourselves if it weren't for Freedom and Nubia.

A jar of shea butter sits beside me, and I wet a thin piece of his tightly coiled hair with a spray bottle. Then I dab some of the shea butter onto the strands, smooth out his hair between my fingers, and twist it into a corkscrew. In that moment, I'm closer to him than I'd ever been. This is better than kissing.

"So can I be the wind?" Chris asks.

"What?" I gently push his head forward to part out another piece of hair.

"I want to be the wind under your wings."

It took me a minute; then I playfully shove him. "Oh, please, Chris!"

We laugh as I finish twisting his hair, getting to know the hidden corners of him without even asking questions, without even talking, really. Chris and I do more kissing than talking. When we find moments to ourselves where our little part of the world is empty and quiet, he pulls me in and I wrap my arms around his neck and our lips exchange unspoken words that are lodged deep in our souls. At this point, I can count on one hand how many of those moments we had. But this is the first time I got to touch a different part of him and read his thoughts.

"How come nobody is looking for you?" I ask as I trace the parted roads on his scalp with more shea butter and secrets.

"Somebody is looking for me all right. It's not the somebody you think it should be," he says.

"Your mother, father, cousins, and them? Where are your people?"

He breathes in deep and responds, "I feel like if I tell you everything, you'll think I'm some kind of tired stereotype."

"Stereotype to who? This ain't the movies, Chris. Your life is your life. I'm not going to judge you for that."

"A'ight, then. My father moved out to Cleveland when I was, like, six. Then he got locked up, came across your father's books, and became a fan. Then I met your father in real life. My mother works at a day care center. My older sister moved down to Virginia with her girlfriend. And I stay trying to get money, and that's where the stereotypical shit comes in," he says. "So being up in this jawn is better than prison."

"Why it gotta be prison, though?" I ask. "A coffin or prison are not the only two options for you in this country."

"Yeah, tell me something I don't know. I told you the rest of my story gets into some stereotypical shit."

"I guess this is better than home, too?"

"This *is* home," he says quietly. "And you want to leave?"

If I give him an answer, I'd be throwing away all the moments we shared and shitting on all his dreams he has for the Movement. So I let the silence push us apart, and Chris is suddenly far, far away, as if the space where my fingers touch his scalp stretches an entire block and all I see is his half-done hair and his strong embrace and his deep kisses disappearing in the distance. I don't even reach for him to pull him back in, to pull him back home to me.

2. MY BODY IS NOT A WAR.

I keep going back to Philly Friends, getting there late and missing some days. I ease in and out of the school day as if this is my life from now on. But my father walks around as if he has a plan. He already knows that I'm sneaking out behind his back and he lets me go. So this school is like a ghost between us. It seems like a dead issue, but it'll show up to haunt both of us at any point.

That's what happened on the Friday before the three-day weekend for Indigenous Peoples' Day. After almost a month of slipping in and out of the Village House, after taking Chris up on his offers to drive me around in my mother's car, and after abandoning the Youth Group members, my days at the Philadelphia Friends School almost come to an end. My father comes to get me. And no one can stop him.

The bass coming from his truck's speakers makes the entire campus grounds of the school vibrate, and maybe he's trying to wake the dead. There's been enough accidental grave site diggings all around Philly to let the world know that Indigenous and Black people were buried under almost every old building in this city, and probably under the school, too. So in that moment, as I step out of Philly

Friends's red double doors with my father beside me, I whisper a prayer asking for courage.

Other cars are approaching the pickup line and my father's truck is in the way, not moving. Uncle Ra, with his thick beard and dark sunglasses, comes out of the passenger-side seat to greet us, as my father walks with his head held high. His Eye of Horus pendant hangs against the Movement's logo on his hoodie.

I look over my shoulder to see if I still have some sort of lifeline to reel me back into the school. Diane is standing in front of the entrance. Our eyes meet, and I plead with my whole face hoping that she understands, hoping that she'll do something.

But Diane couldn't do anything but hand me over to my father when he asked for me at the front desk.

"I'm not going back home," I had said.

"You're a minor, Nigeria. We can't keep you from your father," she had whispered. "Unless we have reason to believe you're in some sort of danger."

I wanted to ask, *Is too much love dangerous? Is liberation supposed to make me still feel trapped?*

But my father had his arms outstretched as if I was a little girl and I'd be running toward him for a hug. I'm not his warrior princess, so I just walked past him and out of the school's doors ahead of him.

The music coming from the truck is that same rapper talking about chemtrails and Black bodies in jails in front of the Philadelphia Friends School; then it switches to an old Beanie Sigel jawn and I'm sure that was Uncle Ra's pick.

"I hope you had a good time," my father says. "I let you get a sense of how it is in there. Was hoping you'd come to your senses and realize that you don't belong in that school or anywhere like it. You can do something revolutionary instead of letting these racist institutions take advantage of your genius. It's time to come home."

I ignore him, and my body is moving on its own, doing as my father says. But my mind starts racing in all directions, wanting to get free again. *What if I say no? What if I just run back into the school?*

Classes had let out, and kids are probably wondering what's going on and who's driving that black Escalade. The front desk security guard, a Black man wearing a navy-blue blazer with the school's logo, rushes past us toward Uncle Ra. They give each other daps and start talking.

"We have to keep the pickup line moving, bruh," the security guard says.

I stay back as my father keeps walking toward them because maybe this distraction is my way out.

"Look, we don't want this to escalate," the security guard continues when my father reaches him. "The parents are already coming out of their cars wondering who's that thug parked in front of the school with that loud music. They don't have to say it; I know that's what they're thinking."

"But I'm here to pick up my child like everyone else here," my father says.

"I know, man, but y'all got to turn that shit down," the guard whispers, but I still hear him from a few feet away.

"Oh, you're one of them Negroes? I guess they're paying you very well." My father walks around to the driver's side. "Don't worry.

We're getting out of here. See, Nigeria? This is exactly what I mean."

Someone touches my shoulder, and I turn around to see Kamau and Sage. I want them to go away.

"Should I call my mother? She could probably talk some sense into him," Kamau says.

"Hey, nephew!" my father calls out. "Can't greet your uncle? How you doing? Send my love to your mother." He doesn't say a word to Sage.

"Peace, Uncle . . . Kofi," Kamau mumbles and looks away.

"My mother can talk to him, too," Sage whispers.

But I'm alone in this fight. My father doesn't care what *my* mother wants. So why do they think that he'll listen to two other women, one of them his sister and the other one white?

Cars are honking, and the music is turned down, thank goodness. The truck is a short distance from where I'm standing and walking toward it feels like parting a sea. I count the steps in my head, my heart is a drum, my breaths are shallow.

"I'm not going back to the Village House," I say when I reach my father. I'd been practicing those words ever since Diane brought up the idea of a guardian. But as soon as I speak them, they don't sound true. My father doesn't believe them. So I clench my fists and stand my ground to let him know that I'm serious. "I'm not going back to the Village House," I repeat. Firm and unmoving.

Someone honks their horn.

"You had your little few weeks of fun, so now quit playing games, Nigeria, and let's go home," he says from the other side of the truck. "Your baby brother misses you, the Youth Group is falling apart without you, and I need you to help me finish my next book and help set up the Freedom School."

More people start honking, and kids just walk to their cars at the end of the line instead of waiting to be picked up at the curb.

The security guard approaches my father again. "Come on, man. You can park in the lot if you're not ready to leave. We need to let these parents pick up their kids."

"I *am* a parent, and I'm picking up *my* kid," my father says, raising his voice. Then he looks at me. "We have to get out of the way so these white folks can get their precious children. And I'm over here just picking up the trash, I guess. How's that for your fancy scholarship?"

I take a few steps back, away from the truck. But my father walks around to face me. He smells like Egyptian musk, sandalwood incense, and last night's weed. And I don't know if my mind is playing tricks on me again, but a deep, deep memory and something that feels like warm hugs and rainy-day vegetable stew, old books and boring documentaries, and veggie burgers on the grill pulls me closer to my father. For a minute. Only a minute as he speaks with a firm and calm voice.

"Nigeria," he says, almost whispering. "I can't get your mother to come back. But you're my daughter. You're my responsibility. You're my own seed. I let you take a little break. And trust me when I tell you that if I wanted to, you would've never left that house. I gave you some space to deal with your mother not being here. But continuing to stay with someone who doesn't love you nearly as much as we love you is out of the question. I'm going to say this one last time, Nigeria Sankofa. Get in the truck. Now."

I don't move and I stand tall, even though his words are supposed to chop me down to someone small and weak.

Right then and there, I can either turn away from him or get into the truck and back to the Village House, where everything that I love and that is supposed to love me back is walled in under my father's gaze.

A car's horn cuts through everything thick, everything layered and dense between me and my father. Then another honk, and another.

I take a few more steps back.

"Mr. Sankofa!" the guard says, almost yelling this time. "My boss already called the cops. I didn't want it to get to this."

My father and I are locked in a staring match as more car horns blare, and I can't read his eyes. I can't read his face. I don't know what else to do but to keep walking backward, away from everything that made me, away from the father, the life, the Movement that I supposedly chose as a returning ancestor. Reaching and reaching back for this school, these new friends so that I can move forward toward a new life.

He can't stop me. He can't hold my body down, scoop me into his wide palm, and hold me like a bird in a hand. Not in front of all these people.

So as I keep walking back away from my father, and even though my feet are firmly on the Philadelphia Friends campus grounds, I feel like I'm flying up to the sky.

3. My body is not a treaty.

Kamau lives much closer to East Falls than I do. So he takes the SEPTA to and from school—the K bus on Midvale Avenue and Fox Street all the way to the corner of Chelten and Baynton in Germantown. This isn't the first time I'm on the SEPTA with him. But I'd never taken the bus to run away from my father.

I hold on to a pole. There are a bunch of empty seats around me. My body is a stew of fear, rage, relief, sadness, and joy. The bumps and sways on the bus ride make everything feel worse—mixing and stirring the highs with the lows. Kamau must see the nausea on my face.

"Your father's not gonna chase down this bus and make you get off, Gigi," he says from his seat in front of me.

I give him the side-eye, letting him know that I won't put anything past my father at this point. "What if he's waiting for me at your mother's house?" I ask, seeing the whole thing play out in my mind. He's probably already there by now—his Escalade parked at the curb, he and Uncle Ra sitting on the stoop.

Kamau doesn't say anything and looks down at his phone. "Would you report him? Like, for abuse?"

"Is this abuse?" I ask.

He looks around to make sure no one is listening. And I'm hoping that no one recognizes me as Kofi Sankofa's daughter, *if* they know who he is.

"I think so," Kamau says.

"That's your uncle and that's my father. I'm not gonna snitch on him just 'cause he's . . . strict."

He scoots to the edge of his seat to get closer to where I'm standing. "Think about it, though. You have a right to be educated. And when we were homeschooled, no one probably knew we existed. He might even get in trouble if they find out you're just helping him write his books instead of learning math and science."

"He already has enough people breathing down his neck," I say. Then I narrow my eyes at my cousin. "You're trying to get your uncle locked up?"

He leans back in his seat. "No, Gigi. It's just . . . all that stuff he put me and my mother through . . . I mean, I used to look up to Uncle Keith. Who wouldn't? But me and Mom don't need to live by his rules. I can tolerate him, which is why I'll come to Freedom's gratitude celebrations and yours. Visit a few times. But that's it."

"You think Aunt Sharon will take my side on this one?"

We reach his stop. Kamau gets up and says, "My mother is on *my* side."

With that, I already know a line was drawn a long time ago between brother and sister. I don't want that line to come between me and my cousin, too.

If my father is a thunderstorm like Shango, then Aunt Sharon is harsh winds like Oya. And they look like twins, too, even though Aunt Sharon is a couple of years older and is much shorter. She works from home as a legal secretary, and she's just as smart and well read as my father. If he had been waiting for me, they would've been at each other's throats already.

"Well, hello, niece. So you think you can run away from that house and come hide out here?" Aunt Sharon says as soon as I step into her foyer. She's wearing a denim button-down shirt over gray sweatpants and is not smiling, so I know this isn't a joke.

Kamau walks right past me.

She's waiting for an answer, and all I say is "Yes. Please, Aunt Sharon. I just need to figure out what's going on. I need some space to clear my head."

She waves me in, but she still has a mean mug, the same face my father makes when he's angry and won't say a word until he's ready. But I've always known my aunt to speak her mind, and when I'm standing in her living room, she says, "I love my brother. I really do. We don't see eye to eye, but one day, we'll make things work. But that day is not today."

I sigh, trying to figure out what to say and what's my next move. I haven't been to Kamau's house since he started Philly Friends, since Aunt Sharon and my father got into a huge argument, since Mama stopped talking to her because of it.

"I don't wanna go back there, Aunt Sharon," I say. I don't know if she ever liked me or not. But she let everybody know that she didn't like how my mother was so *submissive* around my father. Her word, not mine.

"Come get something to eat" is all she says. And I follow her into the kitchen as Kamau takes both our bags and sets them down on a chair.

The row house almost looks like the Village House with all the African masks on the walls and colorful fabric over the windows and on the couches. Kamau and I sit around a table in the kitchen where a cloth-covered baking pan holds fried fish. There's coleslaw in a glass bowl and skillet corn bread on the stove, and that's the only thing I can eat. I don't even ask when they'd stopped being vegan. Kamau and his mom stopped doing a lot of things they used to do when they were members.

Aunt Sharon just stands in front of me with her arms crossed over her chest. I can't look at her. She and my father have the same eyes. I can stare him down, but not her. The overhead lights in the kitchen reflect off the top of her shaved head. She cut her locs a couple of years ago, and it was as if she cut the Movement off along with them.

"You're going to have to make things work with your father, Nigeria," she says. "He loves you. I know it doesn't feel that way with him being so hard on you. And this isn't about you being a rebellious teenager like my son over here." She smirks at Kamau. "You have some legit reasons to not want to be in that house. I mean, I was ready to fight my own brother because of how he's keeping you so sheltered. You and your mother. But you're not my child and he's your father. You two have to work it out. At least until you're eighteen."

"Ma, isn't she legally supposed to be in school?" Kamau says, grabbing a piece of fish with a fork and taking a bite before putting it onto his plate. "Can't we use that to keep her in Philly Friends?"

I smile at him, because at least he's trying to be on my side.

Aunt Sharon just gives him the side-eye, as if letting him know to stay out of this. "I'll warm up some beans for you, Nigeria," she says, disappearing behind a set of cabinet doors.

She's being nice. So this is my moment. "Aunt Sharon, my father's got some new woman in that house, and she's having his baby."

"Well, congratulations to him and you!" she says, but she doesn't sound happy. She places two cans of beans on the counter.

Kamau and I quickly glance at each other. I think of another case to make, another cry for help. "I really like Philly Friends. I just want to be able to stay there. It was Mama who got me in."

"No, you got yourself in, as smart as you are. All this time, I was telling Natalie to put you in that school with Kamau and Sage, but she let your father talk her out of it. She should've started you in the ninth grade and told Keith to kiss her ass. You probably wouldn't be in this mess right now."

Kamau is just like his mama. Their sharp words cut deep.

And I'm related to them. So I say, "You don't have to bring my mother into this, Aunt Sharon. She's doing the best she can."

She quickly turns to me and looks straight into my eyes. "Then you need to go back to your father's house and do the best *you* can. I don't have to deal with him and neither does Kamau. Making my son feel bad for who he is, and giving my number out to his little foot soldiers 'cause he thinks I need a man in this house? My brother has lost his god-loving mind! I was right there with him for so long when it was about culture and changing policies, but now he's taking it too far with this *indigenizing* stuff. I tried to tell your mother."

"My mother has nothing to do with this," I say through clenched teeth. I don't mean to, but it just came out.

Aunt Sharon and Kamau stare at me for a long second. "I'm sorry, baby," my aunt whispers. "I'm sorry you have to deal with this. But my brother made it clear that I have to stay out of his business and to not come between him and his Movement."

"But I'm not the Movement, Aunt Sharon. I'm his daughter."

"I tried to tell him that, sweetie. I tried to tell him," she says, and her face softens.

Kamau reaches over, pulls me in with one arm, and gives me a side hug. "Ma?" he says. "She can do what she wants when she turns eighteen, right? But can't she do something now to show that she doesn't want Uncle Keith to keep her out of school?"

"Well, yes," my aunt says, pulling out a can opener. "When you're eighteen, a parent is not obligated to support you, financially or otherwise. But you can file for emancipation before that. It's hard to do in Pennsylvania. You can't just tell a judge that your father is too strict."

"She can say her father is a hotep," Kamau says, laughing. "That he starves her with juice fasts, makes her write his books, take care of his baby, and uses her to get viewers on his channel."

Aunt Sharon holds a finger up to Kamau. "Boy, that's family. We're not going to just hand him over to people who want to see him dead."

"My bad, Gigi," Kamau says.

I shake my head at my cousin. He's not on my side right now.

Aunt Sharon's phone rings, and we all look at each other. She mouths, "KD," and puts it on speaker.

"Hello, Sharon? I hope you're well, my sister. You probably heard that Nigeria's father pulled her out of school. I'm hoping we can work together to keep her at Philly Friends," KD says.

I'm both relieved that it's not my father and confused as to why she's calling my aunt.

"I think you should stay out of this, KD," my aunt says.

"And this is exactly why Natalie trusted me with this and not you," KD responds.

Aunt Sharon cocks her head and looks as if she's ready to jump right into that phone to wring KD's neck. "KD, we really appreciate everything you've done for Nigeria. Truly. But this is between her and her father. You shouldn't've gone behind his back!"

"This is what her mother asked me to do. She trusted me to see this through until Nigeria graduates," KD says.

Aunt Sharon looks at me, takes the phone off speaker, and walks away with it. But I hear her ask, "Do you have this in writing?"

Kamau squeezes my arm and mouths, "Girl. I am so sorry."

In that moment, I feel like I'm in an empty room with four walls closing in on me. Each wall is a different part of my life—my father, the Movement, the Village House, and my mother's absence. I need to get out of here. I get up to walk out of the kitchen, and Kamau follows me out.

"So much for 'a person is a person because we are people' and 'harambe' and 'kombit' and all these things we had to learn that don't mean shit right now!" I blurt out.

Kamau grabs my shoulder, forcing me to turn around, and says, "Nigeria, it's the system. Some of us want to stay in it, and some of us want to burn it down. That right there is enough to start wars."

"But Kamau. What about me? What about what I want? You get to have what you want. You get to be happy. What if my father was your father? What would you do?"

He takes my left hand and says, "Cuz, you need to call a truce with everybody. I mean, keep the peace until we're both eighteen. You won't miss much at Philly Friends if you can't go. But college . . . Nigeria! We will run any college town. We will take over the world. Do you hear me? We can be whoever we want to be once we're out of here."

I pull my hand away from his. "That's not what I want, Kamau. I mean, yeah, I want to go to college. But I want to be in high school first. My mama knows that. It's so simple, Kamau. Like . . . school! I'm trying to go to a good school, and I can't because my father thinks I'll be brainwashed or whatever. If I tell anybody that, they'll think I'm from another planet."

"I get it. I do. Ever since I told you that I'd be going to that school, I saw the look on your face. But seriously, though. I mean, Philly Friends of all places? It's cool and all, but I personally wouldn't risk everything to just go there for two years."

I step back away from my cousin. For the first time, he's wrong about this; he's wrong about me. "You don't get it, Kamau. You really don't."

"Nigeria, you think I'd be at the school if I did what I wanted? You think I'd even be in Philly?"

"It's not the same. You're treading water, Kamau. I'm already drowning."

Aunt Sharon comes to stand behind Kamau, and they're on each other's side. I'm behind enemy lines—my father and his Movement. "KD reached out to me when your acceptance letter from Philly Friends was mailed to her house," she says, stepping closer to me. "She wanted my help in getting you in without your father knowing. I guess it was her way of making things right after what happened. And, honestly, I don't think she'll stop trying because she still feels guilty. Gigi, if you want my advice, this is what you should do. Forget about fighting your father to go to Philly Friends. Start planning for college now. Get some money together. Look for scholarships, especially the ones for homeschoolers. You turn seventeen in January, which gives you about fifteen months total before you're eighteen. At Philly Friends, you'd only be a senior by then. If you go with this plan, you could be starting your first semester somewhere away from the Village House and away from your father. Can you hold out until then, Nigeria?"

"Fifteen months?" I ask. "Mama hasn't been home for exactly that long and it's been hell."

"I know, honey. But you can pass the time by planning and organizing. You're good at that."

"Gigi, I can help you with anything you need," Kamau says.

I don't want them to keep pushing for this. I don't want them to change my mind and, before I know it, I'll still be stuck in the Village House because too much time has passed and I'll forget that I have wings. I'll stop dreaming of flying. Mama will stop visiting me in strange places, and maybe she won't come home because I didn't follow through with the one last thing she did for me before she left. And Freedom won't remember the sound of her heartbeat. So I just say "Okay" to keep my peace.

I walk out of my aunt's house. Kamau tries to stop me, but I put my hand up. "I'm fine. I'll call a cab," I tell him.

Instead, I head to Germantown Avenue and keep walking down block after block. But my feet are still on solid ground. I don't have a jacket and the early fall afternoon breeze gives me goose bumps. I check my phone to see texts from Sage, Jasmine, Kamau, and Chris. And a recent one from Liam.

I heard you're leaving. We never got to compete in the LD debate. I'll miss seeing you in class, he wrote.

I get goose bumps again. And this time, it's not because of the cold. Here I am trying to find a corner in a Philly where I can just disappear and this white boy is talking about he'll miss my *seeing me*.

I let my mind wander as I cross the street and pass small restaurants and businesses along Germantown Avenue. I think of all the moments in school these past few weeks when I was shining and flexing on the smartest kids in the class. I was starting to speak up more, and Tyler kept reminding me of a class participation grade. Some of the Black girls were saying hi to me. Liam kept wanting to "pick my brain." I went to my very first affinity group meeting. I wrote my first paper on a book called *The Great Gatsby* for English and got a B. It was easy to talk about capitalism and classism in the 1920s, but the teacher docked me for not citing my sources. Someone else besides my parents had read my writing and judged it. I was learning new math and my mind was expanding. I was starting to fit in like a mis-shapen and discolored replacement part on something broken. Most importantly, I was starting to make friends.

So I text Liam back: Where do you live?

4. My Body Is Not an Exploration.

It'll be about forty minutes to walk two miles to this white boy's house in Mount Airy, and I can't believe this is where my body is taking me. I haven't really been to this part of Philly, and I want to go through doors that I've never opened, never even considered. I'm not ready to return to the Village House. I'm not ready to visit any of the other members who will gladly offer me a place to stay. They're still my father's followers, and I don't want to be anywhere near the Movement right now. Not until I can make sense of everything, or Mama gives me another sign as to where I should go. Or maybe she'll just show up out of nowhere. If she does come back to the Village House and I'm not there, she'll know how to find me.

Even as I'm walking away from everything familiar, old thoughts and ideas plague my mind. People and places are always in black and white. Just by being my father's daughter, I've been given glasses where out of one lens I'm supposed to see history; out of the other, I'm supposed to see race. But maybe I don't have to see everything from my father's perspective because it's all as plain as daylight. Old trolley tracks and cobblestones run down the middle of Germantown Avenue, and I wonder how the Germans got here and claimed it as their town. I wonder why there's never a Blacktown anywhere, or an Africatown in every big city and just about everywhere in the South.

There's another Quaker school around here called Germantown Friends, and William Penn's unfulfilled dream of a utopia is seen everywhere in Philly. I think of my father's dream of having his own school, and I wonder if someone like him could ever have a chance for his vision to be fulfilled or unfulfilled. Would Kofi Sankofa ever have a whole city named after him, much less a school? Did William Penn have a daughter who didn't want to be part of his experiment? Did she go off to explore this new world on her own?

The farther I walk away from the hood, the more white people I see. Short buildings and storefront businesses are well kept and look more expensive, and I cross that invisible line into Mount Airy. I make a right on East Mount Pleasant Avenue, and my heart starts to race. *What am I doing here?* But I already told Liam that we can meet to go over the debate resolution, but really, I just want somewhere to go besides the Village House, someone to chill with besides the Movement's members, someone who doesn't know that side of me at all.

Liam lives in a corner town house off East Mount Pleasant, and there's a literal white picket fence around it. Three boys are doing wheelies in the middle of the street. I'm half a block away, so I can't really tell which one of them is Liam.

A Black man comes out of his house, so this is clearly a mixed neighborhood. Once I get closer to his block, I peep Liam and one of the other boys skating with him—Black, tall, and lean, and I don't think I'd seen him at Philly Friends. One of them waves as I'm walking up, and I freeze. I make an about-face because I'm not supposed to be here. I can't be here.

But Liam calls my name. "Nigeria!"

I freeze again, and I'm sure everyone on this block is looking out their window to see the Black girl who's named after an African country on her way to a white boy's house. What are the chances someone will recognize me as Kofi Sankofa's daughter?

But in this moment, I don't want to be his daughter. I am my own self right now and I think of a new nickname. "You can call me Geri," I tell him.

"Okay. Geri," Liam says, holding his skateboard. He changed out of the clothes he was wearing at school today. His hair is messier. It hangs over his eyes, and he tosses it back. He looks at me as if he can't believe I'm actually here. "These are my friends Kyle and Jaden," he says, smiling a little too wide.

I barely say hi to any of them, looking down at the sidewalk. These aren't my people, and I don't belong here.

His friends keep skating, and Liam leans on the fence. "You walked all the way from Kamau's house?" he asks.

"Yep," I say, still not looking at him. I scan the houses on the block and it's nice here, but definitely not trust-fund-and-expensive-tutor vibes.

"Been around here before?"

"Nope."

"Wanna skate, or . . . ?"

"I'm good."

His friends come over to give him daps before they leave, and my eyes meet Jaden's, the Black boy. I look away.

"Nice meeting you" is all he says. Kyle just waves bye, and Liam and I are alone standing in front of this white-picket-fenced town house.

"Next weekend is our first mock tournament," he starts, putting his skateboard down and rolling it back and forth with his foot.

"Why is it a mock tournament and not a real tournament?" I ask, still avoiding his eyes and checking out some of his neighbors. A white lady jogs into another town house across the street.

"We'll be debating each other instead. Practicing."

I cross my arms and turn to him. "So why are you so pressed about debating me anyway?"

He shrugs. "Maybe . . . iron sharpens iron? You're smart. I'm smart. We'll be even smarter if we go up against each other."

"I'm not made of metal. What, you think I'm some sort of *strong* Black woman?"

He smiles and shakes his head as if he was expecting me to throw the race card again. It's a running joke between us. Even with our small talk, I can't let him forget that he's white and I'm Black. Maybe this is something I need to work on, or maybe it's my brand at this point, being Kofi Sankofa's daughter and all.

"Philly Friends has been undefeated for the past ten years," he says.

I nod, unimpressed. "Good for Philly Friends."

Then he stops smiling and says, "I need a win this year. College scholarships are at stake."

"That's tough."

He chuckles. "I know. You couldn't care less about a white boy worried about paying for college."

I nod again. "Accurate."

"So . . . you want to go with the college angle for the debates?"

I lean on the fence, too, and pull my bag up on my shoulders. "I think it's boring. If you want to debate me, you have to dig a little deeper than that."

He squints his eyes at me. "Now I'm worried. What do you mean 'dig a little deeper'?"

The sun is setting over Philly, and some kind of emptiness fills the air. Early fall used to be about collecting vegetables from the local farms, packing them into boxes, and driving around Philly with Mama to give them out to the members. For me, feeding the people around us was school. Community-building was school. Making sure every member was healthy and relatively happy was school. But now I'm unpacking big ideas with kids who don't know my life, and whose lives represent everything oppressive. "I was raised differently. Like, you're the enemy," I say.

"I know," he says.

"What you mean, 'you know'?"

He touches my arm, and I look down to see it's covered in goose bumps. "It's getting cold. You can come inside if you want."

I'm legit curious about his house, so I say, "Sure."

I check my phone to see that Kamau had texted, asking me where I was going. He has my location. So I turn off my phone before I walk in. I don't want to be found. Inside, everything is neat and clean, as if they hardly hang out in this house. Full bookshelves take up a wall in the living room, and I step closer to examine the faces in a huge family photo. In that moment, I learn something new about Liam. Two women, him, and an older boy who must be his brother are in that photo. They look alike. Light brown hair, sharp, angled faces, and big smiles—a strange combination of the two women standing behind them.

"I have two moms," Liam says, exhaling as if this is something he's been waiting to say to me for a while.

"Oh."

"My mom, Candace, and my other mom, Hannah," he says. "And my older brother, Lucas. We call him Luc."

"Cool. Where is he?"

"At Penn State. He's not too far, but we don't really see him. And you might be wondering . . . Candace gave birth to me and my older brother with Hannah's brother's sperm."

"That's what's up" is all I can say, still staring at the photo of them. "I get it. You're not like the others."

"Hence, why I'm at Philly Friends. I got bullied in elementary school. But Luc didn't care. He went to Central High, and he could stick up for himself if anyone said shit."

I finally peel away from the family photo and check out the other stuff in the house. There are lots of novels—thick books whose spines are color coded on the shelves. Pictures are everywhere—Liam and his brother on the beach, rock climbing, in the desert in some foreign country. Some are of his moms holding hands, kissing, laughing. "Cool family," I tell him. "It's just you guys. Must be nice."

"Yeah. We have no choice but to be tight-knit," he says. "So back to the debates. We can go with the family angle. Community standards as the heteronormal nuclear family, or individual liberty as . . . love is love."

I nod and peek into the kitchen with its bright white cabinets and artsy lighting. "Love is love, huh? I see where you're going with this."

"And it doesn't have to be about gay marriage, either. You ever heard of the *Loving versus Virginia* case in 1967?"

I shake my head, pull off my backpack, place it on the shiny hardwood floor, and take a seat on a leather couch, even though he didn't offer it.

"It was a civil rights Supreme Court decision," he continues, "that stated laws banning interracial marriage were unconstitutional under the Equal Protection Clause in the Fourteenth Amendment. He was white; she was Black."

He sits next to me, and for the first time, I look at him. Really look at him. His whole face is lit up with curiosity. Like I'm something he needs to take apart to understand. I get it. I want to understand him, too. *"Loving versus Virginia?* Did love and virginity have something to do with it?"

He laughs a little. "I think that was just a coincidence. The couple's last name was Loving and it happened in Virginia. We can start jotting down some examples and court cases like this one. But the trick is we'd have to argue for and against marriage as an institution that needs to be protected by the Constitution."

Now I'm squinting my eyes at him. "You want to be a lawyer or something?"

"A judge."

"Like on the Supreme Court?"

"I wouldn't mind that."

I look around the small living room for any more signs of who he is and what his life is like. But the place is kind of bland—light gray walls and I think this is what they call a modern design. "Did y'all gentrify this neighborhood?"

He laughs again, louder this time. "You don't mince your words, do you? Just straight for the jugular. But seriously, this was Hannah's grandmother's house. Been here since forever."

"Cool," I say. Then I turn to him. "I think I might want to be a judge, too. It's not something I thought of until now. What if I get to decide the laws of this country? Just change up everything."

He looks away from me as if I've said something wrong. "Nigeria, I've seen some of your father's videos," he says with a low voice.

I pull away a little. Part of me wants to end this now because I feel exposed. I don't say anything.

"He wants this country to burn to the ground? And he doesn't want you in Philly Friends 'cause it's a white supremacist institution? Does he even believe in the Supreme Court?"

I slap my hand on my thighs, making as if I'm about to get up and leave. "Okay. I think it's time for me to go. I guess you got me all figured out now."

"No, no, no!" He touches my arm, gently nudging me to sit back on the couch. "I didn't mean to offend."

I relax my shoulders, exhaling. I'm thirsty and hungry and a little tired from this long day. "I don't agree with everything my father says, but he does believe in the Constitution. I was raised to know my constitutional rights. Which is why I think we can dig a little deeper with these debates."

"So you don't hate white people, too?" he asks, with an even lower voice.

"How did you find out about my father anyway?"

"Sage and Kamau. When he came to pick you up that first day. They were making a big deal about it, and I was wondering why since he's your dad. They told me his name, and I looked him up."

I roll my eyes and shake my head, pissed that Sage and Kamau would put me on blast like that. "He doesn't hate white people. He hates white supremacy."

"You think Philly Friends is a white supremacist institution? The Quakers would disagree."

"I mean, it's not a bastion of diversity, that's for sure." I tilt my head to the side and ask, "You like Black girls or something?"

"I like *you.*"

"Really? I'm Black. Am I the first?"

"No. I don't . . . discriminate."

"Would Candace or Hannah care?"

"I dated a Black girl who lives around the corner. Her name is Ayana. You're acting like this is the fifties."

"I can say the same about this country sometimes."

"I'm not this country."

"You're white."

"A social construct."

"That you benefit from."

He's quiet for a minute, rubbing his hands. They're pale, and I want to put mine against his to see the contrast between deep brown and light pink. "I hope you stay at Philly Friends. You're, like, super smart. You belong at Harvard or Yale or Princeton. And you should definitely be on the Supreme Court. And maybe even the president."

I sigh, rest my chin in my hands, and roll my eyes. "A girl can dream . . ."

"But I know it's the opposite of what your father believes," he continues. "Divest, decolonize, indigenize, right? He says this at the end of his live streams."

"Oh, you're a fan now? Careful. You might be recruited as the first white member. Though you wouldn't be an ally. You'd have to be something like a coconspirator."

"What would he say if he knew you were here with me?" he asks.

"I'm not trying to think about my father right now," I say. I'm also not trying to think about Chris, but Liam can't know that I've got something else going on back at the Village House because that person is Nigeria. Here, I'm Geri.

"Neither am I," he says.

I laugh. I'm trying to stay in this moment, this new feeling, this new self I'm slowly becoming. "So you're not gonna offer me some water, a snack, or *something*?"

"Oh!" he says, quickly standing from the couch. "I'm so sorry. We got . . . sparkling water. Some chips. My mom makes this bomb banana walnut bread. Any allergies?"

I follow him into the kitchen, where copper pots and pans hang from the ceiling. A tiny rainbow flag is in a giant aloe plant pot by the window. A Temple University sticker is stuck to their stainless steel fridge. "My parents went to Temple. Well, my mom for grad school."

"So, wait a minute . . ." he starts as he hands me a can of something that is not water.

"Nope. Not talking about my father."

"Fine. Well, my mom Candace teaches at Temple. Physical therapy. And Hannah is a librarian."

I glance at the front door, hoping neither one of them walks in.

"They won't be back till late," Liam says.

When he says late, my stomach sinks. I'll have to get back home, but I don't want to. I haven't even settled into whatever this is. Then I examine the can he gave me. "White Claw? Is this some white boy juice?"

He laughs and takes a long swig from the can. "Hard seltzer," he says. "We have tap water if you don't drink. But one can won't do anything. You don't have to . . ."

"No, I'm good." I open the can and slowly take a sip. It's cold and bland, and I don't drink, so it's nasty.

"I can order pizza or . . ."

"Cool," I say, and just sip slowly, glad that it's at least quenching my thirst.

He leans on the counter, watching me. I keep looking around the kitchen for signs of racists living in this house—stickers, other flags, books. So I ask, "Where's your room?"

In seconds, we're in the basement, where it almost looks like the one in the Village House with exercise mats, weights, and gaming consoles. A closed door has a poster of an A with a circle around it. I know what it is, so I ask, "You're an anarchist?"

"Well . . . I'm leaning more toward Marxism, but I believe that all forms of hierarchy are oppressive," he says. "I'm not part of any group, if that's what you're thinking. Not yet, at least. There's a group of us at Philly Friends, but not enough to lead a movement. I'm planning to be more vocal in college."

I just nod, wondering if he's a white, younger version of my father. Maybe that's my cue to run up out of here. But I stay.

He plops down on a green futon pushed against a bare white concrete wall. I join him, sitting only inches away, and we place our cans on the floor. He takes his phone and says, "They have a vegan and gluten-free option, too."

"I'm good with actual pizza," I say, and my stomach growls a little. It's quieter down here, cooler and full of potential. Like, right now, anything can happen, and my heart is racing. I swallow hard because I've opened a door wide enough for him to walk in.

I let my body sink into the futon because I don't have to do anything here except exist. I turn to Liam. He's looking at my hair. So I look at his hair. He's looking into my eyes. So I look into his eyes. He's looking at my lips. So I look at his lips. He leans into me. So I lean into him.

I close my eyes. Our lips touch. And before I can take another breath, his tongue is almost down my throat. He's moving too fast and starts breathing hard and he wants to swallow me. I pull back a little and whisper, "Slow down."

He jerks back. "I'm sorry. I'm sorry."

"No, I mean relax. I'm not going anywhere."

He takes my arm and runs his fingers up and down my skin.

He looks at it, probably examining my color and wondering. Just wondering.

So I take his arm and bring it up close. "What's it like to not have melanin?"

"Don't all humans have melanin? Some more than others, obviously."

I keep examining his arm—the tiny blond hairs, the blue veins, the transparency of it all. "How did you convince the world that having this skin is better, more powerful?"

"Maybe because we really aren't better or more powerful. It's a lie we have to tell ourselves just . . . just to survive."

"Destruction isn't survival."

"If we destroy hierarchies, it is." He pulls his arm away and takes mine. He brings it to his lips and kisses the tender skin.

My entire body lights up. "So you don't think there's a hierarchy between me and you?" I whisper.

"Maybe you're more powerful," he says, breathing his words onto my arm.

"I am. Black women birthed humanity." I take my arm back and slide my hand through his liquid hair. His scalp is warm and he's melting under my touch. "What if I were in charge?"

"The world would probably make sense. There wouldn't be a need for anarchists." He leans his head back and looks up at the low ceiling.

"You'd have to convince your people."

"Maybe that's my purpose." Then he takes one of my locs and holds it in his hand. "This . . . feels . . . electric."

I take my loc back. "Don't touch my hair," I say, while pulling him in closer and kissing him, taking the lead, because his body pressed against mine feels like he's about to implode. He tries to unzip my pants, but I push his hand away. He tries to lift my shirt, but I push his hand away. He is everything I was raised to believe is oppression, destruction, and hate. So I study him to find the truth—explore the depths of his soul with just a kiss. He can't do that to me, though. I control the rising tide that he is, keeping him at bay, at sea, and never letting him make landfall on my body.

5. MY BODY IS NOT A MISSION.

Time has wings. It wants to aim for the sky, too. Hours later, even though my body is still in this basement, on this green futon, I am soaring. I can't believe that this is where I needed to be to pause my life. Liam lets me rest. A pizza box and five cans of that hard seltzer are on the floor, and my head feels like it's above the clouds and underwater at the same time.

It's eleven o'clock at night, and no one from the Village House knows where I am, including my father. When Liam's mothers came home, I begged him not to say anything.

"I shouldn't've let you drink that much. I'll get in trouble for having a drunk Black girl hiding out in my basement," he'd said. "I don't usually lie 'cause they're really cool about stuff like this."

"If I meet them, then I'll have to leave right away," I mumbled with my eyes closed. "I just need . . . a nap."

He gave me a knit blanket and a throw pillow. "You never drank like this before?" he asked.

And all I could do was moan and open my heavy eyelids for a second to see him peering down over me.

A single lamp casts a dim light into the basement. I listen for footsteps upstairs, and the voices are muted. I try not to think of my father and the Village House. This is a hiding place for now, and I float. I stretch my wings. I let the wind take me to somewhere far, even though I'm only twenty minutes from home, where no one would ever think of finding me.

Liam leaves me alone, turning on his gaming console and putting on headphones. I'm lulled by the sounds of the video game. It's like white noise in this white space. Emptiness for now. Sleep pulls me down into an ocean, and it feels so good to rest.

But a loud bass forces me to quickly sit up. I look over at Liam; his back is turned to me, and he's lost in his game. I know that beat. I've heard that rhythm.

My entire body sinks.

A tiny window on the other side of the basement faces the backyard. It's dark out. I'll need to go upstairs to look out of a front window to make sure that what I'm hearing is what I'm hearing. But I don't want to see what I think I'll see.

The music is louder now—that rapper . . . My father's mentee. My father. "Shit!" I say out loud.

But Liam still doesn't hear me.

How could my father know where I am? Does he know? I check my phone. It's still off. *Who told him?*

"Kamau," I whisper. I don't dare turn on my phone.

"Liam?" someone calls from upstairs. Then, footsteps.

Shit!

My heart is thumping in my ears. Liam doesn't hear anything. Then the door at the top of the stairs opens and light floods into the basement.

"Liam!"

He jumps up and quickly takes off his headphones. "Hide!" he mouths to me. Then he says, "Yeah, Mom?"

I try to get up, but it feels like I'm walking underwater. I stumble on the floor and crawl to a dark corner near an old pool table away from the view of anyone coming down the stairs. Everything in the basement is swirling. But the music is louder outside, and if it's my father—it has to be my father—I'll have to surrender.

"I think you have some friends outside," a woman says. "Want me to ask them to turn the music down?"

"Friends?" Liam asks, walking toward the stairs. "No, no. Just . . . I'll be up in a minute."

"Where do you know them from? I've never seen them before."

"Um, school," Liam says. I can hear the nervousness in his voice.

"Well, they're making a racket. I don't want them to get in trouble," his mom says.

She sounds nice. Like, she's not even tripping that the music is so loud, not threatening to call the cops or nothing. So I ease out of hiding because this is my father's way of summoning me out of wherever I am and it's working. Even though Liam's mom won't call the cops, someone else might. I'm a hot mess because I can't even stand straight, but I manage to walk over to stand next to Liam.

Liam glares at me, but I just look up at his mom who's looking down at me.

"Hi, um, I'm sorry. I was hiding," I say. "I just needed a place to stay for a bit. I think my ride is here."

She looks surprised for a second, but she says, "Oh my god! Liam, why didn't you say something?"

"I asked him not to. I didn't want him to get in trouble." I lean on Liam so I don't fall. It feels like I don't have legs.

"Sweetie, come upstairs," she says, stepping aside to make way for me.

"Sorry, Mom," Liam mumbles.

I hold on to the banister for dear life, hoping that Liam's mother doesn't realize that I'd been drinking.

When I reach the top of the stairs and I'm face-to-face with her, she says, "Hannah."

I'm afraid to say my real name, so I tell her, "Geri."

The music outside is blaring now. "Are they your friends?" she asks. I nod.

Liam is behind me. "I'll walk you out."

"No, I'm good."

"Have some water before you leave," Hannah says, and his other mom comes down.

Her arms are crossed over her chest, and she scowls as she peers out of the window from behind the drawn curtains.

I don't want my father to see either of them, especially Liam, so I walk to the door and open it. But it's not my father's truck that's parked across the street. It's my mother's car. In the driver's seat is Chris.

I rush out of the house to him because I'm relieved that it's not my father, and I'm horrified that it's Chris. I trip, and if it weren't for the white picket fence, I'd be flat on my face. Chris quickly comes out to help me, taking my arm and walking me over to the car without saying a word.

"Nigeria!" Liam calls from behind me. He's standing in his

doorway holding my bag. "You forgot this?"

Part of me wants to ignore him in this moment and pretend that the last few hours didn't happen. But Chris helps me into the back seat of the car, where I'm surprised to see Jasmine in the passenger seat, and Makai and Danika squeezed into the back with me. Chris goes over to Liam to get my bag.

"Are you drunk?" is the first thing Danika asks.

"Seriously, Nigeria?" Jasmine jumps in. "You were at some white boy's house getting drunk? While we're over here turning Philly upside down looking for you so your father doesn't find out? You lucky he left for Atlanta tonight. Or else we would've all been in trouble."

"I think we should call an emergency Youth Group meeting," Makai says.

Chris is dead quiet as he drives us back to West Philly. But it's a sort of quiet that shouts. He's clutching the steering wheel in a way I hadn't seen him do before. His jaw is locked and his eyes are narrowed on the dimly lit streets. He's seething, and I can feel it from the back seat.

I hold my head in my hands and wish to my ancestors I could disappear. And somehow, I do. I mute all of them out, close my eyes, lean my head back in my mother's car, and keep flying; keep soaring. Because when I step into the Village House and my father returns, he will clip my wings.

6. MY BODY IS NOT A BORDER.

It's Monday morning on Indigenous Peoples' Day. I had brought in the suitcase Mama left in her trunk. It's on my bedroom floor now, wide open with the clothes still folded into neat rows. I don't own a suitcase because I've never gone anywhere far. Freedom puts his little bare foot onto his mother's dresses and I wonder if he remembers the sound of her muffled voice, the feel of her heartbeat against his small, small self. Do I keep Mama's clothes in there and take them with me, just in case I see her along the way? Do I take every single thing that I own? Do I fold my baby brother into the tiny pockets of what our mother left behind?

"Nigeria, please open up," Nubia says from the other side of my locked bedroom door. "Please bring the baby out. He needs his breakfast."

I ignore her. I'm done with her and everyone in this house. My soul is exhausted, and all I want is a place to close my eyes and become someone else. So I pick my baby brother up and hug, kiss, and squeeze him tight. "We're gonna be all right, Freedom. We're gonna be just fine," I whisper into his little ear.

Then he starts to cry. He knows something is wrong. Freedom says "Mama," but I can't tell if he's calling me or Nubia, and that shit makes me mad. Sometimes I imagine myself locking everyone out and that some giant bird will come swoop me and my baby brother up and take us away to a new life. I wish Mama would come back to show me and Freedom our wings so we can follow her to wherever she is.

Nubia finally walks away from my door, and I'm left to deal with all my stuff. Another knock makes me jump, and I catch my baby brother right before he puts a small quartz crystal from my altar into his mouth. I grab him and take the crystal from his little clenched hand. He starts to cry again. Another knock.

"No!" I say, thinking that it's one of the aunties, uncles, or worse, my father has come back from his trip to Atlanta.

"It's me, Jasmine."

I glance over at her bed and all the stuff she's packing to go back to her mother's. Guilt settles in my belly, and I exhale. I don't want to see her right now, but we really do need to talk. I have to apologize.

When I open the door, she pushes me aside, pulls a black garbage bag from out of her backpack, and starts tossing her clothes into it. She's breathing hard and being extra about everything she's doing.

So I say, "Jasmine, you don't have to leave the house just because I'm leaving. But at the same time, I don't want you to lose yourself in here. You still have to make your own path."

"The Movement is supposed to save my life and not yours? I'm supposed to thrive here and not you?" she asks, her words heavy with sadness.

"Yeah, but I was born into this. . . ." I pick up Freedom, who is still whimpering, and hoist him onto my hip.

Jasmine puts her hand up letting me know she doesn't want to hear it. "Rules are rules," she says. "And I followed all of them."

Freedom is finally quiet now, and I put him down on my bed and hand him one of his toys. "Will you be safe back at your mother's house?" I ask her as she packs the last of her things. She plops down on her bed and sighs.

"What do you care, anyway?" Jasmine says. I know her words are about to sting me again. "I feel like y'all talk all this shit about liberating Black people, but here I am feeling like I don't have anywhere to go to be safe. I'm sitting right here, Nigeria. I've been in this house all along. *I'm* the people. Liberate *me!*" Her voice cracks.

And I crack.

"I feel you, Jas" are the only words I offer her.

"Then why are you leaving, Nigeria?"

If I give her an answer, I'd be repeating exactly what she'd said to me and would prove her right. So I let the silence push us apart, and Jasmine is suddenly far, far away, as if my bedroom has stretched an entire block and all I see is her small, small body disappearing in the distance. I don't even reach for her to pull her back in, to pull her back home to us.

7. My body is not a conquest.

Jasmine stands in the doorway of my bedroom holding a giant black trash bag with all her stuff. I don't have any words for her, or an explanation. Just by sharing this bedroom, she's seen parts of me that are raw and messy, but there are no words that can make sense of all that I am. So I let my silence be the goodbye she's waiting to hear. I want to say, *I'm right behind you, girl.* But I'm leaving to step into my mother's dream for me. She's leaving to step back into an old world where her light will be dimmed.

"If you stay, you'll have this room to yourself," I tell her.

"I came here for the people, Nigeria. Not for the space," she says, and walks out of my room, out of the Village House, and out of my life, for good. Maybe. She's not the first. And if I stay in this house, she won't be the last, either. That bed on the other side of my room has seen girls come and go—runaways, strays, pregnant and confused, kicked-out and angry, abandoned and lost.

I wonder if somewhere out there is another house with an empty bed for a girl like me. There are other movements all over this country, and my father knows them and what they do and what they stand for. From here in Philly to Oakland, California, where the Panthers first started; from LA to Houston, Chicago to St. Louis; a bunch in Atlanta and New York; Cleveland and Detroit, and even Boston. They call themselves different things, and some of them have their own Freedom Schools. Their leaders debate my father online, and he travels to their events. All these different organizations are trying to get together in one place for a big Black liberation conference or a family reunion or something. But the thing is, they don't all agree on what liberation is. Some of them want to separate and divest to form our own communities like the Amish. Others want a seat at the table to uphold the same power structures that oppress us.

But none of that matters now because I don't want to be a part of anyone's movement. I want to be my own liberation and break down these walls, tear down this house, kick down the front door, and just walk out and never come back. Like Mama.

But I'm not abandoning Freedom.

He's more active now, getting into any-and-everything. He tore the pages to one of my favorite books—Octavia Butler's *Parable of the Sower*—and was putting bits of paper into his mouth. He cries when I stop him from doing what he wants.

So I let Nubia take him. When I open my bedroom door, she's there again with a bowl of oatmeal and a smile. "I can give him his bath and go out to the park. It's nice outside," she says.

I narrow my eyes at Nubia as I hold my baby brother and ask straight up, "Are you keeping your baby, *Camille*?"

She gasps and looks at me as if I've just insulted her. "Why would you say something like that? Of course! I'm bringing a Black child into this world—a returning ancestor," she says; then her shoulders drop, and she looks at me as if she feels sorry for me. "I get it. You don't like me 'cause you think I'm taking your mother's place. But that's not true, Sister Nigeria. We're a village, and you know that. You should be happy that Freedom has someone who can love him and take care of him. You're only sixteen. You shouldn't have to be fussing over no baby. And he'll have a sibling soon. They'll grow up together."

Freedom starts to cry as if he understood what she just said. I bounce him and shush him and squeeze him tight.

"Can I hold the little man?" someone says from down the hall. It's Chris. "He needs to start hanging with the brothers."

I'd rather Nubia take my baby brother than for him to be part of my father's little army. So I put Freedom down, and he quickly toddles over to Nubia, who picks him up and walks away.

Chris comes into my bedroom, and I don't protest. He gave me the silent treatment the past two days since he picked me up from Liam's house. I guess now he's ready to talk. But I'm mad that he's seeing me like this—sweatpants and a T-shirt with no bra. But it's whatever at this point. He's practically family in a weird way. I haven't seen him all weekend, not since Friday night when I jumped out of the car and headed straight for my room.

Chris leans against my tall bookshelf and starts scanning my books. His baby locs are a mess and I haven't offered to re-twist them. He hasn't asked. He's getting leaner and more muscular 'cause my father has him eating whole, plant-based foods and exercising. So if I'm being honest, he looks good. I'm sure the girls in the Youth Group notice him, too.

"Don't you have somewhere to be?" I ask as I stare at my mother's opened suitcase. I still haven't taken out her stuff to make room for mine.

"I'm supposed to ride with some of the uncles to pick your father up from the airport tonight," he says, pulling out a beat-up copy of Ralph Ellison's *Invisible Man*.

I'm quiet for a long minute; then I ask, "Why'd you decide to come get me on Friday?"

"'Cause I'm the only one in the Youth Group who knows how to drive."

"I would've taken a cab back home or—"

"You were trying to spend the night with some white boy you just met at school?"

"He's a friend," I say, not looking him in the eye.

"A friend? Or y'all talking?" he asks, looking dead at me.

"We're working on a project together. He's cool."

"What kind of project y'all working on that you gotta be drunk?"

Now I glare up at him. "Excuse you, but you are *not* my father!"

"I was worried about you. We all were. And we didn't want King Kofi to find out. Even Nubia was looking out for you. Kamau didn't even want *his* mother to know. And he was the one who told us you might be there."

"Okay," I say, exhaling. "Radical honesty? I just wanted to get as far away from here as I could. Liam was nice to me, and we just chilled. Half the time I was sleeping anyway. And I don't owe you an explanation, but I need you to understand that I'm about to be up out of here and no one can tell me what to do!"

"Nigeria . . ." He lowers his voice. "I feel like you're just doing all this shit—going to a white school, hooking up with a white boy, I mean, being *friends* with a boy—just to piss your father off. I know we just met, like, a couple of months ago, but I think you really need to talk to somebody about what's going on with you. How is it that I'm getting all the help I need, and you're over here pushing everybody away and running to some white boy's house?"

I don't say anything to that, mainly because I don't know what to say. He won't understand. But I try to make him see where I'm coming from. "First of all, I didn't hook up with Liam. And second of all, why'd you leave your family, the people who love you?"

"The people who love me? The way this system is set up, it's hard to love people the way they wanna be loved."

"Damn," I say, because the truth of his words sting. I guess Chris has dug deep into himself, into his soul. Once that happens, it's hard to come back to reality. The men and boys who stay in the Village House are sometimes running from the law or a bullet with their name on it. Or both. They have rough lives and don't often have time to think deep thoughts, know deep truths, or even read big books. Until they start living here.

He slowly pushes the door to my bedroom closed.

"Quit playing, Chris. You know you're not supposed to be in here." I keep myself distracted from whatever he's trying to do and finally pull out some of my mother's clothes from the suitcase.

"You asked me a question and I want to answer it, but it's not everybody's business," he says. "If I tell you what's going on with me, maybe you tell me what's going on with you."

"You heard my father say family business is the Movement's business."

"Yeah, I heard him. So you're family, right, *Sister* Nigeria?"

"I'm your *play* sister."

"Far as I know, ain't nothing about the Movement is a game. You coming to the shooting range with us this weekend?"

"No. I'm tired of *playing* games. I'm never gonna have to shoot a gun in my life, so I don't see a reason to keep going."

"You don't think you'll have to defend yourself one day?" He pushes some of Freedom's toys aside to sit on my floor.

"Defend myself? They shoot, I shoot? Then it'll be an all-out war. That's not what it's all about, Chris. I hope you're not thinking of doing anything stupid. Besides, the way you were shook holding that gun . . . If you're disrespecting everything my father's trying to do for you, then . . ." I catch my words because I'm the last person who should be saying this right now.

He laughs. "I know that's not what it's all about. King Kofi schooled us before he even thought about bringing us to the range. And I wasn't shook; I was just . . . surprised, that's all."

"That's being shook, Chris. Surprised and a little scared. Probably intimidated, too. It's cute, though. Lets me know you're not out here trying to be hard. It's not like in the movies, huh?"

"That's so much power to have in your hand, though. Like, how can it be okay for anyone to just shoot somebody over some petty beef, or 'cause you don't like them?"

"Second Amendment," I say, lowering my voice. "Right to bear arms."

"Right to kill?"

"Or be killed."

"You believe that?"

"It's not about *what* we believe, Chris. It's about our right to believe whatever we want."

He's looking at my collection of crystals, tarot cards, candles, sage bundles, palo santo, and incense sticks. "So white people have the right to believe whatever they want about us?"

"Believing something is not the same as acting on it. They can believe that we don't belong in this country, but they don't have the right to do anything about it. Just like we can believe in the Second Amendment and not want to own a gun."

"'Cause we all have a right to live free."

"Exactly."

"You think your father will let you leave?"

"He has no choice but to. I made my own decision, just like how I decided to keep going to school. And he low-key probably cares more about you than me," I say, and I didn't mean to, but those words just came out as if they're a fully formed truth.

"What? Nah," Chris says. "King Kofi is just teaching me about self-discipline, that's all. Now that I know how to use a weapon, I can respect it. I know how to handle power when I have it. Use it wisely and see its value, like everything else in my life. And I know how to defend myself if it comes down to that."

"And it's not about defending yourself from your own people."

"Yeah, run and tell that to them niggas in North Philly."

"Hey, watch your mouth, bruh!"

"Sorry. My bad. It's a habit," he says, then stretches down on the floor and starts doing push-ups.

I know exactly why he's doing them, so I say, "My father's not here to check you, Chris."

"Nah. Rules are rules. A hundred push-ups for each n-word." He makes it to thirty-three before he collapses on the floor.

"Get up from there. It's covered in dust and Freedom's dirty footprints. This house hasn't been cleaned in months."

"Oh, yeah?" he says, all out of breath and crawling his way over to me. "Why don't you have all the people who live here clean up after themselves?"

"That's my mother's job," I whisper. "She makes the rules."

"Why do you talk about her like she's still here?" he asks quietly.

"She's coming back," I say, just as softly.

"And you're still trying to leave this jawn?"

"Yep."

"Will you come back?"

"I don't know."

"And I'm just supposed to let you go?" He's whispering now, and I didn't realize how close he was sitting next to me on the rug. Our legs are touching. "I'll find you and come get you and bring you back."

"Yeah. Like my father," I say.

"You're just gonna expect that I'll let you go after . . . everything?" He reaches for my hand but only takes my pinkie finger and holds it.

"What you mean 'let me'?" I ask.

"Just like how you *expect* your father to let you go."

"Chris, that's not the same thing," I say, taking back my pinkie finger. "Nobody is *letting* me do anything. I don't need his permission. And I definitely don't need yours."

And now Chris is closer, reaching for my pinkie finger again. "Well, I'm not gonna let you go that easy," he says. "Take me with you."

"Boy, stop!" I say, pulling away my finger.

He takes my finger again. I let him.

"Why do you keep grabbing the smallest and weakest part of my hand?" I ask.

He massages my pinkie, and it's . . . comforting. "'Cause it's the most delicate," he says.

"My pinkie? I have other . . . delicate . . . parts." I smile a little.

"I'm sure you do!" He gives me a once-over with those intense eyes of his. Then, while still holding my pinkie, he pulls me close and wraps his arm around me.

"I'm a whole delicate flower," I whisper, leaning into him. Our entire bodies are touching now.

"You have delicate parts, but you're not delicate, Queen. You're a strong Black woman." His breath is warm and sweet against my face, and I want to inhale him.

"I don't want to be strong, Chris. And stop calling me Queen." My voice is tiny, and my whole soul curls in on itself.

"You want to be weak? And you *are* a queen."

"I want to be . . . free."

"You can't be strong *and* free?"

"Not if I have to fight all the time."

"But you gotta fight to be free."

"I know, and that's fucked up."

"I hate that for you."

"Thank you."

"I'll fight for you."

"No, you won't. You'll fight for yourself."

"Fighting for myself *is* fighting for you."

"It doesn't feel that way."

"Then how are we gonna both be free?"

"I don't know if that's possible."

"It is. You just gotta have my back. You have to work on your aim and start coming to the shooting range again, and stay in this house with us. Don't go to that school. And if you do, it's to help us build our own school."

"See? You're proving my point, Chris. All these things *I* have to do so we can both be free?"

"I don't get you sometimes."

"I didn't give you permission to."

"Oh, I have to ask permission now? Okay, Nigeria Jones. So can I get to know you better?"

"I don't know. *Can* you?" I half smile, feeling his warmth against my body. I take his hand and place it on my thigh, inviting him in further.

He slides up to the bed first, pulling me up with him. I straddle him, and we move with such ease that it feels like our bodies understand what the other wants. Like a trade. I want to feel delicate. So he slips his hand under my shirt and caresses the small of my back. I want to be a flower. So I open wide, wide as if he is sunlight.

He is the sky and I am the earth—quaking slowly, quietly moving continents and shifting my entire world. I kiss him deeply and try to swallow everything that he is—a boy from the hood, mad at the world, but full of liberating dreams, and I want that for myself, too.

When he unzips my pants, he searches for gold. No one has ever gotten this far because I am fertile land whose paths are secret and sacred, and something inside of me is not ready to be explored.

He places his mouth over my right ear and releases his warm breath, and he becomes lightning and thunder. I become high tides and an overflowing river. I didn't know. I didn't know that—

We can be the big bang that created the universe. I release a sound that I don't recognize.

And then he quietly explodes.

I become a fragmented earth. He kisses me along the fault lines on my body.

"You're my queen now?" he whispers, easing off me, pulling the covers over both of us and sliding his arm beneath my body. He pulls me in and makes himself at home here.

"I'm not yours," I whisper. I'm pulsing everywhere. Every part of me is a heartbeat.

"What I mean is . . . we're together now?"

I pull the covers up to my chin because his question is asking too much of me right now and I feel even more naked. "I'm my own self," I tell him. I don't want him to think he's taken something from me, or that I've given something away. Or by doing this, he's completed me in some way.

He's quiet for a bit; then he pulls his arm from beneath me and asks, "Did you do this with the white boy?"

"No, Chris! And he's not just a white boy. His name is Liam."

"Well, I got your father's blessing."

I quickly sit up. "What you mean 'my father's blessing'?"

"Yeah. He told me I would be good for you."

"Good for me? My father doesn't know what I want."

"He knows what you *need*—what we all need. I mean, look at us. We'd be, like, a Black Power couple," Chris says as he runs his fingers up and down my back.

"A Black Power couple?" I say, thinking of my parents. With that, whatever fault lines he's made on my body become deep chasms. I pull away from his touch, climb off the bed, and gather myself, not letting him see my most precious parts.

"What's wrong?" he asks, sitting up.

I ignore the throbbing in the middle of me and quickly dress. Chris gets up, too, only wearing his boxer shorts, and paces around the room looking for the right words, looking for the truth—something, anything more to say to me, but there's only silence and forgotten mother tongues after conquest.

Still, I manage to say, "Are you gonna start calling me your 'queen' now?"

He looks at me and says, "You'll still be a queen to me, even if you're mine or not."

Before I respond, a door slams downstairs, and my stomach sinks.

Chris quickly puts on his pants, and in seconds, he opens the door to leave. Nubia is standing right there, and we both freeze.

She looks into the bedroom and sees me trying to fix the bed. "I won't tell," she whispers, and grabs Chris's arm. "But you have to get out of this room."

And they both leave. I lock my bedroom door again, sit back down on the floor next to my mother's suitcase, and wonder why she never told me that, with the right touch, my body can feel like the creation of the universe and the end of the world at the same time.

So I dump all her clothes onto my bed, where the ghost of my girlhood self is curled up into a fetal position mourning her virginity. I feel brand-new, but not because of Chris, but because of what I wanted for myself—to feel someone's soul touching mine. My world has expanded again.

The suitcase is packed, and tomorrow is school. I'm going. I won't let my father or anyone stop me. I don't want anyone to create borders on my body, rename me, force foreign words into my mouth, and make me forget my mother's dream for me and the dreams of all our mothers who came before her.

8. MY BODY IS NOT A TERRITORY.

I'm leaving the house I was raised in. I'm leaving the village that raised me. I'm leaving the people who claim to love me. And I am broken. Not even split in two anymore. I am shards of glass and jagged little war-torn pieces of earth because this is everything that made me who I am. But I'll piece myself together again.

Jasmine went to her real home, and Makai is off with the brothers of the Youth Group somewhere. My father is coming back tonight, and there's no one to stop me from flying out of this cage called home. I don't say a word as I go into the kitchen to say goodbye to my baby brother. He babbles and laughs as usual, and grabs my locs as if he doesn't want me to leave. So I hold him tight and I don't cry. When I put him back down on the floor, Nubia is pleading with me not to take him. She doesn't have to.

I have enough courage now to leave with myself and only myself. Freedom will be too heavy for me to hold. I have to carry my own weight. So Mama's suitcase is filled with my stuff, her letter to the school, and some of her clothes. My favorite books and laptop are in my backpack. I'd already texted Sage that I needed a place to stay.

The rideshare comes just as Chris steps out onto the stoop. "Need help with your bags?" he asks.

I shake my head.

"You know he wouldn't let you leave, right?"

"I already told you. I'm walking out with my own two feet, Chris."

"He would stop you if he was here."

"Is that what you want?" I turn back only to see his face. But he's just looking at me as if he knows that he'll see me again soon. Maybe he's smirking. Maybe he's sad. I can't tell because he doesn't say a word. Maybe this is a secret he's keeping for me, too.

When I slam the car's door shut and the driver pulls away heading to Chestnut Hill, I exhale long and deep, lean my head back and dream of the horizon on a beach somewhere. Anywhere. Anywhere but that house.

When I get to KD's, I stare at the Black Lives Matter sign on the lawn before ringing the doorbell. This is where my baby brother was born. This is where Mama thought she could find a safe space, and it was her last stop before she journeyed back to herself, wherever that is.

Sage answers the door, and I walk right past her and put my stuff down. She hands me a glass of water and offers a small vial of lavender oil to sniff. "Welcome," she says. "Do you need anything else? Some food, a warm bath?" Even though it's chilly out, she's wearing a tank top and shorts, and her curly hair is up in its usual messy bun.

"Yes to all of that," I say as I take a seat on one of their fabric-covered couches and stare at a coffee table tray of lit candles. Everything feels like thick smoke around me, and maybe this is a dream. I did it. I actually left, and I wonder if I'm going to wake up back in my bed at the Village House because everything about my life right now is playing tricks on me.

"Did your father do something to you?" Sage asks.

"Leave my father out of this," I mumble, not wanting her to bad-mouth him.

She disappears into the kitchen, and I know that she's coming back with some sort of concoction. She's a midwife's apprentice. So at my age, she's seen more babies being born than probably all the sixteen-year-olds in the entire country. Sage can name different herbs, carries around a medicine bag, and sings like a fairy. Like me, she holds the memories of all her mothers who came before her. We both know much more than our bodies can handle.

"Does this mean you're staying at Philly Friends?" she asks when she comes back with a mug of smelly, dark green tea.

I nod and sip the tea—nettle leaves. The warmth wraps around my insides like a tight hug. "I need your mother to help me stay there."

Sage sits beside me. "This is like déjà vu," she says.

"What do you mean?"

"Nigeria, you do realize that you've been brainwashed in that house, right?"

I take another sip of the tea. "We're all brainwashed to some degree."

"Your mother wanted to stay here, too. Remember those sleepovers we used to have when we were little? She didn't want to go back."

"You can't talk about my mother like that, Sage." I squeeze the mug in my hands because I didn't come here to dig up old memories.

"Wait a minute," she says, turning her whole body to face me. "I don't think you even know the whole truth."

"The whole truth? I was right here the night Freedom was born."

"But you weren't here nine months before that. You didn't come with her, and she wanted to leave your father back then. She came here one night and sat in that same spot. And my mother was sitting where I am. You're doing everything your mother wanted to do, Nigeria. But she didn't end up doing the one thing *she* wanted to do. She tried. She really did."

Everything freezes, and the tea suddenly feels cold. "What did my mother do?"

She pulls away, and I know she wasn't planning on saying that much.

"What did my mother do?" I ask again, louder this time.

"Nigeria . . . I'm . . . I'm sorry. I didn't mean to bring that up," she says.

I think of all the ways to force the truth out of her, to know what she knows about my mother. But someone comes down from upstairs.

"Helping your mother get you into that school is one thing, but you staying here?" KD says as she walks over to me. "I don't know about that, Nigeria. I don't want your father coming to look for you." She's wearing scrubs, and she cut her dark-brown-and-graying hair since the last time I saw her. She gets calls in the middle of the night to deliver babies.

I don't tell her that even though I'm part of the Movement where there's a bunch of people to turn to—my village—this is the only place where I can find my own voice without the echo of my father's teachings. "He won't do anything," I say, not believing my own words. Then I glare at Sage and ask, "What was my mother doing here nine months before Freedom was born?"

KD shoots Sage a look that lets me know that this is a secret they were supposed to be keeping for my mother. "None of that really matters now, sweetie. And besides, your father came to get her," KD says. "Just like your father will come get you."

"I'm not going back to him. I'm going to school."

KD sighs and puts a hand on my shoulder. "I know that's what you want, honey. We'll find a way to keep you there. I owe your mother that much," she says in a low voice.

I wish they'd stop bringing up my mother, but I don't say anything. I wish that KD didn't feel that she owes my mother anything, but I don't tell her that, either.

But still, in this house that is a portal for new life, answers aren't given, they're shown. Truth is revealed as if every room is a crystal ball. I'll find out what Mama was doing here.

9. MY BODY IS NOT A CONSTITUTION.

Hours later, in this house that is not my home, I'm in a brand-new world that still feels old. And I'm a little bit more free. Sage takes me up to her room where there's an extra bed, and I swear it's made of angel wings and cumulus clouds. Sage said that they're organic cotton sheets, and the duck feathers in my duvet are responsibly sourced. Maybe here, my body, my mind, and my entire soul will rest.

Mama came here after she left us, and now I know why.

Tonight, a full moon hangs low in the dark sky, and KD has made a dinner of roasted chicken, heirloom potatoes, and wild rice. A playlist of soft-rock melodies paired with wispy or throaty voices blasts out of Bluetooth speakers.

"Who are those singers?" I ask Sage, and she names them—Stevie Nicks, Janis Joplin, Fiona Apple, Phoebe Bridgers, and Maggie Rogers—pulling up a photo of each one on her phone because I'd never heard of some of them. Me and Mama love Nina Simone, Sade, Jill Scott, India.Arie, Erykah Badu, and Solange. So I listen to their words, a mix of sadness and inhibition. And maybe the music in this house is translating my own unsung truths.

I didn't know that other women, girls, and nonbinary people come here to rest, too—to take care of their bodies, or to make space for their wombs. So they come in from outside or from an extra room downstairs and treat me as if I've been here all along. This is almost like the Village House. If we're fighting for Black liberation, then maybe they're fighting for body liberation.

We gather around a long wooden table in the dining room—me, Sage, KD, Corinne (who has a clean-shaven head and is staying in an extra room in the basement), and Naomi (who is pregnant and is staying in the birthing room). KD asks us to hold hands as she recites a prayer. "I am grateful for the mother, goddess, moon, and earth," she begins.

"I'm grateful for my sister from another father," Sage says, squeezing my hand.

When it's my turn, I can't think of anything to say. "I'm grateful for . . ."

"It's okay, sweetie," KD says after a long minute. "We do this every time we share a meal. We know you have so much to be grateful for."

If my father is the king of the Village House, then KD is the queen here, where everything is bells and chimes, folk songs and goddess figurines, bone broth and homemade bread, fantasy novels and tarot cards. During dinner, I chew on a piece of chicken for the first time in my life, and the salty, sinewy flesh unlocks a deep hunger I didn't know I had.

After dinner, I'm in a bathtub sitting in too-warm water, rose petals, and eucalyptus leaves. KD said that since I'll be staying in this house, I need a spiritual bath to banish negative energy and open the way for new possibilities, and Sage already knows what to do.

"You have to look within for inner guidance on this journey, Nigeria Jones," she says.

My clothes are folded neatly over a hamper, and my locs are gathered on top of my head. Sage smudges the bathroom with palo santo sticks and has soft meditation music playing from her phone. When I'm settled and calm, she holds a singing bowl over my head, and the vibrating chimes reach my bones and awaken something deep inside of me. I'm fully alert and aware of everything around, while feeling as if each cell in my body is fast asleep. This is better than being calm; it's transcendence.

"Mama says that wombs are made of gold. You know how gold is made?" Sage asks. Her voice sounds as if it's coming from the bottom of an ocean.

"No. How?"

"They're fallen stars who'd forgotten their way back home. So they get stuck here on earth, sinking deeper and deeper into the soil, until someone finds them. But by that time, they don't remember that they were once stars."

I stare at her for a while trying to make sense of her magic. "What are you saying, Sage?"

"No one can control the stars in the sky, the stars that become gold, the gold that becomes wombs."

Sage talks like Mama and all other mystical women and girls who weave poetry and magic out of English words. I'm fully naked, and this isn't a big deal for her. It's not for me, either.

"You know, my mother used to give your mother spiritual baths all the time," she says. "I used to help prepare the herbs."

"Our mothers were never supposed to be friends. Your mother was never supposed to bring me and Freedom into the world."

"Why? Because she's white? But none of that should matter, Nigeria. My mom told your mom that she's one of us. So you're one of us, too. Free spirits. Women who howl at the moon and know how to talk to spirits. That's why she couldn't be with a man telling her what to do with her body and with her life. You too."

"Me too?" I asked.

"Yes, you too."

"I kissed Liam."

"Oh shit, Nigeria! Seriously? I knew he liked you! Please tell me *everything*."

"And I had sex."

"Whoa, that's fast!"

"With Chris."

"Who the hell is Chris?"

I shake my head, not wanting to say more. I only state facts. Not feelings, not possibilities. Just the truth.

And Sage doesn't pry for more, thank goodness. "Okay. When you're ready," she whispers.

I let the silence stretch between us, leaving only the sound of slow-moving water in the tub and our quiet breaths to fill the space. Then these words pour out of me: "My father doesn't like your mother 'cause he says she's just as evil as white men, that most slave owners were white women and they were the cruelest, and it was a white woman who got Emmett Till killed and they accuse Black men of rape all the time, and white feminism can be just as oppressive as racism, and—"

The rest of the words get lodged in my throat, so instead, a river of tears comes gushing out. I spill it all, and maybe it's the smoke that exorcises my father's words and ideas out of me. Or maybe it's Sage who conjures the truth.

She stays quiet and lets me cry for a moment; then she says, "What if my great-great-grandmothers had nothing to do with slavery? I know some of them came here through a place called Ellis Island way after slavery ended. I know that what white people did was fucked up, and maybe my mother's ancestors were assholes, but we're not all our ancestors' wildest dreams, Nigeria. I help my mother bring all kinds of babies into the world. We make things right and undo some of the terrible things all my ancestors did. We live the lives they couldn't live, or even wouldn't live."

"I don't know if it's that simple, Sage." I calm myself down and sniff back tears. "The life I live is the one I chose. The one I was born into."

"Nigeria, that's not true. If you think everything that happens to you is because you chose it, then that's some serious mind fuck."

I let her words swim around the bathroom for a while; then I gather them, trying to make sense of her truth. "I know you always thought that me and my mother didn't have our own minds, that we can't think for ourselves. But I'm here, ain't I? I'm at Philly Friends, right? I did these things on my own."

"Yeah, but that's basic. Think about it, Geri. You going to school shouldn't be like breaking out of prison. Your mother wanted to keep this whole thing a secret from your father. *School*, Nigeria. It's your right to go to school. And it's not the only thing she kept secret."

"Sage, you keep dropping hints like this. . . . Spill it."

"I'm just saying . . . All those times we used to go to Brooklyn or just hang out, and then we stopped doing things together because your father had these ideas of separating from this country to find freedom. But all I see are a bunch of walls around your life," she says as she sets down the palo santo sticks, reaches for a cloth bundle on top of a hamper, and unwraps it to reveal a deck of tarot cards.

Again, I'm quiet. Thinking. Taking words apart and putting them back together again in a way that makes sense. "We're all fucked up because of what was done to us. And we're trying to find freedom wherever there's room to breathe. And sometimes, I guess, we don't know where those places are. I'm trying to find my own room to breathe."

"I'm sorry, but don't you think you're making excuses?"

"It's not excuses; it's the truth."

"You're probably making excuses for that boy you hooked up with, too. Just like your mother made excuses for your father."

"What did you say?"

"You heard me, Nigeria."

"My body is my body, and my life is my life. I get to decide which story I tell."

"But the only story that matters is the one that's true," Sage says. She motions for me to reach out of the tub to cut the deck of tarot cards. Then she shuffles them and spreads them out for me to choose three.

I take one from the right, one from the center, and one from the left.

"I've been learning about herbs my entire life," Sage starts. "So when your mother scheduled an appointment with my mother, I was the one who gathered the herbs and tinctures."

"Appointment for what?" I ask.

She slowly turns over the first card. It's an illustration of a woman sitting on a throne at the edge of the sea. She's holding a covered golden chalice. "This means that you have many past lives. Or the souls of many women live in you."

"The Queen of Cups. All the women before me have my back," I correct her. I've learned to read tarot cards, too.

"Your mother likes to do everything the natural way," she says. "So she wanted to consult with my mother."

Sage keeps talking as she turns over the other cards: the Two of Swords and the Fool. Each card in her deck has an illustration of a full-figured woman. I don't listen to how she interprets my past, present, and future. But the words to how Mama came here when she found out she was pregnant with my baby brother come alive and I see it all play out in front of me as if Mama has bent time and space to show me her truth. Sage is only a vessel for her story.

So I climb out of the tub and wrap myself with a towel and step out of the bathroom because this house holds secrets and I need to see and hear and feel all that it is telling me.

My insides sink when I see Mama take my place in the tub. Her long locs are tied over her head just like mine. She looks sad and she bows her head as if praying to her body, and I want to console her, to let her know that I love her. But I'm frozen where I stand, and the only thing I can do is call out her name.

"Mama!" My voice sounds as if it's coming from far away, on the other side of this truth that is slowly being revealed to me through the smoke, through the tarot cards, through Sage's words. "When are you coming back? You have to come home. I left Freedom there."

She doesn't look up. She can't hear me.

"Your body is holding the potential for life, Natalie," KD says to my mother with a low, calming voice. She's sitting on the bathroom floor where Sage was just moments ago. "You have to talk to your body to let it know that now is not the right time, and release that potential back to the stars."

Everything becomes smokier and more humid, and I can barely see my mother now. But her voice is as clear as daylight.

"KD, he's going to want me to keep this baby. I just want the one that I got. They'd be fifteen years apart, you know—Nigeria and this baby. She's old enough to help me take care of him, but I need her to go to that school, KD. I need to get out of that house. I can't bring another baby into the world."

Then Mama's voice becomes low, as if someone is turning down the volume to this vision. And she keeps talking, but I can't hear her. I need to know what she's saying.

"Mama!" I call out, and rush back to the tub. But the smoke is white and thick and I can't see her anymore, either.

It's like someone is changing the channel on the TV, and Sage's words become louder and clearer and take up the space again.

"She said she wanted to try herbs first," Sage continues. "They're dangerous and need to be administered by a trained herbalist, but your mama begged for them. She didn't go through with it, Nigeria, because your father came knocking on our door."

The vision of Mama in this bathroom becomes distant and muffled, as if Mama has returned to the clouds, or the bottom of the ocean. This is what she didn't have the courage to tell me? Is this why she left? She didn't want Freedom? She never wanted him, after all?

My eyes well up again, and I want to scream. But I just stand there in the bathroom's doorway and hold it in because this isn't home. Home isn't home. I don't know where I can curl into myself and implode.

It's nighttime, and my father doesn't come knocking on KD's door to look for me. There's an extra bed in Sage's room, just like how I have an extra bed in my room. She calls it a safe bed. The lights are off and so is my phone, and I already miss my baby brother. If I'd brought him here with me, he'd be nestled on this bed listening to me read *The People Could Fly*. So I take the book out of my bag and place it under my pillow.

I hear Sage tossing and turning. The first and last night I spent at her house was when we were both twelve. Sometimes, it seems like yesterday. Most times, it feels like forever ago. Like now. I don't want it to be weird between us after what she told me. But I need to know more, so I ask, "My mother came to your mother for an abortion?" My voice cracks because I can't believe I'm saying it. I can't believe it's true. I swallow back tears.

She's quiet for a second. Then she asks, "What would your father have done if your mother went through with it?"

I don't have an answer for her, and it's none of her business anyway. So I change the subject. "There was this white woman named Margaret Sanger. My father talks about her in one of his lectures. He mentions her in one of his books, too."

"I know who she is," Sage interrupts. "The founder of Planned Parenthood. There's a picture of her in Mama's office."

I get up on my elbow to try to see her through the dark. "Really? Did you know she wanted to weed out Black people? It's called eugenics."

"Maybe she thought she was helping Black women take control of their bodies."

"She believed that Black people are a lesser race and the fewer Black babies being born, the better the world would be."

"Is that what your father told you?" Sage asks.

"I had to learn about her and do my own research."

She moves around in her bed, and I can see the outline of her body sitting up now. "I hate that what started as something bad for one group ended up being good for another group."

"That's the definition of white supremacy, Sage," I say. "And colonization, and even feminism, maybe."

"No maybes. Planned Parenthood is a good thing."

"Almost half this country doesn't think so."

"Your father's part of that half, Nigeria."

"He has different reasons when it comes to Black people."

"How is it different when the outcome is still the same?"

I think about Sage's question, searching the dark bedroom for answers. "You know I don't agree with everything my father says. And he can think whatever he wants, but he doesn't have the power to do anything about it. And he never will have that power. Not in this country at least."

"But it doesn't have to be a country. He has power in that house. Your mother didn't want to have a baby, and he stopped her."

"Don't say that."

"It's true."

"But it's their truth. You don't have the right to speak on it," I say, a little annoyed at her now.

"Your mother came here for help. And now here you are . . ."

"I can leave . . ."

"That's not what I'm saying."

I'm quiet for a minute, remembering all the things I've learned, all the things my parents made me research, all the lectures I've heard my father give, and say, "The laws in this country have different consequences for Black people. Either they don't apply to us or we're oppressed by them."

Sage doesn't say anything. A minute or two goes by. Then she responds, "You're a girl first, Nigeria. You should fight for your rights as a woman."

"No. I'm Black first. Just like the world sees you as Black before they even meet your mother."

"I'm both. I want to be both. I'm not erasing my mother from my identity. And that's a choice I make."

"The world already makes that choice for you," I whisper.

"And that's the problem," she says.

"You made that choice for me. I can be both, too. I can be Black and a girl."

"But it's hard to fight for both, right?"

"Not if I don't follow the rules. If I make my own rules, I am nothing, everything, and both at the same time." I sit up on my bed now, as if my own words are truths I've been waiting to hear all along.

"I'm with you," Sage says. "A thousand percent, I'm with you."

After a long while, we both are tossing and turning before I ask her, "Did you know that Liam likes Black girls?"

"He likes *you*. Do you like him?" she mumbles.

I don't answer that question. "I wanna introduce you to Chris."

"Liam will be good for you, Nigeria."

I clench my jaw and hold in whatever I'm about to say because Sage doesn't know me well enough to know what's good for me. So instead, I take in a deep breath and ask, "Do you want me to read you a story?"

"Yeah," she says with a tiny, sleepy voice.

I turn on the lamp and pull the book out from beneath my pillow while wondering if KD ever talks to her about slavery and masters and the damage they did to Black women's and girls' bodies. So I start, "They say the people could fly . . ."

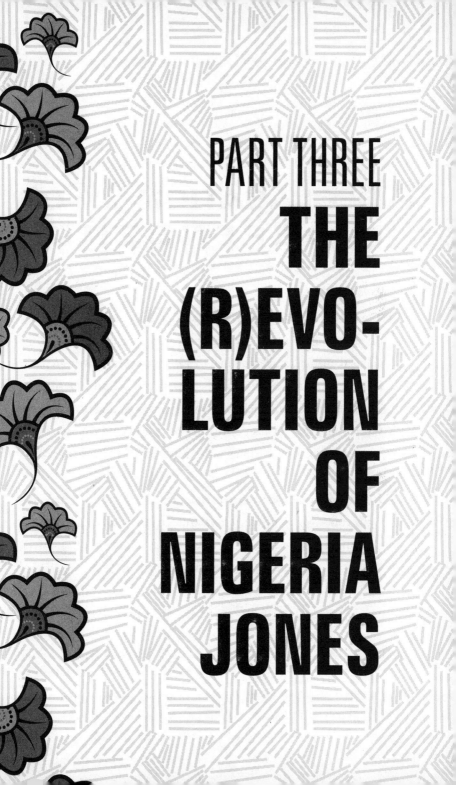

PART THREE

THE (R)EVO-LUTION OF NIGERIA JONES

DECLARATION OF INDEPENDENCE

This declaration of the united states of Nigeria Jones, when in the course of my story, it becomes necessary for me to dissolve the political, mental, and emotional bands which have connected me to others, and to assume among the powers of the earth, the separate and equal station to which the Laws of Nature and of my ancestors entitle me, a decent respect for my own opinions requires that I should declare the causes which impel me to this separation.

I hold these truths to be self-evident, that I am created equal, that I am endowed by my ancestors with certain unalienable Rights, that among these are Air, Water, Food, Land, Shelter, Safety, Freedom, Love, and the pursuit of Joy.

ARTICLE VI
HALLOWEEN
ALL SOULS' EVE

"The devil came to me and bid me serve him."

—*Tituba. Salem Village, Massachusetts, 1692.*
A witch and a snitch, teller of tales, and sole survivor
of those implicated in the Salem witch trials.

1st Amendment

It's Friday, the morning of Halloween, three weeks since I left the Village House, and everything smells like pumpkin spice and patchouli. This is the most time I've spent with white people, and I don't feel the walls closing in on me. Maybe they're expanding.

Sage is already up and getting dressed, and she sings in the morning, too. So does KD. Old songs from their ancestors that sound nothing like our songs. The melodies transport me to a place where I don't belong.

"It's Celtic folk songs," Sage had explained. "Sometimes we sing the Gaelic and Scottish ones, too, and I don't even know what they're saying, really."

"Your ancestors passed them down to you?" I had asked, wondering if she'd lost a mother tongue, too.

"No. Mom learned them from these women who have monthly meetings out in New Hope," she answered. "I joke that Mom's part of a coven. Or else she'd only know the bluegrass and Appalachian Mountains music she grew up on."

So I asked, "Do these songs make you feel more connected to your mother's ancestors?"

"I'm not going there with you again, Nigeria," she had said.

"It's a simple question," I said. "If I'm gonna stay here, then we need to dig a little deeper into the stuff that used to cause arguments between us. We're both older now, and can handle these disagreements."

"It's complicated," she answered. "I know they did terrible things, but terrible things were done to them, too. The Irish were practically starved to death by the British. Did you know that?"

I didn't, and I was curious. My whole life, white people were painted with one giant white brushstroke. And here, Sage has already mentioned her mother being Irish, Scottish, German, and Italian.

"My ancestors were not really part of the whole colonization thing," she'd said. "And my father was born in Senegal, so he didn't do the whole slavery thing, either."

But I had to check her on that. "Germans and Italians had definitely colonized parts of Africa but lost them to the Allied powers during the world wars," I said.

"Well, I'm sorry," she'd said.

"We don't need apologies; we need reparations."

"Stay as long as you need and eat as much as you want."

"I meant institutional and systemic reparations, but okay," I said.

So I make myself at home here, the same way strangers have made the Village House their home, and I wonder if someone has already taken over my bed. I wonder if my baby brother is calling Nubia "Mama" now, and a hole in my belly widens.

My stomach has been a stew of feelings for the past few days, but there's one particular sensation I've been waiting for: cramps.

In the middle of the night, I checked to see if my period came. Nothing. I get up to use the bathroom and check again. Still nothing. The sinking feeling in my belly after each time is not cramps, either. It's been a week. Maybe more. Maybe less. I wasn't keeping track of my period, especially since staying at Sage's house.

"I can't decide between Lilith or Eve," Sage says when I return from the bathroom as she places wigs, leotards, and costume stuff on both our beds. "Lilith was Adam's first wife, and I think when he got with Eve, he kept Lilith as his side chick. Yeah, his side chick, the evil one. Or I can go as Eve. She was ignorant and beautiful in the beginning, but then she talked to a snake—who must've been Lilith—and ate an apple and realized that Adam was cheating on her, and all men are trash, and she was like, 'Fuck the patriarchy!'"

Then Sage pauses, looks at me, and asks, "Nigeria, what's wrong?"

I don't know what my face is doing. I don't know how my body is looking. But if I keep this to myself, I will burst. "My period is late."

Her mouth drops and her eyes go wide. "Oh shit. No!"

I nod.

"Nigeria, you didn't use a condom with that boy?"

I'd already replayed that moment with Chris over and over in my head. He did something beneath the covers. Maybe he was putting it on. And maybe he took it off when I wasn't looking. But I didn't check. I didn't ask. And I didn't know what to feel for. Was it supposed to feel like plastic? Like skin? I don't know. All I remember was a chaos of feelings. I just close my eyes and drop my head because how could I be so stupid?

Sage doesn't say anything and comes over to hug me. "Are we talking two weeks or . . . a month?" she whispers close to my ear.

"It was supposed to come last weekend."

She gently pushes me away. "Nigeria. It's probably late 'cause you've been stressed about everything. You did a huge thing, girl. These past few weeks have been life-changing for you. Your body's adjusting, that's all."

"But what if—?"

"Positive vibes only," she says, making circular motions with her hands. "Not saying that a baby would be negative, but—"

"But I can't handle another new thing now," I whisper.

She takes a blond wig from her bed and places it over my locs and says, "And if it comes to that, you're in the right place to be loved and supported. Whatever you decide. But for now, it's Halloween, witches! A costume will take your mind off things for a while. Please wear this one, please!"

So I swallow the ocean that's threatening to drown me and pack the Eve costume in my bag to change into after school. "Seriously? Eve from the Bible?"

"'Cause you're the mother of all creation," Sage says.

"With blond hair?" I ask, smirking.

She laughs. "We're just flipping the narrative, that's all."

"Not *my* narrative," I say, rolling my eyes.

"The patriarchy's narrative. So fuck them!" she says as she takes two pieces of paper that she'd brought in from her mother's office and starts writing with big letters on each of them: F*CK THE PATRIARCHY. "This is part of our costumes. We'll wear these signs on our backs so when we walk away, we're telling everybody exactly how we feel."

"Really, Sage?" I say. "This is what we're doing? Won't we get in trouble?"

"We absolutely will get in trouble, and that's the point!"

"You're a mess!" I laugh.

We both laugh. And for a moment, like all the other tiny moments in this house these past three weeks, I forget everything. Maybe even myself. And Mama's absence, too.

Maybe a new presence has taken the place of her absence. What if an ancestor has come to remind me of who I am; come to show me that I don't have wings, but two human feet firmly planted on this earth and I have a life to live that is not my own?

2ND AMENDMENT

Liam is sitting directly in front of me around the oval table in our Constitution class. It's the last period of the day before we change into our costumes for after-school clubs and off-campus parties. My nerves are all over the place, and I don't want to admit that I'm excited. Halloween is one of those European holidays that the Movement forbade us to celebrate. But Mama always told me that it's really called All Souls' Eve and it's about the souls who've left us, our ancestors. Capitalism just turned it into a circus, and here I am about to join in on the fun.

Jon, the head of school, didn't want any drama around what we decide to wear on this day. According to Sage, Philly Friends kids are notorious cultural appropriators. Never mind that I'll be going as a white Eve with a F*CK THE PATRIARCHY sign pinned to my back.

Liam keeps looking at me. There's a tiny spark between us, and I know he feels it, too. My insides become molasses when I think about those few hours at his house. Since then, I've been avoiding him outside of school, not answering his texts, and keeping a distance because my mind is plagued with the images and words I was raised on—movies and books about slavery, my father's lectures, the news, and history lessons.

These warm fuzzies can also mean that I feel guilty. Sometimes I wish I never went to his house. Other times, I wish Chris never picked me up and made me feel bad for messing with a white boy. We haven't talked about that time I was in his basement, and it's as if we're starting over again. This time, without the guessing games. He likes me, and I'm . . . curious. Liam gives me the space I need to figure all this out, thank goodness.

In this class, we keep it cordial and pretend that we never kissed and opened a door to the potential of us being a thing. But we're still a thing. Everyone around us can feel it.

Liam has been schooling me on this mock LD debate—telling me to use quotes, name historical figures, and strategize during the rebuttals. Sage calls it mansplaining. Kamau says that he just really likes me.

"Have you thought of an argument for your first real debate, since this one is just for practice?" he asks as more kids are coming into the room. "Maybe we can tie the idea of Quakers being colonists into the resolution. Something like, Quakers: Colonizing individualists or community-minded pioneers?"

I can't hide my smile because my brain is lit up right now. "From the perspective of the Natives, they were colonizers. From the perspective of colonizers, they were pioneers."

"I guess you've never heard of Penn's Treaty," Liam says as he opens his laptop. "A community-minded agreement that allowed for a peaceful coexistence between the Lenape and the Quakers."

"Who told you that lie?" I say, crossing my arms, and still smiling. "Not the Lenape. And I guess you've never heard of the countless wars, massacres, and desecration of sacred land caused by Europeans, including the Quakers, to annihilate the Native population on Turtle Island. All thanks to Penn's Treaty and all the other treaties after that, which were broken over and over again. So like I said, colonizing individualist."

"It's the attitude for me!" Tyler interjects, sitting a couple of seats from Liam. He and some other kids had walked in, including Sage, and were listening to our little debate. "Nigeria, delivery is just as important as content."

I glare at Tyler. "So whiteness is a default for civility and professionalism? Anything else is having an 'attitude'?" I ask him. Some of the kids shift in their seats, but I don't care.

"That's a reach, and you know it. No one said anything about whiteness," Tyler says.

"She's right," Sage jumps in. "Just because she's a Black girl and she's speaking with passion doesn't mean she has an attitude."

I nod. "Thanks, Sage."

"I agree," Liam says. "Nigeria has every right to defend her truth with as much passion as she wants. I'm just . . . white, and stating facts. She may be coming from a lived experience."

I don't need him to defend me, so I say, "I'm good, Liam. Trust me, I'm good."

"Of course you're good," he says, smiling.

I'm thrown off by that. Something in me melts, and maybe the sharp edges in this classroom have been rounded, so I settle in my seat ready for this little battle between us, and I'll fight with all the attitude I want.

Henry had walked in and had been listening to us, too. "Those were some good points," he says. "But let me remind you, friends, that the resolution is 'Community standards are of greater value than individual liberty.' It should be an easy argument for both the affirmative and negative. So let's begin, shall we?" He adjusts his bow tie and takes a seat next to Liam. "Up first, Liam and Nigeria. Best argument gets bragging rights and an exemption for the next written assignment. But this is just to sharpen your skills as we prepare for tournaments."

Everyone in the room buzzes with excitement. Nerds. And I'm right there with them.

Liam stands from his seat, glances at his laptop screen, clears his throat, and begins: "When we think of great movements throughout history, revolutions that have changed the course of human existence, we do not often just celebrate entire groups of people. We do not exalt the nations and armies over the leaders who have led them to overthrowing oppressive regimes to make way for a brave new world. We celebrate our heroes and bright stars. We sing songs and write poems about their bravery and epic journeys. We mount statues in their honor and name whole constellations after them. And thus, it is the individual who first answers the call to battle, and it is the individual who takes the liberty of challenging the status quo to dismantle oppressive systems. Individuals like William Penn, Abraham Lincoln, Karl Marx, Mahatma Gandhi, and Martin Luther King. Therefore, I stand negative that, resolved, when in conflict, community standards are of greater value than individual liberty. I will argue that individual liberty is the foundation for communities and their standards, and individual leadership and bravery will lead and guide those communities to freedom and justice for all."

Everyone claps and nods except me.

It's my turn, so I hold my head up high, stand from my chair, and open my laptop to the document I worked on last night. I didn't give it much thought. It just poured out of me because this is something I spent the last few months thinking about. And I was raised to poke holes in ideas. So I start, "He said that individuals—"

"Please begin by addressing Liam as your opponent," Henry says.

"My opponent," I continue, "says that progress can't happen without individual liberty. Well, I would argue that individual liberty can't happen without community support—"

"Refrain from using contractions," Henry interrupts. "Whole words and proper grammar, please."

I pause for a second, trying not to be offended because I remember what Tyler said about me having an attitude. But I just inhale and make sure to edit my words as I go. "For example, if you take something like the Black Lives Matter movement, there are no individual leaders, really. It's . . . *It is* a collective effort, unlike the Black Panther Party for Self-Defense of the late nineteen sixties. Their leaders were sent to jail or killed by COINTELPRO and other counterintelligence—"

"Nigeria," Henry says. "If you mention acronyms, spell them out. What does COINTELPRO stand for?"

"You don't know what it means?" I ask, a little shocked.

"Oh, I know what it means all right. But your audience, the judge, and even your opponent may not know what it means."

I glance over at Sage, who's scowling at Henry, and I hope she doesn't say anything to take away my shine. I can defend myself. "If I was allowed to finish, you would know that I already said 'counter-intelligence.' Anyway . . ."

Henry starts shaking his head hard. "No. Absolutely not. You do not want to show any sign of defeat. Leave out the snark and quips. Mutual respect is the name of the game."

I pause and take in another breath. I lose my train of thought even though my words are written down. My passion is gone. I doubt my truth, so I read my essay flat with no conviction. I hate to think of him in this moment, but if my father was here, he'd make me start over. But I keep going again, even as my voice shakes. "So, other counterintelligence *program* efforts enforced by the FBI and CIA who believed—"

"FBI. Federal Bureau of Investigation. CIA. Central Intelligence Agency. Go on." Henry isn't even looking at me.

Now I actually want Sage, or anybody, to defend me. Henry is purposely throwing shade at this point. But I keep my cool and sec-ond-guess every word I'm about to read. "Who believed that if you cut off the head of a snake, the body will die. So what happened when the leaders got killed? The whole thing fell apart. But what if there is no head? What if movements are a collective effort where every-body is a leader? That's why I stand affirmative that, resolved, when in conflict, community standards are of greater value than individ-ual liberty. I will argue that war can't . . . *cannot* happen without an army. Presidents *cannot preside* without a country. Protests cannot happen without people in the streets. Movements cannot happen without community involvement. And most importantly, change cannot happen without women, especially Black women."

I had imagined a mic drop after my argument. But I just stand there because I made my voice small and dimmed my light. No one claps. Not even Sage. It's quiet, and I can hear my own breathing. Henry is rubbing his chin and looking up at the ceiling as if my speech is written there. Everyone is waiting for his feedback. Too much time is passing, so the echo of my father's words fills the silence. *Who are you competing for?*

"I'm competing for the past and the future," I say to no one and everyone really quietly. "For untold histories and unspoken truths. I'm competing for myself."

"Exactly!" Henry says, leaning forward in his seat. "And that's the problem. You're competing for a team, Nigeria. You'll be representing the Philadelphia Friends School and not yourself or those other ideas you've already got in your head. Keep working with Liam. He'll get you to where you need to be before I put you on the team."

Uncomfortable silence fills the room and everyone shifts in their seats. I should know what to say. I should clap back. I should drag him with a few choice words. Where is my voice? So I blurt out, "You kept cutting me off!"

"Yes, because you're still learning," Henry says. "There are rules and protocols and decorum . . ."

"Truth is truth no matter how it's spoken and you wouldn't let me finish my arguments."

Sage finally applauds slowly, and it's too little, too late. Liam hesitantly joins her, and then everybody else. I quickly sit back down because this isn't the performance I thought it would be.

Someone knocks on the door just as Henry is about to dismiss the class, and in walks Diane.

"Henry, can I borrow one of your students?" she asks while looking directly at me.

I don't hesitate to leave the classroom with her. My eyes meet Liam's on my way out, and I quickly look away. Something stirs in my belly, and it's not molasses or anything sweet anymore.

When we're out of the classroom, Diane touches my shoulder, leans in, and says, "Jon wants to see you after school. But I want you to come to the affinity group meeting one last time. I'm sorry we couldn't make this work, Nigeria."

If I had dimmed my light just a few minutes ago, then I become a total eclipse in that moment. "There was nothing you could do?" I ask.

"I don't run this school, sweetie. I'm here for the optics" is all she says.

3RD AMENDMENT

"When I was nine, my father made me watch Alex Haley's *Roots*, an old TV series about slavery. When I was twelve, he made me watch *Sankofa*, another old movie about a woman who accidentally travels back in time to be enslaved on a plantation." I say all of this without looking at everybody else sitting in the circle.

No one wanted to come to the affinity group meeting on Halloween, but we've already changed into our costumes and there's a rumor that some of the white kids are dressed as rappers and are calling themselves wiggers. Diane wants to address it with us right away. So here we are. And here I am trying to get them to understand how I was raised because this shit doesn't surprise me.

"I've watched *Amistad*, about a slave uprising on a ship," I continue. "*Django Unchained*, *12 Years a Slave*, a biopic about Harriet Tubman, and just about every other slave movie out there, and I'm not even seventeen yet." It's the first time I'm being so honest with people outside of the Movement, and I'm telling all my business, which is also the Movement's business.

"I've also watched the very first movie in this country that gave rise to white nationalism—*The Birth of a Nation*. And because my father wants me to understand whiteness as much as I know Blackness, I've watched old Westerns, too—cowboys and Indians, shoot-'em-up movies. I know random shit like the president who started the War on Drugs, a political platform that put countless Black people in jail and gave rise to mass incarceration, was also a Hollywood actor who played a cowboy shooting up fictional Indians. My bedtime stories were about enslaved Africans breaking chains and learning how to fly to be free. It's like I'm carrying around a heavy-ass iron-clad library in my head, and I can never put it down." I say this in almost one breath as the other Black kids in the circle stare at me as if I have two heads. I don't know if it's because of what I've just said, or what I have on.

While Sage is sitting next to me wearing a black bodysuit, a black wig with a devil's horns headband, and an orange stuffed snake around her neck, claiming to be Lilith the she-demon, I'm dressed as Eve, the first woman according to the Bible, Adam's second wife, who was created from one of his ribs. I'm also wearing that blond wig, and it's in a single braid over my shoulder, barely fitting over my thick locs. She lent me a nude leotard (which isn't nude against my deep brown skin) and wrapped fake ivy around my chest. A blue stuffed snake hangs over my shoulder and I'm carrying around a Red Delicious apple with one bite mark. The signs are pinned to our costumes. So we are a biracial Lilith and a Black Eve with F*CK THE PATRIARCHY written across our backs, and I look a hot mess.

Diane is opposite from me and looks as if she was holding her breath while I spoke. "Wow" is all she says. She's wearing a church-lady wig, some old-school cat-eye glasses, and a vintage polyester paisley shirt from the seventies. I was one of three people in the entire school who knew she was Shirley Chisholm. Kamau and a girl named Chloe were the other two.

"No wonder," a girl named Madison says, who is sitting diagonally across from me. "I'd walk around pissed at the world, too, if I watched that many slave movies." She has on a red bandanna and a denim shirt, and it was a look I've seen before but couldn't place. She kept taking selfies while flexing her biceps for whatever reason.

Kamau is sitting next to Diane, across from me, and is looking down, fidgeting with his hands. He's the only other person in this room who knows exactly what I'm talking about. But things have been weird between us ever since I found out he was the one who told Chris I was at Liam's house. He's wearing only a T-shirt with an illustration of a Black woman wearing a flower crown on her head.

"Do you go to therapy?" Madison asks.

"Why would I need therapy?"

"You don't have to answer that, Nigeria," Sage interjects. She reaches over and touches my hand. She's been telling people that I live with her now, and I wish she wouldn't.

"Well, it *is* a lot," Kamau says. He's making me feel so different in this circle. He can say the same things about his childhood, too, but he doesn't.

"See? I did all these extra Black things growing up, and I still feel out of place sitting here with y'all," I say. Once I start, I can't stop being radically honest. This is supposed to be a safe space in this white school.

"We're not a monolith," Diane says. "But this affinity group is so that we can share our common experiences here at Philly Friends. I don't want you to feel out of place, Nigeria."

The kids in here make up about half of all the Black kids in the school. Not everyone sees the need for us coming together like this, especially Sage, who claims being white just as much as being Black. We're not a monolith all right, with everyone wearing different kinds of costumes—a vampire, an alien, a rapper, viral memes, celebrities I don't recognize, and anime characters are a few.

"I don't think it's healthy to walk around thinking about slavery all the time," Tyler from my Constitution class says. He's wearing an argyle vest over a white button-down shirt and a bow tie. He parted his short fro on the side, and I thought he was dressed as himself. But he had come into the room doing a silly dance to some white music, and everyone guessed that he's Carlton from *The Fresh Prince of Bel-Air.*

"I'm not thinking about slavery all the time; I'm thinking about injustice," I say.

"I have to agree with Tyler," Madison adds. "It's like you're in a perpetual state of victimhood. It's been almost two hundred years, and we've made progress."

Some of the kids nod and agree with her. I'm trying to make eye contact with Kamau, but he's not giving me anything here.

"Nigeria, I think you knowing all that stuff is a serious flex," Chloe adds. "If we made progress, then why are we even sitting here talking about the dumb shit the white kids are wearing on Halloween."

If I hadn't already run away from there, I'd recruit her for the Movement's Youth Group. She speaks her mind and would probably love a field trip to the shooting range. She has on a turtleneck and a blazer and is wearing a giant afro wig—Angela Davis, of course.

"Because white kids don't see color anymore because of . . . progress," I say, and everyone laughs, and I crack a smile.

"Seriously, though," Madison cuts through the laughter, as usual. "If your father is this big-time SJW on the front lines of every injustice out there—yelling at cops and politicians and posting about white supremacy and what Black people need to do to get free—then are *you* free? Like, what do you do for fun?"

"*This* is actually fun," I say, and it's the truth. "I mean, I get to be myself a little bit . . . And not the daughter of a big-time social justice warrior. At least I *hope* I can be myself."

"He's not an SJW," Kamau quickly adds. "Social justice warriors fight for the rights of all marginalized people, and not just . . . hetero-cis Black men."

"Facts" is all I say, nodding at Kamau.

"Yes, you definitely can be yourself," Diane says, changing the subject. "So, Nigeria, how has it been beneficial, or . . . a burden to have to always think about race in that way? I haven't seen some of the movies you mentioned, and I already feel as if I need a serious movie night."

"It feels heavy sometimes," I tell everyone. "But it was my life. I don't know who else I would be without the stuff I know. I can't unknow anything at this point. I can choose to put it aside so I can . . . have fun." I wonder if I should bring up what happened with Henry in my class, but I put that aside, too.

"Why would you want to push it aside?" Chloe asks. "It should make you angry and move you to action. The way you were raised . . . It's like your father wanted you to be a warrior for our people, and you just want to . . . have fun?'"

And this is exactly like my father asking who I am competing for. In this school, I'm not president of the Youth Group. I'm not the daughter of a Black nationalist leader. I'm not recruiting members and claiming to have all the answers to what will liberate our people. But the issues are still the same. The fight is still the same fight. So I say, "Look, y'all. I'm legit confused at this school sometimes. Like, the message is to be ourselves, but only a little bit so the white kids are not uncomfortable. And we have to find a room just so we can talk about how racist some of the teachers and kids are, but we don't want to tell them to their faces? It's kind of like you have to constantly make a decision between being part of the Black community or the school community. I don't feel like I can do both."

"Kind of like being a girl and biracial at the same time," Sage says.

"Intersectionality," Diane says. "Coined by scholar Kimberlé Crenshaw. We're not all just one thing. This country likes to racialize us without acknowledging the other parts of ourselves. And we can still be all these things within the *context* of being Black in this school."

"So . . ." Kamau interrupts loudly. "Why don't we put all this race talk aside and . . . discuss something else?"

"Wait, Kamau," Chloe says. "I want to hear what Nigeria has to say. Let her finish."

So I say, "I'm good, really. We can talk about something else, like . . . so . . . what are y'all doing for Halloween?"

"And that right there *is* a race conversation," Chloe says. "When are we going to address all the cultural-appropriating costumes and

Halloween parties at this school? Did you see what Liam is wearing? And speaking of Liam, what would your father think about you dating a white boy, Nigeria?"

"Okay. Chloe, you're crossing a line," Diane says.

"Yes, Chloe *Angela Davis*. That's crossing the line," Kamau repeats.

"It's okay. This is a safe space, right?" I ask.

"Well, I can tell he's into you. He was really trying to let you win that mock debate," Tyler interrupts. "You and Liam make a great team."

"*Let* me win? Boy, please!" I say.

Everyone laughs, Sage especially, and I nudge her leg to shut her up 'cause she knows that me and Liam are a thing. She pokes me back on my belly.

And I remember the huge secret we're keeping between us.

"Sorry," she mouths.

As everyone keeps talking, I shut them out to take an inventory of my body. I still don't feel anything. No slight headache. No cramps. I never really got PMS symptoms other than those, so I can't tell when my period comes. I excuse myself to use the bathroom, but on my way out, Diane touches my arm and says, "Don't forget your meeting with Jon."

I didn't forget. How could I forget that my time at Philly Friends may finally be coming to an end? And I wonder if with one thing ending, another thing will begin. This is my life—a cycle of endings and beginnings.

I check myself in the bathroom stall. Nothing. I wash my hands at the sink and stare at myself in the mirror. My wig is lopsided, and the ivy around my chest looks stupid. I rub my temples, wishing a headache would come. Cravings. Bloating. Something, anything that will let me know that an ancestor did not choose me.

Someone comes in, and I pretend to be washing my hands again.

"Well?" Sage asks as she rushes to a stall and closes the door.

"Nope," I say.

"Nope, you're not pregnant? Or nope, your period didn't come?"

"Sage!" I call out through clenched teeth.

"Shit. Sorry," she says just as Chloe comes in.

"Hey, Nigeria. I hope I didn't make you feel bad in there," Chloe starts immediately. "You got up and left after I asked you about Liam."

"I'm good," I say. "I get it. You just have questions, that's all."

She turns her back to the sink, leans on it, and crosses her arms. This should be my cue to leave. "I do have questions. My mother went to Temple with your father. She used to go to his Kwanzaa and Juneteenth events before I was born."

"We still have them." I glance over at Sage's stall. She's not moving, probably eavesdropping.

"Cool, cool. I'll look forward to the next one. I've been watching some of your father's live streams recently," Chloe continues. "I wanna join the Youth Group. I hear y'all go to the shooting range. Shit is getting serious out there, and we need to be strapped. What do I have to do?"

"She doesn't belong to the Movement anymore," Sage says as she comes out of the stall. "And it's not what you think it is, Chloe."

Chloe puts her hand up to Sage's face. "Your name is not Nigeria."

"Hey, don't talk to her like that!" I say.

"Why are you defending her?" Chloe asks. "So let me get this straight. Your father is this big-time activist and community organizer, and you left your people to go live with this chick?"

"Who are you calling a chick?" Sage interrupts.

"Bet. It's none of my business," Chloe continues. "But when your father is out here claiming that liberation starts in the home and his own daughter goes to this white school and is messing with a white boy and living with white people, then it becomes *our* business. We want to believe that your father is not just saying these things just to get subscribers for his channel, sell books, and get money for a school that might not be real."

I don't say anything to that because I hate that she's right. I wish Kamau was in here to defend me. But Sage steps in, and I wish she wouldn't.

"He *is* saying all those things to sell books and make money," Sage says. "If you join the Movement, your voice as a woman will be silenced."

"That's not true," I say because I don't want her exposing my father. "It's just . . . complicated."

"There's nothing complicated about patriarchy. If his own daughter is not messing with him, then don't you think something is wrong?" Sage asks.

"See what I mean?" Chloe says. "She's out here trying to discredit him like everybody else talkin' about the *patriarchy*. You gotta have a certain level of understanding to know what the Movement is all about. And Sage, you're just not there yet."

Chloe leaves on those last words, and Sage asks, "Why are people so quick to follow whatever men say?"

"The patriarchy," I mumble, and I wish I said something to Chloe and had the last word. But I'm not myself right now. I won't defend the Movement, and I don't even know what I'm fighting for anymore. Especially with the possibility of an unnamed and faceless ancestor swimming around in my womb.

"That's what I tried to tell her," Sage says. "Girls like Chloe are so dangerous to feminism. And apparently I'm not Black enough for her. So, yeah. Say it with me, Nigeria. Fuck the patriarchy."

"No," I tell her. "I'm not saying that." Whatever I decide to do with my body, I still have to deal with patriarchy—my father, who controls everything; Jon, the head of school who gets to decide if I stay; Henry, who makes me question my truth; Liam, who is everything forbidden and dangerous; and Chris, who is everything familiar and uncertain. And even my baby brother, who will probably want to be exactly like his father.

"Well, whether you say it or not, you're wearing it and you're living it," Sage says, reminding me of the sign on our backs. "Your body, your choice."

She takes my hand, and we walk out of the bathroom and down the hall together. And in that moment, this sisterhood with Sage is a freedom I didn't know I wanted, didn't know I needed. Sage as Lilith, and me as Eve fucking up the patriarchy.

4TH AMENDMENT

My days at Philly Friends are as if I'm floating on water. The bottom of the ocean is behind me, and the clear blue sky is a canopy over me. The white kids here are the endless sea, and their salty mix of microaggressions and guilt, apologies and audacities are oppressive, like atmospheric pressure. Still, I've learned to breathe underwater. Maybe the silence at the meeting for worship helps—just sitting there and taking in the fact that I was here. I was actually here, and I'm okay.

Sage keeps me close as we walk through the halls arm in arm. She calls me her sister, and I'm her claim to everything revolutionary, everything radical change. That's what Philly Friends likes to remind us—that this school was founded on radical ideas. That's also what Jon tells us when we walk into his office.

"Creative costumes, ladies," he says. "Radical message, but I'm afraid the language taped to your backs may be offensive to our younger, more impressionable friends."

"With all due respect, Jon," Sage responds. "Dismantling the patriarchy is the most radical message we can send to our younger, more impressionable friends."

Jon only chuckles and says, "Just make sure you leave those radical messages with me. I'll make sure to get them to the right people."

"You should tape them to your door instead." Sage gives him a devilish grin and looks as if they've been doing this dance for a while now and he's used to it.

Jon crosses his arms over his chest as if to surrender to Sage's digs. I only smile a little, not willing to rock the boat until I hear what he has to say.

A sign on his desk lets everyone know that his last name is Meisner, he's the head of school, and has an open-door policy. Too many quotes by Martin Luther King are framed on his walls. A portrait of William Penn hangs behind him, and I swear both he and Jon are looking down at me with disapproving eyes. This is the moment I've been dreading for almost two months now. I've managed to stay this long, and I have both Diane and KD to thank for that. But Jon has the last word.

"I'd like to speak with Nigeria in private, Sage," he says.

"No. Whatever you have to tell her you can tell me." She squeezes my hand, and I almost want to cry. Sage knows that I've never been alone in the same room with a white man in my life.

Jon smiles without showing his teeth and motions for us to take seats on the two leather armchairs in front of his desk. His graying hair is cut low and he's clean shaven with deep laugh lines and wrinkles, but he might be younger than he looks. "You two are good friends, I see," he says, and it sounds more like disbelief than stating the obvious.

"Sisters," Sage says. "My mom was pregnant with me when she was delivering Nigeria. She was born in January, and I was born in

June. So I like to think we're sort of like cosmic twins."

She only calls me her sister at this school. Otherwise, we were always just good friends. I just nod, agreeing to be part of Sage's little act if it'll keep me here.

"And this is what I'd like to discuss with you, Nigeria," Jon continues. "I'm sorry, but Katherine Dillon can no longer vouch for you if we can't get updated vaccination records and income verification from a legal guardian. And most importantly, your father has threatened legal action if we don't release you. I'm afraid this will have to be your last day and you will not be able to enter the school."

"Where's Diane?" is the first thing I say to him. "She should be here. She knows what's going on. She can vouch for me."

"It's okay, Nigeria," Sage says, shushing me.

"Diane was instrumental in getting you accepted, but legally, our hands are tied."

"No, they're not," I say, sliding up to the edge of my seat. "They're folded right there in front of you and you can do whatever you want because you're the head of school. That's what that sign says. You can let me stay here, Jon."

"I understand you're upset, but I answer to a board of trustees."

"That's not true. You have all the power in the world."

"Come on, Jon," Sage interrupts. "There are a bunch of kids who we all know should not be here, but you and . . . this board of trustees . . . have moved heaven and earth to keep them."

"Well, that's because their parents actually want them here."

"My mother does want me here. This is all her idea," I say.

"But I thought your mother—"

"She's coming back." Those words seem to echo throughout the office, as if everything in this room has emptied out to make way for a truth I'm not ready to hear. "She's coming back," I repeat, making sure that I believe what I'm saying.

Sage slides her fingers into mine and squeezes again.

Jon looks down as if he's at a loss for words. Maybe he's changing his mind, and a tiny spark of hope lights up in me. But he says, "Nigeria, I'm so sorry. I'm sure you were able to take advantage of all the resources we have at Philly Friends—psychologists, counselors, and I hear you've been attending the affinity group."

"Well, she can still—" Sage starts to say, but I stop her.

"I can speak for myself." I take my hand from hers and tell Jon, "You never really wanted me in this school."

"Oh, we absolutely wanted you here! But your father is spreading negative information to his followers. And we're getting calls . . ."

"I'm messing up y'all's reputation?" I ask, even though I already know the answer. "I can go here as long as I make y'all look good? Never mind what I want for myself?"

"So you're expelling her?" Sage asks. "She can't control what her father says."

I close my eyes for a second and ignore whatever other reasons Jon gives for forcing me to leave the school. I'm trying to make sense of everything. "I get it. You don't want me here because I'm a liability. I'm no longer an asset."

My father's words echo in my head. *Who are you competing for?* Even though he's the last person I want to hear right now, that question forces me to get up and walk out of the office.

"Ladies, please remove those signs from your back!" Jon calls out.

"Jon, please *read* the signs on our backs!" Sage responds, and she catches up to me and wraps her arm around mine again.

Kamau, Chloe, Madison, and Tyler are waiting outside, so I whisper to Sage, "Please don't tell them anything."

"I got you," she whispers back.

I don't want this to end. School was not just about learning new things and being told how smart I already am. It was about these friends and their ideas and questions that force me to unshackle my mind, one chain link at a time.

5TH AMENDMENT

Sage and I check ourselves in the bathroom mirror before we leave school. I stuff my locs under the blond wig as best as I can (they're disobedient and don't want to be contained, too), and I remove the fake ivy from the nude leotard. I'd already been wearing jeans and had borrowed Sage's Doc Martens. And I am not like myself at all. Tonight I'm going all out and celebrating my last day at this school after two whole months of stepping into another world.

"But you don't look like Eve anymore," Sage says.

"Yeah, but it's still a costume," I say.

"Well, who are you supposed to be?"

I take another look at myself in the mirror. I undo the wig's braid and let the hair fall over my face and shoulders. Not gonna lie. The yellowish-beige color looks good against my deep brown skin, and I wish I had some makeup. "Geri," I say, softening my voice. "I'm supposed to be Geri. Geri Jones."

Sage laughs. "Okay, Geri Jones! I see you!" She tucks her own curly hair beneath her jet-black wig, and we stand next to each other doing sexy poses and pouting our lips in the mirror.

But Sage kills the mood by asking, "You wanna get a pregnancy test while we're out?"

I sigh and say, "No."

"Your period came?"

"No," I tell her, and walk out of the bathroom ahead of her.

A bunch of us get on the SEPTA over on Henry Avenue, heading downtown. It's only the Black kids who are taking the bus, and we're noisy and cracking jokes on the scenic forty-five-minute ride. We get off near LOVE Park, and I used to come to this part of Philly— with its historic row houses, expensive boutiques, and restaurants with white tablecloths. Other kids went to Rittenhouse Square, and I wonder if Liam is there because he's not with us. I don't ask about him.

A couple of years ago, I'd walk through other Philly neighborhoods with members of the Youth Group as part of our homeschooling—going to the Philadelphia Free Library, browsing the Black bookstores, Uncle Bobbie's in Germantown and Harriet's Bookshop in Fishtown; and on nice days, going down to the Delaware River Waterfront. We practically lived at the African American Museum on Arch Street. With all the school groups touring Independence Hall and all the historic sites, our entire city is one big classroom, so we never missed real school.

We take pics next to the huge LOVE sculpture and show off our costumes. And right here, right now, walking with Kamau, Madison, Chloe, Tyler, Sage, and a few other kids from Philly Friends, this is better than homeschool. This feels like the real world—a rainbow, and not my father's black and white with no grays.

I feel like I'm flying high above Philadelphia, gliding with the changing leaves, riding the autumn air, and spreading my wings wide. Who knew I could walk the streets and float in the air at the same time?

Kamau is the star of the show as he cracks jokes and makes everyone laugh. But he's not wearing a costume, so I guess he's just being himself. He was always like this in the Movement, but here, he seems even freer, funnier, and brighter. And Sage is bringing down the mood with all her talk about ghosts and opening the threshold between the dead and the living.

"Samhain is where this whole Halloween thing came from," she says with a wide smile. "So everybody is honoring my Celtic ancestors." She takes my arm in hers because we're a duet, like the couple dressed as Bob Ross and a paint palette. Except now, instead of Eve and Lilith, we're just a blond and a brunette.

"No, we are not honoring your white ancestors," Chloe says, walking a few steps ahead of us. "I'm honoring Angela Davis."

"Not with that fake afro you got off Amazon dot com you ain't," Kamau adds. "We're celebrating capitalism, just like with all the other holidays."

And we all laugh. The air is crisp, and I'm in a bubble that will never burst. I forget everything and hold on to this feeling like my life depends on it. It does.

A group of tourists are waiting to take pics near the LOVE sculpture, too. We're about to cross the street toward city hall with its towering statue of William Penn. Liam is there with another group from our school.

"There go your boyfriend," Chloe says as she slows down to walk next to me. She took off her Angela Davis fro because of Kamau's joke. Her hair is in short twists, and she has smooth brown skin like mine and full lips. We almost look like sisters and we should be friends, but talking to her is like talking to Makai. I don't feel radical enough.

"He's not my boyfriend," I say, wanting to avoid her. "But if he was, it's not a big deal, right?"

"You talking to the wrong person."

"Chloe, I hope you know that I'm not like my father."

"Clearly," she says, looking me up and down. "But sis, what are you even doing with that blond wig?"

"It's Halloween," I say, and I know what she's getting at.

"Don't come to this school and get whitewashed."

"I'm not. And why would you say that?"

"Nigeria, you are so obvious right now," she says as our group walks ahead of us, and we're face-to-face as passersby move around us. "I already knew who you were when you came to this school. Kamau had told everybody that Kofi Sankofa is his uncle. I really thought you'd be running Philly Friends by now 'cause everybody thinks they're so radical and far left and socialist and anarchist. . . . But it's all talk and keyboard activism. You *lived* it. You're doing the work. Everybody should be bowing down to you. But here you are—"

"Here I am living my best life." I cut her off.

"And that's sad, to be honest." She shakes her head at me.

I feel that hard blow in my gut. "I'm not a radical activist, Chloe. And I don't wanna be."

"Well, it just looks like you're lashing out. I'm sorry about your mom."

"Please don't bring up my mom, and you don't know me like that."

"I know enough to see that Liam is fetishizing you, just like you're fetishizing him." Then she walks away, not letting me have the last word again.

"Nigeria, come on!" Sage calls out before she crosses John F. Kennedy Boulevard, and I don't move. The passing cars, the chatter, and the late-afternoon sounds of downtown Philly become louder.

"Did Chloe just say some shit to you?" Kamau asks as he walks closer to me.

"It doesn't matter," I say, and we cross the street together, arm in arm. I don't know what comes over me as I look up at that giant statue of Pennsylvania's founding father, but I tell Kamau, "I think I'm pregnant."

He stops right in the middle of the busy street, but I grab his hand and rush to the curb where everybody is waiting for us. Kamau's mouth is wide open, but I hope he doesn't ask me to say more while all these people are around. I shouldn't've said anything, but it just came out.

Liam walks up to us, and Kamau is still in shock as he looks at him, then looks at me.

I shake my head to let him know that it's not Liam's, but I don't think he gets it.

"Cool hair," Liam says.

Then I see his costume.

Before I can say anything, Tyler runs up to him and gives him a dap. "What's good, bro!"

He and Liam start doing this stupid dance and singing "Jump on it! Jump on it!" and everything starts to make sense. Liam is wearing a blue-and-yellow cap that says, "Philadelphia Born & Raised." That, along with the round sunglasses, a neon green striped T-shirt, and sweatpants with a nineties graphic design, lets me know that he's the Fresh Prince of Bel-Air. And Tyler, of course, is Carlton.

I glance at Chloe, and she smirks. "That's all you," she whispers.

So Liam, Tyler, Madison, and some other girl are the cast of the *Fresh Prince*. Liam is the only white boy, and I don't know if it's funny or offensive.

We stroll around East Penn Square and down Market Street, and it feels like someone pricked a tiny hole in my bubble. That joyous, free air is slowly seeping out. I make sure to stay behind Liam and his friends, and he's being extra right now. Laughing hard, making corny jokes that I'm glad I can't hear, and being way too friendly with both Tyler and Madison, and I wonder where that skateboarding anarchist with a weird affinity for William Penn went.

Then he stops, turns around, and waits for me. We're side by side now, and I don't know what to say.

So he starts. "Chloe doesn't like my costume."

"You look ridiculous." I didn't want to be so mean right off the bat, but I'm being honest.

"It was Tyler and Madison's idea."

"Bad idea."

He slowly takes off the cap and sunglasses. "I didn't think it was cultural appropriation."

"You didn't think. Period."

"If you'd answer my texts, maybe I could've double-checked with you."

"Are you guilt-tripping me for something you're doing wrong?" I ask, moving away from him a little bit.

"I wasn't sure about this, but I love that show! Plus we're both William. He's Will, I'm Liam."

I just shake my head at him, and even though it feels wrong, I can't help but smile a little.

Kamau had been next to us all this time, listening. "Liam, you should've double-checked with Wikipedia Black over here," he says. "If she says it's cultural appropriation, then it is."

"My bad. This was stupid," Liam says, looking down at himself.

Tyler is a few feet ahead of us, and he turns around. "Hey, Will! What happened?"

"Nope," Liam says, looking deflated. "Not playing anymore."

He gives me a half smile. My stomach tightens; my heart starts racing. I look around at everyone with their silly costumes, on our way to the waterfront, and I'm over here feeling like I'm doing something wrong and doubting this path that's laid out in front of me. In this moment, I'm not trying to think about white supremacy.

This is my own revolution.

So I walk closer to Liam and purposely bump his arm. He bumps me back. Now we're playing some sort of touch-and-go game and we're both smiling. He takes my hand. I don't pull away. His hand is warm and smooth, and I want to look down at our skins touching. But I don't.

Chloe glances back at us, and a surge of guilt runs through me.

I still don't let go as we walk past the wide buildings and stores along Market Street. My wings spread even wider taking in my city and claiming every corner, every rooftop, and even this boy who's holding my hand.

A sudden sharp pain below my belly button forces me to remember that I don't have wings, but two feet. And a womb.

I squeeze Liam's hand because a life that I haven't lived yet surfaces in my mind—a light-skinned baby with curly hair and two different worlds in one tiny body. If I'd gone all the way with Liam . . . and let him explore me . . . and it was his . . . and I fell in love . . . my father would disown me . . . he would be angry . . . and I would prove him wrong about black and white . . . good and evil . . . war and peace. . . . Prove him wrong about everything. *Everything.* But it's not Liam's.

And he doesn't know that, but he asks, "Can I kiss you?"

"Here? Now?"

He nods.

I nod, too, slowly, feeling a warmth take over my body even as a fall breeze blows and goose bumps form on my skin.

He takes me to an empty spot against a tall building with a wide awning. He turns me around so that my back is against the brick. He holds my face in his hands and kisses me long and deep. And I melt. Right there on Market Street. For all of Philadelphia to see.

But our friends clapping and cheering "Woohoo!" kills the whole vibe.

We stop kissing, and he hugs me, whispering, "I've been wanting to do that."

I close my eyes and rest my chin on his shoulder and let him wrap his arms around my waist and allow myself to be held close. I inhale deep, and Liam smells like everything that is opposite of familiar. But I stay here for a second because exploring strange, new places is a freedom I didn't know I wanted, didn't know I needed.

I open my eyes and see Chloe watching us with an attitude. Her shoulders drop and her eyelids are heavy, as if she had high hopes for me and I've disappointed her. Liam gives me one last squeeze before letting go, and someone walking by smiles at us.

I slowly pull away and refuse to look at him. He thinks we're a thing now. And another sharp, pulsating pain stabs at my womb. I put my hand there and remember my future and my past.

Our friends are several yards away and Liam tries to take my hand again, but a Black guy stares at us. A white girl looks back and sizes up Liam. Another boy shakes his head at me, and suddenly, it feels like all of Philly is judging me and maybe they know whose daughter I am.

"You good?" Liam asks.

I'm not, but I don't tell him. Maybe people see us from their apartment and office windows, and from their cars, and I watch every person going by, too. A white man, an Asian woman, another group of teens . . . They're judging me.

Liam starts to put his arm around my shoulder, but I pull away and—

A whirl of blue and lavender colors across the street catches my eye.

It's too cold for a summer dress. It's too late in the year for pastel tie-dye. And everything, *everything*, comes to a stop because Mama is walking down Market Street and she must be on her way to the waterfront.

My heart falls to the ground, and my feet lead me to her. "Mama?" I whisper, and rush to the curb.

She turns to look at me. She sees me. *She sees me!* I wave and start jumping up and down. "Mama! Stay there, I'm coming to you!"

But she turns and keeps walking, gliding. Her dress is blowing with the breeze. Her locs sway like they always do. I run to the corner even as Kamau tries to stop me and ask me where I'm going. The light is red and cars are speeding, and I want to run to her. I want to run to her so bad.

But she keeps walking, gliding.

The light turns green and I dart across the street. My blond wig flies off. But how did she move so fast? She's down the block now, not looking back. Not waiting for me.

I keep running, bumping into people, dodging slow walkers. And I swear she's leaping from one block to the next. She walks past 8th Street and Market, and I need her to stop. I'm almost out of breath. I don't respond to my friends calling out my name. I need to get to my mother before she forgets me.

And she finally stops. I pick up my pace because finally she wants me to catch up to her. Mama is looking up at a building, and from where I am, I notice the giant portrait of one of the founding fathers—Thomas Jefferson. I'm a few yards from her, and I stop to take in whatever she's contemplating. Thomas Jefferson's words are written in script near the drawing of his face: *We hold these truths to be self-evident* . . . The last words, *Life, Liberty, and the Pursuit of*

Happiness, are more prominent.

I know this building—Declaration House. The portrait is against a newer structure that stands besides a redbrick tenement with off-white shutters. It's supposed to be from the colonial era—the site where Thomas Jefferson drafted the Declaration of Independence.

"Mama?" I say, careful not to get too close so I don't scare her away.

She looks younger, as if the last few years never happened; as if she was never pregnant with Freedom and her face wasn't puffy and glowing like how I remember her those last few months before she left. She's taking good care of herself, and she looks happy. Almost. "Mama," I repeat.

She still doesn't turn to me, and looks away, and glides down 7th Street, past the Declaration House's entrance, down and down and down the block until we both reach Washington Square.

No matter how fast I run, no matter how slow I walk, she's always the same distance away. Close enough for me to smell her lavender-and-patchouli scent, far enough that I can't reach her, can't touch her.

She disappears. So I call out to her again. "Mama! Where'd you go?"

"Nigeria!" Kamau shouts from behind me, but I ignore him.

I walk into the park with its canopy of earthy orange, yellow, red, and green leaves. And in the middle of it all is the blue-and-lavender tie-dye dress standing in front of the Washington Monument at the center of the park. Mama is just standing there again reading the inscription: "FREEDOM IS A LIGHT FOR WHICH MANY

MEN HAVE DIED IN DARKNESS."

Mama once told me that this space used to be called Congo Square because it's an old burial ground for Africans, both free and enslaved. Revolutionary War soldiers and Philadelphians who died from the yellow fever epidemic of 1793 are buried here, too. Some of whom were Haitian, like her, America's first refugees.

"History lives and breathes and so do our ancestors," Mama's voice says.

She said this then, and she's saying this now. Her back is to me and I can't see her face, but I hear her words.

I want to forget history now and touch my mother, let her embrace me and tell me that she's coming back home. So I step closer, but she moves away. I keep reaching for her, and she's nearer to the statue now, on the other side of the chain link guarding the marble tomb.

"Mama, why are you here?" I ask. "Turn around, Mama. Let me see your face again."

And she does. She finally does!

Tears are rivers streaming down my cheeks. But she doesn't cry. She's smiling and looking at me. Mama sees me. She sees me and I should be running to her but she's ephemeral and transparent. The statue behind her is visible through her presence.

"History lives and breathes and so do our ancestors," she repeats, and I swear it echoes throughout the park and all over Philadelphia because it sounds like a thousand voices are saying this at the same time.

"Mama, how did you conjure yourself here?" I ask, because only now, on this All Souls' Eve, am I realizing that everything is not what it seems. "Mama, how are you in the past and the present at the same time?"

Then, as if a crack in the universe widens, Mama glides to me and tries to lift me up with her, to fly us both into the clouds. But cramps force me to remember that maybe she forgot to give me wings. I can't stand on my own two feet, either, so I collapse while still holding on to her memory, the scent of lavender and patchouli and the sight of blue and lavender tie-dye dancing in the wind.

Mama always told me that energy doesn't die, it transforms—

—into unrest souls beneath cities and mothers who can never rest because their daughters and sons forget that they can fly, too.

I don't grow wings, and I don't feel so free anymore. Or maybe this isn't the liberation my ancestors dreamed for me, because history is the ground and my two feet are the future.

I don't need wings to fly. Just my own free mind.

The first arms to wrap around me and lift me from the ground are my cousin's. "We have to get you home," he whispers. "I have to call your father."

And I black out.

6TH AMENDMENT

"You are such a damn witch!" Kamau says, looking relieved. "Catching the holy ghost in the middle of Washington Square! I know, I know. It used to be called Congo Square, where our ancestors did the same thing. But still, it's not the seventeen hundreds, girl!" He's hovering over me, and he knew that I'd be happy to see his sunshine face when I woke up.

"It's Samhain, Kamau, and she was a vessel for the spirits, that's all," Sage says, holding a bundle of sage and swirling it around all up and down my body as I lie on a couch.

I look up at the ceiling and recognize the wooden-beaded chandelier and macramé wall hangings. The bittersweet scent of the smoke is suffocating but relaxing at the same time. I'm on the velvet sofa in Sage's house, and I close my eyes again, not ready to see my father after almost a month.

But he would've said something by now. Besides, would he have wanted to come in? This birthing house traps a memory we're all not ready to confront. Or maybe it's just me.

"What happened?" I ask, sitting up to look around at who's here. "I remember being helped into a car, but that's it."

"You fell out right in front of America's first president," Kamau says, and he makes it sound funny.

But I'm embarrassed. I hold my head in my hands, thinking that I must've looked insane. "I'm sorry y'all didn't get to hang out."

"You're more important, Nigeria." Sage sets the bundle on a small plate and fans the smoke toward an open window; then she extinguishes it.

"What was I saying?" I ask.

"You were calling your—" Sage starts to respond.

"Gigi, don't worry your little head," Kamau cuts her off. "None of that matters now because my mother is on her way."

"Not my father?"

"I couldn't bring myself to call him. People were trying to get you an ambulance but—"

"No!" I shout.

"We didn't," Sage says, taking my hand. "We knew it would be triggering, and you were responding when we called your name. So we got in a cab and came here."

"Does he know?"

"Mom said he's in New York. He's coming back tomorrow," Kamau says.

I think of Freedom, and I'm mad that I haven't been there for him.

"Hey, drink some tea," Sage says, holding out a mug.

"Got anything stronger?"

"Like what?"

"White Claw?"

They both laugh, but I'm serious. I need something to drown out everything because today my entire life changed. Again.

"White Claw? Did Liam put you onto that?" Kamau asks. "He wanted to come, but . . . this is family business."

"And I don't think alcohol is a good idea. In case, you know . . ." Sage glances down at my stomach.

I touch below my belly button and ask, "Who else is here?"

"Everybody's out. You have time to rest and tell us what's going on. At least until your aunt comes."

"Okay. So . . . who else knows?" Kamau asks, side-eyeing me.

I motion toward Sage.

"I could've sworn you told Liam, the way he was kissing you in public like that," Kamau says.

"It's not Liam's."

"Thank the ancestors."

"Why'd you say that?"

"Your father would kill him; then the government would kill your father."

"Kamau!" Sage shouts. "Are you serious?"

I throw up my hands and stand from the sofa, though I'm a little dizzy. "I'm done. I'm going to the bathroom."

"Wait." Sage reaches for something on a nearby tray table. She hands it to me and says, "Follow the directions on the box. My mother has a bunch of these in her office in case you miss the stick."

I examine the contents—a pregnancy test—and stuff it into the pocket of my jeans.

"So are you having a Black Jesus or what?" Kamau asks. "Are we talking a virgin birth here?"

"It's Chris," I say on my way to the upstairs bathroom. "Christopher Fauntleroy from Strawberry Mansion who's staying at the Village House."

"What? You lying!" is all Kamau says.

In the bathroom, I place my hands over my belly. I want to feel if an ancestor has chosen me; chosen us. I want to feel the potential for life—the cells dividing and coming together to become soul, then body, then mind. I look at my face in the mirror—deep-sunken eyes like my father's, high cheekbones like my mother's, hair like DNA strands, and I wonder what another version of me in the world will be like. An ancestor returning back to me, back to fight for our liberation, and to heal our generational wounds.

Then I hear moving water behind me. I look up at the mirror to see a reflection of Mama sitting in the tub. Her belly is flat, too. Her eyes are red with tears. I don't turn around because I know this vision of her is not real and she's only on the other side of this mirror.

He's going to want me to keep this baby, Mama's honey-sweet voice echoes again from some other place. *It took so long for me to get pregnant, mainly because I didn't let it happen. He wants his little African tribe. I just want the one that I got.*

And I remember what she wanted to do, what my father stopped her from doing. Mama didn't want Freedom. And if it weren't for my father and his ideas, I wouldn't have a baby brother. If it weren't for my father and his ideas, Mama would've had a choice. If it weren't for this country and its ideas, I would still have my mother.

Voices come from downstairs, and I'm not ready to see people just yet. But I recognize Aunt Sharon's hard words and gruff tone. So

I brace myself for whatever will happen from this point on. It's been a good three weeks of living in this birthing house.

I look around this bathroom. Mama was here, and she was making the hardest decision of her life. A choice that would change all our lives. And here I am standing between her world and my father's world. But I have to make my own world. I have to reach for my own past so I can move forward.

I sit on the toilet, open the pregnancy test box, and brace myself for a brand-new life. But when I look down, I see my period came. Finally!

I didn't know that I'd been holding my breath all this time because I let out a moan so loud and so deep that I'm sure the ancestors hear me. "Thank you," I whisper, looking up at the ceiling.

When I get downstairs, Aunt Sharon is standing by the door. She's looking around as if this place is a museum. Sage and Kamau are looking at me with wide eyes, waiting for me to give them a sign for the test result, but I just look away.

"Hi, kids!" Aunt Sharon says. "Taking my time to come in because, well . . ."

"A lot has changed since you've been here last," Sage says, fluffing pillows and picking up empty mugs.

"You were here?" both Kamau and I say together.

"Don't be judging me, y'all," Aunt Sharon says, always keeping it one hundred. "KD provides a service, and I was in need of a service. It's just that I haven't been in here since before . . ." She looks up at me; then she comes in. "Nigeria? What happened, honey?"

I want to tell her that she turned her back on me and on my mother. I want to tell her that the petty beef between her and her brother has forced me here, a place that holds Mama's last memories. But I just say, "Nothing happened."

"Yeah, right!" Aunt Sharon says with a smirk, and we all laugh a little. She comes over to give me a hug and says, "I'm so sorry, niece. This has been so hard on all of us."

I clench my jaw so I don't cry.

"Can you give us a minute?" she asks Sage, who disappears into the kitchen. Then she motions for me and Kamau to sit on the couch with her. Her nails are always done—bright colors and patterns that she changes every couple of weeks. Her burnt-orange crochet hat sits stylishly over her buzz cut, and she smells like rose oil. I wish I'd gotten to know her better, to know how she was able to break away from my father, her own brother, after being part of the Movement for so long.

Kamau starts playing with my locs, and I look back at him. He still wants to know what I found out in the bathroom, but I don't give him any clues.

Aunt Sharon reaches into her designer bag, pulls out a folded piece of paper, and just holds it in her hands. "If you hadn't left that house," she starts, "I don't think my brother would've reached out to me. We've been talking every single day since."

My heart opens up. I close my eyes, waiting to hear what she'll say next. Aunt Sharon reaches over and takes my hand.

"Nigeria, I had told your mother to leave him, to take you with her and abandon the Movement. But then she got pregnant with Freedom. And I think she tried to still get out, but . . ." She sighs and continues. "He said he thought I was trying to break up his family and sabotage the Movement by telling your mother to leave. He was hurt by that. Nigeria, I want you to know that even though your father is hard on you and he's tough, and strong, and has all these ideas, and does all these great things for the community . . ." She pauses and seems to be getting choked up, so Kamau goes over to her and places his hands on his mother's shoulders. Aunt Sharon doesn't say anything more, and she unfolds the paper she'd been holding and gives it to me.

I take it and read four short sentences: *To my daughter. Warrior Princess. I want you home. I miss you.*

I fold the paper back up. He's written entire books, and this is all he writes to me?

In that same moment, the front door opens and in walks Corinne and Naomi with her round belly and a witch hat. KD is right behind them, and when she sees us, she nods in my direction as if to say that it's time. It's finally time.

"Nigeria, pack your things," Aunt Sharon says with a really low voice. "Now that my brother and I are talking . . . Come stay with me."

KD, Corinne, and Naomi join Sage in the kitchen, giving me, my aunt, and my cousin some privacy. The truth of this moment settles in my bones, and I should feel sad. But I just feel . . . relieved.

Aunt Sharon reaches into her bag again and pulls out a yellow manila envelope and gives it to me. "Take a look at this. I've already done the research at my job. There'll be lots of paperwork, and the courts will have to get involved."

The first sheet is a printout of a web page with the title: "Emancipation for Minors."

I scan all the bullet points. There's a court process for sixteen- and seventeen-year-olds who want to be legally emancipated from their biological parents. I bring the stack of papers to my chest because this is a door and a window, and I didn't know that the sky could be so close.

I look at Kamau, whose eyebrows are raised high, like we both can't believe that this is possible. And maybe, maybe I'm finally ready. In a few minutes, I'm upstairs opening my mother's empty suitcase.

"You have to fight to stay at Philly Friends," Sage says as she helps me pack.

I remember my last few hours at the school today. Henry. Jon. And even Liam. "Do you have to fight to be there, too?"

Sage pauses for a second, holding a pair of my tattered jeans on her lap. "Hell yeah, I have to fight to be at that school."

"Is there anywhere you can be where you don't have to fight?" I ask.

"Here. Home," she says. "I don't have to fight at home."

"Well, I do," I say. "Me and my mother had to fight the world, the men that came in and out of that house, white supremacy, oppression. . . . I guess that's why my father calls me a warrior princess. I'm supposed to spend my whole life fighting."

And I don't say this out loud, but I wonder if this is why Mama wanted to fly away. I wonder if this is why she keeps showing me a way to freedom even if I don't have wings.

Downstairs, everyone gathers in the living room to say goodbye. KD motions for us to join hands and form a circle. Aunt Sharon walks out the door ahead of us, saying that she needs to start the car, but I know she's just not feeling whatever we're about to do.

"Nigeria, I am so grateful for the time you've spent with us," KD starts. "You've brought so much light and love to this birthing home. And . . ." She swallows hard and squeezes my hand, and so does Sage on the other side of me. "And healing."

When it's my turn, I hold my head high and close my eyes. It's quiet for a second. I conjure Mama's face in my mind. Her moonlight smile. Her long locs draping over her shoulders. Then her voice fills the space. Not her words, but her cries—distant and muted as if she's crying on the other side of this threshold. So I quickly open my eyes because I don't want to see her again. Not yet. And I say, "I'm grateful . . . I'm grateful for . . . closure."

This Halloween night is supposed to be filled with ghosts and darkness and fear and the onset of winter. But there's a lightness to this moment. Like, this change might be the threshold between the new life ahead of me and the death of my old life behind me.

After I give my last hugs to everyone, Kamau helps me with my suitcase. Mama's suitcase. I remember finding it in her car. So I quickly turn to KD and ask, "Was she coming here to stay?"

"I think so, honey," she responds. "I always kept my door open for your mother."

KD's was the last house my mother had been in before she left— this white woman who ushers babies into the world and reminds people with uteruses that they have power over their own bodies. But my father sees black and white as ideas. KD is white, and he thinks that the closer to whiteness we as African people are, the closer we become to death. Systems and institutions like schools and hospitals rob us of our sovereignty, he says. Never mind that education is how we move up in this world, but they don't teach us our history and so many of us are still behind. Never mind that modern medicine and surgeries save our lives, but Black women are still dying and they don't believe us when we say we're in pain.

That's what happened to Mama.

By the time she got to the hospital, she had lost too much blood, something inside her broke, and they weren't able to save her.

She died. Mama died in the hospital that night.

Just as I'm walking out the door, everything comes rushing back to me like the midday sun after sitting in darkness for so long, like a piercing scream after being silent for so long.

"Baba, please slow down!" I shouted from the passenger seat of his truck.

The police had let him go, but I didn't want any others to come chase him down again. He was holding the steering wheel as if it was the only thing that would get us to Mama fast enough. He tried following the ambulance, but he had to stop at the red lights. He cursed the red lights. Beads of sweat formed on his forehead, and wetness streamed down the side of his face and his neck. His T-shirt was already drenched.

"Baba, we can put on the AC," I said, being very careful not to shift the universe by saying the wrong thing in that moment.

He was a quiet storm, focused on the road. It was the night of July Fourth, and everyone was out. Fireworks kept lighting up the sky, and everything about that felt wrong.

I had stopped crying so I could keep it together for my father because he looked as if he was about to burst.

"Where do I park? Where do I park?" he shouted when we

reached the hospital, and those were the first cohesive words he spoke since leaving KD's.

I wished I could drive so I could tell him to run in.

"Turn here," I said, pointing to the signs.

He bumped a car while trying to fit into a narrow parking spot. He couldn't get the truck straight.

"Baba, breathe. Please breathe," I said.

He didn't breathe and kept trying and trying because he was so close to the other car, he couldn't open his door. I wished I could park so I could tell him to run in. It took way too long for him to do something he'd done a million times.

Before that moment, I couldn't remember the last time my father grabbed my hand so we could run together. His hand was sweaty and slippery and I was wearing flip-flops and he was already out of breath and his entire body was an ocean. The sky was on fire. All of Philly, and the entire country, too, was one huge party, and that felt wrong.

"My wife! My wife!" is all my father could say when we reached the front desk in the emergency room.

KD was already there because she had ridden with the baby in the ambulance. She came to console my father, but he turned her away. I touched her arm to let her know that she should leave him alone.

"Where is she?" I asked.

"Surgery," she said.

My father heard her, and I didn't want to turn around to see the look on his face.

Time can either have wings or two legs. And on July Fourth in that hospital, in that emergency room, everything walked along the edges of my memory like an aging elder. Slow. Deliberate. Careful.

My father refused to drink water. He refused to sign papers or show proof of insurance.

I looked to KD for answers. "She paid cash when I delivered you," she said, shrugging.

People came and stayed. People came and left. People were hurt, crying, shouting, rushing, and I didn't know that hospitals can be portals for life and death, too.

The uncles arrived, and I wished that this moment belonged to us and only us. But my father has followers, and soon, our entire village knew what was happening to Mama, and KD was the enemy. This hospital was the enemy. The system was always the enemy.

Auntie Fola brought food. I couldn't eat. She held a prayer circle, but everybody's ancestors and gods were already summoned here. When a team of doctors came out, and my father rushed to them like he was about to fight, and they said a few words in that language that made us forget our mother tongue—

—the universe shattered.

I split in two. Then four. Then eight. And fell to pieces because my mother . . .

My mother left her body there in that hospital, left her new baby there in that hospital, left me here in this world, and flew away to the land of first mothers. The Motherland. Mama's soul went back to Africa like a Sankofa bird, and maybe this is where she found freedom like the people in that story.

But she's supposed to come back because ancestors return over and over again.

ARTICLE VII
GRATITUDE DAY
(INDIGENOUS PEOPLES' DAY II)

"Flower between two streams."

—*The Algonquin meaning of Matoaka, the true name of Pocahontas. Daughter of the great and powerful Powhatan. Caught between the world of her ancestors and the world of her colonizer.*

I feel you, beloved.

ATONEMENT

At Aunt Sharon's house, I pause everything. School. Home. Homework. Missing my baby brother. New friends. Kissing boys. The Movement. My father. And I grieve. Again.

She didn't let anyone come visit me, and she gave me white dresses to wear. I wrapped my locs in white, too, and drank teas, ate salads, and listened to all the songs that remind me of Mama. Soft, soulful melodies and voices that forced me to turn in and slowly, slowly grow wings.

Today is Thanksgiving, and food is spread out across two tables and a countertop and this is the first time in my life that I'm in the same room as a big, brown, juicy turkey. I feel guilty. I was raised not to celebrate Thanksgiving, of course, to be in solidarity with our Native brothers and sisters. But this is Aunt Sharon's house and she's not part of the Movement and she can do whatever she wants in her own damn house. She's been saying this for the last three weeks I've been here, like it's a mantra.

"Why'd y'all start celebrating white supremacist holidays?" I ask Kamau.

"First of all, we call it Gratitude Day. And real talk, it gets lonely sometimes, Gigi," he says as we make a pan of mac and cheese (real

340

cheese) together. "I hate being the only one to know things and not everybody is ready to liberate their minds. It's just easier to do what everybody else is doing because people are more important than ideas. Plus, my mother makes a mean jerk turkey!"

Even though it doesn't feel right, I know what he means.

"And I remember those days of fasting on carrot and celery sticks and driving all the way to New York to go to that museum," Kamau adds.

"The National Museum of the American Indian," I remind him. "Black people in this country were eating collard greens and ham, turkey and rice and peas. Meanwhile, we were hungry and spent the day talking about genocide."

"Gigi, you think we were traumatized?" he asks. "With everything we learned."

"We learned about it, Kamau. We didn't live through it."

"Facts. And I can't believe your father's coming," he says. "King Kofi Sankofa is celebrating the white man's holiday and the revolutionary ancestors are turning over in their graves!"

We both laugh, but it's a little scary that my father is bending his own rules like this. There's definitely a shift, and maybe it was all because of me. And Mama, too.

I'm exhausted from cooking all day, and I'm making all the meals Mama would've made—Haitian black rice, fried plantains, and a beet salad. The last time I cooked this much was for her repast after her funeral, which we didn't call a funeral but a homegoing, where everyone was dressed in white and we had drummers, and it was a celebration that I'd buried deep in my memory, until now.

Everything has been coming back to me these last couple of weeks: the hospital, the rage, the grief, the denial, the memory loss.

Aunt Sharon says that I need to go to therapy. But someone would have to pay for it. So she has me sit on the floor as she reads the messages my guides and my ancestors are trying to send me through tarot cards, palm readings, cowrie shells, kola nuts, and cigar smoke because we honor our African deities, even though they're not always enough to get us through our traumas.

The doorbell rings, and it's my father. It's the first time I'm seeing him in person since I left the Village House. When Aunt Sharon opens the door, he looks thinner and more fragile, as if the work has been slowly chipping away at him.

Behind him is Nubia, and she's showing now—her round belly is hidden beneath an African print caftan and I can't help but think of Mama. My father is holding her hand, and it hurts a little to see that. But I force a smile.

My entire soul lights up when I see little Freedom toddling up the front steps on his own.

"He swears he's grown," my father says, smiling. "Don't want nobody holding him."

I run to him and pick him up and shower him with kisses. "What's up, little homie! I missed you so much!"

He fights me to get down, and my eyes are welling up with tears. He's grown so fast, and a part of me doesn't want to miss another day of his life.

Inside, Kamau greets my father with an awkward dap and hug. I can't remember the last time I saw them that close.

"You getting tall, boy," my father says, pounding Kamau's bony chest, and I know that hurt.

"Greetings, Uncle Kofi," Kamau says, deepening his voice and avoiding my father's eyes. He cuts that uncomfortable exchange short by taking my baby brother to the sofa to get him out of his little coat, and Nubia joins Aunt Sharon in the kitchen.

I'm left to deal with my father in the dining room. He calls me over to him and places his arm around my shoulders. "How you doing, baby girl?" he asks with that deep voice of his.

"Better," I say. I lean into him, taking in the scent of sandalwood and everything about him feels like soft air.

Aunt Sharon comes back out and motions for us to take seats on opposite ends of the dining room table before it's set for dinner. I know what this is about. She'd told me that I need a come-to-Black-Jesus moment with my father. And it would happen today.

"Y'all gotta start working this out before we break bread," she says.

So we're facing each other. She lights a white candle and places it in the middle. Then she gives us each a glass of water, and she leaves us alone. Everyone else gathers in the kitchen.

"Go on and start, warrior princess," my father says as he folds his hands on the table. He finally got a haircut, and he has dark circles under his eyes. He looks sad, and I think it's because of me.

"I'm not a warrior princess," I say softly.

"I call you that so you can remember your power. Everything you're doing right now lets me know that you're a warrior. Be careful what I ask for, huh?"

"What power, though?" I say. My heart starts racing because all the words and all the truths are rushing from the bottom of my soul and up to my throat chakra and out into this room. "Baba, when we say all power to the people, what does that even mean? What did it mean back then, and what does that mean now?"

"It means that power belongs to us," he says.

"Does it, though?"

"Okay. This is what we're doing? Ask all the questions. It was my mistake for assuming you know all this already."

"But I don't want a lecture, Baba. I just want to be able to . . . question."

He nods. "Okay. Shoot."

"My mother . . ." I start, and the words get stuck in my throat.

My father extends his hands out across the table. So I take them and hold them there.

"Mama wanted to leave the house, and she didn't want to have another baby. . . ." I can't continue, and my father squeezes my hands.

"What am I supposed to be fighting for?" I ask after a long minute of pranayama breaths. I let go of my father's hands and let everything, *everything*, ride the waves of my tears because I crack open and become a torrent. "I don't know what the Movement is all about anymore. If all this stuff keeps happening, then what are we even fighting for? It feels like we're . . . we're always punching brick walls, and throwing stones into the air and they never land. They never land . . . and we can't save everybody because . . . we're still hurting each other and we can be just like them sometimes and . . . And I wonder if this was the plan all along and maybe we've already lost because . . . Because this doesn't feel like freedom to me, and my mother couldn't even make choices for her own body without thinking about liberation for our people, without thinking about if she's making it worse for us just by choosing herself . . . And maybe her back was breaking from carrying everything and everybody on her shoulders and she just wanted to go lie down somewhere . . . And . . . and maybe she flew away because there's more freedom in the skies and old memories of Africa, or out there in the universe, or somewhere in the past when we didn't have all this . . . all this . . . And I don't know if we'll ever be like it was back in Africa 'cause it feels like they'll always be coming. They'll always be coming for us, to steal us and own us and press us down into the earth until we're buried six feet deep, and . . . Because they can't survive without us and we can't survive without us, we're always going to be fighting this war, and . . . my mother. How come you didn't love Mama enough to liberate her? How come you chose the Movement over her? And me?"

My entire body starts shaking. I didn't know that telling the truth is like an exorcism or the holy spirit or a trance or an old African deity coming down to mount my soul.

My father gets up to come over and hug me, and says with fragmented words, "Nigeria. Baby. I love you, and you're . . . okay. You're okay. You're fine, young queen. You're strong. You're going to be just fine."

I'm not. I'm not.

His voice is the ocean floor and the edge of the sky all at once—sinking me and lifting me at the same time.

"I'm not always strong, Baba," I say, with my voice still trembling like aftershocks.

My father and I sweep the mess we've made of ourselves beneath the table as we set it, gather around, and give thanks to the ancestors before we eat.

"I am grateful for freedom and Freedom," I say, looking over at my baby brother sitting on my father's lap. Then I glance at Kamau looking down at his plate, probably thinking of saying something that won't offend my father. "And I'm thankful for Kamau and all that he is—my lifeline, my rock."

"I am so grateful for you, Nigeria," Kamau says. "For challenging us in more ways than we know."

It's supposed to be Aunt Sharon's turn, but she stays quiet, leaving room for my father to say a few words. And he does.

"Sharon, I love you and I'm grateful for you," my father says with a soft voice I haven't heard since after Mama died. "And thank you for pointing out my flaws, my sister. My actual sister. Revolution starts in the home and in the soul. And Kamau . . ."

I can feel Kamau tensing up in the seat next to me.

"I love you, too, nephew. I do. I really do" is all he says.

Kamau just nods, and we all collectively exhale.

I set out a plate of food for Mama and place it on one of Aunt Sharon's altars, and we eat. Nothing is the same. Small talk is awkward, our hearts are heavy, and I am growing. This will take time. But we are getting better and my father is right when he says liberation starts in the home. And in the soul.

ARTICLE VIII
NEW YEAR'S DAY
KWANZAA: IMANI (FAITH)
HAITIAN INDEPENDENCE DAY
BIRTHDAY

"Everything I do is for my people."

—Attributed to Sacagawea, the new
mother whose land became her body,
and her body became this land.

EMANCIPATION

My parents named me Nigeria Sankofa Jones, and today is my seventeenth birthday. I dab a mix of patchouli and lavender oils onto my neck and wrists to remind me of the scent of places I know, faces I can name, and secrets I remember. Everything my mother taught me.

We're having my gratitude celebration at the Village House to mark the seventeenth anniversary of me choosing to be the daughter of Kofi Sankofa—the Black nationalist, revolutionary freedom fighter, and founder of the Movement, whose mission is to divest from oppressive systems and create an all-Black utopia.

The gag is, though, my birthday is always on New Year's Day, the last day of Kwanzaa, and Haitian Independence Day.

"Then why didn't you just call me Imani?" I remember asking my parents one day when I was little. "Or Haiti, or New Year?"

"Because we want you to remember further back," Mama had responded. "Way past slavery, way past Haiti, to the land of the Yoruba and the Igbo, where both our people are from."

But later, when I was older, Mama said that my father named me, and she and him were just young and they could've been more creative than that.

But I'm personally celebrating going out on my own and beginning the process of emancipating from my father. Even after Philly Friends, there's still college and grad school if I choose, because I want entry into a world that my father wants to divest from. I want to chart my own journey.

My father and I had made enough amends for him to celebrate me today. "You're still my daughter," he'd said. "And whether you believe it or not, you're choosing this path. But I have to stay true to my own purpose, baby girl. I hope you understand that."

I do. He chose the Movement because he's a Black nationalist, revolutionary freedom fighter. When I don't fit into his visions of liberation for our people, I have to get out of his way and find my own liberation. This is the only logic that makes sense of our messy relationship. He chose his life, and I will choose mine.

When I get to the Village House before the day's celebrations, I grab my baby brother and head straight to my old room. Freedom is happy and plump and independent and Mama's defiant energy is all over him, too. He toddles to the door, not wanting to be stuck here with me as I smother him with kisses and baby noises. I don't blame him. I smile while opening the door to let him out. He can climb down the stairs on his own, too. "That's right, little bro. Find your own path," I tell him as his little feet pitter-patter away.

I look around at everything I didn't take with me to Aunt Sharon's. Some crystals, tarot cards, photos of me and Mama. I think of Jasmine and how I left her hanging. I hope she comes today. I hope she understands that I didn't have enough to share with her at that time. I was grieving and healing.

Then I stumble on an African baby names book on my shelf. I need a new name for my new life. This is what my father said he did when he changed his name to Kofi, which simply means "born on Friday" in the Twi language of Ghana. So I let my spirit guide me, and I land on a Yoruba definition that suits me: "one with a history."

Enitan. I rename myself Enitan. Enitan Sankofa. I am reaching back to tell my story.

It'll be a few hours before people start coming, so I go downstairs and slip into my father's office to look through some of my mother's things, and maybe find more clues she may have left behind. I don't know all that I need to know about her. Her story was still unfolding before her life was cut short. But still, she grew wings.

When I open the door, Chris is there.

We lock eyes for a long minute before he says, "Peace, Sister Nigeria."

"Hey, Chris," I say, trying not to look thirsty, because I'm not. I'm glad I look decent, though, wearing a Well-Read Black Girl hoodie with leggings. My locs are tucked high into a colorful head wrap, and Kamau has me wearing makeup these days—eyeliner, mascara, gloss.

I had ignored texts and phone calls the entire time I was at Aunt Sharon's. So this is the first time I'm seeing and talking to him since that day in my room. I never told him about my pregnancy scare.

"Happy Born Day!" he says. His locs are forming and he's trying but failing at growing facial hair. Glasses, a black sweatshirt, and a copper ankh necklace give him a different edge, like he's settling into being part of the Movement, looking like a young, passionate Black hippie activist. And maybe we look good together.

"Thank you." I step in and close the door, knowing that we're not alone in this house. I wasn't ready to speak to him just yet.

"Also, habari gani?"

"Imani. And please don't say 'Happy New Year.'"

"Happy New Year to you, too."

"Funny. But seriously, what are you doing in here, anyway?" I walk around to my mother's desk in the corner of the office. It's covered with papers, and I'm glad my father hasn't moved her desktop. There's so much work that was left unfinished, and I know most of the Movement's programs and activities have been at a standstill. But I guess that's what Nubia is here for, and maybe Chris, too.

"Remember the research you were supposed to do for your father's book?" Chris asks.

I look over at his laptop to see the title on the first document: *A Black Man's Constitution*. "Yeah, but you should definitely be the one to help him write it."

"It's almost done and it's gonna be a bestseller. Every Black man and boy in America should buy it."

"So is he paying you, or . . . ?"

"I'll be touring with him. Like, TV. Radio. This'll put me on the spot. I'll get something out of this, for sure."

I nod, unimpressed. "Cool. Cool. He's setting you up to take over one day, huh?"

"That's the plan," he says with a wide smile.

I shake my head and smile, realizing that the patriarchy isn't going anywhere. And neither are my feelings. No doubt that Chris is looking really good right now, but did he forget about us? What we shared? I want to ask, but I don't. "Okay, then. I'll get out of your way. Hope you come have some cake later."

"No. Wait."

My heart pauses. I didn't think I'd still be catching feelings, but we have unfinished business, too.

"You think you can help me with this? My sentences don't sound right."

My heart deflates. "Really, Chris?"

"I found some notes from your mother. I tried to copy what she wrote, but I don't think they make sense. Maybe you could—?"

"Chris, don't copy my mother's work. And my father should be writing his own books. . . ." It's pointless to say this to him now. "What notes?"

He motions toward a black notebook on my father's desk, one that I hadn't seen before. I quickly open to the first page to see written in Mama's handwriting, *A Black Woman's Constitution.* I close it and hold it to my chest. "Where'd you find this?"

"Your father had it." He looks at me as if he wants my help, like he can't do this without me. "King Kofi needs this to be published in time for Juneteenth. We need some funds for the Freedom School, and we're moving the trip to Africa until next summer."

How do I tell him that none of this will happen without my mother's organizational skills? I don't want to burst his bubble, so I just say, "You'll figure it out, Brother Chris." And turn to leave the office.

"Nigeria?"

"It's Enitan now. I'm changing my name."

"Oh, word! Me too. I'm thinking of . . . Che. Like Che Guevara, the Cuban revolutionary . . ."

"Argentine," I correct him. "He was from Argentina. He fought in the Cuban revolution." I start to leave again.

"You still with that white boy?" he asks.

"I was never with . . . Liam. His name is Liam."

"Some girl from your school named Chloe DM'd me asking about the Youth Group. Then she told me how you sold out and was messing with a white boy. I mean, you were at his house claiming that he was just a friend. So I thought it was over between us."

I'm not surprised that Chloe would do that, but I am a little surprised that Chris is even asking. "No. It was just . . ."

"I get it," he says. "Do you, Queen. Do you." He goes back to his laptop, looking as if he's trying to make sense of a puzzle.

So I leave with my mother's notebook, forcing this chapter closed because that moment with Chris belonged to a girl named Nigeria who was trying to find herself.

"I'm here, though," Chris says, getting up from behind the desk and walking toward me. "I'm here when you're ready. I still wanna figure us out."

He's standing a few inches from me now, and our bodies want closure, too. So he steps closer, and I step closer, and we hug each other real tight, swaying from side to side. I inhale him—Egyptian musk and shea butter, revolutionary dreams and rage, sweetness and confusion in the body of this eighteen-year-old boy.

"I miss you," he whispers.

I don't say anything.

He kisses my forehead, and I pull away. We look at each other for a long minute, and I want to swim in his eyes.

"I have my own revolution to fight . . . Che," I whisper back. And I turn and close the door softly.

I have to share my gratitude celebration with the last day of Kwanzaa, so this is also our annual karamu. Mama would make a huge pot of soup joumou—pumpkin soup for Haitian Independence Day. So Nubia and the other aunties have taken over all the meal prep, and I hope they've included that soup. I'm half Haitian, I'm independent, *and* it's my birthday.

The Village House was my house but not my home. It belongs to everybody and no one. Auntie Fola, Auntie Gloria, Auntie Ama, and Auntie Yvette embrace me as if I've never left, as if this was all just a blip in our fight for liberation.

"Happy New Year! Happy birthday, and habari gani?" Auntie Fola sings.

"Imani!" I respond, and I'm flooded with memories of my childhood when this was my favorite day of the year. Mama would be in the kitchen making all kinds of vegan dishes, and we kids couldn't wait to open our zawadi—Kwanzaa gifts.

The aunties all gather around Freedom to dote on him, and I feel like a stranger in what used to be my house that is not my home. I miss the food most of all. I'm eating chicken and fish now, but I make a beeline for the fruits because I've been going hard on junk food with Kamau. I take a plate of fruit and chips with me and walk past all the eyes, all the questions, and slip out into the backyard and onto the deck, my favorite place in the world, where what used to be my mother's garden is covered with a thin veil of snow.

Makai, Travis, Danika, and Jasmine are out there, and my heart lights up.

"How you been, Sister Nigeria?" Makai asks, making room on the deck for me.

I just nod and stuff some chips into my mouth because I don't want small talk. I want to just be here with them. "I missed you guys so much," I mumble with food in my mouth.

None of them says anything for a long minute; then Makai says, "I'm happy for you, Nigeria. I know a lot of shit went down last year. So new year, new you. Right?"

"I'm sorry," I say. "I'm sorry to each of y'all."

"We're sorry, too," Jasmine says. "I didn't know, like, how hard it was for you."

No one else says anything more, but they pat me on the back, hug me, nudge me, take food from my plate and this is all the apology I want, all the closure I need.

Then, as we all get up to go back inside 'cause it's brick out here, Jasmine asks, "You like it there? Your aunt's house? Your new life?"

"Yeah. I mean, I'm changing and growing. And I just needed to deal with stuff in my own way. You know?"

"Yeah, I know," she says.

"How 'bout you?" I ask.

"I need to stay in the Youth Group for now. It's giving me something that's . . . keeping me . . . alive. You know?"

"Yeah, I know," I say, and I give her one last, tight hug.

Back inside, the festivities have begun, and it's my time to shine. I spot Aunt Sharon and Kamau. Then I pause to see Sage standing with them. She holds out her arms for a hug, and when we reach each other, we almost lift each other up from the floor. "Habari gani?"

"Umoja!" she says, really loud, and everyone looks at her.

"It's Imani," I whisper. We both laugh, and I'm so glad she's back to celebrating these moments with me.

"Habari gani?" my father says, calling everyone to order as he stands next to the elaborately decorated Kwanzaa table with its kinara, kente and Ankara print fabric, ears of corn, and bowls of fruit.

"Imani!" everyone responds.

"And what does that mean?"

"Faith!"

"Any volunteers?" my father asks.

Jasmine steps forward. "To believe with all our heart in our people, our parents, our teachers, our leaders, and the righteousness and victory of our struggle."

"Nigeria Sankofa Jones," he says. "Come do us the honors." He steps aside to reveal another table covered in white linen with plants and vases of flowers and other stuff that honors the spirit of who we are also celebrating today.

All this time, my mind had made me believe that this table was just a corner of our living room that held a bunch of my mother's photos, and I was waiting for her to come back. But it's an ancestor table. My mother's stuff is here. Her crystals and trinkets, jewelry and handwritten notes, and photos of her face—her eyes, smile, hair, and soul are there to remind me, to remind us, that she never left. She was always here with us. And maybe, through one of our children, she'll come back as an ancestor.

I stand next to the table and hold a glass of water in my hand and say, "History lives and breathes and so do our ancestors."

"Ashé!" everyone sings.

I pour out some water into an African violet plant, Mama's favorite. With each drop, I shed a tear. Freedom toddles over to me as if he already knows that we are calling our mother's name: Natalie Pierre.

The members won't let us stay in this sorrowful space for too long, so they start clapping and singing our song, starting with my baby brother.

"Look at Freedom! He's Black and beautiful!
Look at Freedom! He's Black and beautiful!
Look at Freedom! He's Black and beautiful!
Singing power to the people! Power to the people!
He's Black and beautiful!"

But I'm still crying, I can't contain the river I'm becoming as I look out at all the faces of the people who love me back. I didn't want to be a part of this anymore. Yet they still love me. They love me enough for me to leave to go find myself. And maybe I'll be back.

They start to sing my name, but I stop them.

"I am now Enitan," I say, sniffing back tears and holding my head up high. "It's Yoruba. And it means 'one with a history.'"

Auntie Fola comes to give me a hug, then Aunt Sharon, then the

Youth Group. I am engulfed in love by my people. I catch Chris smiling at me as he leans against a wall, taking in all of this. Just by being here, he's seeing the messy love that we have for each other, and how love and war can coexist under the same roof, in the same revolution.

"Look at Enitan! She's Black and beautiful!" everyone starts, and I do my little two-step dance, and I swear my smile is like warm sunshine on this cold, winter day.

But I spot my father becoming his own river of sorrow. He's trying to wipe his face and blink back tears. He doesn't let himself cry, and he clears his throat and climbs back onto his revolutionary throne.

"A luta continua!" he says, calling everyone to order. And I know that this gratitude celebration will also be another one of his lectures.

After we light the candles on the kinara; after we open our zawadi (books, crochet hats and scarves, homemade soaps and jars of shea butter); after the members sing "Happy Birthday" to me (the Stevie Wonder version, of course); after we eat baked tofu, greens, vegan mac and cheese, soup joumou (that Aunt Sharon *tried* to make), vegetable gumbo, and rice and beans, I head back up to my room to give myself a birthday gift.

I find my bag and dig for my phone where a bunch of texts wishing me a happy birthday flood my screen. But I only open the one from Liam.

Hope you enjoy your day of birth! he texted, followed by a GIF of a Black girl being swept up by balloons.

I shake my head and laugh, knowing it must've taken him a while to come up with that. I scroll up to see all the other texts from him I didn't answer. Arguments for the next debate. Who won the last debate. One text wishing me a merry Christmas, and another one wishing me a happy Kwanzaa.

So I text back, Thank you.

And this is enough closure for me. For now. Philly Friends was a key that unlocked a door on this journey to find myself.

Then I remember what I came up here for. I go into the bathroom and find my father's clippers.

I clear my dresser and wipe the mirror to take one last good look at this girl. Did I choose to be here? Did I choose my parents? Did I know that I'd lose my mother and I would have to give birth to myself again? Did I know that I would have to learn how to fly on my own?

Either way, from this point on, everything that I claim and can claim me will be my choice.

I find a pair of scissors and start with one loc, snipping it close to my scalp. I hold the long loc in my hand and look at it. Memories are coiled into it like a DNA strand—Mama's hands and fingers, her homemade shea butters and oils, her songs and prayers, and even her own ancestral memory.

But I can't carry this weight with me into the next phase of my life.

So I snip more locs, one by one, feeling the weight of a thousand ancestors lift from my head. When they've all been cut, I still feel them with me, hovering, though, and not bound to me like puppet strings.

Then I take the clippers and buzz the little fro down to the scalp. My entire face beams. I can see myself, and I am born again.

I feel like air.

I walk down the stairs with my newly bald head as if wings are slowly growing out of my back. I open the front door, and the sky is calling my new name. So I walk down the front steps, onto the sidewalk, and toward the edge of the world because I am flying and flying and flying, freeing myself.

Who knew that I could soar even while my feet are firmly planted on solid ground?

The people could fly long ago in Africa, and even here where chains are not around our wrists and ankles but around our minds, we can still break free and fly.

So I grow wings, invisible like memory. I remember, invisible like wings. I am free, visible and present and taking up all the space that I need, like my body. And I have a story to tell.

My story becomes herstory. And I fly high above Philly, soar over Pennsylvania and Ohio, Chicago and the Midwest, Oregon and California, and all the way to the Pacific Ocean. My body becomes this land, and this land becomes my body. All of it is mine, claiming the world like the wind as it lifts me high to touch the edge of the universe. This is the sky map my mother, and all her mothers before her, have charted for me.

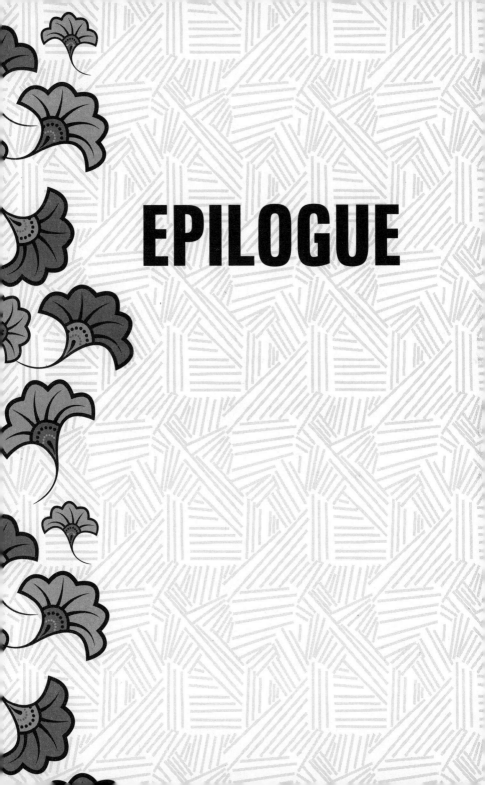

EPILOGUE

ARTICLE IX
FATHER'S DAY
JUNETEENTH

"If the first woman God ever made was strong enough to turn the world upside down all alone, these women together ought to be able to turn it back, and get it right side up again! And now they is asking to do it, the men better let them."

—*Sojourner Truth, always keeping it one hundred and speaking truth to power, as told to Harriet Beecher Stowe for the* Atlantic Monthly, *1853.*

(And there still isn't a national holiday honoring any Black or Native woman's contributions to this country.)

Reparations

A few days after coming down from the high of the Odunde Festival, where Philly streets were packed with Black people and culture, music and food, we try to create a smaller version at Malcolm X Park down the block from the Village House to celebrate Juneteenth. I don't live there anymore, but I still get sucked right back into managing the Youth Group as they direct the vendors, set up tables with food, and come up with activities for the kids. Cutting off everything about my old life is not as easy as I thought. I lived and breathed the Movement, so I have to slowly, slowly cut the cord so I can still breathe.

But I still spread my wings and fly whenever I need to.

Red-black-and-green flags are propped up near trees and benches, and djembe drummers are unfolding chairs near the podium where my father will be speaking. The aunties are organizing the food and drinks, and part of me misses coming to these events so bad.

I'm here on my own terms. I'm helping because I want this to be a successful event and Mama was always on the planning committee. This is for her, too.

"You're ready to set up?" Kamau says, rolling a hand truck

stacked with boxes toward me.

I nod, and we head to an empty table and start to unpack my chapbooks. "Here goes nothing," I say, sighing deeply.

"Got everything you need?" Kamau asks. "Square, apps, bills, coins? And please don't agree to barter. Money in exchange for knowledge. Don't trade an incense stick for your book in the spirit of Ujamaa. I know how we do."

I laugh at my cousin. "Yeah, can't pay for the white man's university with incense sticks!"

So we put out my chapbooks, spread them out over Ankara fabric, and I can't believe I'm doing this. Five months ago, I set out to finish what my mother started. After all these years of writing my father's books for him, she wanted to write her own. I take a copy and hold it in my hand. It's not as polished as my father's books, and it's much thinner and low-budget. Kamau is also helping me turn it into a video essay, and I can't believe I'm about to be like my father, except not like my father.

"Don't worry, cuz," Kamau says, turning my poorly designed book over in his hand. "We were raised not to judge a book by its cover."

"Shut up, Kamau!" I laugh and nudge my cousin because he illustrated the cover for me and I designed it. There's a silhouette of a girl with an afro set against a backdrop of an intersecting American flag and the Black Liberation flag, and in the middle is the Haitian flag. It's not perfect, but it gets the job done. I set up the typeface for the title: *A Black Girl's Constitution* to look like the real Constitution, and if I'm being honest, this is one of my proudest accomplishments.

We're selling them for ten bucks a pop, and below it is both my and my mother's names: Natalie Pierre and Enitan Sankofa. People will know that I'm Kofi Sankofa's daughter. They will also know that I'm doing my own thing and that my mother had her own ideas, her own voice.

I look up to see Che, Makai, and Jasmine carrying boxes to an empty table. My entire body smiles the closer Che gets to me, and I wait for him to say something first. He scans my table, looks at me, and says, "Proud of you."

We're still figuring us out—texting, talking, kissing, disappearing, and reappearing in each other's lives. He's too close to everything I'm running away from, but there's something there and I can't cut him out yet, just like everything else about my old life. "Thanks, babe" is all I say.

"Okay, lovebirds," Makai jokes. "Let's get this bag! We trying to get free."

Jasmine comes over to check out my book and is the first customer to buy a copy. "Okay! I see you, Kofi Sankofa Jr.!"

"Please don't say that," I tell her.

"I mean, apple . . ." She motions toward my books. "Tree . . ." She motions toward the books Che and Makai are putting out.

The copies of *The Black Man's Constitution* are ten times as thick as my little chapbook and the design quality is much more professional, of course. Then I spot the bylines on the cover. Kofi Sankofa and Che Sankofa. I try not to roll my eyes, but it's whatever at this point.

"Really? All this time, my mother never got her name on the

books she wrote, and here comes the son he never had," I say to Che, straight up. Even though he's something like an on-again, off-again boyfriend, I'm not afraid to call him out on his bullshit when it comes to my father.

"That's 'cause I asked," he says. "And I'll help him reach a younger audience."

I can't lie; he was smart to do that. But I know even if me or Mama had asked for the same things, we wouldn't get the same response. Or maybe we wouldn't even know to ask for what's ours. But that shit ends today.

"Hey, Che? Makai? Wanna buy a copy?"

And they do.

We're having a low-key contest to see who can sell the most books, and our tables are side by side as more people come into the park and the drummers start drumming and the music blasts from speakers—the Roots, Jill Scott, Jazmine Sullivan, and Musiq Soulchild spread that Philly love all throughout the park and in the surrounding streets.

Jasmine comes over to my table to help me sell copies because it's Father's Day and my father's books are selling like Hot Cheetos.

Then I spot Sage walking up with Chloe and Tyler, and I immediately start squealing and jumping up and down. Sage and I run to each other like long-lost sisters.

I couldn't go back to Philly Friends. It wasn't like I was expelled, more like disinvited. And I wasn't trying to beg to go back, either, not after how Henry and Jon treated me. I'm following Aunt Sharon's plan instead and putting all my energy into college. I've already taken GED classes, and I got my high school diploma last month.

Kamau was jealous, of course, and I take every opportunity to rub it in his face that I just had to take a test to graduate high school. "Are you serious? And I'm over here still busting my ass . . . for what?" he had joked. "This whole thing is a scam."

So I'll be applying to college in the fall as I work and save up money to live on campus, hopefully far away from Philly but close enough to visit my baby brother, come back to family, and community, if I need to.

Sage buys four copies of my book. "To keep in the birthing house," she says. "And we'll get more, too."

It's weird between me and Chloe, so I just give her a free copy and keep it moving. "Thanks," she says. "And I like your buzz cut."

I pass my hand over my clean-shaven head and give her a genuine smile.

Tyler doesn't buy any books, but he's looking around like he's out of place, taking it all in, and I wonder if he'll start listening to my father's podcasts and watching his videos. But I doubt it. "This is cool," he says. "Could expand it. Get some corporate sponsorship."

"You're joking, right?" I ask.

Then he laughs, and I playfully shove his shoulder.

Still, I'm happy to see them. Sage can tell that there's one person I'm curious about, even though me and Che have become a thing these past few months.

"He asks about you sometimes," she says in a low voice, stepping closer so no one hears.

"I know. Kamau tells me. I just hope he's doing good."

She nods, and we leave it at that because I don't know if Liam would ever come to something like this. We had a moment when I'd stepped into his world at Philly Friends and even Mount Airy. But what would we be if he had to step into my world—the Movement and all its teachings about white supremacy and decolonizing? He'd probably be into it with all that socialism stuff. But reading and posting about it on social media is way different from trying to live it.

I spot my father walking up to me pushing a stroller with my brand-new baby sister. Her name is Harriet, and she is a ray of sunshine. So my father calls her his little freedom fighter, and I'm glad that my baby brother will have a sibling that he can grow up with.

It still hurts a little. Healing takes time.

I quickly grab a copy of my book. When he gets closer, I hand it to him. "Happy Father's Day, Baba!" I say with a big smile.

He laughs and shakes his head. "All right, now. *A Black Girl's Constitution*, huh?"

"That's right," I say.

"I'll take my gift, thank you very much. And can you please autograph it for me?"

And I do, carefully writing: *To my father, the revolutionary. Love always, your peaceful princess, Enitan Sankofa.*

He pulls me in and kisses my cheek and holds me tight. I'm still going through with the emancipation even though I'll be eighteen in six months. I don't want to have to ask him for permission to fly. He doesn't believe in systems, and I want to be in the system, to maybe change things from the inside, like *The Spook Who Sat by the Door*. But that's our little secret. Our little master plan. By competing for myself, I am competing for us. I am because we are.

My father taught me that.

When it's time to start the day's events, I take Freedom from Nubia and hold him in my arms. He's heavy and a lot more talkative now. I don't correct him when he calls me "Gigi."

The park is getting packed, and I look out at all the brown faces who are celebrating freedom today. Whether they're from Philly or Haiti, down south or West Africa, all of our ancestors had to do something to get free. And we are here trying to stay free.

The aunties begin by leading the crowd to sing "Lift Every Voice," and our song rises up to the clouds. Then it's time to start our affirmations. My father calls the Youth Group members to stand next to him, and I stay put next to my table of books. Chloe joins them, and I'm happy for her.

Jasmine steps up, with her hair in fresh braids and wearing the Movement's T-shirt.

She looks over at me, so I mouth, "You got this."

She nods, and then she shouts over the crowd "All power to the people!" with her fist in the air, her brothers and sisters by her side, and her people in front of her, hanging on her every word. "In honor of the legendary Black Panther Party for Self-Defense, we invoke their vision of Black liberation in the twenty-first century. Now say it with me, family."

"All power to the people!" we all say with one voice.

ACKNOWLEDGMENTS

This was, by far, the most emotionally challenging book I've written. There are so many people to thank who have instilled in me a sense of purpose and pride in what I hoped to achieve with this story.

First, I am forever grateful to all the resilient, self-determined, and autonomous communities all over the world—from the maroons throughout the Americas, the quilombo in Brazil and the Caco in Haiti, to the Gullah Geechee, the Garveyites, and the Panthers. The children in these spaces grew up to understand the true price of freedom. I would not be who I am and understand the world as I do without the spiritual, cultural, and political communities that shaped me. Thank you to the Black womanists and feminists who have paved the literary and intellectual way for all of us—the Combahee River Collective, bell hooks, Audre Lorde, Alice Walker, Octavia Butler, and all unnamed fanm djanm (strong women) who are fighting for reproductive rights. To the midwives and birth workers—Tioma, Memaniye, and Denala, thank you.

To my husband, Joseph, who is always an anchor and the best supporter and creative partner. My two daughters and son remind me each day of why this work is vital.

To Tunu, I could not forget Nigeria Jones and the story of so many girls like her. Thank you for that first seed of a story so many years ago. To Denala, Ayo, Christine, Tahnia, Meena, Neffie, Kala, Mama Marimba, Atilah, and Mama Bayyinah, I love you all to Africa and back!

To Leah Henderson, this book would not be this story without your sisterhood. Thank you for being a friend, as well as an auntie to my children. That means the world to me.

My agent, Tina Dubois: Thank you for being in my corner and championing this story every step of the way. Emotionally and intellectually, I feel seen and understood.

Alessandra Balzer, editor extraordinaire: I am so grateful for the care and understanding that you've given to not just this story but my body of work. Thank you for your wisdom and insight and challenging me to grow creatively with each project.

Huge shout-out to my team at Balzer + Bray/Harper, especially: Patty Rosati, John Sellers, Audrey Diestelkamp, Sabrina Abballe, Mimi Rankin, and Caitlin Johnson.

A special thanks to the phenomenal Nettrice Gaskins, whose stunning cover illustration fully captures the energy of this book. Thank you to Jenna Stempel-Lobell for the gorgeous design and lettering.

To some of my first readers, Frederick Joseph, Candice Illoh, Malinda Lo, and Nic Stone, I am so grateful for your kind and generous words.

To the ancestors of the Middle Passage—before and beyond—whose shoulders we all stand on: Each time we honor you, we are a little bit taller.

A Luta Continua!